'*The Plague Letters* is a riotous delv

world of Restoration London and



...lean, author of *The Seeker*

'With its endearing, comic characters and crisp, spirited prose, this witty portrayal of seventeenth-century Britain pulls you into the gruesome underworld of the London plague. *The Plague Letters* is a gripping whodunnit with a sinister twist'

Jennifer Ryan, author of *The Chilbury Ladies' Choir*

'V.L. Valentine drops us deep into a single deadly year, 1665, into a sickening, increasingly desperate London wonderfully evoked. With meticulous detail, excellently chosen, she compels us to experience a squalid and horrifying world that ultimately reaches hope through its two sympathetically drawn principal characters. A terrific read!'

Alix Nathan, author of *The Warlow Experiment*

'Dark, haunting and unexpectedly witty – a journey back to seventeenth-century London, where a serial killer is even more terrifying than the raging sickness. Suspenseful from start to finish'

Susan Elia MacNeal, author of *Mr Churchill's Secretary*

'A gorgeous, darkly witty novel that transports the reader to the London of Charles II and the bubonic plague. In this richly layered tale of a rector who teams up with a maid of rare gifts to find both a cure and a sadistic killer, Valentine takes the reader to squalid back alleys and serene country estates with equal aplomb, creating a marvellous cast of ghosts, inebriates, brave tots, licentious aristocrats and misguided lovers. Those looking for a wonderfully entertaining escape from our own dark times need look no further'

Mariah Fredericks, author of *A Death of No Importance*

'A funny, fascinating and gripping adventure tale. It's as if V.L. Valentine holds up a magic mirror to reflect a lesson in time for us now'

Janice Hallett, author of *The Appeal*

'A glorious whodunnit. I loved the characters, and fell in love with its world'

Leonora Nattrass, author of *Black Drop*

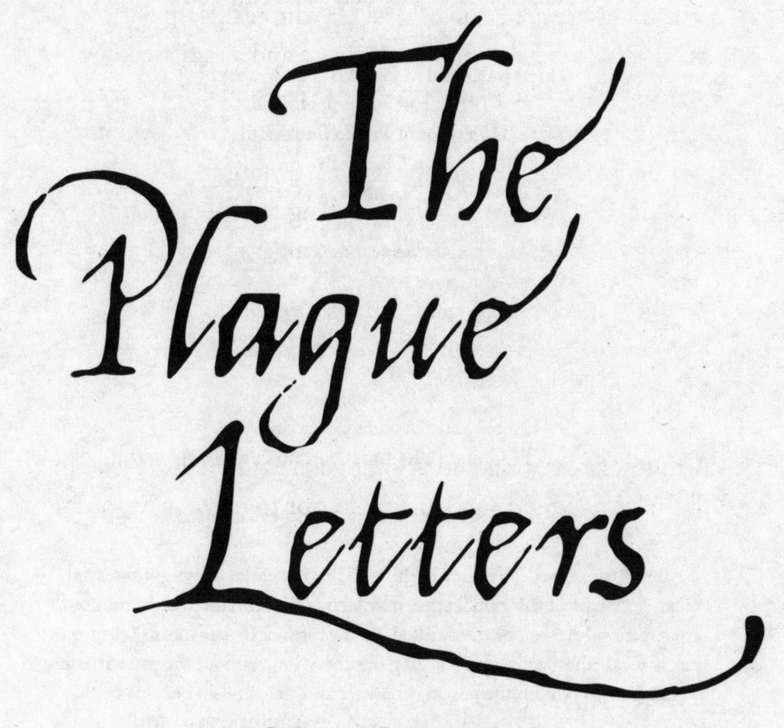


V.L. Valentine

This paperback edition first published in 2021

First published in Great Britain in 2021 by
VIPER, part of Serpent's Tail,
an imprint of Profile Books Ltd
29 Cloth Fair
London
EC1A 7JQ
*www.serpentstail.com*



1 3 5 7 9 10 8 6 4 2

Printed and bound in Great Britain by
CPI Group (UK) Ltd, Croydon CR0 4YY



A CIP catalogue record for this book is available from the British Library.

ISBN 978 1 78816 455 9
Export ISBN 978 1 78816 454 2
eISBN 978 1 78283 656 8

For Sylvan

*That Man nev'r breathed yet, Nor ever shall*
*That did all well, and had no fault at all.*

The Distichs of Cato

# CAST OF CHARACTERS

*All Loyal [Mostly] Subjects to King Charles II*

## IN LONDON

*The Rector's Household, James Street, Covent Garden*

Mr Symon Patrick, Rector of St Paul's Church, Covent Garden

Joan, Housekeeper

Nell, Maid

Jack, Errand Boy

Mite and Tripe, the Cats

*The Society for the Prevention and Cure of Plague*

Dr Alexander Burnett, Fellow of the Royal College of Physicians, of Fenchurch Street

Mr Lodowick Mincy, Surgeon, by the Maypole, the Strand

Mr William Boghurst, Apothecary, at the Sign of the White Hart, Holborn

Mr Valentine Greatrakes, Irish Mystic, Temporarily of Pall Mall

*The Staff, St Paul's Church, Covent Garden*

Francis Bernard, Sexton

Penelope, Misc.

*And . . .*

Sir Denis Gauden, Navy Victualler, Little Tower Hill

General George Monck, Duke of Albemarle, Overseer of the Western Outparishes

Lady Katherine Digby, Heneretta Street, Covent Garden

Mr Unthankes, Sexton, St Gabriel Fenchurch

Theodora Thurgood and Family, of Leg Alley, St Martin's in the Fields

**IN BURNTWOOD, ESSEX**

Lady Elizabeth Gauden, Temporarily of Hutton Hall, Burntwood

Mrs Abigail Pheasunt, Sister to Lady Gauden, Hutton Hall, Burntwood

Mr John Evelyn, Fellow of the Royal Society, Naval Commissioner, of Sayes Court

# LONDON

# 1665

# PRELUDE

*The Parish of St Paul Covent Garden*

He checked his pockets, started out. *Such a clean, crisp time of day*, he thought. Just before daybreak, the world no longer black and not yet that garish yellow, but the colour of a deep sea. A subtle glow suffused the sky, but it was still dark enough to hide whatever needed to be hidden.

He took a deep breath, the morning mist soothing his lungs. Plucked a leaf off a young elm, crumbled it, coating his fingers with its tangy scent. London belonged only to him at this moment, and he was in love with it. Well, there were a few others out. He tried to catch the eye of the early-morning clerks and servants passing by. *They are like me*, he thought, *immune to sloth and joyfully springing out of bed at this godly hour. And for our dutiful efforts, we will be rewarded with the companionship of this blessed and luxurious dawn. We are special.* He smiled. *Yes, we are.*

He turned on to Long Acre. A newer lane, separating the parishes of St Martin's in the Fields and St Paul Covent Garden. Not quite London, not quite Westminster. Not yet crooked and festering. The land ripped from the Westminster monks to make a royal road that connected the king's palace at Whitehall in the west with the ancient walled city in the east. Not that merry King Charlie ever made the journey. Why would he? So dismal that end of town.

He surveyed the shops and homes lining the street, inspected them for the day's first signs of life. A candle flickering behind an upstairs curtain, a dog let out a door. The homes and businesses were tall and proper, made of brick; the dwellings of sturdy, prosperous folk – carriage makers, furniture makers, drapers. Still, the lane was a little too exposed for his taste. He headed south towards the heart of Covent Garden. He had seen so many possibilities on earlier walks, a veritable banquet! But he would skip the sweets. Go for strength. Look for those with an inviolate air. One in particular had stood out.

He walked by a saddler's shop, a sempstress, a tavern. A gust of wind, a creaking of hinges. He looked up to see a green dragon swinging over his head. Perhaps afterwards he would come back for breakfast. Some oysters, some ale, then a rest. He peered through the window. A bent bone of a girl, chest caved in, behind the bar, spit-shining the pewter. Consumptive. No doubt they shoved her into the kitchens come opening time.

He turned on to James Street, a lane even newer than Long Acre. A wide, well-cobbled street that led right into Covent Garden's famed piazza. He closed his eyes, said a prayer then quietly made his way to the corner of James and Hart Street and, ah, there she was, as expected. The clergyman's maid. Up early (good girl!), sweeping the front step. He fumbled around in his satchel, pretended to search through his papers, all the while taking her measure out of the corner of his eye.

She wasn't long from the country, this one. Thick wrists, thick ankles. No cap to cover her head, luscious knots of buttercup hair on display for all. He wanted to part little sections of it and hide things in it. Shoulders so broad and straight he could use them as a bookshelf. He knew the clergyman. A plain man, her master. Plain, like his church. The clergyman did have good hair and a handsome calf, he would give him that. But the man was also in a bit over his head. He was not yet five and thirty but already a rector in one of London's wealthiest, most prestigious parishes. God knows why. He supposed it was because the man was affable. Pliable. An unwitting pawn for his patrons. Why he himself was about to take this risk with the man's maid. How could he not? She was so perfect! He had searched and searched, was running out of time, and he really did need the best.

He hurried up to her, took a quick breath. Began.

'My dear! Oh miss!'

She broke from her sweeping, looked him over, then turned back to her task. A positive sign. Strong-willed. That flash in her eyes, fascinating. A jutting chin, must be some Prussian in her. Or a lot. He needed to know these things. Know anything and everything about her.

He tapped his cane on the cobbles. 'Would you like a better sort of work? Something less dreary? Would you like to come work for me?'

She gave him a ferocious look.

He knew exactly what she was thinking. 'No such thing, bless us, no! The girl who watered my plants, she's left me. Gone to care for sick family. I hope it's not *the* sickness, but if it were, it is for the best that she's gone, I suppose. It's just . . . I have a great deal of plants.'

Her arms went slack, the broom dangled from her hand.

'Sir, you feeling all right?'

'Quite serious, my child. I have so many plants. Big house. Lots of stairs. Inside and out. It is a lot of walking. But no other duties required. Well, if you could write, that would be helpful. Can you write?'

She looked ready to spit. She had good instincts then, a keen mind! Could such traits be protective?

'Course I can't write.' She snapped the broom upright and started sweeping again.

He stepped closer, angling his cane between her legs and the broom. 'I could teach you! Would you like that? And in the meantime, you only need to make an X on the chalkboard for each plant you water.'

She stopped. He could see her working out the calculations in her head. The promise of lessons would be hard to resist. He fetched the coins from his pocket, held them out to her. 'An advance payment, perhaps, to seal the deal? A little more if you come with me now?'

She was beginning to waver. Why? She'd learn to read. Get a small purse. What more could she want? Ah . . . yes, of course.

He smiled, a twinkle in his eye. 'Might I ask, do you like almond cake? Curd cake? We always have plenty.'

Quick as a whip, she knocked his cane out of his hand with her broom. 'Scut off, you old mackerel,' she said, taking another swipe at him before fleeing down a passage between the houses.

He sighed, bent over to pick up his cane. He'd misjudged her. Not Prussian blood at all. Irish. He took out a kerchief and polished the brass handle, then followed her into the passage.

# JUNE

*In the evening home to supper; and there, to my great trouble, hear that the plague is come into the City; but where should it begin but in my good friend and neighbour's, Dr Burnett, in Fanchurch Street: which in both points troubles me mightily.*

Samuel Pepys, Naval Clerk, Seething Lane

# I

## *A Departure From Half Moone Street, Covent Garden*

PENELOPE DRAGGED HERSELF towards the church. Her strength nearly gone, the world before her in shadow. She leaned against a hitching post to catch her breath; she wouldn't let herself sit, no. If she could get to the church, the rector, she would have a chance. Mr Patrick was his name. Symon Patrick. A good name. Pleasingly plosive. P-P-P Patrick. But Penelope was a better name.

The night her luck turned ill had been as hot as Satan's belly, the winds stolen away. She cursed her master, the baker on Half Moone Street, as she thought back upon it. That doughy old hairball. Cursed his wife, cursed the ghosts, too, for there had not been a whisper from them of what was to come. One was by her side now, a young woman with a sorrowful face and dressed in a gown of ashes. The wraith tried to take her by the elbow and guide her along. Penelope had long since stopped wondering whether any of these phantoms often about her were real, or a distorted attempt by her mind to ease her loneliness. For no matter what she tried, she could not be rid of them. 'Do you mean to help me,' Penelope hissed, 'or take me to Hell?!'

That night – how many days ago was it now? – she had woken up with a terrible itching. Tore through the knots in her hair to get at her scalp. Scratched her toes against her shins. Shot out her arms like a possessed marionette to get at her shoulders, her back, behind her knees. She was used to sharing the baker's garret with all sorts of creatures. They scuffled and clicked around her in the dark. In the mornings, she'd sweep up their dried, feathery little corpses. But that night, something had agitated the fleas and she woke up with welts the size of pinpricks all over. Perhaps it had been the full moon, low in the sky and swelled up to thrice its size, pulling on them, provoking them all.

She had liked the baker's garret in a way, surrounded by sacks of yeast and sugar, barrels of wheat flour, rye, barley and lots of white flour – most of the baker's customers were rich and preferred their loaves fluffy and white. (She herself was partial to oatmeal; she had stitched up a half-empty sack of it for a pillow.) When a new sack or barrel was needed downstairs, they would hook it to a pulley outside one of the garret windows and lower it to the ground. It was one of the better places she'd stayed. Dry and clean; the nutty smell of baking bread warmed the air most hours of the day.

She remembered getting up to search for a balm to stop the itching, and she'd heard the baker and his wife stirring below. A jolt of panic. Had she overslept? She looked out the window for the moon, judged it to be two in the morning. Nearly time for her to wake up, get the ovens going, but why was the family awake? They were never up until the ovens were hot. She had pulled a tub of lemon balm out of her bag and rubbed it on her legs and arms. Threw on her dress, wrestled her hair under a cap. Tugged out a few greasy clumps for show, tied on a dirty apron and bumped her way down the stairs.

Light had flickered from under the door of the master's chamber. She knocked, called out, 'All's well?'

The door flung open, Mr Gilbert stood before her, night-shirt over his breeches. 'Penelope!' He eyed her snake's-nest hair in disgust. *He was one for faces*, she thought, forcing herself not to comment on his own thick mat of hair creeping out from under his shirt and up his throat. 'I . . . you . . .' He looked over his shoulder at his wife, who was fluttering around behind him. He turned back to Penelope. She lifted up her chin, dared him to comment on the lard she'd deliberately smeared on her apron. 'Go downstairs, clean the ashes out of the ovens. We're closing shop, leaving town.'

She had worried about this. Their custom had dropped to a trickle as the parish emptied out. And she had heard the day before there was sickness at the other end of Half Moone Street.

The Gilberts' maid elbowed past Penelope and dumped a pile of linens into an open chest. She was a pretty thing, Deb was, a buttery little biscuit. As she swept out of the room, she refused to meet Penelope's eye.

'The cloth!' her mistress yelled after her. 'The curtains!'

'And the plate!' Mr Gilbert said. 'When Mark gets back with the cart, get him to packing the plate!'

'What are we to do about my mother's chair?' Mrs Gilbert asked, more to herself than anyone.

'And the dogs, are they tied up? There's no time to chase after them! Penelope, see to it.' Mr Gilbert started to close the door on her; she thrust her foot out, blocking it.

'Where are we to go?'

He paused. Looked back at his wife. 'Canterbury. Cousins

there. Be fast about it, girl. Anything of metal we'll need to lock up.' She heard horses clopping up the street, heard them stop in front of the bakery.

'What time are we to leave?'

The baker gave her an exasperated look. 'You're to stay; we haven't enough space.'

'Shall I watch the stores?' Her eyes lit up, she imagined herself standing guard by the door, a big club in her hand. Or swinging down from the pulley, bashing intruders on the head.

'Mark is to do it.' He stared down at his hands, stabbed his fingernails into his thumb.

'I'll watch him, then.'

'A girl like you, here? Unsupervised, with Mark? Heavens, no. You'll have to find another place . . . though who will take you in, looking like that . . .'

'Looking like what?' *Go on, say it,* she thought.

The baker moved to shut the door. She put both hands out to stop it, pushed it back open with her shoulders. 'Is Deb going with you?'

'The ovens, Penelope!' he yelled, trying to shove her back. She craned her head around his fat arms; she'd get one last word in, she would. She cried out to his wife, 'Oh mistress, did you know? When you go to visit your mother, Deb keeps the bed warm for the master.' She heard the crash of a ewer followed by a murderous scream. She let the door slam shut and ran up the stairs to collect her things. Not much there; she kept her treasures elsewhere.

She had been sorry to lose her garret, the chimney that kept it so warm in the winter. She'd settled right into a decent routine after she'd dealt with the baker's cockle hands. Poor Deb, she wasn't as skilled. Didn't know how to fend for herself.

Penelope, however, always had a plan. She was going to cross the river, spend the summer helping in the fields, wait out the sickness, wait for the baker to return, then burn him down. But now, she needed help.

She dropped down to her hands and knees. She could do this, get to the church. *It's not so far*, she tried to convince herself. The rector would help her. He had done so before. She had been on her way to deliver a sack of bread over at Hart Street. A boy had darted from the alley, grabbed at her skirts, then another took her by the shoulders and spun her around. Next thing she knew she was surrounded by them, filthy boys, pawing at her, pinching her and then a blow to her back that knocked her down. The beggars ripped the bag of bread off her shoulder and as fast as they had come they were gone. She had stayed on the ground for a moment and closed her eyes; she wanted to remember their faces so she could find them again. Of a sudden, two hands slipped under her arms and she was ready to kick, but then she heard the whisper, 'I've got you.' It was the priest, Mr Patrick. 'I saw them,' he said. 'My man Bernard, he'll find them. They'll be worse for it.' She stared at him, waited for the trick; there was always a trick with men. 'I expect your baker will blame you for this,' he continued. 'Here is what we shall do.' He asked her to take him to her shop then bade her to wait at the corner. He went inside and came out with a dozen loaves, a replacement for those stolen from her. He bowed and left, asked nothing more of her. Except that she come to his church when she could. And now, that was exactly what she was trying to do. When she reached the piazza, reached his church, she would ask him for a dry, clean corner. Some water. A home. A safe one. A place where she wouldn't have to die alone.

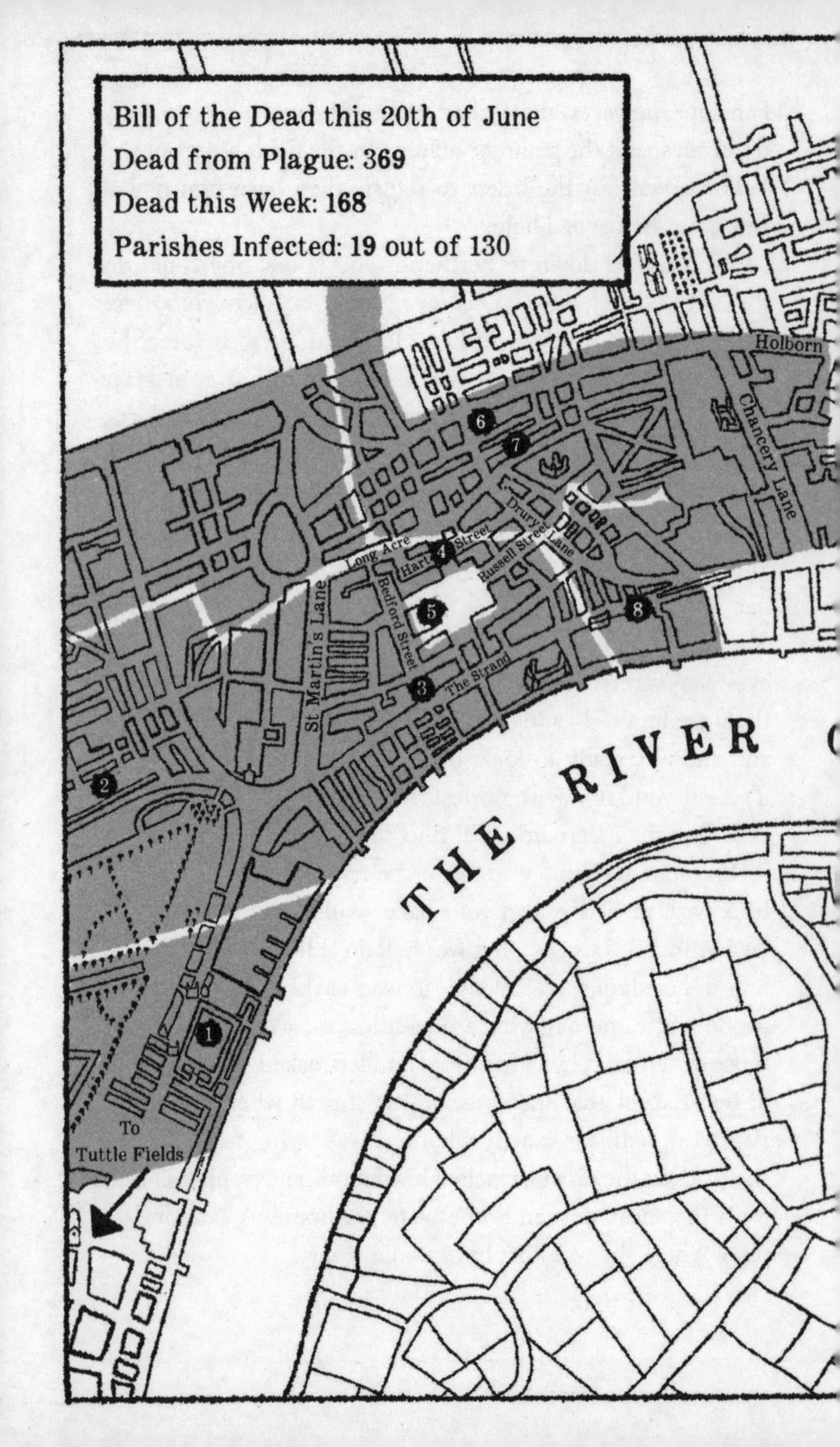

Bill of the Dead this 20th of June
Dead from Plague: 369
Dead this Week: 168
Parishes Infected: 19 out of 130
Holborn
Chancery Lane
Drury Lane
Long Acre
Hart Street
Russell Street
Bedford Street
St Martin's Lane
The Strand
THE RIVER
To Tuttle Fields
1
2
3
4
5
6
7
8

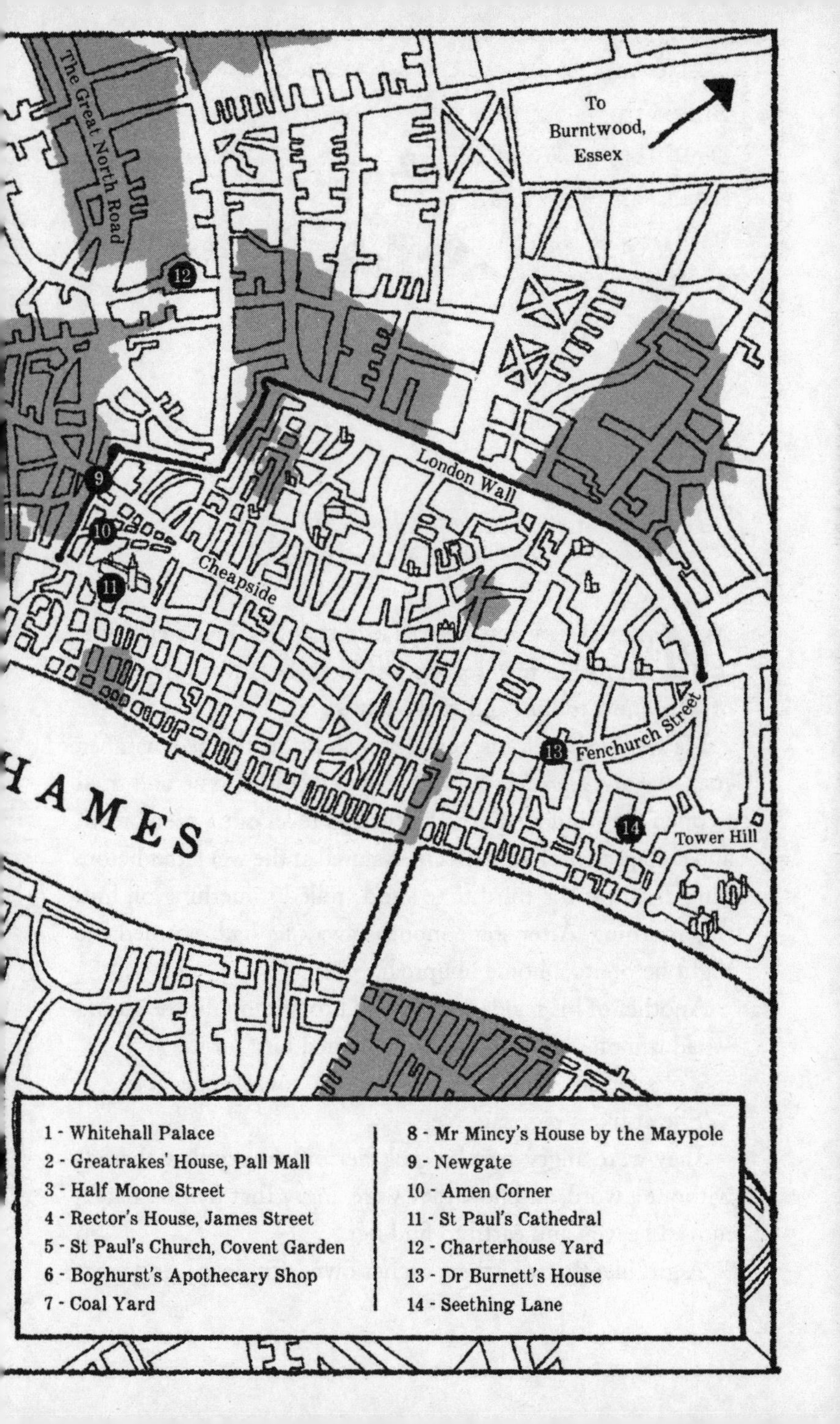

The Great North Road
To Burntwood, Essex
London Wall
Cheapside
Fenchurch Street
Tower Hill
HAMES
1 - Whitehall Palace
2 - Greatrakes' House, Pall Mall
3 - Half Moone Street
4 - Rector's House, James Street
5 - St Paul's Church, Covent Garden
6 - Boghurst's Apothecary Shop
7 - Coal Yard
8 - Mr Mincy's House by the Maypole
9 - Newgate
10 - Amen Corner
11 - St Paul's Cathedral
12 - Charterhouse Yard
13 - Dr Burnett's House
14 - Seething Lane

# 2

*Saturday, June 24th*
*James Street, Covent Garden*

MIDSUMMER. THE HOTTEST DAY Symon Patrick ever did feel in his life. His girl Nell slammed down a cup of whey next to him and stalked away.

He was sitting in his new little closet off the bedchamber. *Roasting was more like it.* He frowned. He bolted up and tried to open the window more. It refused. He let out a deep breath and collapsed back into his chair, stared at the wet letter before him. This was the third time she'd spilled something on him this morning. After some months away, he had returned the night before to a home in uproar.

Another of his maids – a girl he'd brought on for the spring – had run off and his household blamed him for it.

'Told you she were no good,' said his housekeeper Joan.

'She et like a pig,' said Nell.

They were angry that he took her on. Angry that she left without a word, and now they were angry that Symon hadn't moved heaven and earth to find her.

'A girl like that, out there on her own,' said Joan. 'And what with the sickness spreading so! It ain't right! Trouble clings to her like soot on linen.'

'I don't know what you mean, Joan,' was all he said. Though he knew exactly what she meant. He had taken the girl on as a favour to his brother, who lived across the Thames in Battersea. His brother claimed a need for economy, but there was such an urgency behind the request, and the girl so beautiful – a perfect peach of a thing – that Symon suspected his brother had done with her what he would and been found out by his wife. Symon couldn't afford to take her on permanently, but he agreed she could stay until another place was found for her; she could help Joan and Nell give the house a thorough cleaning while he was away. He rubbed his eyes; he would have no peace until he found the girl. 'And then have her beaten for her cheek'! Joan demanded. 'And tossed back out!' Nell added.

The girl had been gone for several weeks now; Symon had written to his brother when he first heard, hoping she had run back to him. But all Symon got in return was a vituperative letter blaming him for his carelessness. He had his sexton ask around the parish, and then returned to the business of restoring his health at the spa in Northamptonshire. He thought the matter well behind him – maids running off, it wasn't unheard of! – until he walked through the door last night.

'If we was to go missing, is that all you'd do for us?' Nell's voice had quivered. 'Write some letters? Then disappear back to your spa?' The girl was all knees and feet and gangly hands. She needed a new dress, Symon thought as he looked at her. She was a severe-looking thing, all in all. Her hair winched back tightly in its braided bun, the way she'd hitch up her cheek and squint her eye when you were talking to her, like she was taking aim. The other eye was no longer safe either, for it threatened tears.

'Of course not,' said Symon. He gave her an awkward pat on top of her head. 'I'd—'

'Take his dagger and stick whoever took us!' yelled Jack. He had an eye like his sister's. But his peeked out from behind shaggy blond hair and was more quizzical, like he was trying to square something, not shoot it.

Symon had given them both a kiss atop their heads, then gladly closed the bedchamber door on them. But his household found one excuse after another to intrude. Breakfast in bed, which ended up being breakfast on the floor. The gift of whey that turned into a milk bath for his letters. 'Fie,' he snapped. He would write again to his brother, take a sterner tone this time. His brother started this trouble; he should be the one on the hook.

He picked up the soggy letter by the corner and dropped it on to the cold hearth. He gave a quick mop of the desk with his sleeve – damp linen was a blessing in this heat – and pulled out a fresh sheet of paper. Wrote a quick note to his brother, then turned back to his original endeavour. He had been writing to Elizabeth. Or not writing to Elizabeth. He couldn't get past the opening. He tried again:

*My Friend,*
*It happens to be such a busy time that I cannot say all that I would.*

He took a sip of the whey, chewed on his quill. He could say nothing that he wanted. The truth would work no magic.

He could not tell her of this foul situation his brother had landed him in. Nor would he frighten her with a tale of his journey home to London the day before. The Great North

Road clogged beyond belief, stuffed with carriages stuffed with people; carts and wagons piled high with chairs and tables, bedding and trunks; crates of chickens and rabbits jammed into the cracks. Nothing moving beyond a crawl. The heat near to unbearable. Through unforgiving clouds of dust, he saw mothers with their eyes closed and fanning themselves uselessly under trees while their overdressed children nipped at each other for the waterskins. Drivers yelled their right of way, oxen refused to budge – the miserable bulldogs and pocket beagles sheltering under them in agreement. Symon's little coach – he was the only one in it – was constantly forced to pull over to make way for those leaving London. Each time he was stalled, he wondered what madness had seized him that he should agree to return when the whole town was fleeing.

A cramp flamed through his belly. The only remedy, his letter. Quill to ink, quill to paper and let the soothing scratches begin.

*With what little time I have to mee, I shall tell you that I am troubl'd with the thoughts of what this friendship will do to mee. Am I to believe the dreams that I have lately had of you?*

'Mweep.'

Down at his feet, his little cat Mite stared up with her spring-green eyes. 'Mweep,' she said again, cocking her head. She had missed him so. Was she getting fatter? How embarrassing.

'You want some pets? Come here, kitlin.' He gave some quick strokes to her cheek, then resumed his letter.

*This evening I shirk no longer. This evening I begin burying the plague dead so that you will not know mee to bee . . . or think mee to bee . . . the most weak, most pathetic, most . . .*

No. That wouldn't do.

He could tell her of Astrop, a new and most miraculous mineral well in Northamptonshire. As soon as the muddy spring roads were passable, he had gone to drink the waters there. The winter had not been kind to him; a cough sitting in his chest, many a parishioner ailing about him. He had walked amongst them every day, doing what he could. It was not plague; no, not yet. But a winter fever, a ferocious one that killed indirectly, through starvation. For it made even the strongest feeble, stranded them in their beds for weeks. Their families went without bread; the poorest of his parish would not have survived save for the funds and provisions raised by his church, St Paul's, Covent Garden.

By the first blooms of the crocus, that miserable fever disappeared and so Symon had set off to recover his health. He had hoped to stay a good while at Astrop, though with each new letter from London, a panic grew. They told of a dribble of cases in February, a rivulet in May, a torrent in June. Plague. There had not been such an accounting of the disease in near to thirty years, and while there was much hope most would be spared . . .

He heard a rip, the sound of claws tearing cloth. His cloth. Mite had hooked her claws into his stockings, then his knee breeches. She was pulling herself up, paw by paw, until she reached his lap. Stepped on to his desk and was now walking over his letter to Elizabeth. Wretched cat. He picked her up – she shrieked as if she were being gutted, she hated being touched – and gently placed her on the floor. She had a bad back, or else he would've thrown her.

Astrop was no more than a day's ride outside London, but it had taken him two great dusty turns of the clock to make it home. And then the driver refused to get too close to the city; had kicked him out of the coach with his bag at the edge of St Giles in the Fields, the parish to the north of Symon's. He walked the rest of the way, arriving home to his seething household in the middle of the night.

He had slept but little, there was much to do, and was up betimes. He had been writing letters since daybreak: to his sexton; to his patron; to Elizabeth, to let her know he had returned and was safe.

He stiffened. Sniffed the air. Made a face. What now? He smelled cold grease. He smelled sausages. He smelled Lodowick Mincy.

Mincy was a surgeon with a wealthy clientele, including several at court. He had inherited his distinguished list from his father, who had been a royal surgeon. A face without guile, a face that never registered the state of disgust he carried his own person in. The pudgy little surgeon wibbled through the door; two panting badger dogs trundled behind. Mite hissed and ran from the room. Symon took a long sip of whey, hoping to steady himself.

'I've come to watch your burials!' Mincy picked up Symon's parish register and paged through it. 'You see, I was at my breakfast and I had the most extraordinary idea. I could get a body a day off you.'

Symon spat out his drink. The surgeon was a most unusual man, Symon had long known this. He was blunt to a fault; said whatever was on his mind, and then seemed shocked that others didn't agree with him.

'I was frying up some sausages for Hans and Otto here.' He nodded to the two miniature dogs by his side. 'They're exquisite, aren't they? My brother sent them over from Hesse. Such dark velvety hair! Don't you adore them?' He gave each a stroke between the ears. 'And I'd heard you were back, and

I know you never say no to anything. You always help when asked and so if I am to end this plague of ours, I'll need bodies to experiment on and you'll give them to me.'

Symon raised both eyebrows. What new madness was this? He was to supply the surgeon with bodies? How did the man even know he was back? Symon decided to ignore him. Started to take off the stockings Mite had ruined. Used them to wipe up the whey he'd spat out.

'The slowness of my inquiry, it's killing me,' the surgeon went on. 'I find I'm filled with an irritation and a fretfulness that won't ease. It's caused me to resort to methods that really are not of benefit to anyone.' He frowned and looked at his dogs. 'A treatment will not be found through pen and paper. It requires blood. Man's blood. You have to help me. Or I'll be forced to cut up another dog.'

Symon dropped his stockings in horror; the surgeon nodded in agreement. 'I know! It's terrible! I've already tried with so many other dogs and I know it's useless . . . But I have to do something! I can't sit idly by; I have to get my hands into something. You understand, don't you?'

'No,' Symon said slowly. 'Not at all.'

The surgeon fell quiet for a moment, doubt spreading across his face. 'You won't help me?' He picked up a dog, began talking to it. 'You see? I don't understand people. They are so irrational. Uncharitable! They don't think clearly. I wonder what nonsense this rector is about to say, his defence of why he can't help us? Why he thinks it's better that I kill you than give me something already dead?' He kissed the dog, put it down, turned back to Symon. 'Lord! You have an irritable look about you. How is that possible? You've had two months' idleness!'

'I was recovering my health!' *Yes, most decidedly*, he thought, *the man be lunatic*. The surgeon would not hurt him, he knew, but he did fear for those dogs. He would stall. 'I am sorry, but we have no burials tonight.' He looked down at his cravat. *Whatever you do*, he thought, *do not look him in the eye*. Symon untied the loose knot, attempted to arrange it and retie it so it flowed like a soft waterfall down his shirt front; he had so admired the look at the spa.

'I'm surprised at you!' Mincy slapped his thighs. *They were rather like plucked goose legs*, thought Symon. Bony below, bloated and bulbous at the top. Raw ones, for they jiggled when the surgeon moved. 'I saw your sexton and he told me you had two bodies. You are an awfully ill-informed rector for such a rich parish. Three earls, four barons, eight marquesses and at least two of the king's sprats—'

'Is that what I've got?' Symon sighed and stopped fussing with his cravat. The ends flopped down like tiny crooked arms. When he first met the surgeon, he found him filthy and rude. Years later, he still found him filthy and rude. Over time, he realised the man wasn't like most people who said rude things, he wasn't trying to upset. But if that wasn't the case, why say them at all?

'Is that whey?' Mincy grabbed Symon's cup, took a sip of the yellow liquid, held it down for the dogs to lick.

'Yes.' Symon snatched the cup back.

Mincy shrugged, walked over to Symon's shelf and examined one by one the dainty objects on display. Symon groaned, he would have to have them cleaned; surgeons had such sticky hands.

'If I could get a steady flow of bodies, I could cut through this problem so much the sooner.'

'But you have so many patients, living ones, who can talk and tell you things the dead can't.'

'Not really. Plague kills so quickly, by the time I'm called a delirium has set in. And then the family takes possession of their bodies before I can come to any significant conclusions. Maddening.' Mincy plopped into a chair next to Symon, gave an exasperated roll of the eyes.

Symon had made a promise to himself during his time away. He would no longer engage in ridiculous ventures simply because it was easier than to decline. He had come back a stronger man. He didn't need to help everyone who asked. Especially people like Mincy. He closed his eyes, imagined himself in his churchyard, the plague bodies before him. He saw this pudge-pot of a surgeon waddling up to them, squatting down. He saw the man's greedy eyes roving underneath that thick hair cut straight across and too short on his forehead. Saw him prodding the dead, sniffing them, pinching them, squeezing them. Scraping off crusty bits and putting them in a pouch. Then he saw the surgeon tearing off carbuncles and whole pieces of flesh to study later. Oh, there he goes, popping a particularly meaty bit into his mouth. Anything was possible with Mincy. Then Symon imagined Lady Digby, one of the few nobles who hadn't yet fled the city, leaning out of her back window and screeching, 'Devils!' If he helped Mincy, at best, Symon would be out of a position; at worst, staked and burned.

'How I wish I could help you!' Symon lied. 'But it's simply not possible! You know as well as I do that bodies are God's sacred vessels! Even if I did agree with you, rules are rules . . .' Symon was looking past Mincy, going into a trance that enabled him to talk and talk and talk, his words becoming more banal as he went along. A new practice of his to wear down unwelcome visitors.

'But, Symon,' Mincy cut in, 'you dump them! Could you be any more wasteful?'

'I don't dump anything. I bless them and place them in a loving eternal rest.'

'Yes, a waste!' Mincy was in a full fit now, his arms flapping, flesh wobbling, his voice rising an octave. 'In the name of God, you must do this!' The surgeon's fit appeared to be taking flight; he was trying to lift himself out of the chair but kept falling back into it.

'I would be thrown out!' said Symon, half wondering if he should help the man up. 'The parishioners wouldn't stand for it; you don't cut up the bodies of the rich. We have none of the poorer sort . . . well, we do get some wandering over from St Martin's and St Giles . . . I suppose you could approach them. Now please leave.' Symon hooked him by the elbow, dragged him towards the door.

'Not even a little one then?' cried Mincy. 'One little body?'

'Revolting, Mr Mincy!' Symon's breath was getting shorter, he was feeling faint. Air, he needed air. A strange smell was growing in the tiny chamber. Uriny. The smell of nervous sweat. His sweat. *Lord, please help me*. He felt a fit of his own coming on. 'Are you going to jam things in them and pull and stretch and burn them? Are you going to peel off their skin to see what the infection has done, telling everyone I got you the bodies, all the while not bothered by the ghosts watching over your shoulder, planning your death? Not bothered what God may think of this desecration?' Sour juices pushed up his throat; he would be sick all over himself if this didn't end soon, he was sure.

Mincy peered over Symon's shoulder.

'Is that for Lady Gauden? I will say, you do have an uncommon beauty there!'

'I'm sure I don't know what you mean.' He shifted to block Mincy's view of the letter.

'She might like you more if she knew you helped find the cure.'

Symon flushed. 'Get out.'

'You'll come Thursday night?'

'Out.'

Mincy picked up one of his dachshunds and kissed it. 'Look at them! You like them, don't you?'

Symon pointed to the door.

'Didn't I tell you?' Mincy said to the dog. 'People! Most confusing creatures! All sentiment and emotion and circular reasoning! I tell you to sit and you do because you know it's suppertime! I tell you to bed, because it's bedtime. Now, if I tell that man there' – he pointed the dog's snout towards Symon – 'to sit. He says, "No thank you, I'd rather cut off my toe!"' He kissed the dog, threw the other one under his arm. 'I suppose it's up to us to solve this thing. Apparently this one' – he nodded at Symon – 'doesn't want to do anything other than mope over letters to Lady Gauden.'

Symon jumped at the insult, turned the surgeon around and shoved him through the door.

'They say you won't come on Thursday,' Mincy said over his shoulder. 'That you're not what you were. I am afraid I have to agree with them!'

'And I'm all the better for it!' Symon kicked the door shut behind him, heard Mincy say to his dogs as he went down the steps: 'To think I defended him! He should thank me for it. This is the greatest invitation he's ever had in his life! And he looks at me like I'm the lunatic? Now, how about we go for a nice walk and then a bath? More sausages? After that, what if we . . .'

Symon didn't hear the rest. He walked over to a little table that held the afternoon wine, poured a glass, downed it. He had no idea what Mincy was talking about; he had received no invitations for Thursday. *Do not let him in*, that's what he would tell his household. The surgeon was to be barred from James Street. Sweat pooled under his arms and ran down his chest and back. It wasn't even ten of the clock and the heat was gaining on him. What a terrible idea, this closet! Before he left for Astrop, he had ordered the builders to box in a corner of his bedchamber. A mistake to think he needn't supervise them!

He turned his mind to Astrop. Ah, Astrop. Its mineral waters most delicious. Such gentle conversations, such delightful supper partners. The tender care of the famed Dr Willis, the thought of future comforts. The idea of coming back to his home on James Street in Covent Garden, newly decorated, remodelled. To wrap himself in the fashionable new closet that now darkened his bedchamber because it stole the light from one of his windows. Not that there was any light in London. Gloom and murk and drizzle and smoke from hundreds of thousands of coal fires. At Astrop there was sunshine nearly every other day! The fact that the sky was as bright as heaven's courts today, the fires out with half the town gone, did not help. London was never what you needed it to be. He eyed his little shelf of treasures. A miniature of Mite's mother, Inky, painted by Elizabeth. A shiny toadstone and a devil's finger; he'd bought them in Portsmouth, they'd come out of the sea cliffs. A jawbone, pitted, of a fantastical beast. He found that one himself on the beach along the Dorset coast; the villagers there declared it a bad omen, for a priest to find such a thing. Bah, he told them. Who better than a man of the cloth to complete the inventory of God's creatures? They wanted him to give it to them; safer for all that way, they said. And then you'll sell it right back to me at a lofty price, he said. They tried to trade for it a coiled and ribbed imprint of a worm on a rock, a fright of a thing. He ended up giving them a few coins just to stop their grumbles. The shelf, despite being new, threatened to come off the wall. The room itself stifling. Yes, he could see it now, the treasures were stealing his air.

He had wanted more time at the spa. His health had improved there, his mind eased, but he still felt them, the holes, the tiny crevices where things could seep in, or his will could seep out. And such a terrible time to return, with this insidious miasma flicking all around them. But his patron, the Earl of Bedford, had sent him a note, gave him no choice: *'I can think of no better person to lead us through this most evil time than he who watches over and cares for our souls. My love to you as you safeguard my heart, which lies within the peoples of our parish.'*

A postscript got closer to the matter: 'We must think to our reputations!' The earl's father, with the old king's backing, had cut out the very centre of a venerable and beloved parish, St Martin's, to make what he called a jewel of a parish. The old earl had financed wide roads, built a church, St Paul's, Covent Garden. A mistake, that name! At best, people confused it for the far grander and ancient St Paul's Cathedral in the heart of the old London. At worst, when they wanted to insult Symon, they said he was rector at 'small Paul's'. Or the 'barn', on account of its plain appearance. But the old earl had cared not and invited the richest of the rich to build their worlds anew in the 'most spacious aeyres' of Covent Garden. St Martin's never forgave the earl, had looked for every opportunity since to create scandal. An empty pulpit during a time of plague would exactly suit St Martin's purposes.

Symon had bristled when he read the earl's letter. Then comforted himself with Elizabeth's reaction at the courage his return would signify. He imagined their reunion after this insidious miasma had left them. It was never far from his mind, this idea that he would seek out a smaller parish, a more amiable one. A hamlet deep in the countryside, away from the quarrel of London. A place Elizabeth could be fond of. There they would meet. She would take him into her arms, put his head upon her breast ... A sulphurous smell filled the room, his daydreaming cut short. He looked down. It was Mite. She had found her way back up, was sleeping on his letter. She grunted as he picked her up. She was a beautiful cat, her fur the colours of a blazing autumn: burnt oranges and ochre crossed with charcoal, a hint of the winter to come in her snowy paws. Rather, her once snowy paws, for they were now covered in ink. In addition to poisoning his air, she had smeared the ink, and thus was true to her mother.

He crumpled up the stained letter and threw it out of the window. The spa. There everyone asked after him, cared for him, encouraged him. Here it was nothing but need.

Symon took out another piece of paper, shouted for his boy Jack – the only one currently talking to Symon, for Nell's little brother was too young to hold a grudge – told him he would have dinner in his room and gave him a note for Bernard, the church sexton. Once the boy had gone, Symon ripped off his clothes – they'd become too damp and clingy – and pulled on a fresh linen nightshirt. Climbed into bed.

The note:

*My Dear Bernard,*

*I shall not bee able to attend the burials this evening or the morrow. A reoccurrence of my old troubles. Please seek out the curate.*

*Your affectionate friend,*
*S.P.*

# 3

*Sunday, June 25th. Symon's Bed, Then, a Charnel Ground*

SYMON SPENT THE DAY sweating in bed, staring at the canopy. That it was new gave him little comfort. His housekeeper, Nell and Jack clucked around him; they feared he might truly be ill and thus had called a temporary truce over the matter of the missing maid.

'He's gone green as the curtains,' said his boy Jack.

'Drab all around,' said Nell, picking up a bowl of untouched meat and broth. 'Look at his hair. All flat. Limp. Used to be such nice hair. Such a spring to it, like those clown in the boxes.' Symon scowled, put his back to them. 'For a minister to take to his bed on the Lord's day . . .' She sat down at the foot of the bed and he could feel her eye on him, assessing the situation.

'He's done lost it,' Jack agreed, scooping up with a finger some of Symon's half-eaten syllabub. Joan, Symon's housekeeper, had tried – and failed – to chase away his melancholy with the sweet, spiking the sugar cream with sack and lemon.

'Then we're done for as well. Better eat while we can.' Nell pushed her brother away from the dish so she could have it. Jack grabbed for it, jumping around her as she held it high above him.

'What nonsense! How is he to get on with all this squabbling?' Joan seized the syllabub from Nell. 'Downstairs with you both. If those coals go out, I'll slice off your fingers and make a jelly out of them.'

*They are right*, Symon thought as he listened to the sister and brother race down the stairs, pushing each other, *if I do not rise now, I might not ever. And then what will they say of you, Symon Patrick?* Eventually he forced one heavy leg then another out of the bed. Dragged himself to the top of the house, past the servants' rooms and out on to the roof. Some peace, some quiet, an adoring wife, adoring friends, intimate dinner parties, breezy days. That's what he wanted to come home to. Not this. He did have the view to himself, his neighbours all gone. But who wanted it? Instead of the caresses of a night breeze, he itched with the flicks and bites of insects, for the swifts, the swallows, the house martins, they would not settle in London this year – their disappearance one of the early harbingers of the great sickness. He had watched them fly over, a great widow's veil, shimmering across the sky. Their absence was soon filled by an explosion of frogs popping about the town's streams and swarms of ants filling the roads.

Symon called for Jack to set up chafing dishes of coals and juniper to smoke out the insects, and then for hours he scanned the night skies, hoping for a blazing star like the one that had brought London to a standstill Christmas Eve last. But this one, he prayed, let it be an omen of good fortune. The winter's comet had appeared in the east. A blue and purple cloud full of leprous spots, said some. No, said others, 'tis a coffin, large enough to hold us all. By three o'clock the comet had vanished, only to return every night for a fortnight. In February, another ill omen: flames filled the night sky, a celestial fire that lasted for hours. In March, the brightest comet yet, and with it the surety that plague was well upon them. The comet stayed all night, and would only leave when the sun came pushing in. And it was the sun that woke Symon the next morning, curled up on his roof, with not even a cushion under his head.

*This won't do*, he said to himself. He went downstairs, set about reframing his outlook and the work ahead of him. This missing maid. He would find her. Reassure everyone that he was capable, in charge. He studied himself in the looking glass, wet his hair, pulled and fluffed it with his fingers. Drab? Limp? Nell and Jack knew nothing. His dark brown hair was as thick as ever. He snipped off a bit that refused to behave and shook the scissors at the wavering face looking back at him. Plague dead? He would not fear them. It is a privilege to see to the dead. *Here is how to think of it*, he lectured his reflection, *a body in a coffin was an opportunity to reflect, take inventory. A warning. Even more so with plague.* He frowned, the memory of his last burials before he left coming forth. A late-winter freeze had set upon the town and he had been called to the house of the parish's most beloved physician, Dr Ponteus. Upstairs, next to a fire, Symon found the doctor sitting next to his daughter. She was lovingly wrapped in furs, curled up with her favourite doll. Her eyes were closed, she was gone. Symon had not arrived in time to help her out of the world. She had died of plague; the next day, her father and mother joined her. Symon was required to report any plague death to the authorities and he did record the deaths in the parish ledger. The cause, he left off. *Let them go quietly*, he had thought.

Symon spent the afternoon writing more letters. Again to his brother, to neighbouring clergymen. Asking for reports of his girl, of plague, of provisions for the sick. When the sun dipped towards the horizon, he put on his cassock, wrapped the black belt around his waist, and took a sip of the tonic prescribed him at the spa. He thought again of those last burials, the doctor, his daughter, his wife. How he had hidden their secret, given them peace. It was no longer possible to hide the sickness. All deaths were to be treated as plague now. *My dear Symon*, he thought, *it is no longer possible for you to hide, either.*

*

'About time,' Bernard grumbled. The sexton from Symon's church was waiting outside, scraping away at the stucco with his stick. Symon looked up in dismay at the cracks; they ran all the way to the roof. It was never-ending, this business with the house! He looked at Bernard out of the corner of his eye. The sexton was in charge of keeping the church and grounds in order. Would he perhaps help Symon with his house repairs? A more diligent and inventive sexton – particularly with the limited church funds – Symon had never met. He handled everything, with little need for direction. Or rather, he resisted all attempts at direction. Still, if Bernard ever stopped for a moment to clean the mud off his boots, pick the meat out of his teeth or comb down his porcupine hair, he could well take over for Symon in the pulpit. *What a roaring sermon that would be!* Symon thought. Hellfire exploding from every word.

'Thought I was going to have to drag you out like a breeched calf.' He gave Symon's house a last great bash with his stick, causing an explosion of plaster chips, then started walking towards the church. 'Should've spent the money for that silly closet on a good coat of paint, keep the damp out. Makes me sick to think of the money you wasted. Damn fool.'

*Ah, perhaps not*, thought Symon, hurrying after him.

'Found your girl,' Bernard said when Symon caught up.

'Oh, thank the Lord. She's upset a good many people, you know. Where is she now?'

Bernard only grunted. 'Tailor's daughter come in, too.'

'God help us, not Alice Jones?'

Bernard nodded grimly. 'Shut the whole house up 'round Saturday. Guard out front, lock on the door and all. The rest'll be dead by midweek, God save them. One house after another going down over there.'

Alice and her father had only a few months ago made Symon two new cassocks and a suit. Durable wool, yet of a fine cut. Elizabeth had wanted silk for him, but he didn't dare. The tailor had done the measurements, but the stitches were the daughter's elegant work. He frowned. She hadn't been pretty, that crook in her neck, but there was an apprentice who asked for her hand. Her father's money the lure, no doubt; he bit his lip and scolded himself for his harshness.

'Now, what's this? Move on!' Bernard stopped at the corner of the church. 'Shoo!' Stuck between the steps and the churchyard rails was a tiny black package, a cobweb of a blanket draped over something the size of a fawn. The smell was monstrous.

'I'll thrash 'em bloody,' Bernard muttered. 'All I ask is that they drop 'em off at the side. Leaving them here for all to see, scarin' everyone off.'

He swung his boot at the body and Symon grabbed him by his jacket to stop him, but he was too late. The boot hit, the bundle cried out.

'Bernard! For God's sake!' Symon crouched down and

reached for the edge of the cobweb. 'There, there, we're here to help you,' he said, hoping to calm whatever foul beast the sexton had awoken. 'You are amongst the blessed and have a home with the Lord.' *Bless this creature, dear Lord, for anything that smelled like that . . .* He pulled back the rag. A bony thing. Not a boy. A breathing fright of a girl. He couldn't tell how old she was, she could be twelve or twenty. Matted black hair hung down over her face like a shield. Pinpricks of ivory-white skin here and there, the rest of her covered in what he hoped was only mud. Bernard shoved a twig in her mouth to see if she had any teeth left; she screeched, opened a crusty eye and shat herself.

'Heaven help us. We're going to have to take her inside. Someone from the pesthouse can come and get her.' He hoped they still had beds open over at Tuttle Fields. Dried blood under her nose, a purple tint to her fingers – rot already setting in. Plague.

'Tell us your name,' Bernard barked, 'and where you come from, or I'll kick you again.'

A bare arm poked out of the rags and clawed more of her sticky hair over her face.

'Tell us your name now or I'll stuff you under the stairs and be done with you!'

'Penelope,' she mumbled.

'Takin' a lady's name!' Bernard raised his fist to strike her. 'Tellin' lies will only get you to Hell quicker!'

A pale grey eye sized them up from between two gloppy ropes of hair. 'Won't make me wash, will you?'

Symon gently pulled Bernard away. 'It won't do any good to beat her.' The girl had closed her eyes again, her mouth had fallen open. Dead or asleep, Symon didn't want to know. He looked around. 'We can't leave her here.'

Bernard huffed and disappeared through a gate, came back with a wheelbarrow. 'Get in there, turd blossom.' He prodded her with his stick. Symon pushed him aside and stooped to lift her into his arms. She let out a sigh. 'Hush now, my little one, we have you.'

Symon placed her into the wheelbarrow. *A hard bed indeed*, he thought. 'Bernard, a blanket, if you please.' The sexton stomped off again through the gate, swearing under his breath all the way. Symon looked down at their unfortunate discovery. 'Penelope, does it hurt?' He frowned at his own stupidity.

'Sleepy,' she peeped, then pulled the tattered blanket over her head.

Bernard was back; he threw one of the shrouds for the dead on her, took the wheelbarrow by its handles. 'We'll have one of the diggers take her down to the pesthouse.' He waved for a yard boy to follow him.

Symon could see she had no more than a few hours left. He couldn't let her spend her last moments being driven down a rutted road and then dumped in a house of death. He laid a hand on Bernard's shoulder. 'Take her inside the church, put her in the parish office.' The vestrymen, afraid of any kind of gathering these days, weren't likely to meet there soon. 'Set up a pallet for her, get someone to look after her, see her out, the poor puss. Some broth. She won't last long. Let's see what we can do to make her final moments a little more bearable. Think of it this way, it will save the pesthouse the work of bringing her back after she . . .' Bernard was already wheeling the fright into the churchyard, passing her off to be someone else's bother.

Symon took a deep breath. How were any of them to survive this? He continued on, past the church's towering double doors (they didn't open, they were fake – all for show – fit the parish to a T, said Bernard) and entered through a dwarf door on the far left. He rushed down the centre of the nave and made for his vestry, where he took off his soiled cassock and washed his hands. He quickly scanned the interior of the church. Bernard had said he'd found Symon's missing maid. Was she here? Or had she moved on to work for someone else? Perhaps Bernard hired her to be his own maid, she was a comely thing.

Outside, in the churchyard, he peered through the falling night. The yard boys – orphans Bernard collected as workers – were gathered in the north-west corner. Near them, Symon could see two long forms on the ground. The plague dead. One of them must be Alice, the tailor's daughter. Bernard had set torches all around the yard, their light flickered over the corpses, illuminating them one moment, plunging them into shadow the next. They weren't in coffins, not even in shrouds. They were just there, waiting for him.

Symon had been staring at the bodies for he didn't know how long, a hand resting on a companion for strength, the stone of one *Gilbert Cragg, dyed 31 October 1653, in the 49th Year of his Age,* when Bernard returned.

'No more coffins, Bernard?'

'Ran out.'

'Surely we can buy more—'

'With what money?' Bernard asked impatiently, tearing weeds away from a grave with his stick. 'Come on now, got something to show you.'

They walked closer to the bodies. Symon hesitated before looking down, afraid of the accusation he might see in their faces. At least they hadn't been stripped yet. The Lord Mayor had ordered all clothes from the plague dead removed and burned. The stockings, the stomachers, the doublets, the ruffs, the ribbons, the bows, the wigs – all of it was infested with plague seeds. Bury them and you'll breed more plague, the doctors said.

He looked at the nearer body, recognised the tailor's daughter. The crook in her neck hadn't relaxed in death; her chin thrust up towards the sky, giving her a look of defiance, anger. It made sense, for even in death, God had denied her a last chance to be pretty. Her hair wasn't lovingly braided, but a bird's nest. Instead of the pallor of angels, she had blackened patches of skin on her nose, her cheeks. Her fingertips were crunched and shrivelled. Symon felt ill. Bernard had laid her out next to the paupers' grave. Her family had not sent money to guarantee a private grave. They were not able to, sick as they were . . .

He glanced over to the other body, started to ask who it was, then shook his head in disbelief. A girl who had once been plump and merry was now a wasted corpse, lifeless. The thick braids he knew to be the colour of the summer sun had been cut off, the rest of it shorn unevenly to the scalp.

'Bernard . . .' Words failed him in his shock. He knelt down beside her. Thin little lines criss-crossed her hands, her face. A trick of the light? No . . . they were too even, too steady. They had been drawn on her by a human hand. His stomach cramped as his eyes fell to her neck, the plague bubo there. He picked up her cold hand, vainly attempted to warm it in his. His fingers touched strands of twine twisted around her wrist like some primitive ornament. He hadn't seen these on her before; but then again he'd barely seen the girl at all before he set off for Astrop. He traced a rope burn from the bracelet, she must have fretted it so in her misery, like some sort of a pagan rosary. Dazed, he looked up at Bernard. 'Mary. My brother's maid . . . my maid. How did you find her? What happened?'

'What happened?' Bernard snorted. 'Plague! And I didn't

find her. She found me. Dead cart brought her in, picked her up somewhere over around Long Acre.' They heard a great crash and a scream at the other end of the churchyard. 'Ho! Hedge-pigs! What now?' Bernard ran towards the yard boys; they had been playing with a tombstone, now toppled and cracked in two.

Symon looked back at the girl, touched a stub of hair. She went missing at the end of May. He stopped. Not missing. Fallen sick. Likely she had gone on an errand and the fever came upon her suddenly, she hadn't been able to make it home. A pain ignited behind his eyes, his vision blurred. He had abandoned her, hadn't taken her disappearance seriously. He should have come home. Maybe he could have found her in time. Got her some help. Someone had found her, though, had tried to help her. Cut her hair to cool the fever. There was that, someone had cared for her as she lay dying. Mind swirling, his gaze travelled down her legs. She had twine trinkets tied around her ankles similar to those on her wrists, but the illness had swollen her lower limbs and the twine had become too tight, cutting into her skin there, too. *Oh Mary*, he thought. He took out his prayer book and Lord help him, he didn't know why, but he nudged her skirts up with the book, past the knees. He fell back, dropped his book in fright. Her thighs were covered in a series of circular burns, some small, some terrifyingly large. He yelled again for Bernard. 'Good God! Did you see this?'

The sexton took his time coming back, his big arms now filled with white linen shrouds. Symon pointed at the girl's legs. 'Something horrible happened to her. These burns . . .'

Bernard shrugged it off, throwing a shroud to the ground and shaking out another. 'A ha'penny quack. Lucky she got even that.'

Symon's temper was rising. 'Your boys. Did they interfere with her? Cut her hair, sell it—' He stopped. The girl was rolling into the grave. Bernard had kicked her in.

Symon grabbed him savagely by the arm. 'What's wrong with you? That's my brother's girl, Mary, his servant!'

'That's what you call it, eh? He'll send money for a grave, then? I'll fetch her back out – once we've got the money.' He dropped a shroud down in the grave over her, then rolled Alice in.

'There was something wrong with her,' Symon yelled after him. 'I've never seen such . . .' His voice trailed off. The sexton paid him no attention. He stared at the grave. 'What she must have gone through,' he whispered. The yard boys were swarming around him now, shovelling lime and soil on top of the bodies, erasing them from this world. A boy tugged on his sleeve. 'Ready, Rector?' Symon picked up his prayer book and opened its worn leather covers. He fumbled for the right page, and began. 'I am the resurrection and the life, saith the Lord: he that believeth in me, though he were dead, yet he shall live: and whosoever liveth and believeth in me shall never die . . .'

As he turned from the paupers' grave, another dead cart rolled in.

# 4

*An Empty House, the Parish of St Giles in the Fields*

He put a hunk of dried bread on the table, a knife and cup beside it. Something to give the place a feeling of warmth. It had been in a terrible state when he'd found it. A house in Coal Yard, the caretakers long gone. Nothing left but a few dead plants on the windowsill, mouldy rushes on the floor, an overturned table. Through the back, sacks stuffed with straw in the corner, someone's old bed. He had checked upstairs to make sure no one had left an ailing granny behind. Peered out of each window to make sure not a soul looked back. The whole yard was abandoned. Perfect. He started a fire in the hearth, and to pass the time, took a broom to the front room and stairs.

Coal Yard, a woeful sight! A dusty court off Drury Lane, the arched stone entrance no wider than his shoulders. He'd nearly missed it, had walked by it many a time. But that morning, some wildling shop boy had nearly run over him with a cart; he was knocked right into the entrance. Fortuitous, really.

*

Once dusk fell, he ventured out to see who he could find. Those who hadn't fled, they wouldn't be paying attention, their minds focused on reaching the safety of their own hearths. The shadows stretched. He stood in the darkness. Waiting for her.

Too short, too thin, already infested. He needed the uninfected, so he could follow the progression of the disease, including the state of the patient before onset, for there was already too much guesswork in the matter. The evening neared its end; if the light were to pass entirely, no one would dare heed his call, that of a stranger beckoning in the night. He was starting to think of his own home, and the comforts that awaited him, when he saw her. Dandelion locks. Ample hips. Significant bosom. Much like the other one. He looked at the girl before him, what a pretty little step she had! Fine material indeed. He hunched over, limped right into her arms.

'Ack, my cat! Miss? Miss! Do you know anything about cats?'

Her mouth formed an O, her cornflower eyes showing innocence. And concern. 'I suppose I know something about the rascals. What's the matter?'

He pawed at her arms, pawed at his hat. 'She's gone up the chimney! I can't reach her. She won't stop meowing. I can see her, but my arm, it isn't long enough.' He held out the limb, giving a good tremor to it. 'Could you come and look?'

She crinkled up her nose, thought for a moment, then said slowly: 'I can try.'

*Good girl.*

He led her through the empty courtyard and into the house, dragging his foot.

'This way, this way,' he whined, taking off his cap and twisting it in distress.

He got behind her, still hunched over and patted her towards the back room with feeble pushes. He pointed at the hearth. 'There, she's up there! And with the coals going. Wicked cat.'

'Are you sure she's up there?' the girl asked. 'I don't hear her.'

'Wicked cat, she's up there! Can you get her?'

'She jumped up a hot chimney?'

'Yeeeessss, wicked puss! So wicked.'

He was learning that these scenes shouldn't make sense. Confusion distracted people, made them miss things.

'I don't think a cat would do that. Perhaps she went upstairs?'

'No, she took the cheese right off my plate' – he pointed to the table – 'and up she went. Owww. Go on there, look up there!'

She stepped closer to the hearth. 'I don't hear her . . . she's probably scaddled already. What's her name?'

She bent over, backside pushing out, and sing-songed up the chimney, 'Puss, puss, are you up there? Time to come down, my love.'

He picked up a wooden mallet from the chair, took a deep breath, and slammed it against the side of her head. She cried out and went down on one knee, crying out again as her hands fell against the hot hearthstones. He lunged forward, pulled her back by the collar and hit her again with the mallet, this time knocking her out. He laid her down on the ground and grabbed his sack from under the table. He took out the rope and tied her up, stuffed linen in her mouth. He shimmied the sack over her body and dragged her out to his cart.

Back inside, he swept up the coals and put them into a tin bucket for safekeeping. He pissed on what was left. No sense in burning down his new home. He put on a billowy labourer's shirt and coarse breeches. Left the hunk of bread for the rats, closed the door behind him, and pushed his cart down the back lane. God, she was heavy.

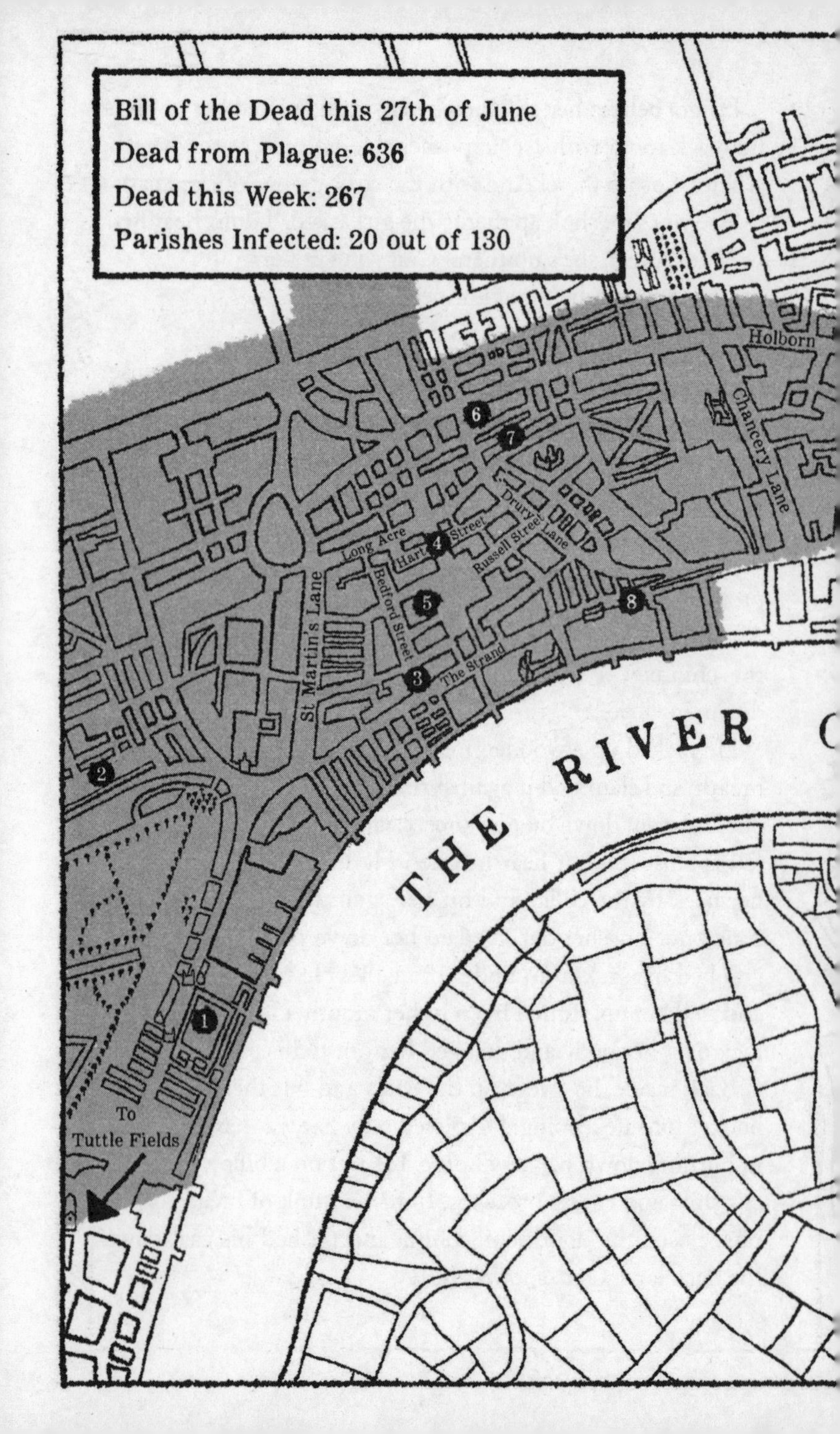

Bill of the Dead this 27th of June
Dead from Plague: **636**
Dead this Week: 267
Parishes Infected: 20 out of 130
Holborn
Chancery Lane
Drury Lane
Long Acre
Hart Street
Russell Street
Bedford Street
St. Martin's Lane
The Strand
THE RIVER
To Tuttle Fields
1
2
3
4
5
6
7
8

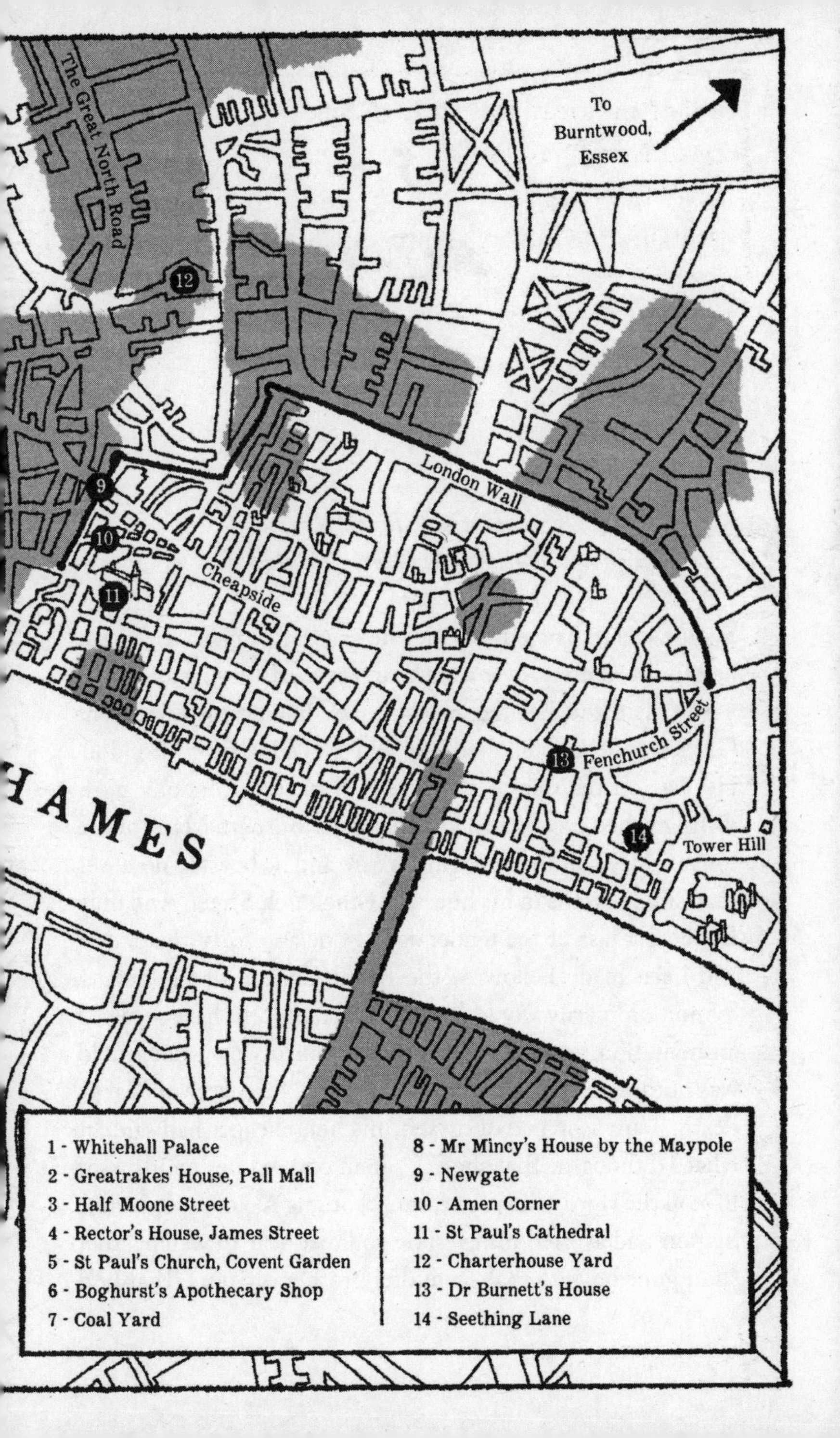
The Great North Road
To Burntwood, Essex
London Wall
Cheapside
Fenchurch Street
Tower Hill
HAMES
9
10
11
12
13
14
1 - Whitehall Palace
2 - Greatrakes' House, Pall Mall
3 - Half Moone Street
4 - Rector's House, James Street
5 - St Paul's Church, Covent Garden
6 - Boghurst's Apothecary Shop
7 - Coal Yard
8 - Mr Mincy's House by the Maypole
9 - Newgate
10 - Amen Corner
11 - St Paul's Cathedral
12 - Charterhouse Yard
13 - Dr Burnett's House
14 - Seething Lane

# 5

*Thursday, June 29th*
*The Parish of St Gabriel Fenchurch*

Symon's teeth banged together, he grunted in pain. The coach had thunked down over a crater in the road, serving as official notice that he'd left the smooth, new boulevards of Covent Garden and had entered the old walled city of London. He was on his way to the house of one of London's most distinguished physicians, Dr Alexander Burnett. Many of the town's oldest families were in his care and he boasted no fewer than nine hearths in his house in Fenchurch Street. And only December last, at the tender age of one and forty, the doctor had been made Fellow of the Royal College of Physicians. Symon ordinarily would have been flattered to have received an invitation to such a man's house. But his own household was nothing but tears these days with the discovery of Mary's death. 'I am ashamed of myself,' his housekeeper had said, 'at what I'd thought. That she'd . . .' Joan covered her mouth as if to stop the words, the pain from becoming too overwhelming. Symon had averted his eyes; he couldn't bear to watch. 'That she'd gone back to that scoundrel brother of yours. That he'd hidden her away, put her up in a nice set of rooms. Why didn't I search her out?' Her husky voice finally cracked; she turned her back to them. 'Never thought that she were out there alone! Dying! That she needed me . . .'

'You should've been here!' Nell had yelled through her own heavy sobs, her arms wrapped fiercely around her little brother. 'You said you would keep us safe.' Symon reeled even more at this. She was referring to what he had told Nell and Jack when he took them in a few years back. He tried to comfort the girl, but she pushed him away. He understood. She was frightened. They all were frightened. He had let them down.

'Mary has a nice spot at the church, don't she?' Jack had asked, rubbing his sister's apron strings between his fingers. 'One near the flowers?' Then he buried his little blond head in Nell's apron. Symon stared at his family; felt nothing but the scorching ache of his own failure. He leaned over and kissed the boy. 'The best of spots,' he whispered. He would pull Mary out of the paupers' grave himself. He was not so foolish as to think he could have saved Mary from plague; her final hours had been nothing but agony, that was clear – he hid from his household the hideous burns and cuts on her body. But he would right her burial.

As he left them, he heard Nell say to Jack, 'Don't you worry, I've got you. I'm no milksop!'

*No, girl, you are wrong,* Symon had wanted to say, *for I am not made of mush, but jagged straw.*

And so his heart was indeed heavy, his list of failings still growing when he had received the letter requesting his presence at Dr Burnett's house. The invitation was actually to join a new society the physician had formed that spring, the mission being to find a cure for plague. That was what that pushy little surgeon Mincy had been on about the other morning.

Symon had considered saying no. He couldn't afford any more distractions. Besides, what had he to offer these medical men? He doubted they were interested in prayer.

In the end he decided that he should go. Surely it was his duty to help in such a matter. He looked out of the coach window. The Cheapside shops were dark, closed. But he was surprised to see so many candles in the windows above; the shopkeeps and their families sitting down to a late supper. A contrast from his hollowed-out end of town. As if there was nothing to fear here. Perhaps there wasn't. Perhaps the pest would pass the old city over. So far there had been fewer than a dozen cases inside London's walls. The tavern trade certainly seemed to take an optimistic view; as his coach rocked past the Bear, the Greyhound, all winding down for the night, he saw a steady stream of workers – the more reliable ones – heading home.

The approach to Dr Burnett's house offered more balm. A most pleasing sight! The doctor had a corner house on a merry little street of the old style. Unlike the strictly symmetric houses of Covent Garden, these houses grew at their own leisure; new rooms, new floors added as needed over time, not a straight line to be found. Nothing pinched or forced to behave. Two were newer brick houses, but most were custard-coloured plaster criss-crossed with frayed timbers and topped with red-tiled roofs, including Dr Burnett's. Floors refused to match up with each other; even within the same house windows were placed half a man higher or lower than the next one over. The gables were cheery and broad, like old gossips chattering over the goings-on below. Chimneys from the kitchen fires puffed away, sending soft tendrils up into the night. Shaggy trees stood watch over the cloth-covered food stalls set on the corners. Empty now, but during the day they were filled with chickens, rabbits and birds of all kind, fish, sausages, big wheels of cheese, and midsummer vegetables. They hadn't been shut like the markets in Symon's parish. Here, he was once again in the land of the living. He dared to think of Elizabeth. Would she prefer to live in this part of town? *There is so much more warmth here*, he thought, even as his coach swerved around a mud hole big enough to swallow a pony, *than my perfect piazza*. Or nearly perfect. His church was one of the newest in the city. The old Earl of Bedford had been tired of finding vagrants squatting in his garden, so he guaranteed himself a better sort of neighbour by transforming his garden and surrounding fields into a replica of Venice. He built fine, tall townhouses of brick and stucco and arranged them around what he called a piazza. The earl's mansion formed the southern border and Symon's church, with its Grecian portico, was to be an elegant finale on the west side of the piazza.

The trouble was, said the Bishop of London, the church entrance was on the wrong side. All proper Houses of God had their entrances facing west. The earl's new church faced east. But the bishop didn't say this until the church was nearly complete. The earl said it was of no matter; there was nothing in the Bible ordering churches to face west. 'Well, if you don't mind being branded a heretic . . .' the bishop said. The next day, a new set of double doors was cut out of the back of the church; the old front doors sealed. The earl, however, refused to dim the splendour of his new piazza by knocking off the columns and pediment on the original entrance, so what was now the back of the church continued to look like the front, leaving Symon, like his predecessors, to have his sermons interrupted by poundings from visitors trying to enter through the sealed doors. Not their fault, Bernard said when Symon complained, they didn't build the church arse-backward.

As his carriage rolled past Dr Burnett's parish church Symon wondered which was better for prayer, his nouveau temple or that crusading old barnacle, St Gabriel Fenchurch? 'Whichever's warmer,' he could hear Bernard saying.

He paused as he stepped out at Dr Burnett's house; there was an exceedingly tall, thin figure holding open the front door. It was a confusing gesture, for the man had not acknowledged Symon and he could see no one else around. For whom did he hold the door? He squinted through the dusk; the man wore a large pale cavalier hat, its ostrich plume long and rippling in the night breeze. Thick, ballooning curls fell past his shoulders, but they were light in colour. *The hair must be his own*, he thought, *for the fashionable wigs mimicked the king's preference for black curls.* Symon approached, heard the man murmur warmly, 'My darling . . .'

There was an Irish lilt to his voice and the pictured formed fully. It was Valentine Greatrakes. Symon felt his nerves wind even tighter. The man was a court phenomenon; Symon would indeed be in esteemed company this night. But Symon also considered him a royal nuisance. Greatrakes had arrived in London the summer before and Symon had met him at several dinners around town; he was always petitioning for testimonials to his powers. Greatrakes was considered to be a most powerful mystic. One who claimed kinship with kings; God bestowed upon kings the power to heal with the touch of a finger, and for some reason He had also deemed Greatrakes most worthy of such a gift. ('Oh, I don't know why!' cried Greatrakes. 'Our Lord doth move in a mysterious way . . . Though I might add, I have to use all ten!')

'Good evening, Mr Greatrakes,' Symon said with a short bow.

The man was startled at first, but then swooped in to kiss

Symon's cheeks in the French manner. 'Come now, we're more than that to each other!' Greatrakes said.

Symon tried to play merry, too. 'The door, good sir, do you hold it for me? Most kind of you.'

'Goodness, no!' Greatrakes threw his big head of white curls back and laughed. 'Didn't even know you were invited! But now that you're here, I couldn't be more pleased!' He lowered his voice. 'I know you feel . . .' He searched for the word. '*Things* . . . as keenly as I do, Mr Patrick. So I do not mind telling you that I hold the door for my dear wife.'

'But she's d—' Symon stopped himself, mortified at what he had been about to say.

Greatrakes stood his full height and looked down at Symon. 'Yes, thank you for reminding me, Mr Patrick. Nonetheless, she is with me wherever I go.' He threw up his hands in a grand show at the brightly lit mullioned windows above them. 'And she would not miss such an adventure as we are to have this night!'

Symon looked over his shoulder to see if his coach was still in sight. *It's not too late*, he thought, *I don't have to go in* . . . He lurched forward; Greatrakes had put a paddle-sized hand on Symon's lower back and shoved him through the door. Symon stumbled up the stairs, not sure what bothered him most. That he had clumsily reminded the man that his much beloved wife was dead; that the man thought she was still here; or that he was once again allowing himself to be pushed around.

He took a moment to catch his breath before pulling back the pocket doors to Dr Burnett's dining room; he could hear the gathering in full force inside. But Greatrakes let out an impatient sigh and stepped around Symon. Cheers went up as Greatrakes entered; he swept off his hat, put a pointed foot forward and bowed to the company. 'At your service, my most dear friends!'

*The man really is too much*, Symon thought; then jumped as someone shouted his name. It was Lodowick Mincy, the puffy little surgeon.

'Symon! I knew you would come!' Mincy was kneeling by the sideboard, feeding tartlets to his odd little Hessian hounds. 'Look ye! He's braved the quarantine!' The surgeon swayed to his feet and trotted over to embrace Symon.

'Quarantine?' Symon looked around, perplexed. He knew of no quarantine in the old city. There had been that strange case of the two manservants who had come down with plague. One had died, the other had gone missing. Symon paused . . . it was like what had happened with Mary. Except no one knew about her. The case in the City, everyone had heard of it. It was in all the newsbooks, though it was still a rather mysterious affair. There was some suspicion of foul play, that the master had been so incensed that his servants had brought plague into his house, he had beaten one to death. Perhaps both of them, since no one had been able to locate the second manservant. Though the master had been considered a most respectable man, a doctor even. Oh no . . . Symon's knees buckled as he recalled the name. Dr Burnett.

'Indeed! Right here.' Mincy had gone back to the sideboard and grabbed a tartlet for himself. 'This very house, most extraordinary!' Symon looked at their host, Dr Alexander Burnett, who was standing by a blazing hot fire, his wiry copper hair and complexion fit to match.

'Now I have asked you repeatedly, Mr Mincy, to leave the past in the past,' said Dr Burnett. 'Such talk! Shall my wife be thrown back upon her bed, melancholic and aggrieved, because of your insensitivities?'

The room started to spin; Symon put a hand against the wall to steady himself. He was in a plague house. A steaming one that smelled like a shambles. It was one thing to stand over the plague dead in his churchyard. Quite another to be in a house were the disease had lived and bred. Why were the windows closed? He stumbled over to open one. Dr Burnett ran past him and slammed it back shut. Symon recoiled, bewildered. 'Mr Patrick! Thrilled you could join our happy little gathering. Your contributions will no doubt greatly increase our chance of success!' The doctor smoothed his copper coils back into place, whispered, 'You do understand, I only recently got the miasma out of the house. Wouldn't want it wandering back in, would we?'

'Buck up, Symon, it's safe. Enough.' Sitting at the far side of a long walnut table was William Boghurst, apothecary to be found at the sign of the White Hart Inn, and one of Symon's oldest friends. They were from the same village in Lincolnshire and had known each other since boyhood. Symon's father was a shopkeep there and Boghurst's the local apothecary. They had bonded over the bitterness of being the children of tradesmen in such a small place. No one ever paid their fathers, everything always in arrears, which made for many a cold evening. The family stews were thin, and the prospects for the children even thinner. Boghurst complained that the scarcity of meat – it was only served on birthdays, and only to the birthday child, while the eight other brothers and sisters were forced to watch – was the cause of his hummingbird stature and colourless hair. These days, he liked to say it had all rather been a blessing. Taught him how to get by without much food, or the sleep that goes with a full belly, and so he could do a supernatural amount of work and thus keep his own family plump and pretty. Symon had left the village – at a young age he discovered that he could sit and write all day without stopping, and so he wrote himself into Cambridge on a scholarship. No one could understand much of what he wrote, but they said Cambridge would work that out – and so he lost track of Boghurst. Deliberately. A disturbing incident that he didn't like to think on, involving the village animals. When Symon took up his position in Covent Garden a few years back, he discovered his old friend had a shop nearby. Symon decided to renew the friendship, they had been children after all, and it was a child's nature to be cruel. Surely time had corrected this flaw in his friend. *Or not*, Symon now thought, for the apothecary had his boots propped up on the table in a roguish way, and was looking all too pleased with himself. Boghurst had ever since been a frequent visitor at Symon's house and church. 'Good Lord no!' he had said when Symon once asked him if he would like to join him in prayer. 'A nice chat about the old village! That's all I want. And a drink?' Boghurst had been over several times since Symon's return from Astrop; he was in fact the one to convince Symon to come out this evening. Never once did he mention the meeting was to be held in a plague house. Of course.

'We must, as Dr Burnett said, think to his wife and not talk of that matter. Will Annie join us?' Boghurst asked the doctor, a look of eagerness on his face.

'Do not call her that,' the doctor bristled. 'You've missed her by a good few hours. She's gone to our sister's.'

'Another time then, a family supper perhaps? I would—'

'I think not,' Dr Burnett said, taking his seat in the middle of the table.

Symon was still standing by the window. The bells of St Gabriel's struck the hour. He would give this a half-hour then make his excuses.

Quill in hand, spectacles perched on the tip of his ruddy

nose, Dr Burnett opened the ledger in front of him. 'Let's see who is here, shall we? Mr Boghurst?'

Silence.

'Mr Boghurst? Is there a William Boghurst here?'

Boghurst leaned over, whispered, 'Yes, my copper badger, sitting right next to you.'

Dr Burnett ignored the slight. 'Wonderful, I shall mark you as present. Did you secure a body?'

'No, the body had a previous engagement.'

'Unfortunate.' Dr Burnett scratched a note in his ledger.

'Mr Valentine Greatrakes? Are you here?'

'What? My grand bow wasn't enough?' Greatrakes was squished between Boghurst and Mincy, his arms slung convivially around their shoulders. Symon, thoroughly annoyed, wanted to ask him where, exactly, his dear wife was now. On Mincy's lap? Or Boghurst's? The man looked far from a portrait of grief. While the others wore clothes and faces stained and dirtied by their day's labours (Dr Burnett in particular had the look of a drowned spaniel – what with those bulging eyes and sweat-drenched curls), Greatrakes appeared fresh as a day-old baby. There was nary a wrinkle in his suit of lavender silk. His curls were full, indefatigable, much like Greatrakes himself. Another shiver of distaste ran through Symon. He had been caught off guard by Greatrakes' rare display of vulnerability earlier. The man was not known for his depth of feeling. He was one of the Anglo-Irish; he had a vast estate back in Ireland, near Cork. His family had been given land by one of the English kings, in exchange for sending back reports and bringing God's true word to the Catholic heathens. In thanks, Greatrakes had told him, the heathens burned his family off the estate. Greatrakes also liked to say it was all his father's fault; when he himself had gone back to soothe the natives and reclaim his land he found he could get them to do whatever he needed as long as he told the mothers their children were beautiful. As to their complaints about lack of food, well, he would point out that small meals were better for the digestion. His father's great failing, he said, was to not recognise that love solved all. Greatrakes made sure it infused everything he did. And for that, he said, God had given him this great gift – the power to heal. With God's love working through his hands, he travelled from town to town, always residing with some minor aristocrat to whom he had restored the use of a leg or ear or bladder. He would hold forth in village squares, running his giant hands over the bodies of the ill. Symon had attended one of his shows – partly forced by Greatrakes, partly out of curiosity. He had watched Greatrakes' hands and enormous white curls swish back and forth over one ailing soul after another. They all jumped up at the end, claiming a miracle, that they had been healed. Symon had not yet made up his mind on this. Greatrakes made much ado about the fact that he healed for free at his public shows. But for those not blessed enough to be in the front of the line, he would stroke them with his healing hands in private for a fee. A fat fee. Symon tried to like him, they were both men of God. But . . .

'Did you bring a body?' Dr Burnett continued, making another mark in his book.

'My body,' Greatrakes said as he inspected the ends of a white lock he had twisted around a spatulate finger, 'sad to say, much like Mr Boghurst's body, had other plans. Prior commitment to play Yorick over at Drury Lane. Couldn't talk him out of it. One rarely gets that kind of attention after one's dead.'

'Spare us the sprankles, Mr Greatrakes. This is a business meeting, not one of your shows.' Dr Burnett drew his pen down the list to see who was next. He looked over his spectacles at Mincy, who was busy nibbling on one of his own thumbs. 'Mr Mincy, have you secured a body or must you, too, fail us?'

Symon groaned. A meeting to collect bodies. This is why he had been invited. Like Mincy, they thought he would be their supplier.

'I tried. I really did,' Mincy whined as he stroked the hound on his lap, the other asleep under his chair. 'I had six people die on me this week. I offered all the families money. They refused me.' He looked at the dog as if it understood him. 'I explained and explained, it was so very frustrating, wasn't it?'

To be such a famed surgeon with so many rich patrons and such a repulsive lack of feeling; Symon couldn't understand it.

'Symon!' the surgeon abruptly shouted. 'The cream and cakes!'

'Pardon?'

'Where are they?'

'What do you mean?'

'Well, if you didn't bring the cream and cakes, did you bring a body? No? I heard you had a dead servant, too. What about her?'

Symon blanched, was about to scold the surgeon when Dr Burnett cut in. 'We will have no talk of servants, dead or alive, at this meeting! I will not stand for such disrespect to my family!'

Mincy, looking disappointed, whistled to wake up his dogs. 'I think the boys and I should go home. This meeting is most confusing to me. No one did what they said they would do.'

'Sit back down, Mr Mincy!' Dr Burnett racked a stack of papers against the table then passed them around. 'You didn't bring a body, either.'

'At least I tried. Very hard.' He took one of the papers, started to read it. 'Seems to me no one else did. So why show up?'

Symon peered down at the list scrawled on the paper shoved into his hand. At the top: *Anatomical Examination.* Symon handed it disdainfully to Boghurst.

'All of you have an agenda before you, copies courtesy of my house,' said Dr Burnett. 'We've agreed five meetings running now, excluding the interval between the second of May and the twenty-fifth of June when I was . . . preoccupied, to dedicate ourselves to securing a body for group examination. I quote from the meeting of the first of April.' He held up the ledger. '"To further our study of this Dreaded Visitation, which worsens by God's Holy Minute, to procuring one body, if not more, per meeting for systematic investigation." And yet we have no body.'

Greatrakes bobbed his head, acknowledging the awful truth of the ledger.

Dr Burnett pulled from the back of the book a piece of paper and shook it at them. 'I am quite sure, my esteemed colleagues, that you have made it a priority to consult the latest bill of mortality, out today. Has anyone not seen it yet? I would be happy to give you my copy.' The bills were compiled each week by parish clerks, tallying the number of people who had died in the 130 parishes in and around London, breaking down the deaths by cause and separately by parish. The bills came out on Thursdays, and most weeks dropsy, consumption, griping in the guts, worms in the teeth and fevers led the causes. But as of mid-June, plague was the biggest killer; it had been likely stealing away mothers and fathers, babes and grandames for some time now. The first case spoken of came on Christmas Eve. Searchers, old women paid by the parish to examine the dead, were called to a pinched court in St Giles in the Fields. There, in a cellar, they found a woman neatly washed and dressed, laid out on the table. Her children, heads lowered to hide their tears, sat in chairs along the wall. Their father sat on the floor next to them, staring blankly at the corpse of his wife. Surely there were other deaths, Boghurst had said, recounting the story to Symon one night over a late supper, deaths passed off as smallpox or spotted fever, people claimed anything to avoid having their houses shut up, or in the richer parishes, the scandal of a disease born of filth. Symon had a twinge of guilt, as he thought of Dr Ponteus and his family, how he hid the cause of their deaths.

'A doubling in one week's time!' Dr Burnett read from the sheet, his poppy eyes near to exploding. 'Three score and two hundred dead in one week alone! Gentlemen, it's happening. The sickness is here, around us, upon us!'

Symon did not like the look of the doctor at all. He whispered to Boghurst, 'He's gone purple and his eyes, they flutter so, I wonder he can see at all. Are we sure he wasn't infected?'

Boghurst ignored him and turned to address the group. 'It's not that simple. It is similar to what our dear surgeon Mr Mincy said, though not quite as Mr Mincy said, for as usual, he fails to account for the delicate side of human nature.'

'Delicate?' Mincy replied. 'We are one of the hardiest creatures that ever walked God's earth!'

Boghurst took a sip from his glass, swallowed. 'Yes, I will try again, though you never seem to catch on.' *Rudeness*, thought Symon, *a cornered man's wit*. His friend was sinking. Served him right.

'Delicacy. It is often the lack of such refinement that is the first sign you are in the presence of a surgeon.' The apothecary's gaze followed his finger as it traced the rim of his glass. One that was now without wine and likely had no wine in its future; the sideboard had not been replenished. Boghurst cut off from drink was a dangerous thing. That was the real secret to the apothecary's heavy workload and long hours, Symon knew. 'A lowly calling, because he is trained at best by a line of surgeons, the first of whom was no more than a barber. Who then turns butcher. A butcher, who, upon discovering how easily he can sever a beast at its joints, decides he is amply experienced to apply this work to God's highest creation, man.'

'Don't you have some cats to milk?' shot back Mincy.

'Gentlemen, come now,' Symon said. 'We've got rather off topic and perhaps—'

'Must we pull a crow? I recall you to our business!' Dr Burnett took out another paper from the back of his ledger and threw it down the table. 'This, from my dear neighbour, Mr Pepys. He left it yesterday.'

Symon picked it up and read it aloud: 'Lord! To see how the plague spreads. It being now all over King's Streete, at the Axe . . .'

'It is the very heart of Westminster he talks of! The Palace! Parliament! The Axe, a most favourite spot for refreshment!' said the doctor. 'Given that the very foundation of our great land is in jeopardy, I ask you, I ask all of you, why have you not secured a body?'

Boghurst raised a finger to silence the doctor's sputtering. Then he reached over for Mincy's smudgy glass and poured its wine into his own. He took a sip, swished it around his mouth, studied the chandelier for a few moments, swallowed the wine. Cleared his throat. 'It is this. The family calls for you, hoping that you will save their loved one. Perhaps it is the mother, she who brought them into this world. She who holds the family together. Or perhaps it is the father, upon whom all of their fates depend. Or worse yet, the littlest babe. You try your best, you fail, inevitably' – nods from around the room – 'and then you must interrupt them when they are at their most tender, most vulnerable, and ask if you can take their precious beloved, that plump little piglet they called Grace . . . or Hope, to be handed over to a drooling, insensitive, dirty, double-fed' – he aimed his finger at Mincy – 'sneak.'

Symon was appalled. These petty rivalries, such meanness!

'You mean the boil-covered, blackened corpse that no longer resembles humanity?' Mincy shouted. 'I don't get it. The body has lain there, smouldering, complaining, erupting. Threatening to wipe out the whole family, their neighbours for that matter. The family's dog has long escaped, with much good sense. You'd think they would beg us to take the body, throw it at us!'

'You had a body,' Boghurst snapped, pointing to Dr Burnett. 'Possibly two bodies, your manservants, if I recall correctly. Why did you not keep them?'

Dr Burnett's eyes were pinched shut, his fingers manically massaging the bone around them. 'You are out of order, gentlemen!'

'Is it not also odd,' Boghurst continued, 'that the sickness happened here, in your home, but nowhere else in your parish? Did you fail to follow proper fumigation procedures after visiting patients? Did you bring it home with you?'

Dr Burnett, eyes still jammed shut, got up and went to the door, called for a servant. 'Coats, please!'

He put his hands out in front of him to feel his way back to his chair. 'Have a care! You vex me so!'

Much to Symon's disappointment, the servant did not appear and so on and on it went. The bickering. Notes written down, then crossed out. It was endless, they could agree on nothing, and after they tired of attacking each other, they attacked colleagues not present. Ad nauseam comparisons of the plague in Athens, the plague in Constantinople, of Venice, of Antwerp, of Slough. Had anyone had any success with any treatment?

'A cure, we need a cure, people!' screamed Dr Burnett.

'What about Thomson's Buffo frog remedy?' Greatrakes asked.

'The antithesis of all good physick,' said surgeon Mincy.

'Yes,' agreed Dr Burnett, 'I have no time for hanging toads by their legs until they die, then pulverising the beasts and force-feeding them to my patients. Cold beer works much better, the medicine of ancient Greece at its finest – treat a fever with its opposite, a cooling agent.'

'Plus doctor and patient can both partake of the remedy. I see your logic now!' Greatrakes added. 'Most pleasant! But I ask you,' the Irish mystic continued, 'is plague carried in seedlets or miasmas or atomical effluvia or epidemical aers?'

Symon spoke up, an attempt to put an end to their useless discussion. 'I remind you that there is one and only one origin, and one and only one treatment. Plague comes from God, a punishment for our sinful ways.'

'Rather harsh of you,' Greatrakes sniffed.

'Too right,' Dr Burnett said. 'How dare you insult my family!'

'I only—' Symon's cheeks were burning now.

Dr Burnett went back to the door and screamed again for a servant to bring his guests' coats.

'Another one dead?' Boghurst said drily.

'The bowels of the earth!' Mincy shouted, disturbing his dogs who were now yipping frantically. 'Have they not opened? Spewing centuries of clogged-up faeces upon us all, taking the form of plague?'

'No, no,' said Dr Burnett, who heard it from his patient and good friend Mr Pepys that it was all to do with Holland. ('Enough of Mr Pepys,' Boghurst said. 'I've never met a more pumped-up bootlick.') The country had sought to deliver a fatal blow to its English enemy by sending over a very fine parcel of silks, with pestilential steams buried in the layers.

'Brought it on yourselves, didn't you then?' Greatrakes made a moue. 'The best silks come by way of France, and if England doesn't know this by now, then Heaven's pity on all of you.'

The cockpit was in full fury. Symon was compared to a drangled goose; Greatrakes to a weeping wen; Boghurst to a ripe, round jar of pickled testes, at which point he pulled out his own to show they were ripe and round, but not pickled. Mincy called for a trial of knives. Boghurst tucked his testicles back in. Fists thumped, chairs fell over.

Symon slipped out, tiptoed down the stairs and out into the cool night air. *What pother!* he thought. *To squander an evening so!* He flinched as he heard the sound of breaking glass, threw a disgusted look up at the strange shadows flailing past the dining-room window. 'That,' he yelled to them, 'is the last time I shall attend a meeting of the Society for the Prevention and Cure of Plague!'

# 6

## *An Upper Floor, West End of Town*

NO FAMILY TO HELP HIM. No assistants, no nurses. He was tasked with the entire care and well-being of his patients, day and night. Frankly, he wondered if he had the stamina to pull this off. He'd been hoping for a quick solution. One of his pet theories was that hair of gold prevented plague from taking hold. But he had scooped out infectious material from the buboes of an active case and managed to infect four angel-haired beauties now and still no breakthrough. Still, he wasn't the type to give up. He was soaking the hair in a solution, trying to distil and concentrate its gold. He was worried he didn't have enough; the hair didn't boil down to much. He should offer to buy hair from girls. Why hadn't he thought of that before?

He looked over at his patient. She was unconscious. He had felt very alone for a long time now. Alone with his thoughts, alone in his soul, alone in his heart. Hadn't fully realised how blessed he'd been all of those years. The coldness he felt now, being cast away. Would he spend the rest of his life feeling thus? No, of course not, that would be unbearable. He had made a mistake (But which one? Or all of them?), he would make things right. He would show himself worthy again, this current venture, no ordinary man could succeed in it. He could.

Over on the bed, his patient stirred and he braced himself. He didn't mind the weeping and the crying, but when she talked, it made it harder to focus. She lacked conversation, only had complaint. So he had put her out for a bit. He stretched his hand, his knuckles bruised and swollen. Foolish. Some linen stuffed in her mouth would've served the same purpose. This was tough work, but he would prevail.

# JULY

*I met this noon with Dr Burnett, who told me, and I find in the newsbook this week that he posted upon the 'Change, that whoever did spread the report that, instead of the plague, his servant was by him killed, it was forgery, and shewed me the acknowledgment of the master of the pest-house, that his servant died of a bubo on his right groine, and two spots on his right thigh, which is the plague.*

Samuel Pepys, Naval Clerk, Seething Lane

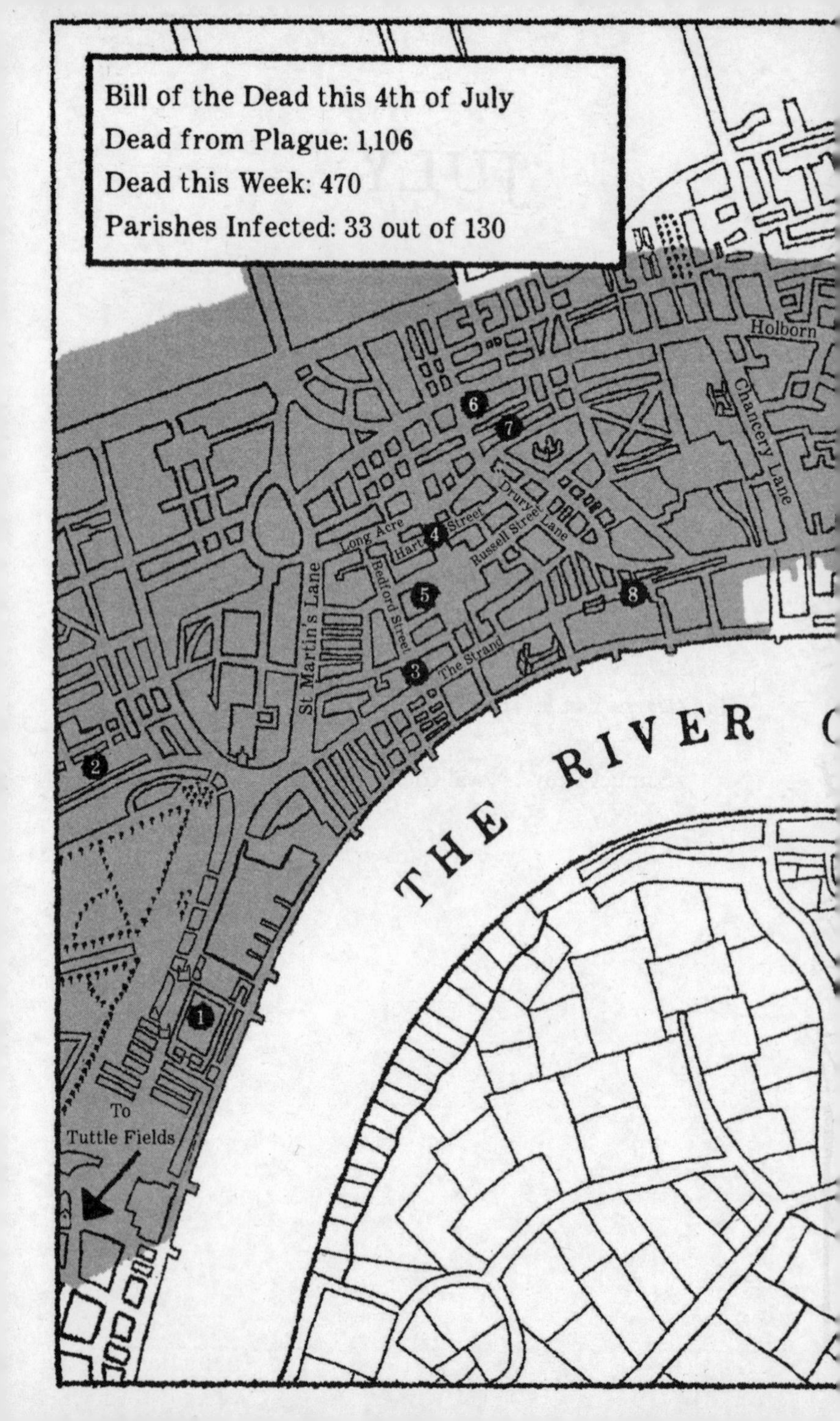
Bill of the Dead this 4th of July
Dead from Plague: 1,106
Dead this Week: 470
Parishes Infected: 33 out of 130
Holborn
Chancery Lane
Drury Lane
Long Acre
Hart Street
Russell Street
Bedford Street
St Martin's Lane
The Strand
THE RIVER
To
Tuttle Fields
1
2
3
4
5
6
7
8

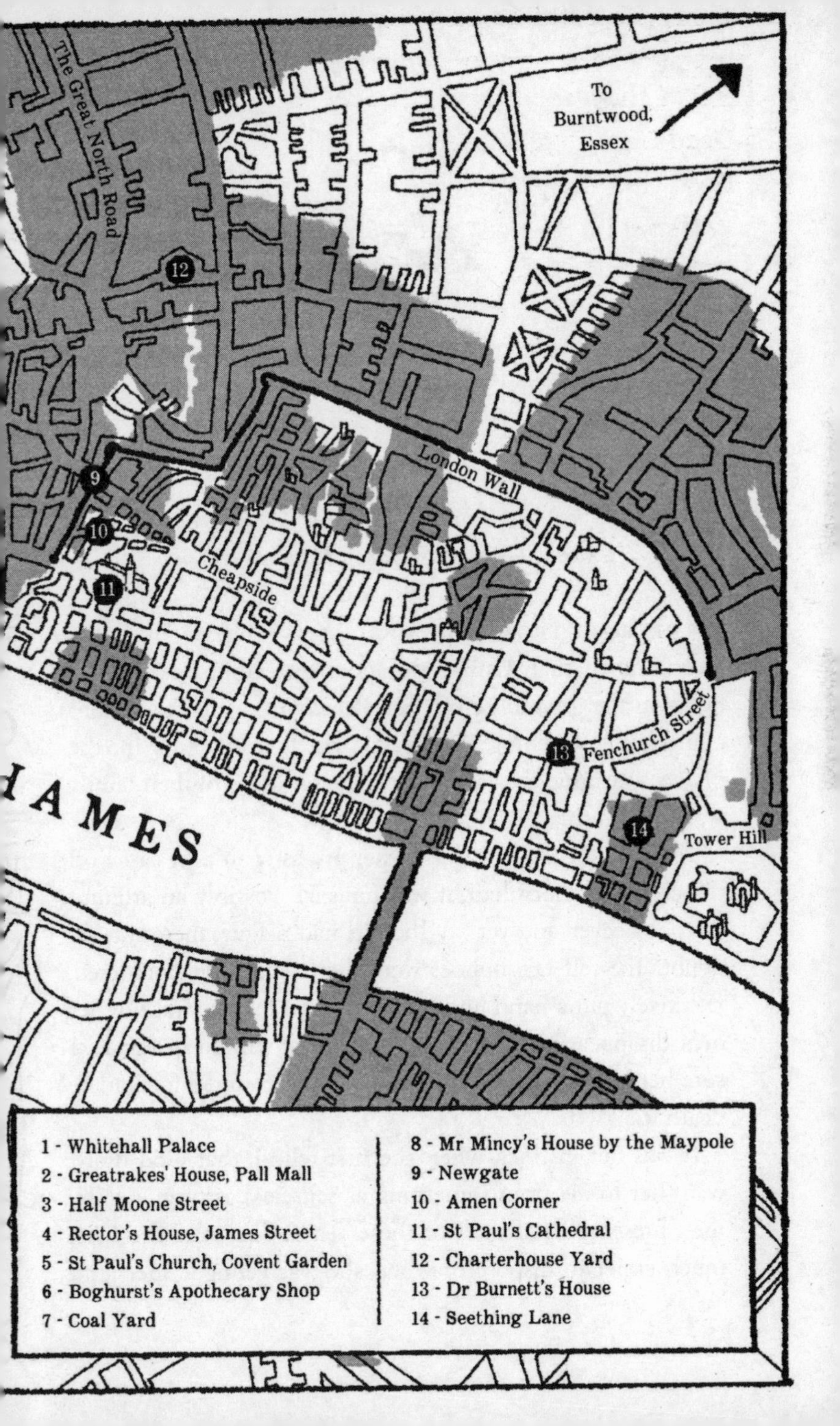
The Great North Road
To Burntwood, Essex
12
London Wall
9
10
Cheapside
11
Fenchurch Street
13
14
Tower Hill
HAMES
1 - Whitehall Palace
2 - Greatrakes' House, Pall Mall
3 - Half Moone Street
4 - Rector's House, James Street
5 - St Paul's Church, Covent Garden
6 - Boghurst's Apothecary Shop
7 - Coal Yard
8 - Mr Mincy's House by the Maypole
9 - Newgate
10 - Amen Corner
11 - St Paul's Cathedral
12 - Charterhouse Yard
13 - Dr Burnett's House
14 - Seething Lane

# 7

*Friday, July 7th*
*Charnel Ground, St Paul's, Covent Garden*

SHE ROSE FROM THE DEAD. Yes, Penelope liked the sound of that. Unlike this poor girl. She stared at the body on the ground before her. Penelope was in the rector's churchyard, watching the dead carts as they came in, the ghosts swarming the carts, looking to see if any of their family were to join them.

The body of the girl caught her eye as soon as it came off the cart. The shorn hair, it was unusual. Possibly an attempt to cool a fever, and yet . . . The girl had plague, there was no doubt. The tell-tale buboes were there. Penelope shuddered, reflexively put a hand under her arm and felt the trace of her own disappearing sores; then patted the white cap to make sure her black hair was still lumpy and accounted for underneath it.

It was her instinct, when she first fell ill, that God didn't want her to die from something as senseless as plague. Why then preserve her for all of these years? She would've been much easier to dispose of when she was younger. Her aunt and uncle did try. The scraps of food. Penelope never really got over that period of starvation. She was as thin and scraggly as an old bush from a long habit now of hoarding her food instead of eating it.

Her aunt and uncle had attempted to beat dead her heart; but it had already been broken with the loss of her parents. They did like to tell her she was clever, but they did not mean it as her father did. They hissed it and followed it up with a slap. She hadn't been there a month when she stumbled upon it, an overheard conversation late one night. She had taken to sneaking downstairs after they were in bed, to steal from the larder. That night they were still awake, and she heard her aunt talk of the profit they would have if Penelope were not to live. She didn't understand why, but the intent was clear. They wished for her demise. So she left. She had been twelve, and told herself she would from that point on consider herself fully formed. Her father had already taught her more than most women – and men! – would ever know. Time to put it to use, she had said to herself, make her father proud. That she could read – English, Latin, French, German, Greek, though she kept the Greek to herself – and do sums made all the difference and she found one small job after another. And left one small job after another because the masters thought they owned her, body and soul. *That was putting it mildly*, she thought.

She moved her torch over the body before her. This poor girl, she had no blessings at all. The razored hair, the buboes broken and sewn back up, wrists and ankles rubbed raw from tattered ropes. A grid inked over her entire body, some of the squares encasing buboes, others surrounding burn marks of various sizes and depths or symmetric slashes of a knife. Penelope had never seen anything like it. But she had heard of something like it.

Penelope had spent more than a week in a cot near the rector's office, had overheard things. The rector reading a letter from his brother to Bernard. A younger brother, furious with Symon. He cursed Symon, ordered him to call upon the family of some poor servant who had suffered a horrible death, pay them money.

Penelope later read the letter and pieced the story together from Symon's conversations with Bernard. A maid named Mary. She had worked for Symon's brother; but his wife caught him with his hand in her skirts and ordered her dismissed. The brother still had some feeling for the girl and couldn't throw her out on the street (*rather rare of him,* Penelope thought) so he sent her to Symon; only Symon didn't really seem to know much about her, not even if she was a good maid. She had gone missing, then a dead cart brought her in, but she bore the signs of mistreatment, of strange markings. Very much like those on the girl before her now. Penelope had heard Symon and Bernard argue over Mary, the grotesque marks about her. Bernard told him he was a time waster and assigned him a new duty every time the rector brought it up. But now there were two girls, both with shorn hair, too many incisions, too many burns and a grid drawn upon their bodies.

She needed to find Symon and tell him. And thank him. He had saved her; she knew he would. He had some of the other orphan girls look after her; made sure they didn't skimp. They brought her broth, kept her warm, kept her company. Told her what new street the visitation had reached, which new house, who was dying, who had survived.

Penelope pulled a dark blanket over the girl's body; a white shroud would be like ringing a bell for Bernard. She dragged the corpse into the alley off the churchyard, just outside the north gate. Since no one recognised the girl, the yard boys had tried to throw her into the paupers' grave straight away. (Bernard had attempted the same with Penelope, she wouldn't forget that, dear Bernard!) But she bribed the boys, so that they would leave the body alone until she could get the rector. He hadn't yet come to the church that evening; she would have to fetch him. Bernard, she realised, was about as hawk-eyed as they came and it wouldn't be long before he found the corpse.

She let herself into the rector's house and stopped to listen. Downstairs in the kitchen, she could hear the quiet chatter of the household, cleaning up from the evening meal. She took a step up the landing; heard a series of deep sighs, the sounds of someone struggling with an intractable problem. It was a sound she recognised from her childhood; that of her father working late into the night on a law brief for a particularly difficult client. Usually his brother, her uncle. She climbed the rest of the steps and gave a hearty knock on the door.

'Hallo, Mr Patrick!'

Symon swivelled in his chair and jumped.

She saw the confusion in his eyes flicker into awareness as he realised who she was. 'You're alive! Blessed be! But how?' He ran over and offered her an arm for support. 'Should you be up? Why you're just as black and filthy as the day we met. I told those girls to take good care of you! They could've at least wiped you down. But I am glad to see you solid on your legs!'

'Is that nice' – she gave him a ferocious look – 'telling someone they're filthy?'

She would not let on how hurtful his remark was; she had been quite proud of herself for changing out of her rags into a good brown dress and fastening her hair under a cap.

'I do apologise,' he said with a gentle smile. 'But you are rather filthy.' He reached out to touch a loose strand of hair and made a face. 'And sticky.' He picked up a cloth from the basin to wipe his hand, turned to settle down again with his papers. 'I'll talk to Bernard; he'll get someone to help you with all that.'

As he went to sit, she pulled the chair out from under him. He hit the floor with a thud. 'No time for that, you're to come with me,' she said.

He looked up at her in shock. She snapped her fingers, held out a hand to pull him up. 'Come now! Bernard's orders!'

He hurried to his feet, but took a step away from her, a look of alarm still on his face.

'You know very well we must do as he says!' She shook a finger at him, like a nursemaid. 'Or he'll eat you for breakfast.'

*

'Bernard' – Penelope tapped on his monstrous shoulder – 'one of the yard boys started a fire in the church. Shall I put it out?'

'That's master to you, you wicked imp! I'll beat thee next time you forget,' he shouted at her as he ran towards the church.

'Quick, over here.' She directed Symon towards an alley and gestured to a sorry shape under a blanket.

'What's going on?' Symon grabbed the torch from Penelope. 'Who put this here?'

'Exactly, Symon.' She squatted down and pulled the blanket back. 'The boys were unloading the bodies and I saw her. It's similar, isn't it, to what you saw on Mary?'

Symon stood dumbfounded, stared at Penelope. 'How do you know about Mary?' They heard an angry oath and a great wallop of wood against stone and looked over towards the church; the sexton was barrelling back their way, brandishing his walking stick like a cudgel. 'Bernard!' Symon shouted, undeterred. 'What do you know about this girl?'

'I know that one's dead and the other ought to be.'

Symon scowled. He knelt down beside Penelope and picked up the body's stiff wrist. She was wearing a rope bracelet, like Mary. Hair shorn. He moved the torch closer – there was something on her face, her cheeks, her neck. Lines of ink. Another grid. He held his breath, raised her soiled skirt. A puzzle of wounds, each one encased in an inked square.

He slowly covered the girl back up. 'Heaven help us.'

'Yes,' said Penelope in a sad voice. 'For who would murder the dying?'

*

It was close to midnight. Symon was feeling violent. He had sent for Boghurst hours ago; he very much wanted his opinion on the matter. But the apothecary had yet to arrive. Where was he? Drunk somewhere. The man was always drunk these days. God help his patients. Weary and raw, Symon longed for his bed. His head felt like to split, each of Bernard's roars threatened to break it altogether.

'Damn ye to hell!' he heard Bernard yell from the shadows. The yard boys were exhausted, knocking into each other, the graves, the bodies left to bury – the dead carts had brought more in – and Bernard had no pity for them. Symon had to repeatedly put himself between the boys and Bernard's stick, until he decided to take the stick away from him altogether. He was leaning against a tree, rubbing his bruised arms as he watched several boys struggle to lift another corpse. They staggered over to the grave and made to fling the body into the hole, but one stopped short, his little legs giving out, and the corpse's head hit the ground with a crack before the body tumbled into the grave. Bernard ran towards them. 'Bloody bastards! I'll bust your jaws!'

'Bernard! Have care! Such grim work! They shouldn't be doing this at all!'

'Would you rather 'em run wild in the streets?' Bernard growled back. 'Thieving and starving? Get inside where you belong!'

Symon gave the sexton a last look of warning then headed for his office. He would order extra provisions for the boys. More bread, more cheese, more cider. Fresh cloths. Whatever could be had, God save them.

Penelope was curled up in a corner, asleep on a pink pew cushion. Symon shook his head; he'd have to have it cleaned in the morning. He had tried to order her back to her cot in the vestrymen's office, but she was as stubborn as Bernard. As foul as him, too.

Symon sat down at his desk and pulled a piece of paper towards him. The bodies flashed before his eyes. The burns and cuts. The ink netting drawn around them. The same twine bracelets cutting into their swollen wrists and ankles. Had they known each other? He had considered asking Dr Burnett about Mary and her wounds the other night but there had never been a proper chance at that disaster of an evening.

Symon scraped his pen tip with his knife, dipped it into the ink, sought distraction:

*My friend,*

Lady Gauden. Elizabeth. What if he told her what he did every night? The corrupted bodies. The burials. Would she think on him more? Or would she grow cold? He imagined the fine linen close to Elizabeth's skin turning icy with the turn in her feelings. The silk layers on top becoming brittle, uncomfortable. She would need to take them off ... He sighed, how he missed her. No one could bring a smile to his face as readily as she. She liked to toy with him, tease him ... taunt him for being too serious. She would hold his hand as they walked through her gardens – 'Put some warmth back into you,' she'd say – her auburn hair radiant in the sun; how he had longed to run his fingers through it, then trace the gentle curve of her throat. She would dance in front of him along the path, pick flowers and thread them through his cravat, his shirtsleeves, anything to get a smile from him. Midsummer the year before, she'd woven a crown of meadow orchids and placed it on his head with a kiss. 'No thorns for you,' she'd said, 'you've had far too many in your poor little life.' He hadn't seen her in some time now, not since March when he'd gone to Astrop. She'd left her manor house in Clapham soon after, part of the great London exodus to avoid plague.

Why hadn't Symon sent his household away too? He could've saved Mary. Why didn't he send them now? He stayed his foot – it was tapping maniacally on the floor – looked out of the window. Where was Boghurst? He thought back to the plague society meeting. No, he wouldn't seek their help. He didn't think he could stomach another meeting with them. Dr Alexander Burnett. Lodowick Mincy. Valentine Greatrakes. William Boghurst. All recognised as most talented healers in their own right. Each came from a different training – a matter largely decided by who their fathers were and what connections they had. As a university-educated physician, Dr Burnett had the most expensive training, which meant he could also charge the highest fees. His father had been a royal physician, though Dr Burnett himself had not yet reached that standing. Next, Lodowick Mincy. Physicians looked down on surgeons (physicians looked down on everyone); surgery was a trade and surgeons were called hacks for a reason. Though Mincy's father was a royal surgeon and, much to Dr Burnett's chagrin, Mincy had long ago gained entrance to that most elite of clientele, Dr Burnett still found ways to snub him. 'You're elbow deep in livers every day of your life, there is no art to this!' he would say. Illness was solved by the application of a clever mind, not by brute force. And that was where Symon's childhood friend came in. Boghurst was the lowliest of the group; apothecaries were seen as nothing more than the servants of physicians and surgeons. They were men who didn't have the money for the lengthy years of education or apprenticeship required by the other branches. They were supposed to keep their distance from the sick, leave the hands-on healing to their betters. Boghurst said this was a sham conceived by surgeons and doctors to protect their purses. He refused to follow the established rules and treated patients himself – he knew his medicines best, he said. He was somewhat of an outcast amongst the medical community for not observing the hierarchy, but at the same time his medicines were much sought after by the likes of Mincy and Burnett for the simple reason that they worked better than anyone else's. Symon once asked Boghurst why, if his medicines were so successful, was he always in want? Six daughters and a wife, Boghurst replied.

And Valentine Greatrakes. A healer nonpareil, claimed the man himself, because his gift came straight from God. The Irish mystic didn't need books or knives or herbs gathered under a fairy moon. He had only to close his eyes, put out his hands and let God's healing love flow. The gift of kings, but not all kings wore crowns, he'd say with a wink. Symon at first had been flattered that they sought him out for membership;

it was rather fashionable to belong to a society. And while these men were not of Royal Society calibre, they were a solid stepping stone. Elizabeth would be impressed indeed to know that Symon counted them amongst his friends, that they sought his aid in this most terrible of matters. Never mind what they were really like. Never mind what he was really like. *Now Symon*, he chided himself . . . He turned back to his letter.

> *Your last brought mee a great deal of good news.*

Yes, let's start off with Elizabeth as the subject. She'll like that.

Elizabeth.

She had written to him the other week, pleaded with him to leave Covent Garden, to shelter at her manor house over the Thames in Clapham. A wine cellar, a root cellar, a cheese cellar – any kind of cellar you could wish for. Its own brewhouse, its own bakehouse. His housekeeper, Joan, would be so happy there. He could even stay in Elizabeth's bed. Wrapped in her nightgown. No one would know, no one was there. They had dismissed the staff when she left for her sister's estate, Hutton Hall, in Burntwood. *Dearest Elizabeth,* he would write, *about this lump in your bed . . .*

Hrmph.

> *Your last brought mee a great deal of good news, and made amends for the past before, which brought mee none. I told you, if we can just stay a little, all will be well. Patience is never badly paid. It seems a very dull virtue yet . . .*

Yes, dull, like his supper. He had told Joan – in a moment of madness – that it would be best if he confined himself to boiled beef and cabbage for the foreseeable future. A plain diet was considered the safest in these times, Boghurst advised him.

*. . . but 'tis rewarded with great joy.*

Would God in fact reward his diligence at eating boiled meat by delivering Elizabeth to him? What if he cut his boiled meat in half and donated the rest to the pesthouse? Would God reward him for that?

Boiled meat. Boils. Boiled boils.

Boiled Elizabeth.

Would he still love Elizabeth if she were boiled?

*My Dearest Elizabeth. I would love thee even if thou were boiled.*

Yes, she would smile at that.

Just in case, he would add,

*But I prefer thee candied.*

He hadn't her ease of manners, her ease with the language of love. He could write day and night of God, but his letters to Elizabeth were halting, awkward, aborted. Elizabeth. She had nearly ruined him. How she swung like a weathervane in a criss-crossed storm! He never knew her mind, her heart, from one day to the next. This constant change in feeling left him with worse than nothing. She hadn't reduced him to a shell. On the contrary, he felt everything all too keenly now. The pain of loneliness most of all. She was the reason he had fled to Northamptonshire, though he would admit that to no one. He needed to recover himself and he could not do it in

Covent Garden, where he must give to anyone who asked.
He picked up his pen again.

*We live and yet whilst I write this word, whilst you read it, perhaps we dye. Is this a land of the living or of the dead?*

'This won't do, Symon,' he said as he looked over his words. 'Such silliness, it will leave you a mad old fool.'

'I agree,' he heard a voice answer back. Startled, he looked down at Penelope; but she was still asleep, her eyes firmly closed . . . It was the late hour, a trick of the mind. He held the corner of the letter to a candle to burn it when he heard a great crash outside, then shouts. Who was Bernard warring with now?

*

Penelope opened an eye and watched Symon leave. *He is a dull fellow*, she thought. He'd been scribbling away all night. She'd tried to engage him in conversation but got little more than grunts for her efforts. She picked up the letter he'd been writing, only its edges burned. A love affair, then. She pulled another letter out of her skirt pocket. Symon's boy had delivered it earlier. She had meant to give it to Symon, but forgot. It was from Burntwood. This didn't bode well. She cut through the wax seal with Symon's knife, shook her head in disgust as she read it.

She heard Symon coming back, so she shoved the letter under a book and returned to her corner. Watched him sit back down in his chair and put his head on his desk. He was asleep within minutes. She tiptoed over and put her blanket over his shoulders, then left.

*

A deep rumbling woke Symon. He limped out into the thick night air, looked up at the tower clock and cursed Boghurst. It was well past three in the morning and the man still hadn't shown up. There on the front steps sat Bernard, the source of the rumbling. He was singing a mournful old Welsh tune in the deepest of bass voices. Next to him sat a yard boy, sharing his pipe.

'Don't you let them sleep at all?' Symon howled. 'Have mercy, Bernard!'

The yard boy snapped his head around to face Symon. 'What are you whining about now?'

It was Boghurst, even more a dwarf beside Bernard.

That he was sitting there casually, having a smoke, made Symon even angrier. 'How long have you been here? Never mind.' He pushed Boghurst off the step with his foot. 'Down in the crypt. Now.' Symon had earlier asked Bernard to put the girl in the crypt, where they could examine the body in private. Halfway down the stairs the smell of earth and damp, the coolness of death, came up to meet them. The crypt was not large, but its edges were lost in a furry darkness. A lantern hung on the wall cast a weak halo of light on the girl's corpse. Squatting next to the body was a slight figure holding a flat board and surrounded by sheets of paper. Symon peered closer. She turned to Symon and gave a small nod. Penelope.

'What's she doing here?' he asked Bernard.

'Not my wench.'

Symon picked up one of the sketches from the floor. Penelope was drawing the dead girl, in perfect detail.

'A record,' she said. 'You'll need it.'

'Where are you from?' he could only think to ask. He couldn't piece it together. Not long ago she had been moments away from death. Now here she was, next to a girl who was dead, showing no emotion and sketching the body with unnatural skill. 'Penelope, who are your family? Do you know this girl?'

'Like a sister,' she said.

Boghurst interrupted. 'Let's get on with this.' The apothecary took the lantern off the wall and directed its light over the dead girl's head, her neck. He lifted one arm, looked at the bubo in her armpit, then checked the other side.

'She's got seven little purses sewn up on her,' Penelope said. She leaned in closer, her face almost touching the corpse. 'There's a square drawn around each, with a little number. Two . . . seven . . .' She moved around the corpse. 'Three . . . There are squares drawn around the burns, too . . . and some of them go deeper than the others; some are clearly superficial, what is the point of them? Why is this one no bigger than an acorn cap but this the size of a dish—'

Boghurst frowned. 'Time for your pet pigeon to leave.'

'She can stay,' said Symon. 'She's not hurting anything.'

Boghurst shrugged and pulled a suede pouch from his bag, unfolded it on the floor. Slid a small knife and forceps out from under their lashings.

Symon was sitting on the clammy stairs watching Boghurst's examination when he felt something large and soft push into him. He groaned. It was Mincy. He had come down the crypt stairs and was standing next to Symon. He nearly retched at the surgeon's smell, a combination of cooked kidneys and old blood. *Whose blood and whose kidneys?* Symon wondered, as he looked at the surgeon's expensive silk chemise, spattered with dried muck.

'I heard you had a body,' the surgeon said.

'Who told you?'

'Who didn't!' Mincy walked past Symon and shoved Boghurst out of the way, citing surgeon's privilege. The apothecary refused to cede his knife and took a place on the other side of the body. Working their way from head to foot, they delicately cut through each of the stitched-up buboes, fished out their contents and dropped them on to the bunched-up shroud. As Boghurst removed the last object, he suggested they move upstairs to discuss. 'Agreed, fresh air makes fresh minds,' Mincy said, wiping his knife and forceps on his shirt.

Upstairs in his office, Symon poured them wine, even Penelope. Boghurst took a deep drink, then another, and held his glass out for more. His eyes brightened, the colour came back to his cheeks – *The countenance of a mad gnome*, thought Symon. Mincy, refusing drink, had squished himself into a chair in the corner and watched Boghurst with a look of aversion. Symon thought this rather hypocritical. Boghurst finished his second glass, then unwrapped the shroud on the floor. Penelope perched next to him to get a better view. Bernard lit a pipe and started to spit-shine his walking stick. Symon wondered at their coolness, then turned his head away; he could only bear to watch out of the corner of his eye as the apothecary arranged the objects in an orderly line.

Boghurst sat back, resting on his heels, and began his report. 'The sickness, no doubt. Buboes in all the usual places – neck, armpit, groin. Blackened extremities – fingers, toes, ears. And what we have here, my dear friends, in no particular order are' – he pointed to each with his forceps as he went – 'foot of a hare, foot of a frog, toe of a dog, claw of a cat, wing of a bat . . . and this one—' He picked up a small, square object with his forceps and held it up for their inspection, it was beige, nearly see-through. 'I'm not entirely sure, but I'm going to guess it's the fingernail of a virgin. The victim's, for she is missing a fingernail. And last but not least, an eye. Thankfully, not hers, I checked. Possibly that of the dog that also lost its toe.'

'Fiend,' said the surgeon.

'God help us,' Symon agreed.

'Yes, help us,' Boghurst said, 'from the superstitious beliefs of peasants. The girl is dying and someone, God knows who, sewed these things into her.'

'Peasants?' Mincy spat. 'That's one word for it. I have another. Charlatan. Here's another: quack.'

'Oh, I know what you mean,' agreed Boghurst. 'I remember with not a small bit of embarrassment the days when I had yet to root out the old beliefs from my practice. But after I had advised the tenth consumptive patient in a row to hold a puppy to the chest—'

'How many dogs did you kill with that nonsense?' Mincy asked in horror.

The apothecary scowled, continued, 'And saw no improvement, I gave them up. My father swore by this method, but I didn't see it made a damn bit of difference. And then the puppies always seemed to piss on the patients, more mess to clean up. No, my false friend' – he practically spat at Mincy – 'I didn't kill any dogs.'

'Didn't you?' Symon asked.

Boghurst grimaced, let the accusation slide. 'Now this particular fellow is inventive. I can see him thinking. The grid he's painted all over her. He's a man of the new science – attempting a reasoned, systematic approach. One experiment per section, keeping track with the numbers. I will admit, to categorise and isolate the results in such a way, it's rather clever of him. Quite an innovation. Wish I'd come up with it myself. Both the cuts and the burns, all of his treatments.' He paused, seemingly lost in thought, then remembered himself. 'But no. It is odd. You are right, Mr Mincy. Not a peasant. Some of these cuts are quite skilled and made by good blades. This is someone who can read, who knows something of the old and new practices. Maybe it's not enough simply to place these relics on the body. Maybe the skin is too much of a barrier, preventing the magic, or what have you, from reaching the inner seats of disease. So he cuts open the bubo and places the relic directly in the infection, then sews it shut. And' – he scratched behind his ear with his forceps – 'he's not sure which of these objects has special powers of remedy for plague. So he tries them all. Some cuts are older, have healed a little. He's putting one object in, waiting to see what happens, and if nothing, moves on to the next.'

'How do you know it's a man?' Penelope asked.

Boghurst snorted.

'It's barbaric,' Symon said. 'She was already suffering so.'

'That's why he had to tie her up,' said Mincy.

'She was tied up?'

'Didn't you see the rope around her wrists?'

'I thought it was some sort of decorative country charm,' said Symon. 'There was a prettiness to it.'

Mincy stared at him in disbelief.

Symon tried to recover his dignity. 'We need to find this man, alert the authorities.'

'Agreed.' The surgeon prised his fleshy hips out of the chair and started pacing. 'Most disturbing. What I propose—'

'Quite the opposite, Mr Patrick, Mr Mincy.' Boghurst clasped his hands behind his back, drew a stern look. 'Plague is what killed her. What you see may be misguided attempts to save her, whether you call it medicine or magic, but in the end, plague sealed her fate. There is nothing for us to do here.'

'But what of the burns?' asked Penelope. 'How random they are! Wanton torture!'

Boghurst shook his head. 'To a crude mind, perhaps. The trained mind can see that he seeks to create exits for the poison. But what is the most effective size of the exit? And what is the most effective agent to entice the poison through the exit? They are not burns, so to speak. He did not take fire to her. But rather various caustic agents to create ulcers through which the venom could escape. It's impossible to tell at this point what he used. A mustard? Poisonous leaves? A bezoar? Sulphur? He is excessive, I will give you that—'

'Excessive? How polite you are!' Symon interjected. He told them about Mary. That she too had shorn hair, knotted ropes around her wrists and ankles, grotesque burns, the ink grid, which to Symon's mind made it all the more gruesome. 'Someone studied her in her pain!'

'Where were the girls found?' Mincy had stopped his pacing, fixed his eye on the apothecary.

'Both came from around Long Acre,' said Symon. 'Most of the dead carts are coming from the north, that's where most of the sick are.'

'Don't you live there, Mr Boghurst?'

The apothecary hesitated.

Mincy motioned for Bernard to get up. 'Block the door, please.' Then he took a step towards Boghurst. 'You are correct. It is obvious. You know well enough the method and *excessively well* the thought behind what was done. That was an admirable performance you gave. But then you stopped short of the logical conclusion. You call it the work of peasants, pagans. I call it malpractice. Criminal. A healer who has gone too far, who is aping procedures well above his training. The knife cuts. You say some are quite nice. Hogwash! The uninformed opinion of an apothecary. Look at this ragged edge! This is a person without the education – the intelligence – to attempt such work.'

Boghurst picked up his satchel, his face unreadable.

'You don't need your things,' said Mincy. 'In fact, you should never have had those things! This is what happens when you license people without submitting them to the most rigorous training, without testing their mental capabilities. Gentlemen' – he turned to Symon and Bernard – 'this is the man who tortured these poor girls. They came to him sick and in need. They had no money; he took advantage of them.' He pointed at Boghurst. 'You knew no one would come asking for them, question your treatment. A bungler of the worst kind. Arrogant and untrained. You are the one crude in mind! Degenerately crude! We must detain him until the authorities can deal with him. Lock him in the crypt!'

Boghurst threw his bag down and went for Mincy's throat. But Bernard stopped him; grabbed the apothecary's arms and twisted them behind his back.

'What's it to be, Rector?' the sexton asked.

Symon looked from one face to the other. What had happened? Mincy was accusing his oldest friend of murder. Of murder most cold, most cruel. Yes, Boghurst was avaricious. But to the point of mortal sin? And Symon was to be his judge? Mincy did have more experience, a higher rank in the medical profession. He was not the type to let feelings cloud his judgement. Mincy was unpleasant, true, but quite methodical in his own bloody way. Boghurst, on the other hand. He did play it fast and loose. He was always short on coin. Always wanting. His past was not clean. And he had read the butcherings on the poor girl so well, explained them in exquisite detail.

'Symon,' yelled the surgeon, 'this is a most easy decision. Lock him up!'

Symon started to speak, hesitated.

'Symon!' Mincy yelled again. 'Pretend you are a dog. It is most simple! Listen to me, then act!'

'Dogs indeed!' shouted the apothecary. 'I'll kill yours if you don't stop this foolishness!'

'More proof you are unfit,' Mincy yelled. Somewhere deep inside, Symon felt a jerk. Something old, something painful from his boyhood. He looked at Penelope; she was chewing her thumb, watching them all carefully. Suddenly, it was clear what he should do.

'Take him to the crypt!'

The apothecary roared as Bernard dragged him out of Symon's office. 'Come easy, only hurting yerself if you kick like that,' he warned Boghurst. They heard a bell clang in the distance.

'Look at the time.' Mincy tutted in satisfaction. 'Four in the morn!' He congratulated Symon on a job well done, said he'd write letters to the appropriate authorities soon as the sun was up, put the items from the shroud in his pockets and left.

Symon lay down on the floor. He already regretted sending Boghurst to the crypt, because he would like to be down there himself. The stones were cooler, the company more still.

'No, they're not,' said Penelope. She had sat down beside him.

'What?'

She shrugged her shoulders. He closed his eyes, let out a moan. 'Indeed,' she said. 'What are we to do?'

# 8

## *Symon's Church*

'HOW COULD YOU LOCK him up?' Penelope asked. 'Your dear friend?' She was leaning against the door to Symon's office, a chamber pot in her hands. He wouldn't ask, he refused to be provoked. He thought back to his life a year ago. The blessings that came with a glorious July day. The height of summer, the air warm and fragrant. How he loved this month for making morning visits around the parish, then closing the day with long talks amongst friends on rooftops or an impromptu supper by the river's edge. This year, he would be blessed indeed if he managed to survive it. He had rushed through morning prayers; he wanted the parishioners out of the church before any could hear Boghurst's screams from the crypt. And now this, the urchin stood before him, boldly detailing his mistakes. He fixed his eyes on Penelope. She was in a silk bodice of a rich burgundy and matching skirt. A chaste white kerchief of fine linen was draped over her shoulders and tucked into the top of the bodice. Where had she got them?

'He's not my dear friend.' Symon turned back to his letter. He couldn't stop reading it. He had found it stuffed under a book on his desk; he would have a word with Jack. It was from Mrs Pheasunt, Elizabeth's sister. Elizabeth had dictated it to her.

He sighed and began to write his congratulations:

*The fruit of my thoughts was entirely with you the day before, and now I have such a reason why, for it seems you were in labour. I am at the greater ease to heare how graciously God hath dealt with you. It makes my heart a great deal lighter, I assure you, than it was before, and will serve mee as an antidote in this dangerous season.*

Yes, his heart was light, as light as a leper's shrivelled foot. She'd had the baby. A little girl. He had offered to be there for her, to wait the baby's arrival, but Elizabeth had declined. He knew her husband was not there. Sir Denis never left their house in the City these days; he was a victualler for the Navy and the war with the Dutch didn't stop for plague or babes, he'd said. Symon imagined Sir Denis at his townhouse by the Tower, saw him before a table groaning with roasted venison and claret, reading a similar letter and sending out his own.

*For you know, Solomon saith, 'A merry heart doth like good medicine.' I believe it will give mee much joy to reflect upon your preservation.*

*Forever,*
*S.P.*

Was he a good liar or a bad one?

'Are you listening? I said he's not the murderer.'

Symon looked up. Penelope. She was still here; had put the chamber pot down on his desk and was tapping the lid impatiently. This wouldn't do.

'Penelope, I am pleased you are better. I think it's time we set you to work, don't you?'

'I've done nothing but work for you since I got up from my deathbed. Now tell me, why did you lock him up?'

He didn't answer, she wouldn't understand. He didn't think Boghurst was guilty. That had been his first thought when he woke up this morning. Fatigue, tensions, old feelings had confused his mind the night before, allowed the reopening of an old wound. The two had fallen out when they were boys. Symon had found him one day in a shed surrounded by several of the village dogs, and a few cats under weighted-down baskets. On the table before his friend was a lifeless dog. Symon pushed him away, tried to shake the dog back to life. 'What have you done?' he shouted. The dog didn't move, and Symon quickly set about untying the other dogs and kicking baskets over to free the cats.

'Stop,' yelled Boghurst. 'Leave them! I'm treating them!'

'You're killing them and you should run, before I kill you.' Even as a boy Symon towered over Boghurst and with the rage he felt inside, knew it would not take much to beat him down. Symon's own dog had gone missing several weeks before. A brindle terrier, she was an old dog when he found her in a hollow in the woods behind their house. He shared his bread with her, he could count each of her ribs, and so she followed him home, gave no indication she had any other. Symon sneaked her into bed with him every chance he could, but one night his father caught them and dragged her outside, raging about fleas and mange. His father had said he tied her up outside, but the next morning his little old dog was gone. Symon hadn't known what to think. Had his father drowned her? Sold her? Eaten her? Or had she wandered off to be someone else's pet? Symon had hoped the latter was true, it was the least painful. But that day when he caught his friend, he knew her fate. After he freed the animals, he started to swing at him. The boy was small but quick and Symon's blows glanced off him. Symon reached for the knife on the table and lunged for him. The boy ran away shouting, 'He was already dead, ask Farmer Cox, I got it off him this morning. What do you think me?'

'You kidnapped them, you stole my dog, you killed her!' Symon screamed as he chased him. 'I'll cut you down!' Symon's fingers were within inches of the boy's collar when someone grabbed hold of him from behind and yanked him off his feet. Symon's father. He took the knife out of his hand and marched him home. Symon stopped the memory there, why recall that pain? Later, lying in his pallet, his eyes closed, too sore to move, he heard Boghurst's father in the house. The boy had told no falsehoods, he said. The treatment of the animals was done with permission of those involved. Symon didn't believe it. He was sure there was some evil afoot and could not forgive his friend. Shortly thereafter, Symon was sent up to Cambridge. When he saw Boghurst years later, it was the first thing on his mind. The apothecary's, too. He pleaded his innocence and Symon knew it petty to think otherwise. But last night in the crypt, the body before him, the blood, the accusations, the denials, his old rage had come back and he saw a cruel boy who had grown into a cruel man.

Possibly. There was no evidence. Symon had been rash and unfair in his decision.

Still. How would Penelope have any insight into the nature of his friend?

'A murderer wouldn't show up and give such an intimate

accounting,' she said. 'He came to help you. And you ignore it, as you ignore my help.'

'You don't think it a ruse?' Symon asked. 'A devious cover-up?'

'I know of devious people. My aunt and uncle. The baker I used to work for. His wife. The baker's man. They never give you the time of day unless they want something. Ever since I got here, I've seen your friend buzz about you like a love-sick court page. All he ever wants is your attention. Well, and drink. So, no, I do not think he is pretending.'

He allowed a small smile. 'You're right. You'll be pleased to know that I agree with you and plan to let him out shortly.'

'I already did.'

Symon bolted from his chair and rushed to the door. 'My God! When? Where is he now?'

'During morning prayers,' she said. 'I thought it safest. He wouldn't hit you in front of all those people. I followed him, just in case. He went straight home and started drinking.'

'Damn!' Symon had been planning to keep the apothecary in the crypt until noon. If nothing else, it would dry him out.

'You should visit him soon.' She turned to leave. 'Find him before he finds you. That way you'll see it coming.'

Symon scowled. He stared at the chamber pot. She'd left it behind. He would ask Bernard to get rid of it. He wasn't going to touch it; she was capable of anything.

*

Penelope went out into the nave and floated along the aisles. She opened the white panelled door of a pew box and stepped inside. Touched a cut on her cheek, a thank-you from the apothecary that morning, delivered by one of his filthy fingernails as he swung at her. She'd known he'd come out swinging, tried to jump out of range as soon as she drew back the bolt, but hadn't quite been quick enough. After that first graze, she'd kept him at bay with her torch – she was waiting for him to calm down and recognise her for what she was, a saint. But he never did. 'I'll thank you not!' he spat at her. 'You'll get no coin from me!' She shook her head as she watched him limp up the street. Another disappointment of a man.

She sat up as straight as she could in the pew, bowed her head in that modest look so practised by the young ladies. Raised her eyes a little, a gesture so small yet so daring that it could ruin a girl's reputation if the wrong person saw it. She pretended to gasp, blush, and look away quickly, as if Symon up in his pulpit had caught her eyes, had seen that she risked her virtue for him. He would look back at those girls with a quizzical, slightly flattered smile – the look of a simple-hearted preacher. She saw all this from up in the gallery at the back of the church, this game the young ladies played with Symon. They knew his value. As did their mothers and fathers. He had a good living. Well-shaped calves. Broad shoulders. Wavy, brown hair – his own. Strong jaw. And such empathetic eyes, as if he knew where you hurt. The slightly sidewise tooth and an eye that wandered a bit, his only flaws – and that he was easily fooled and therefore susceptible to the likes of Lady Elizabeth Gauden.

Penelope pulled a notebook out of her pocket, consulted her agenda. Watch Boghurst. Despite what she had told Symon, she wasn't entirely sure he was innocent. Visit around the parish and up to St Giles. Discover the names of all practitioners of physick working in the vicinity, including the group of quacks in the piazza. Find out where they lived. Anyone who dabbled even slightly on the wrong side of things. Make a map. Stop by pesthouses for latest gossip.

She needed a change of outfit for her inquiries, however. Something more sober. She went up to the attic where she kept her wardrobe these days, picked out a black bodice and skirt. The church was shaping up to be a most marvellous home. The dry attic for clothes, the crypt for perishables. She planned on moving her cot into Symon's office. The watchmen guarding infected houses would be her first stop, she thought, as she put on a fresh cap and tucked every last bit of hair under it. She'd ask them for the names of all the healers who attended, all the so-called officials, visitors, religious folk. Then draw a sketch of the apothecary. Knock on doors and show it to the nurses to see if they recognised him. Find the dead-cart men. People working so closely with the dead generally had a good idea of which healers were helpful and which were not.

But first, while Symon was busy, she should check his house. See what he was writing to Elizabeth. See what she had written back. He spent entirely too much time writing to her, had fallen victim to her siren ways. Penelope needed Symon. She needed him to find this most vile of thieves, one who stole life from friendless girls. She refused to let Elizabeth dash him on the rocks.

*

Outside, it was a dark day; the clouds, agitated and fuming, crouched over the city. Penelope walked through Symon's front door and went straight to his bedchamber. His morning letters lay opened on the table. She picked through them. One from his mother, taking his brother's side over Mary's death.

Another from the limp one at Burntwood. She sat down in his chair and wrote her own little note to the rector. Signed it, *Elizabeth.*

Penelope placed the note on his pillow, and slipped out.

# 9

*The Rooms Behind the Apothecary Shop, the White Hart Inn, Corner of Holborn and Drury Lane, the Parish of St Giles in the Field*

'NEVER MET A MORE misguided fool!' Boghurst yelled as he staggered home from his night in the crypt. 'The man finds a few strange deaths in his parish, and what does he do? Accuses his dearest friend of murder! Never mind the hundreds dying every day of plague, the scourge that said friend is trying to save them all from. My head hurts, my arms hurt. I need drink!' He'd been up all night. As much as he was used to sickness and death, even he couldn't manage to fall asleep in a crypt. 'Is there something wrong with my eye?' He pulled his lower lid down and turned to Penelope so she could inspect it, but was surprised then hurt to see she'd disappeared. The wench had been trailing him after she let him out of the crypt, but now she'd abandoned him, like all the rest. He needed her. He needed a crutch to get home; Symon's ogre had near to crushed his leg.

This action of murder. He saw its uses. He imagined

plunging a knife into Mincy's fatty little heart. Too quick. And Symon? No, he wouldn't kill him. Shave his head and burn his scalp so his hair wouldn't grow back. Club his ankle and give him a permanent limp, knock a few inches off him. 'Liberty!' he yelled to no one. 'There's nonesuch in England!' *A country of tyrannies*, he thought; he was not so foolish as to shout that. They all knew the truth, though. The money, the lineages, it warped the soul. Made the powerful side against clever apothecaries, whom it was in their best interest to befriend, and then plot together to keep said apothecaries down. Symon wasn't rich, but he had many other advantages. The tyranny of tall men with good hair. Everyone assumed such people were natural leaders. A bit of time with Symon and anyone would know that this was a ridiculous notion. Yet the clergyman continued to climb further and with more ease than Boghurst. Symon had written an essay that won him a church prize to Cambridge. Boghurst hadn't even been invited to try for the prize. No one bothered with short men with snot-coloured hair. Snot, that had been his father's nickname for him. Then the rest of the family started calling him that. Even his mother. Boghurst didn't need them. Didn't need any of them. He could write just as many syrupy lines as Symon, only it made him sick to do so. He wouldn't compromise his integrity. For all his height, Symon had no backbone. A pawn of the rich, that's all he was. A floppy, soppy pawn, who lived in great comfort. He had traded his soul for petty favours and soft beds.

That guttersnipe. She knew the truth of it. And if she had stuck by him, he would have stopped in a tavern and stood her a drink. But the wench was gone. *Another one weak of mind*, he thought as he unlocked the door to his shop and yelled for his wife.

Louisa Boghurst greeted him with a small kiss, an afterthought. Nothing more. 'Woman, do you know where I've been?'

'In the muck,' she said. 'Isn't that where you always are?' She put a mug on the shop counter and joined her daughters in the back room. They were laughing. Had they been playing a game? Heartless wenches. Not even bothered he'd been gone the whole night without word of his whereabouts. He drained his mug, knocked it to the floor and listened for a reaction. Nothing. He stamped into the parlour, yelled for his breakfast.

They ignored him. His eldest daughter was nearest, in a chair by the fire paging through a book. 'Get me another drink now or I'll—'

She let out a cry of protest and slammed her book shut, ran upstairs. His eldest daughter was the prettiest, and she knew it. Emerald eyes. A tidal wave of black hair, she was forever brushing it. Refused to put it up, shaming him every time she stepped out.

He sat in her chair, looked around. Six daughters and not a one of them helpful. After the first four, they'd had to farm out the rest to relatives. Perhaps it was time to swap them around. His eye fell on another one. She squeaked and flew out the back door. Minxes. All of them. Where were those sweet little girls who loved nothing more than to help out their papa? Cutting the mugwort and moonwort from the back garden. Setting the toads to drying. Running out to collect pennyroyal from the cracks in stone walls or the hound's tongue growing wild along the lanes. At his work table in the front shop, they had crushed the dried leaves for him, measured out his powders, handed him his bottles. Braided garlands of lavender and rosemary and ivy to hang from the front window. Where had he gone wrong? With them. With his choice of friends. Symon.

'Shippon. Snellock. Staggons. They all owe.' Now his wife. He didn't want to look at her. Louisa was at the table, doing the accounts. She flipped back a page, flipped forward and scribbled something. Let out a whistle. 'Makes a good dozen who haven't settled up.'

'Hard to collect off the dead.'

'Want to add in the dead ones, do you? I've already marked those as a loss. But my darling, let me get that number for you, since you bring it up.' He stole a glance and regretted it instantly. The top of her bodice unlaced. Her curls, of a wilder kink than her daughters', were breaking free from her knot. Why could she never keep them tidy? One spiralled down over her eye. Sorceress. What had she done to him?

'That would be a good two pounds six we're out.' She stroked her cheek with the feather of her quill. 'To think what I could do with that . . . Nice roast pig to begin with. Nice burgundy frock to dine in. Nice black stockings . . . You like those, don't you? New bed curtains to finish off the evening with.' She smiled at him. Such poison! It got her out of almost anything.

He laughed. Then snarled. 'I know what you're thinking,' he said to his wife. 'That I'm an im—'

'Impossible?'

'An imp.'

'No, dear, of course not.' It was true; he had said it merely to hear her shoot down the idea. Louisa didn't see his height as weakness. Said it saved them money on cloth. Her mother, however, pointed out this deficit every time she saw him. But she was dead now, so that had put a stop to her.

'But you are improvident. Could send your daughters out

to collect the payments. They'd bring it home and more. Shall I call them?' She turned back to the ledger, started humming. He thought back to his first love. Anthea Day. Annie. She wouldn't have treated him this way. He had been an apprentice then, not a farthing to his name. Annie had been the daughter of one of London's most prominent physicians. (Louisa was the daughter of no one.) He had met her in the garden of her father's house, he'd been sent to deliver some medicines to him. He came in through the back gate and there she was, cutting flowers for a bouquet with a dainty pair of scissors. Her golden locks were fastened with pins of tiny amethysts; so that when kissed by the morning light, the effect was dazzling, that of a celestial halo. Her perfection – she the mortal daughter of Astraea and Aphrodite – so complete he was struck dumb and could do nothing more than hold out the package of medicines. He rallied . . . and was back the next day. Eventually he was so bold as to hide letters for her in the garden in the morning and throw stones at her window to catch a glimpse of her at night. And then, that day, when she allowed him to unpin her hair, a waterfall of silk in his fingers. Annie. She never faulted him as Louisa did, never made him feel mean and low.

But she had been taken from him, before he could even steal a kiss.

He rubbed his eyes, cried out, 'Drink! What does it take to get a drink?'

'Can't get you one, so stop your fussing.'

A good throttling. That's what they all needed. Or even better, he'd hide their ribbons.

'And why, my dearest, can't you get me a drink?'

Louisa looked at him. That infuriating smile. 'Because, love, I just drank the last of it.' She went back to humming.

'That's it! That's it!' Boghurst kicked over the stool, fought with himself. He couldn't decide whether to beat her or bed her. So he stormed out of the house. He had better things to do.

# 10

*The Surgeon's House, the Strand, Near the Maypole*

IT WAS WELL AFTER the witching hour and Penelope was standing over the surgeon Mincy's bed. He was snoring, with his sausage dogs snoring on either side of him. *And you're the biggest sausage of them all*, she thought. *But why did you behave so? Why were you so quick to condemn Boghurst?* The incident in Symon's office had been troubling on many fronts, and she couldn't make out Mincy's behaviour. It had been rash and senseless for him to order Boghurst locked up in the crypt. The accusation wouldn't hold water in court, and Mincy was intelligent enough to know that. So why do it? To distract from his own actions? Or did he have other evidence that Boghurst had indeed killed the girls? She slowly looked about the surgeon's room, took inventory of what she could. She'd been following the surgeon on and off for days now and had just about had enough of it. Sitting outside the homes of his patients, listening to them scream. He'd leave them as if he'd done nothing more than drop off his dough at the baker's. She couldn't risk watching through the windows, but she could hear enough all right. Mincy was unflappable. After he was well clear of a home, she would go in and check on the patients. He was tying them up, she discovered. But he untied them as soon as he finished whatever cutting or lancing or sawing or cleaving or piercing he fancied the situation called for. There was something else, however. Something more troubling. He was drawing on his patients. Ink grids, like they'd seen on the victims. A dark little box drawn around whatever procedure he'd performed. This was most confusing, for Mincy himself had said the other night he'd never seen such a practice before. And yet, here he was, wielding the pen with his own patients. Had he been lying? Or eager to pick up any technique that might aid his work, no matter the rotted source of it? She made a face; the surgeon had broken wind in his sleep. Boiled pig of a man. *That's right, Muttle-Butt Mincy, rest while you can.* She couldn't stay long – the dogs could wake at anything – so she tiptoed out of the room. She had wanted to look inside his medical bag, it was beside his bed, but she couldn't risk it.

She decided to try the front room below. She had already gone upstairs; Mincy lived with his mother and her rooms were on the floor above. But she was a deaf old woman who slept most of the time. *My God, this is tense work*, Penelope thought as she headed down the stairs; she found herself unable to fully breathe. And what vile men they were! Mincy. Boghurst. She would condemn them both as murderers if she could. Why must they be so barbaric? Why not give their patients a nice salve, a herbal cordial? Why add pain to pain? She was glad Symon had not ordered their services when she was ill. Yes, she got better with ale and sugary turnip cake. Plus a few spoonfuls of London Treacle. She could most certainly come up with a better-tasting tonic. *Penelope Potter's*

*Plague Popper*. But she didn't really want to change her last name to Potter. She would go into business with Joan, have her make the turnip cakes and provide the ale. Come up with their own recipe for treacle. A few peppery herbs mashed and soaked in sack. Perfect. Get the herbs from Symon's garden, the sack from his cellar. Give Joan a third, no, a half of the profit. Perhaps a small written acknowledgement to Symon on the bottle. *T.Y.R.*

She slipped into Mincy's front room and in the thin light of the moon read an unfinished letter on his desk. If she'd been the frail sort, she would have gasped at its contents. Instead, she eagerly flipped to the next page, hoping that what she had before her would end her investigation this very night. She felt a catch in her throat; there was something wet running over her ankle. She slowly looked down. One of Mincy's hounds was sniffing around her shoes. *My dear girl,* she thought as she quietly rolled up the letter and put it into her pocket, *how will you get out of this one?*

# II

*Lord's Day, July 9th, a Sweaty Pulpit, St Paul's, Covent Garden*

THEODORA THURGOOD'S LITTLE brother pushed her into the pew box. She ducked back and tried to shove him in front, but her mother swatted her with a folded-up China fan and told her to get on with it. Theodora bent a knee in brief prayer before entering, pulling her little brother down with her, then froze. A ridiculous stranger in a most awful suit of canary-yellow silk was sitting in their pew. He gave her a toothy smile and she shivered, he must be near to a hundred, and – Lord! – those fat white curls! Entirely false. The teeth, too. She sat as close to her brother as possible. This interloper seemed suspiciously cheerful for a Sunday morning. When it was time to stand and sing a hymn as Mr Patrick and his assistants walked in, the stranger managed to usurp even more of the pew!

This would be Theodora's last Sunday at St Paul's for some time. Her family was leaving shortly for a village in Kent, where they would stay out the visitation at her uncle's. Her father was a draper and had originally planned to see his family to safety, then come back to tend his shop. But now with nearly half the houses in the parish shut up, even he dared not stay.

Theodora pulled her bunched-up skirts out from underneath her and set about straightening them. Her mother, without shifting her gaze from the pulpit, reached across and swatted Theodora with the fan again. She sighed, which brought a third swat from her mother. She turned her eyes to Mr Patrick. She would miss him. She longed to put her arm through his. He was as a man should be. A constant smile spoke to his good humour; downcast eyes to his modesty. Although a man of letters, he had evaded the stooped and pasty look so common to clergy and lawyers. She had never heard a cross or pompous word out of those most Grecian of lips. A most kind man, a most thoughtful one. Early that spring, she had been walking by the church in quite a state, for her mother was in a severe mood and had threatened to end her dance lessons. The rector had seen her frown and picked several daffodils from the church garden for her as consolation. The gesture of a true gentleman. In her mind, the flowers came with a kiss. Never mind her grandmother. Granny was Irish and raised with masses said in Latin. She told Theodora that when she came to England and heard priests speaking in English, she realised they were foolish as farts. Though some were worse, she said, such as Mr Patrick. Theodora didn't talk to her for a week after that.

The very afternoon Mr Patrick had given her the flowers, she had ordered her father to make her a new dress. It was the colour of daffodils and she had worn it every Sunday since. All the more reason she should have asked that old man to move. His canary suit clashed so violently with her gown it threatened a headache. Would Mr Patrick be able to see her at all through that glare? She tried to pinch her cheeks to bring out more colour, without her mother noticing. Before church she had squashed a mulberry between her lips – she made sure to lick the front of her teeth so that they wouldn't be wine coloured too. Theodora had left her lace collar at home, to better show off her bosom. It was coming along very nicely these days. But her mother had produced it on their walk to St Paul's. How she would attract a husband with that woman checking her every step, she didn't know.

She noticed the stranger's hand was resting on the cushion between them and scowled. Today would be her last chance to talk to Mr Patrick for some time, perhaps for ever. She stifled a cry. He had only just come back and now she was going away. And he might not make it through. She should offer her help to him after the service. Tell him she would minister to the sick with him, that no matter what evil should appear during this plague time, she would not falter, would never leave his side. He couldn't turn down such a Christian offer. Could she get her pledge out before her mother stopped her? Theodora didn't know if she could live without seeing him for . . . Lord only knew how long. At the very least, she could remind him of his earlier promise. After he had given her the flowers, she had asked him for guidance in her Bible study. He said he would like nothing better, but was soon leaving town for a time to recover his health. She had waited every day since his return for a note announcing the start of their sessions, but none had come.

Theodora felt a scratch against her thigh. The stranger's hand was now brushing against her gown with a bejewelled and preternaturally long little finger. She inched even closer to her brother and turned her attention back to her divine

Mr Patrick. She had heard he was poor. She didn't mind. Her father's money would carry them. Did he know her father had money? She could see her father out of the corner of her eye. His face was flushed, he kept looking at the door. How could he be so cruel as to separate her from Mr Patrick? Why did he not work harder to make this match for her? Could there be a better match than a rector? She was fifteen, if she waited any longer, no one would want her. Surely they understood this?

She suppressed a fit of anger. The hand was now tugging at her skirts, trying to slip under them. She reached up to her hat and took out one of the long pins holding her ribbons in place . . .

Symon jumped at a yelp from the back of the church, squinted to see what was the matter. Was that . . . ? Yes, it was Valentine Greatrakes, sucking on his hand, sitting next to pretty little Theodora Thurgood. Was he an uncle? He didn't know Greatrakes had family in town. Theodora was in the gown she wore every Sunday – the colour of egg yolk. Not quite the complement to her red locks. Greatrakes was in a matching suit. Perhaps that was it. The gown was a gift from Greatrakes and she was forced by her family to wear it. No wonder she was frowning so much. Symon thought he was the only one who frowned over Greatrakes. Most ladies thought the Irish mystic handsome. Men thought him bold of look and pleasingly proportionate. Symon thought he looked like an upside-down broom. He found everything about the man exaggerated, as if he feared God would overlook him somehow. Symon saw his horse teeth flash as he leaned over and whispered something to the next pew. His paddle hands, his fleshy lips. Knobby cheekbones. All set to his disadvantage in some jarring colour. The person in the other pew mumbled back testily. Dear God, it was Dr Burnett. And Mincy. Was the surgeon eating something? In church! And was that a yip he heard? Had the man brought his hounds into a house of God? Between them sat a boy. Who would trust their child to them? He could only see a few spiky tips of hair. Ah, that was Boghurst. He tried to read his friend's face. Was he here to make peace or to make trouble? Symon had gone round to his house, but the apothecary had slammed the door in his face. He then sent letters of apology, cheese from Joan, wine from Spain, promises of silver shoe buckles and Flemish linens, heard nothing in return . . . He looked over at Mincy who was making very odd faces at him, mouthing something to him; then he heard a snicker from the front row. *Good God, I've been rereading the same passage*, he thought. He cleared his throat, began again.

'Lord of all power and might, who art the author and giver of all good things: graft in our hearse . . . hearth . . . I mean heart.' It was the heat. He was suffocating in here. The doors were closed. Who closed them? He stole another glance at the plague society. Why were they here? Silly question. They were here to molest him. Demand more bodies. *What about you, my murderer, are you here?* He searched the sea of faces before him, dull with the thickness of the air.

'The love of thy name, increase in us true religion, nourish us with all goodness, and of thy great mercy, keep us in the same; through Jesus Christ, our Lord.'

The crowd swayed to life, murmured an 'Amen'.

Insanity. Pure insanity. People dying all around them and some barbarian says, *Let's make this even worse.* Why?

It was a full house despite the great sickness, the orders to avoid gatherings. He didn't recognise many of them, and there had been tussles as strangers took up the pews of the absent, only to find that some weren't absent, but late. He could ask for volunteers to help him in the hunt. He looked back at the plague society. Would they help?

He watched as they squirmed, yawned, belched – *Yes, Mincy, I see you!* He took them through the Gospel of St Mark, the nice bit about food, turning loaves and a few small fish into enough to feed thousands. He'd like a simple dinner like that. But this horrid heat. He was his own meat pie, the church the pastry coffin inside which he was slowly steaming, turning to mush.

He pressed on. 'We believe in one God, the Father, the almighty—'

The crowd murmured back, 'maker of heaven and earth, of all that is, seen and unseen'.

'We believe in one Elizabeth, Jesus Christ, eternally begotten of the Creator . . .' Laughter erupted from the back. The plague society. Symon gave them his dirtiest look.

The congregation began a hymn and Symon unfolded the Lord Mayor's plague orders. They were to be read from the pulpit in every church across London today. Announcements like this always came just before the sermon. The idea, Symon supposed, was you would have half a chance of people still being awake. He looked over the pages, the orders were quite lengthy. This would run the service over by a good half-hour. His clothes were wet already, he was itchy. He sniffed. Was that his stockings? He slipped his foot back into its shoe. He looked up at the gallery, where the servants and riff-raff sat. He did a double take. Wiped at his eyes. Thought for a moment he'd seen his maid Mary there, and the other dead girl, too. Sharing a prayer book, glaring at him. He tried to clear his mind, searched the gallery for Penelope. He was frightened to think of what she was up to, what harm she might bring to herself. She had said it herself. She was like a sister to those girls. Alone, vulnerable. Defenceless. Prey.

He tried to concentrate, picked up the first page of the orders and read it to the congregation. 'The Master of every house, as soon as one in his house complaineth, either of Botch or Purple or Swelling, shall send notice.' And his family is to be locked up at once. Who would do that other than those as unbalanced as Dr Burnett?

Streets to be kept clean – good luck with that. The giant laystalls where everyone dumped their rubbish were to be moved out of the city – by whom? – along with the beggars. All lodgers living in cellars to be thrown out. All plays and games to be prohibited.

'What foul practice is this?' came a shout.

'A piss-pot practice it is,' the reply.

Bernard thumped his stick, growled for the crowd to settle.

Coffee houses and ale houses and taverns were to close at nine. 'No tame pigeons, conies, hogs, dogs or cats be suffered to be kept within any part of the city. And that the dogs and cats be killed by those appointed for this purpose.'

He heard a howl of protest from the congregation; it was Mincy. He met the man's eye, recognised his pain. Mite? Kill Mite? And her brother Tripe?

*

Symon was standing under the portico afterwards, trying to mask his embarrassment with over-enthusiastic handshakes. What an awful service that had been! He had stumbled through the sermon and then it ended abruptly; he had forgotten to finish writing it. He had never been good at impromptu speaking, which is why he tended to shine in the pulpit and not in person. He'd always found it rather easy to put clever words down on paper – an ability that he believed was behind much of his good fortune. But none of that mattered if one didn't remember to *put* the words on paper.

The parishioners were shuffling out of the church now. He said a loud, hurried goodbye to the Cockdills, the Midborns, the Widow Delapears, the Thurgoods. He was pondering how he would get out of a thoughtless promise to their daughter Theodora when Lady Digby, the crowning crone of the parish, thrust her icy hand out for the customary blessing. He shook his head, smiling, 'Oh no, we mustn't; the sickness, you know.'

He grimaced as the skin over her bald eyebrows stretched and contorted in outrage. He must buy her one of those fashionable wide-brimmed hats – to hide her plucked old head.

'You're of the cloth and you deny me God's touch!' she bawled in a squishy voice.

'Yes,' Symon said softly, wiping flecks of spittle off his face. 'It's a shame really, but orders from on high.' He turned to the next parishioner. 'It's to protect you now, isn't it?'

Bernard, who was standing next to Symon, reached out to grab Lady Digby's hand. 'You'll always have me, m'lady; I'll always be here to shake your hand. I'm no coward.'

'You dare to touch me! You lousy ass!'

'There, there,' said Bernard, savagely picking her up – she was a tiny old bone – and depositing her at the foot of the steps. 'Time for yer nap.'

Symon threw Bernard a knife-edged look. He was in no mood for the sexton's blatant rudeness. Distracted, drenched, hungry, he said his final goodbyes and quickly headed down the path for his house. Halted. There they were.

Under Symon's favourite cherry tree, perched on a stepstool, was Boghurst. He was speaking to a group of ladies. Under the magnolia, Dr Burnett stood with another group. Down by the front gate with the largest crowd yet, was Valentine Greatrakes, waving his famous hands through the air like tempest-tossed palm fronds.

'We shall talk to their families, recapture their lives, who they loved, what they were most loved for,' he could hear Boghurst saying as he handed out pamphlets. 'What their daily lives were like, their habits. We'll write it up. They will not be forgotten!'

Symon picked up a fallen pamphlet.

*Wondrous [And Godly] Experiment*
*To Devise A Famous and Effectual* MEDICINE
*To Cure*
PLAGUE
*Seek Us Out And Wee Shall Deliver*
[*through God's blessing, etc., etc.*]

Symon stuffed it in his pocket, avoided the apothecary, hurried over to Dr Burnett. He had a black bandage over an eye – What had happened? Symon wondered – was pounding fist into hand. 'They shall become even greater in death, giving to those they left behind the most miraculous gift of all. The gift of life. And this would mean your parish, Covent Garden, could get a certificate, claiming that you good people—'

'It's not my parish,' someone interrupted. 'Where are the apples we were promised?'

'No matter' – Dr Burnett smiled – 'we can make you an honorary member. Give me your name, I'll enter it into my book and we shall ensure that you get a certificate. Now, does anyone know anyone currently visited by the pestilence? Does anyone know of one such someone who has died, but whose body has yet to be collected? Whose family might be willing to part with said body in exchange for, potentially, their name on a cure ... Now I do say potentially. No guarantees ... still ...'

This was an outrage. Where was Bernard? He would have him chase these men out. He searched the crowds for the sexton, saw the surgeon Mincy, there on a bench, eating an apple.

'Delicious!' Mincy held it up. 'Candied!'

'What's going on here?' Symon snapped.

'We've come to help. You. Now frankly it is a cut and dried matter.' He turned to the dachshund at his feet, said in a babyish voice: 'It's as plain as the snout on your face, isn't it!' He playfully honked the dog's nose, then looked back at Symon and shrugged. 'But the others thought we should do this anyway.'

Symon stormed over to Greatrakes, who was surrounded by a crowd four deep. 'My dear man, would you honour me with a moment of your time?'

'My dear Rector, nothing would please me more.' He turned to the crowd. 'I'll be at Charterhouse Yard this Thursday, I do hope I shall see you there! You'll be there, Mr Patrick, won't you? And don't forget what we talked about! Send a note to Mr Mincy, by the Maypole on the Strand, if you would like to join our great and blessed effort to stamp this thing out!'

Symon was now tugging not so gently on the crook of Greatrakes' elbow, pulling him over to Mincy and his sticky apple. 'You've gone too far. Directly appealing to my parishioners for anatomy bodies?'

'Oh, Symon.' Greatrakes threw an arm around his shoulders. 'What's needed here is a sense of brotherhood. Communion! You were so right; we should be transparent in our actions! We should enlist your parishioners, not hide from them what we're doing! Show them how noble a donation of a body is!'

'I never said any such thing.' Symon pushed the man's arm away. 'Why don't you bribe the dead-cart drivers? Get the bodies off them. And leave me be!'

'That's not a bad idea,' Mincy said as he bent over to give his dog a lick of the apple.

'Now you're thinking!' Greatrakes agreed with a stretched smile. 'Then again. Isn't it far better for the future of physick, for the future of humanity, to establish this, to make this acceptable? To have everyone go in for it?'

'Why me? Why my church? Why must you annoy me so?'

They laughed.

'The vicar over at St Martin's threw us out,' said Mincy.

'My parish is too conservative,' said Greatrakes. 'But Covent Garden? Well, everyone knows you have no backbone, that you're weak-willed! Incapable of taking a strong stand, a hard line and such!'

'Why if the Devil himself showed up in Covent Garden, you'd be the first to go hiding under your bed,' Mincy added.

'Now, now,' Greatrakes said, seeing Symon turn red with anger. 'We don't mean to pick a hole in your coat. We're being uncharitable. We're applying to you because we know you care. You're not stiff like most of your kind. Parched and dried! Besides, we don't like it when people call you feeble! We want to change that!'

Symon could bear it no longer. 'You must all leave at once. I cannot have this.'

'I really don't understand.' Mincy handed his apple core to Symon. 'You let Boghurst, a rogue, a murderer, an affront to God, roam your parish free. Why not us?'

Boghurst had joined them and was about to belt Mincy with his stepstool when Greatrakes slid between them. 'Never mind all that, my good men. We've tried Symon's patience long enough. Listen, how about all of you come to my house, we can talk this over some more, we'll make a great time of it, bring your nightgowns and nightcaps, so you won't have to worry about finding your way home in the dark . . .'

'Very well,' said Mincy, 'and Symon, bring more of your apples. And cheese.'

Symon stared at them.

'No? Well, you think on it, then.' Greatrakes bowed and bounced away on the tips of his toes, Mincy and Dr Burnett trailing behind. Boghurst cuffed Symon on the back of the head and stamped off without a word.

# 12

## *An Attempted Rescue*

THE IDEA HAD COME TO Symon moments after he had read the fatal lines in the plague orders. He hurried home after the service and up to his bedchamber to pack. He would save Mite and Tripe by taking them to Elizabeth at Hutton Hall in Burntwood. That very afternoon. He would only go for the night, to save the cats, to gather himself. He dashed off a letter and yelled for Jack to find a courier who could deliver it that afternoon. He was not running away. No, not he. A regrouping of his mind, his soul. To plot a plan of action. Consider his resources. He must think carefully about his next steps. *I will seek her advice*, he thought. The two of them, together in her chamber. Making lists, drawing diagrams, plotting avenues of exploration. She would want to come back to town to help him. He would put his arm around her, tell her it was too dangerous. Her head would fall to his shoulder in fear, he would stroke her soft auburn waves, then tilt her chin up—

'Don't do it!' Penelope shouted, arms outstretched. 'Why must you go?'

Symon's head jerked up. What was she doing here? He threw the shirt he'd been imagining was Elizabeth into his bag and reached for another.

Penelope ran across the room and slammed shut the door of his clothes press, nearly crushing his fingers.

Symon put his hands on his hips. 'I'm not going anywhere.' He didn't care how obvious the lie. His affairs were none of her business.

'I saw you. At the church. You said Elizabeth every time you meant Jesus. It was terrible! Oh, Symon!'

'Mr Patrick, Penelope, Mr Patrick!' He went over to his wash basin. What was he to tell her? 'This place, all these faces, I must have a rest.'

'Oh, you can see them, too?'

He paused a moment, brush in hand. What did she mean? No, he wouldn't ask.

'Nothing good ever comes of these visits,' she said. He stopped again. How did she know this? How did she know anything of his life? Who had she been talking to? Bernard? Boghurst? Joan? *Don't be silly,* he thought, snatching up his tooth stick and comb.

She walked over and took the brush out of his hand; he saw his opening. He bolted to the clothes press and quickly grabbed another shirt, breeches. He would get a pillowcase from the wardrobe in the hall; Joan kept them soft as a late-spring breeze. (He never knew what kind of linen he would find, even at the grandest of places. And Elizabeth had just had a baby; he couldn't tax her with these trivial things.) He took the brush back, threw everything into his bag. Penelope took it all back out. He gave her a dirty look. Today she was playing marchioness. She had wrapped herself in many layers of dark green silk and topped it off with a turban the shade of a lime. She looked like a grasshopper, for two long antenna sprouted from her turban – his stockings. A terrible thought. Her clothes. Did she get them from the dead? No ... she wouldn't dare. She pulled out his breeches and was putting them on now.

'You push me too far, Penelope.'

'Not far enough.' She tied his shirt around her waist.

He eyed her as she slid his comb down the top of her bodice. His tooth stick went into her stocking.

She stopped. Stared back at him. 'Symon. She's married.'

He let out a long breath, collapsed into his chair. 'What of it? She asks my advice. She's quite disordered in her mind, seized with melancholy. She's had a baby. It's a delicate time. If she sinks deeper she may cross into fits. It is my duty to help her.'

'Your duty is here. I assure you, she does not need you.' Penelope sat down beside him. Softly she said, 'Do not ruin yourself for her. What could you possibly be hoping for?'

Should he confess? He looked at her. She was barely a woman. Of half-addled mind. Of dubious origins. He slowly got up and returned to his packing. She didn't know what Elizabeth wrote to him. The nature of their relationship. The thoughts most often in his mind these days. The one newly come to him, in middle of the night, when the veils were at their thinnest, when one could not tell the difference between dream and reality. That Elizabeth's husband would soon be dead of plague. She would be free to marry.

Penelope, sensing a change in him, stood up and grabbed the bag out of his hand, threw it out of the window.

'Fine,' he said. 'I don't need them anyway. I'll borrow something when I get there.' He heard a horse stamp the ground outside. His coach had arrived. She sat down in the doorway, barred his exit. 'You'll have to go out the window.'

'Really, Penelope, this is too ridiculous.'

'Symon! You must wait. I must tell you about Mincy! I've seen his patients. I've been in his rooms. I've—'

'Mr Patrick, Penelope, Mr Patrick!' he yelled. He grabbed his shoe from her hand and stepped over her.

'I'll give you one day away,' she shouted down the stairs. 'Any more and I'll fetch you back myself.'

Symon paused, hand on the banister. *Resist*, he told himself.

'Think of Mary!' she yelled after him. 'The other lass! Who will be next, Symon? Their deaths be on your head!'

He kept on going, ignored her even when he thought he heard her whisper, 'Think of me.'

# 13

*A Coach to Essex, Window Seat*

ELIZABETH, SYMON BREATHED, letting the cool air rush into his lungs. Elizabeth. His coach had left the poisonous streets of London and the city heat had given way to fields. Out with the black thoughts, out with death, breathe in Elizabeth, love and light. It had been months since he had seen her, and her last letter had unsettled him so. She had written only a few lines:

> *Love meenes nothyng to mee nowe. It interests mee nott. Mourn mee nott. My most fonde and deepest wish is for you, verilye my guidyng angel, to find truthe and hapiness and comfort in another. For I am not worthye.*

He did not believe the letter. Alone and isolated as she was in Burntwood, she was sinking into melancholy. And what of the babe? Would he know her as his own? Elizabeth denied it was his. He wasn't sure he believed her there, either.

On the seat next to him, his cats wailed away, echoing

his own internal state. He searched his mind. A happy recollection was what he needed. He chose their first meeting. Over the Thames in Battersea. He had been the vicar at the church there for only a year but had gained a reputation for his sermons – people said they enjoyed the hopeful, friendly nature of them after so many gloomy and thou-art-sinners years under Cromwell and his Puritans – and visitors from other parishes were coming on a regular basis. That was how Elizabeth and her husband came to his church one Sunday. He was shaking hands after the service, and a rather kindly lady had remarked that his sermon was like a fine French stew on a frosty night. Another agreed but wondered why they should bring the filthy French into it? ''Tis more like a good dish of broth when you are felled by an ague.'

Then a young woman of Titian hair and honeyed eyes stepped forth and said, 'Nay, his sermons are a shade tree, ripe with fruit . . .' She didn't lower her eyes as she said this; she would not be demure. He returned her smile; he had never seen such radiance. Her features changed as she looked upon him; her liquid eyes shimmered, her very countenance warmed – as if she had been sifting absentmindedly through rocks and found a gem. Was it possible? No one had ever bestowed such a look on him. He stammered a response, a shallow, safe one – what did she think of his little church? She told him it seemed most ideal and turned to her husband – an imposing man who looked in a rush – to ask if they could come again. Then she took Symon's hand and asked him if she could write to him, to seek his spiritual guidance.

He gave a hoarse 'yes' and quickly turned his gaze away. He shook hands with her husband, blessed them both, then nodded to the parishioners behind them before he betrayed himself any further.

Symon saw them in his church every Sunday after that. He watched her, and his heart swelled to see that she was indeed amiable in every way and attracted the esteem of all. He awaited a letter from her that would start their spiritual relationship, but it did not come. Then about six months later, he came home to find her waiting in the front room of his lodgings. She had been crying, and could do little more than put a letter into his hand before turning away. The letter told of how she came to marry her husband. A most grievous tale—

The coach suddenly swerved; the horses whinnied and bucked. Symon held on tight, then there was a loud crack and the coach dragged to a stop. He jumped out to see what was the matter. The driver was trying to calm the horses. 'A damn deer bolted 'cross the way,' he said. 'At least 'ee left us with our heads.' The driver nodded towards the front wheel, splintered by a rock they'd hit by the side of the road.

Symon took off his hat and mopped his brow, looked around. It was well dark and he had seen no one on the road for some time. *I will be late*, he thought. *Quite late.* The woods around were thick, he saw not the welcoming light of a simple cottage or farmer's hut. Perhaps he would walk the rest of the journey, it was not too far . . . *No*, he thought. He would wait. An agitation sparked in his chest, followed by a boyish dread. Who walked in these woods? What manner of beast? Then: what demon would come forth, ghastly and cold, to damn him with Penelope's accusation? That he had run away again.

# 14

*Righting a Washstand, Then, Fetter Lane*

PENELOPE REACHED FOR the comb inside her bodice; its teeth had been digging into her chest. She plucked the tooth stick out of her stocking, a similar situation. After she had watched her little rector drive away and disappear in a cloud of dust, she had gone back into his house to return his things. She put the tooth stick and comb back on his washstand. It wouldn't do to leave his bedchamber in disorder and upset Joan. She untied his shirtsleeves from around her waist, retrieved his stockings from her turban. She blew a loose black tendril away from her eye. She thought they had begun to make progress. Yet Symon still hadn't learned that he should always listen to Penelope. *Well, Mr Patrick, no one shall die on my account.* She had much work to do and in truth did not need Symon for any of it. She still had many a question about Mincy's affairs. And she must watch the apothecary, too. She needed to expand her inquiry in many a direction, for there was every chance the killer was neither one. But first she had a small personal affair to attend to.

She took the silver buckles from Symon's shoes, added them to her boots and made her way to Fetter Lane outside the City's western gates. The church service this morning had been quite useful, for it was there that she learned that her aunt and uncle had left town. She was watching Symon from the servants' gallery, but had an ear to the gossip around her. Too far away to hear much of Symon's service, and not that interested anyway, the servants whispered of old ladies found dead because they had been so horrid no one would take them in. That strange lights were seen in the abandoned houses at night. (*I'll have to be more careful*, Penelope thought.) They talked of how plague had breached the old city's western walls and all living there had fled. Her aunt and uncle lived near there. That meant their house would now, too, be empty.

*

It was but a mile's walk from Covent Garden to Fetter Lane, albeit a scorching one. Once there, Penelope took a long drink from her aunt and uncle's well, then set about breaking a back window with a rock. After she had knocked out most of the shards, she took off her skirts and used them to cover the edges and climbed in. Her victory at gaining entry was short-lived; the place was near to bare. She kicked a wall in frustration. She had hoped to sell whatever they had left behind. The pricks of a deep and ancient rage returned, the hatred that she felt for them; then a searing new pain burst forth. *Symon thinks the baby is his.* She took out her pocket knife and started to gash the wood panelling. Penelope thought this was highly unlikely. She knew Elizabeth's kind. Ensnaring everyone around her to fill up her time, her life, because she could not suffer to be alone and think on the miserable condition of her soul. Penelope's aunt was a version of this. Not a siren, like

Elizabeth. Or a damsel in distress. But a demon in distress. Elizabeth, she could tell by her letters, drew people in with pretty words and coquettish sobs. Her aunt snagged people with her claws, and the only way out was to leave behind the flesh her nails had caught. How that woman would rage and spit and slap and scream. Hell. Penelope had lived there. Someday she would give her aunt real flames.

She looked around. Yes. The minor Dutch paintings. The Flemish cloth. The burnt red charger that once sat over the hearth, the glazed blue bowl beside it. All gone. She had loved that bowl best. It had a purple flower shining in the bottom. One day, she took it out into the garden and filled it with flowers so it would have friends. Penelope had heard a shriek, looked up and saw her aunt flying towards her, crying that she was a thief. She stooped and picked up a stone, threw it at Penelope's head. Penelope had dodged it, which made her aunt all the angrier.

Penelope wrapped her hands around the back of a rickety chair, one of the few things left behind. She let out a guttural scream and slammed it against the staircase, taking out several spindles. *A satisfying start*, she thought. It was that very night after her aunt threw the stone at her that she heard the woman contemplating her death. *I would be a fool indeed to give her another chance at my head*, she remembered thinking.

She went up to their bedchamber. The bed was still there. A great old oak four-poster thing. They probably thought it too heavy for thieves to trouble with. Penelope smiled; she would get several pounds for it. She hated that bed, its posters carved with intricate little vines and leaves and flowers. Its marquetry borders. Impossible to dust. Each time they made her, she would select a different flower and scratch her initials inside it. They never knew. Once, she gouged out a lion's face from the headboard and took it to her own room. *Now that*, she sighed, *they had noticed*. She moved on to search her uncle's study, the cellars. Opened all the cabinets, cupboards, drawers. Knocked on the walls for secret doors. Penelope had tramped through many a deserted house in the past weeks. She had found trapdoors, priest holes, false walls hiding the family's valuables, but never what she was looking for – the murderer's lair, where he had kept Mary and the other poor girl. Or his new victims.

She went back out to the garden. Around the stone walls, a dozen shrubs formed a border. They were all recently planted, she could tell from the little mounds of fresh dark dirt around their bases. A smile crept across her face. This was most promising. She walked to the shed to fetch a spade. When she was finished, she would use it to break all their windows. Lord, what a miserable life she'd had here. There had been no other relatives to take her when she was orphaned, and what a brutal shock her new home had been. Her father had been a fine City lawyer, but he had a weakness for his brother, a hapless, silly man who was always in one mess after another. Her father bailed him out time and again, until her uncle found himself in such a situation that even her father could not untangle. He tried, and was briefly sent to gaol for it on charges of obstruction. It was a terrible mistake. A fatal mistake. He died there on the third day, of a fever. Her mother passed away not long after. That is how Penelope knew one really could die of heart break. Her uncle took Penelope in because, as she found out late one night prying through her uncle's papers, her father had left her a small fortune. *Accidents have happened for less.* That's what her aunt said. *Children are always falling down wells.* Her uncle told her to hold her tongue, but Penelope had heard enough and left within the fortnight. She spent her final nights there repeatedly reading her uncle's papers, gathering evidence of her father's fortune, so she could claim what was hers. There were locked boxes; she tried to pick the locks but failed. That is what she was searching for now, the chance they might have left something valuable behind in their rush. Many a time over the years, she had come back under the cover of darkness, getting as far as the back door, an open garret window, but had stopped short of venturing inside. She often thought of murder, often thought of torture. And as she sketched that body in the church crypt, she imagined her aunt and uncle mutilated before her. But she would not go down that path, she would not lose her soul for them. But she would make them suffer. Soon.

The shed was locked and it was getting on in the day. She needed to get back to her inquiry, puzzle out the strange habits of Mincy and Boghurst. She put a hand to her brow to shield her eyes from late-afternoon sun and looked back at the house. She'd come another time. With one of Bernard's spades. And a hand axe to make her own carvings.

# 15

## *A Lonely Country Eve*

SYMON AND HIS COACH SAT by the road for hours; Mite and Tripe had thoroughly soiled the rushes in their wooden cage twice over. Eventually a surly groom, fetched from Elizabeth's house, came in a carriage to get him.

Once in motion again, he felt his mood shift from recrimination and shame to something much softer. The sweet damp of the woods reached into the carriage and settled around him. He breathed in the grassiness of the air, the warm scent of oak and hornbeam carried him the last mile to Elizabeth's. He had stowed Mite and Tripe on the roof of the carriage, and, blessed be, they had finally gone quiet. The low hoot of an owl, the rattling of underbrush, the scream of a fox; the otherworldly sounds of the July night no longer frightened him. Rather, he took comfort in them, they were signs that plague had far from destroyed all. He closed his eyes and let the growing chorus of crickets and frogs soothe him.

Elizabeth. That day in his lodgings and the letter she'd brought. A confession, she wrote, about a wickedness in her past. She had been living with her grandmother, her parents having passed some years before, when she met the man who would become her husband. Through a family friend, she had been introduced to Sir Denis Gauden. He was married and seemed a kindly uncle to her. He presented himself as devout and most eager to instruct Elizabeth in the many rules for conducting a good Christian life. To which she readily submitted. She gave herself so absolutely to his guidance, she wrote, that at last he persuaded her never to marry, so that she could remain always pure and true to Christ. She found no difficulty in giving her consent, for though she was already twenty, she had never felt the least desire to be joined to a man. He drew up a contract and gave it to her: *I promise and vow that I will live a virgin, and never marry any but thee.*

These last words startled her, why did he write them? Sir Denis was past the fiftieth year of his life and with a wife and children. He told her that it was no more than to say she would not marry at all. The great opinion she had of him made her sign the paper, which he kept. Then his wife died. He brought her the contract and told her she was honour-bound to marry him. She was confused, she knew not what to do or in whom to confide. Sir Denis visited her every day, reminding her of their contract. As much as Elizabeth loathed the idea of marrying him, her grandmother, who knew nothing of the pact or how it came about, approved of the match. Elizabeth saw no way out that wouldn't destroy her honour and yielded. But the very night after they sealed their vows, her spirit could not rest. She slipped from their bed and took the paper, tore it up and threw it into the fire. There her written account ended.

Elizabeth bowed her head while Symon read her letter. When he finished and looked to her, she refused to raise her eyes. Her cheeks were flushed with shame and tears. He gently questioned her about the present state of her marriage, and her answers were full of piety and good nature and understanding. He told her she must accept her marriage and continue to be a most excellent and pretty wife to Sir Denis, but that she should turn to God, through Symon, to help her find peace on earth and in her unfortunate situation. He did not blame her for not revealing the pact to her grandmother, he doubted it would have helped at the time. He was sure the old woman would have been blind to all except Sir Denis's wealth and connections. That Sir Denis was a man of extraordinary deceit he did not say. But Symon knew from that very moment that he had fallen in love with her. That he would be a constant for her as long as she needed him, a truth in a life that had been built on trickery.

The country lane curled through a last stand of forest, and there, as the road curved again, was Hutton Hall. This was his first visit to Elizabeth's sister's house in Essex, and while it was not as fine as Elizabeth's new home in Clapham, he still considered himself quite blessed to be the guest of such people. Hutton Hall was centuries old, built and burned down many times over. The current incarnation was three storeys of severe grey stone, topped by three oversized gables. He searched the oriel windows for a flicker of light, but nothing. Completely dark. A lump in his throat. He had imagined – before the unfortunate delay with his coach – that Elizabeth would be waiting for him; that they would begin their evening with a quiet supper. Perhaps a boiled egg, good country bread, some hard cheese. Then he would lead her through evening prayers and they would sing the baby to sleep. Once she was nestled away – what had Elizabeth named her? Isabetta, a version of her own? Miranda? Or Minerva? Yes, Minerva, that would suit her – the music would continue. He would play his flageolet; she would play the virginals. Perhaps before bed, they would share a pot of warmed and creamy egg posset, spiced with a hint of nutmeg and not too much wine. Ah, but it was so very late, and Elizabeth surely must still be exhausted from the birth. He must let her know at once that he was there to help her, not burden her. He would make himself her servant during this short visit and provide for her whatever she needed.

The carriage rolled to a stop, a footman opened his door. 'These?' He was holding up Mite and Tripe. Their night hunt interrupted, the brother and sister were at it again, caterwauling. Symon hadn't thought about what to do with them once he arrived; he assumed Elizabeth would have arranged it for him. 'The stable?' He suddenly felt very foolish.

He was shown to a bedchamber and his spirits fell further. No fire, no basin of water to wash off the journey's grime, no supper. Clearly he was an inconvenience. Of course he was, how thoughtless to make this journey. Elizabeth must look to her babe. She had no time for him. And yet . . . He asked for some ale, some bread. Some scraps sent out to the cats. The food never came; Symon fell asleep in his chair, waiting.

# 16

*The Charnel Ground, Covent Garden*

PENELOPE WIPED HER BROW, tried to free her eyes from the sting of the smoke and lime. In between carts, she had been helping Bernard and his boys set lines for a new burial pit in the churchyard; there was no space left for even family graves. Bernard considered sending the strangers at least over to the big pit at Tuttle Fields, but he banished the idea after one look. A massive thing, he said; the air so thick with lime he couldn't make out the edges. A sad place, an unholy home for those forgotten even before they died. 'Won't do,' Bernard kept muttering as they dug their own pit. 'It's not right.'

Penelope ladled a sip of water from a bucket, then picked up her spade and flung another load of dirt into a wheelbarrow. She was digging out the border of the pit when she heard the clop of horses nearing, the bell toll. Another dead cart had arrived. She let her spade drop and walked over. The yard boys scrambled up on to it. *What a terrible garden they had for play!* she thought. She pulled the littlest boy off and told him to go to dig instead.

There were four or so bodies in the cart. A bigger boy took hold of some arms and she grabbed the ankles and walked backwards until the body was free from the cart. They handed it to another group of boys and Penelope reached in for another set of ankles and stopped. Something had rolled under her fingers; she looked down. There was twine with a complicated little knot tied around the ankle. She looked up at the wrists held by the yard boy; she saw strands of twine compressed under his fingers. She jumped into the cart for a closer look, a heavy misery overtaking her like lead cooling in its mould.

'Oh, my poor pixie,' Penelope whispered. The hair had been shorn; ink lines crossed her body; there were scores of cuts. 'My poor poor pixie; who fated you such a wicked fight?'

''Ere's another one,' said the yard boy. Penelope looked over and lifted the arm of the corpse next to her. The signs were all there. The twine, the odd sores, the stubbled hair, the ink marks. She tenderly held the girl's roughened hand, then leaned over to straighten her long and stained apron. Mixed with smells she didn't want to think on, she could detect a familiar scent – that of an autumn meadow turning to rot. *Ah,* thought Penelope. Old ale. The stink of a serving girl.

'Did you know each other?' she asked the dead girls. 'Did you work together? Did you have each other in the end?' She let the hand fall and slid out of the cart. She gave orders to the boys and headed out to find a horse.

# 17

*An All Too Merry Party, Hutton Hall, Burntwood, Essex*

SYMON WOKE THE NEXT morning to a knock at his door. Elizabeth? 'Come in!' he shouted eagerly. A maid walked in with a tray and a note.

*Deareste,*

*My heart breakes that I can nott yet greete you, an event most extraordinary requyres my attension. But what a feast I have planned for you! Soone . . .*

*I carry you with mee, always.*

*Yr Elizabeth*

*There you are, Symon,* he thought. Last night was an oversight. After all, he'd given her such little notice. He wondered, would she have the baby with her? He would seek out the child. He changed into his new suit, then frowned. It was the one the tailor's daughter, Alice Jones, had made for him. He tried to hurry the thought away – of Alice, his servant Mary. All the deaths he had left behind, all of those yet to come. Those he could prevent. *Fie!* he said to himself. This was not a delay, but a restoration. He would look for the baby, little Minerva, then send directions to Bernard to keep the work apace.

*

Symon enquired after the baby's whereabouts, waited patiently in the garden for answer, but after a good deal of time with no news, decided to seek her out himself. If he met with Elizabeth in the course of his search, so much the better. He went inside and to the upper floor and listened for sounds of cooing, or fussing, or crying – whatever sound it was that babies made. He heard a soft singing from down the hall, prayed it was Elizabeth, called out and let himself into the room. There indeed was the babe, but it was not her mother holding her. The nurse smiled politely at Symon and he crept up to the sleeping infant. He searched her face, her fingers, her toes for a likeness. She looked a plump old man, and that was all he could say. Red cheeks and nose, a bit of fuzz on the head, but he could detect no familiarity – he laughed to himself – with anyone. How funny these little creatures were! He dared to touch a finger, brush her angel-soft cheek, then whispered that he would be back anon.

His heart full of happiness, he made his way downstairs, where he was met and directed by a servant towards a room that at last, he thought, would contain Elizabeth.

He paused as he entered, however, for the room was full of men and smoke. Two stood near the hearth and looked equally aggrieved at seeing him. One was dressed in a vermilion doublet, the other in a suit of robin's-egg blue. If it hadn't been for their costumes, he would've thought himself at a wake by the severity of their looks. They turned back to their conversation without so much as a nod. A third man was slumped in a chair, eyes closed. A fourth was seated next to him, dismantling a pocket watch.

Symon cleared his throat. 'I trust all is well?'

The man with the watch stood up and came towards him. He was a good few years older than Symon; tall, with waves of salt-and-pepper hair flowing back over his crown, and a long, sloping nose.

'Lady Gauden asked me to look after her clergyman,' he said with a bow. 'I assume by the plainness of your dress, that is you?'

Symon was taken aback. Who was this? Where was Elizabeth? 'I'm afraid you have me at a disadvantage, Mr . . . ?'

'Evelyn. John Evelyn. Welcome to our merry party, Mr Symon.'

'Oh no, it's Patrick.'

'Yes, why not? Call me John,' the man said through a half-smile.

Symon was quite at a loss. Perhaps these were friends of Elizabeth's husband?

'Sir Denis,' he ventured, 'did he arrive with you? I am most eager to hear the City news from him.'

Mr Evelyn arched an eyebrow, shook his head. 'Best he stay away, don't you think? I have my own business in town, but I find I can safely conduct it from a distance. I don't go back and forth, too much risk, wouldn't want to be the one blamed for spreading it about. I believe Lady Gauden's husband is of the same mind, but from the other end of the stick; he prefers to stay in London to oversee his business.'

Was the man toying with him? He claimed he knew nothing of Symon, except that he was a clergyman. Did he not know that he had come from London? Symon paused. Elizabeth must have sensed it would upset her guests. He had barely given any thought to this, that he could be a danger to others. Yet this tall, handsome man – who was he? The name sounded very familiar – had implied . . . No, this was nonsense, Symon had not brought plague with him. Did the man think he carried it in his pocket?

'Are you from the neighbourhood, then?' Symon continued.

'Not at all.'

'Is Mrs Evelyn with you?'

'She's at home, tending to our children. Have you seen Lady Gauden's new babe? Most precious.' He walked back to his chair and began fiddling with his timepiece again. 'Gorgeous girl, named her Johana.'

'Johana?' Symon repeated slowly. 'Yes, indeed. How lovely. God is Gracious.' He struggled to recover himself. 'Well chosen.'

Evelyn saw Symon's confusion and added, 'What with her husband in town, we didn't want to bother him. His favourite aunt was named Johana. We were sure he'd approve.' *We?* thought Symon. *Evelyn was here for the baby's birth? Had helped name the baby?*

'Do you like to tinker about, too?'

Symon frowned. Evelyn was holding up his timepiece. 'Let me put the glass back on.' He fixed the cover into place and handed him the watch. 'Built it myself.'

'Most handsome,' was all Symon could manage. Lord! That was how he knew of Mr Evelyn. He was one of the founders of the new Royal Society, a group of wealthy gentlemen and virtuosi who got together and messed about with lenses and devices – yet another group who liked to experiment on dogs; the poor beasts! And that painting. Evelyn as a dreamy young scholar. Dressed in a fluffy white shirt and resting a head of long, thick black hair, all his own, on his hand. The other hand laying across a skull, a black velvet cloak draped across the shoulder. A portrait of melancholy, the signature of an exalted mind. When it was painted, Evelyn was the talk of the town. He had just brought back some ancient drawings of anatomy – why anyone should care was beyond Symon – from his studies of dissection in Padua. The skull was meant to remind viewers that even handsome and clever and wealthy men like John Evelyn would die. Symon as a boy had seen the painting during a visit to Oxford; how his mother and cousins gushed over it! Nearly twenty years had passed, Evelyn's black hair had receded deeply and weakened to much grey.

He invited Symon to take a seat while he explained the parts of the watch. The man in the chair next to them was Elizabeth's brother-in-law, Symon realised. He had met him once prior. Mr Pheasunt, squire of Hutton Hall. *A rather rude squire,* thought Symon. The two men standing by the hearth were brothers, Evelyn mentioned, though brothers of whom he did not say.

'I shan't pretend, I'll pay anything for a good pair of boots,' the taller brother was saying.

'I've easily paid four pounds,' said the other.

'Yes, I have done just the thing, extraordinary cost,' the taller brother rejoined, not to be beaten. 'But there can be no other way.' He lowered his voice. 'A new pair, every season. Sometimes twice. My one weakness.'

Symon very much doubted that. And he had never paid more than a few shillings for his boots. He had been tempted once to pay a guinea, but such extravagance. Should he be paying more? Surely not four pounds. Who could afford that? It was thrice as much as he paid Nell for the entire year. Symon himself had 150 pounds per annum through his patron the earl, and then another 100 pounds in the form of a yearly stipend from the parish. A comfortable amount, to be sure, but not so comfortable as to spend such a portion on boots. He tried to sketch a fuller picture of the men, without revealing his curiosity. He needn't have bothered; the others were quite practised in their ability to ignore him. And yet Mr Evelyn. He was staring at Symon, with that half-smile of his. What did he mean by it?

The conversation dribbled on to gloves. The question: what was the right size of a fringe? Apparently the ladies (*Which ladies?* wondered Symon. For who else was here?) had earlier remarked on the importance of a gentleman's glove being well fringed, large and graceful. One of the brothers was now pointing out that large was difficult, for it could cross over into buffoonery. The other disagreed; it was down to the art of a man to pull it off, no matter the size.

Symon was increasingly annoyed. At their rudeness, their empty talk, that he should feel he was in the wrong for venturing out of London. He would find the steward, arrange to be driven back to Burntwood and take the afternoon coach home to London. He saw Penelope rising up before him, calling to him, pointing to the graves, stomping around in boots – cheap ones – the soil of the dead flaking off with each step. Her angry curses were washed out by peals of laughter. He looked up, he could hear a flurry of steps, the rustling of silk skirts from behind the door. His blood seized and there she was. Elizabeth, followed by several other ladies. The men jumped to their feet. She walked straight up to Symon and, to his great pleasure, kissed him on the cheek.

He noticed first her bosom. It was much plumper, cradled in a white silk bodice, the sleeves billowing off the shoulder.

Then her face: a look of rapture, the one he had seen on their very first meeting. Her eyes were like stars; her face glowed as if dusted with gold. Persimmon lips, beckoning him. Auburn hair, made all the more ravishing against the white silk. How he longed to touch her . . .

'My dear Mr Patrick, how I have missed you!' She kissed him again. 'The Lord is too good to me, you are too good to me!' She searched his eyes, frowned, then said, 'You poor dear, are you so tired? Have you nothing to say to me? We must fix this at once!' She turned to Mr Evelyn, who was waiting next in line for her attentions. 'A drink for our rector, something strong, that's what's needed. Could you, Mr Evelyn?'

The man smiled warmly and bowed; he too considered every order from Elizabeth ambrosia from the gods, Symon realised. *What trouble was this!* Symon thought, for Mr Evelyn, it seemed, was also in love with Elizabeth.

'And why didn't you send word he was in such a state?' Elizabeth continued. Symon stood up straighter at this; did he really look so poorly?

She suddenly wrung her little gloved hands, as if overcome with anguish. 'All of you! How famished you must be!' Symon stood transfixed as her amber eyes briefly returned to him, his body cried out to know the message hidden in them. She smiled, then twirled around and said with a laugh, 'Let us head straight to dinner before you eat each other!'

*

Symon had been placed next to Elizabeth during the meal, but he grew increasingly irritated. The complaint no doubt starting in his guts. He had been hoping for good country fare. Some asparagus, an arrangement of lettuce, perhaps a roast chine of beef, a nice wobbly cake. But before him, the offerings of a cook with aspirations. Jowl of salmon. A dish of mincemeat hash with almonds and rosemary. Boiled pike with pomegranate. Stewed oysters. The centrepiece, a hare with pudding in its stomach. The second course, a fricassee of chickens. Neat's tongue roasted in a caul. An omelette flavoured with tansy. Peas, an orange blossom snow cream, lobsters. He hadn't had such a rich dinner in months, not before he left for Astrop, when the town was full of people and invitations to dine. A slight smile eased the pressure building in his bowels. Was this for him, this feast? Elizabeth making up for his horrid journey, his horrid reception? A physical manifestation of her esteem, even as she was forced to split her attention amongst the guests?

She appeared quite recovered from her confinement and in full spirits. She drew her guests out, one by one, praising them, making sure the conversation never stayed on too dull a subject. 'Do you keep a diary?' she was asking. 'Mr Evelyn keeps the most marvellous diary.' Symon shook his head no. With each new question he feared that she would reveal to the table that he was from plague-ridden London; he caught himself flashing between relief and anger that not a one showed any interest in him. Instead, all the guests vied for Elizabeth's attention, everyone looking for her favour. *Surely these are all guests of Elizabeth's sister*, he tried to tell himself, but this seemed as unlikely as a snowfall in June.

The sister, Mrs Pheasunt, had none of Elizabeth's beauty or charm. She was a frizzled thing and seemed content to let Elizabeth host. She sat on the other side of Symon, gabbling out of the corner of her mouth. She met his vague affirmations with an arch of the eyebrow, a look down at her plate and more mumbles of an incomprehensible but clearly pointed nature. One of the younger ladies who had arrived earlier with Elizabeth was the near to grown daughter of Sir Denis, from his first marriage. As for the others? No one had introduced them.

Symon felt he couldn't sit straight enough at the table or eat genteelly enough. The food was so rich, he was nearly out of control, something primitive in him urging him to rip into the dishes even though they were forming a heavy pool in his stomach, even though the company called for a more indifferent approach. He tried to slow himself, tried to match the languid pace of Evelyn and the other gentlemen. He felt like a cow amongst stallions.

'Any progress, Mr Evelyn?' Elizabeth asked. The honourable gentleman sat on the other side of Elizabeth.

'Not a bit. Most shameful. Our seamen who are sick die like dogs in the street. No provision to care for them. Our prisoners starve in their chains. I should hope our own abroad are not treated as such.'

*Ah*, thought Symon, *a Navy man. Who serves from the sidelines. A courtier.* His mood lightened.

'The king, surely he will help?' she asked.

'Every day I ask for more hospital ships to be set up on the Thames, for more food, for more medicines. I know none amongst our court who care for our state. It was intolerable before the sickness took hold; it is all I can do now to keep it out of our fleet.'

'What a burden on your soul!' Elizabeth cried, placing her hand over Evelyn's.

*He looks nothing like a man burdened,* Symon thought, stabbing into a slice of tongue.

'And his pocket,' Mr Pheasunt added. 'I hear our king pays back none of his commissioners. What is his debt to you?'

'I do not wish to single myself out, I can shoulder whatever

God chooses to place upon me.' Nods of admiration from around the room. 'But I will say this, those of us who do the king's work, we're all under by thousands of pounds.'

'Good heavens,' one of the brothers said. 'What's needed is a good prize ship to pay these things off.'

'Or a dozen,' said the other.

Mr Pheasunt leaned over to one of the brothers and Symon heard him mutter: 'My lady's husband has the worst of it. I hear some hundred thousand pounds he's put out in the name of the king, none of which our merry Charles has bothered to repay.'

Symon dropped his fork to his plate and looked at Elizabeth with dismay. She was lifting her glass in a toast to Mr Evelyn. Symon lifted his as well, choked down the wine. A hundred thousand pounds in debt? It was an unfathomable sum for anyone other than a monarch. Sir Denis was in charge of supplying the Navy with food in all of its various outposts. To secure contracts of that size, out of his own pocket! A servant filled Symon's glass. Hand shaking, he swallowed it down.

For the rest of the dinner, his mind was filled with nothing but black worry for Elizabeth and her future.

'Symon, are you quite well?' It was Elizabeth, her hand on his arm.

'Yes, forgive me, I was . . .'

'I said we have a special treat for you.' Symon's heart leapt. She turned to the rest of the table. 'A sugar banquet! Out in the garden! And after that, Mr Evelyn will entertain us with one of his latest experiments with the Royal Society.' Symon's heart crashed.

The guests followed Elizabeth like puppies towards a little octagonal house shimmering in the afternoon sun; a jewel box with a frame so slender it looked to be spun from spider's silk.

The walls and conical roof were filled with glass panes, many of them levered open at different angles and reflecting the blue of the sky, the orange of the sun, the green of the garden. A gift from her husband, Elizabeth said, to help her pass her summer exile. The ladies had put the finishing touches on it that morning – fresh-cut vines with purple flowers twisting up the wooden supports. Inside, on a table, stood a replica of the banqueting house made of sugar, with a gilt Medusa head on each of its eight sides. Around the marzipan house, a miniature garden, its hedges and borders made of tart. Its flowers of fruit and preserves. There were little clusters of dates, figs and strawberries, and little dishes made of sugar, too. In each one, a sugar playing card, delicately rolled wafers and slices of candied orange. It must have cost a small fortune.

Chairs were set up in intimate couplings in and outside the house. Symon waited to pick his until he saw where Elizabeth would sit, but Evelyn beat him to the seat next to her. Symon skulked over to a chair in a corner and bit into a playing card. Mrs Pheasunt joined him. She stank of lily.

'Do you keep a garden?' he heard Elizabeth ask one of the brothers. 'Mr Evelyn keeps the most amazing garden.'

How his head ached, how the afternoon dragged on. He watched Elizabeth float from one guest to the next, laughing, smiling, happiness itself. She excused herself to see the baby; Symon tried to follow but was pulled back by Evelyn. How ill-prepared he was to deal with this man. How the quips and comebacks were never there for him. How the guests clapped and shrieked over Evelyn's tedious experiment on the nature of fire. Was it so interesting that a fire died if deprived of air? Then Evelyn suggested a walk, he would be their guide and illuminate the secrets of the wood for them. Symon loathed country walks. But he wasn't about to let Elizabeth out of his sight.

Once they were back, Symon was subjected to more squeals of delight as Evelyn brought out tea and little porcelain egg-shell teacups. The China drink was new to Symon, it hadn't filtered out much beyond the court. He took a sip, deemed it detestable – thick and bitter. 'Your digestion will thank you,' Evelyn said. And it soon did: the drink proved to be an effective purge. He would give Evelyn credit for that.

The men became saucier as the claret flowed and the light faded. A supper was served – a grouse pie, cherries, stewed prunes, a cheesecake, cold meats, more wine. It appeared he would have no time with Elizabeth this evening. He tried to lift his melancholy by soaking up the warm glow of the candles set all around them. Beeswax, a comforting, pure smell. Then he recalled the pig-fat candles of his youth, the dreadful meaty stink of them, their thick black smoke, the embarrassment. His dear mother whispering to his father that if he didn't pay the creditors soon, they would be forced to eat the candles. *Surely it couldn't have been that bad*, Symon thought. But with that memory, he was at the end of it. He got up to make his excuses but Elizabeth took his arm before he could get the words out.

'A walk under the heavens?' she asked. He would decline, a punishment for her. She saw his hesitation and added, 'I only wish to ease your fears, my poor Symon, I've watched you struggle all day.'

He looked at her, astonished, relieved. She knew him well; he was not alone in this world after all.

'You're worried they'll discover you've come from London, aren't you? I told them you were a vicar from Lincolnshire, no one's much interested in that.' She gave him a mischievous smile. 'Your secret is safe with me.'

Did she think he was boring? If as a boy in Lincolnshire he'd known that he'd grow up to be anything so grand as a vicar, he'd have considered himself most blessed indeed.

She lowered her voice. 'It's time we talked, isn't it? I promised you a confession.'

A catch in his breath as he remembered what had followed those words before. The day she had come to him in Battersea and told of the wicked foundation beneath her marriage. Then again last summer. At Elizabeth's house in Clapham. Cherry brick trimmed with white stone. The whole mansion floating on a bed of white roses, as if kissed and lofted by angels. Elizabeth's husband had originally built it for his brother who was soon to become Bishop of Winchester, but he met an early death and so Sir Denis kept it for his own.

Symon had been spending the week there, praying with the family, taking long walks with Elizabeth and her spaniel and Sir Denis' children from his first marriage. Sir Denis had left not long into Symon's visit to see to business in the City. At meals, Symon often imagined it was his own family he said grace over.

On the day of Symon's departure, Elizabeth announced she was riding back to London with him; she wanted to surprise her husband. They were settled comfortably into her carriage, her spaniel in her lap, and chatting about neighbours, gardens, the delights of the country versus those of town. Then quick as a sunshower, she began to cry. She talked of her unhappiness, of her husband's coldness. Of the warmth she'd felt with Symon, a warmth she so very rarely felt in her life. Symon pulled her towards him, to comfort and calm her. He truly did not mean for the embrace to be more than that of one dear friend to another, but . . . She looked up and, through her tears, gave him a smile so beautiful it stopped his heart. He felt a mixture of shame and rapture at what had happened next. Afterwards, she had put her head on his shoulder and they were silent together the rest of the way to London. Her warmth, her trust in him, it had been perfection. And he hated himself, vowed he would never take advantage of her again. Except he did. Then she wrote to tell him she was with child.

He went to her immediately; he knew it to be his. He did not say so outright. He had looked at her belly, started to tell her how very glad he was . . . and she quickly put a finger to his lips and hushed him. 'Let's not think on such things, my darling, not yet . . .' He did not press her, and then he did not see her much after. They had been separated for months by one cause or another.

But now, here in this country garden, it appeared, they would finally talk of it. She would assure him the child was not Sir Denis'. Not John Evelyn's. But his.

Elizabeth was leading him towards a stone bench sheltered by a hedge; Symon halted as they neared. He thought he saw a face, a familiar shape at the side of the hedge. He blinked and the face was gone. Penelope? Or a sprite? He became angry, weren't they the same? He put this silliness out of his mind and lifted Elizabeth's hand to his mouth, kissed it. The moon was clear and lusty, not a cloud in sight. 'Look at the stars. In thy presence is fullness and joy.'

'Such blasphemy,' she replied with a laugh. She pulled him down to sit beside her. Symon felt every inch of his body relax. Her gaze, her touch, it calmed him. She looked into his eyes, kept his hand in hers. 'Thou art powerful medicine.'

''Tis God who is the powerful medicine.'

'And you brought me to him. What I mean to say is, He brought you to me. I cannot speak enough of what your love has meant to me, how it holds me. To have met a love such as yours, that seeks nothing but to ease my soul.' She turned her gaze to the night sky and they sat in silence. He noticed her lower lip was trembling.

'Elizabeth—'

She shook her head, her eyes still on the heavens. 'A sea of diamonds. It pains me that I cannot touch such brilliance.'

'But you can. They're in the celestial kingdom, your eternal home. Elizabeth—'

She turned to look at him. Words left him as he looked into her eyes. They were shaped like fat teardrops, full to bursting in the centre. A thick fringe of dark lashes curled around them, the longest lashes he'd ever seen. He could spend a thousand moments on her eyes alone. She smiled, aware that he was lost in her beauty, and that his eyes were now on her mouth.

'It means so much to me that you came here, Symon. I've been so lonely. So confused. I do not know ... Your letters' – she squeezed his hand – 'they brighten my day. With you next to me, I feel such happiness. I never ... understood God, I never understood his magnificence until you showed me.'

Symon melted. 'Whatever comfort I can bring to you, pleases me, pleases God.'

Elizabeth's eyes had lowered, her lips slowly moving closer to his.

'Symon ... there's something about you that makes me want to open my heart to you, tell you everything. There is something you must know.'

Symon had stopped breathing, held her hand tightly in his. She would tell him now. About the babe. 'Please, what is it?'

'That you're very inconsiderate for a clergyman, keeping her all to yourself.' Symon's head jerked back. Mr Evelyn was standing over them, hand out for Elizabeth. 'Come, Elizabeth, I would be most honoured if you would help me light the fireworks.'

She grabbed for his hand. 'Oh my darling, nothing would make me happier! And there is a wine from Greece to put out. A gift from my husband. Symon, you shall have the first glass!'

# 18

## *A Prowler's View*

PENELOPE LISTENED FROM behind the hedge, gave a silent hurrah when she heard Symon decline Elizabeth's offer of wine and bid her goodnight. She had been quite disgusted that he hadn't yet left this sugary party and didn't know how much longer she could contain herself.

Faced with the brutal murder of two more friendless girls, Penelope had decided in a fury that she would come to Burntwood and drag Symon back to his duties. She had taken a horse from the Bedford stables – it was but a few hours' ride to Burntwood; a sign indeed of Symon's dangerous lassitude that he himself had sought a coach for such a short journey.

But it was a cold, calculating fury, safely trapped inside Penelope; she had long ago learned never to act in a hot anger. Her plan had not been to interrupt the party, as much as she liked a good show, but to find Symon alone and make her demands. He was a proud man and could be surprisingly stubborn when put on the spot. He was more likely to come quietly if she didn't make a scene. She had arrived late afternoon and more than once had to douse her temper at what she witnessed. A country party while so many suffered in London? She stuffed her ears with grass when Elizabeth sat down at the virginals, a dashing older man with salt-and-pepper hair howling beside her. Symon sat alone in a corner, and it gave Penelope a small comfort that he, too, seemed horrified at their merriment. She waited outside the parlour for hours, hoping to grab Symon if he left, but he never moved. When they sat down to supper, Penelope could take it no longer and slipped out to the garden. She found a distant tree and sought to rethink her strategy. She must have nodded off, because she was quite shocked to wake up and find her head resting in a cold and spongy substance. The lap of a ghost. Penelope bolted up and grimaced. The wraith wore a look of extreme distress and a gown of ashes. She looked familiar. Had Penelope seen her before? Ghosts tended to follow Penelope, and she tended to ignore them. They thought she understood them because she could see them, but they were often muddled – they talked of mustard seeds when they meant widow's weeds. Patches of black ate at the ghost's sleeves; sooty pieces of skirt broke off as she moved. The signs of a painful death – she was swallowed by something. *Fire*, Penelope thought. The woman tugged at Penelope's arm, then pulled on her hair, trying to keep her attention. Penelope slapped away her hand. 'Mind your manners. Come back when you've sorted yourself out.' The ghost wailed and Penelope heard the music falter in the distance. Supper was over and the company were back in the parlour, playing merry again. She clapped a hand over the ghost's mouth. 'Crying about it won't solve anything.'

Penelope was about to venture back inside when she saw Elizabeth leading Symon by the hand into the garden. They were coming her way, so she ducked behind a hedge. She wanted to brain Elizabeth as she listened to the syrup she poured on Symon; wanted to brain Symon for being such a fool. Her own courage nearly failed her, worn down by such thick slatherings of superficial feeling, thought to go home without speaking to Symon. But when she heard his rebuff of that final glass of wine, Penelope thought there might be hope for him yet. She rallied as she watched them walk back towards the terrace and saw Symon bow and turn for his room. But which was his?

*

A strong, chill wind came in from the east and Penelope bided her time as the guests peeled off and the servants snuffed the candles. She waited a while longer then went in and up the stairs. The upper floor was dark, the storm outside growing. She looked at the doors along the corridor and frowned. What a guessing game this would be! And the storm to wake them all at any moment! She heard the creak of hinges and took cover behind a hall table burdened with a hideously bushy plant. She watched as someone left one room and crept into another. This happened several times over. *Revolting!* she thought. Then her heart sank. She saw a familiar figure come out of a bedchamber. He was tall, square-shouldered, his thick brown hair standing up. His cravat was gone, his shirt untucked. He walked hesitatingly towards a door across the corridor. A door that she knew to be Elizabeth's, because she had already seen her come out. He stood before the door and raised his hand to knock. He paused, looked over his shoulder and that was enough for Penelope. She stood up and audibly snorted in disgust, no longer caring if she were seen. Throwing good after bad, she'd never understand it. Unless there was nothing really good about Symon, after all. She hammered down the stairs and out to get her horse. Symon was welcome to stay as long as he liked; she cared not.

She took an oilskin coat and cap from the stables and headed towards the wood where she'd tied her horse. Halfway down the lane, the sad little ghost with her gown of ashes reappeared. She seemed sorry for Penelope and in the tone of an apology murmured, 'Put them in the office.' Penelope blinked, then brightened. ''Tis an excellent idea!'

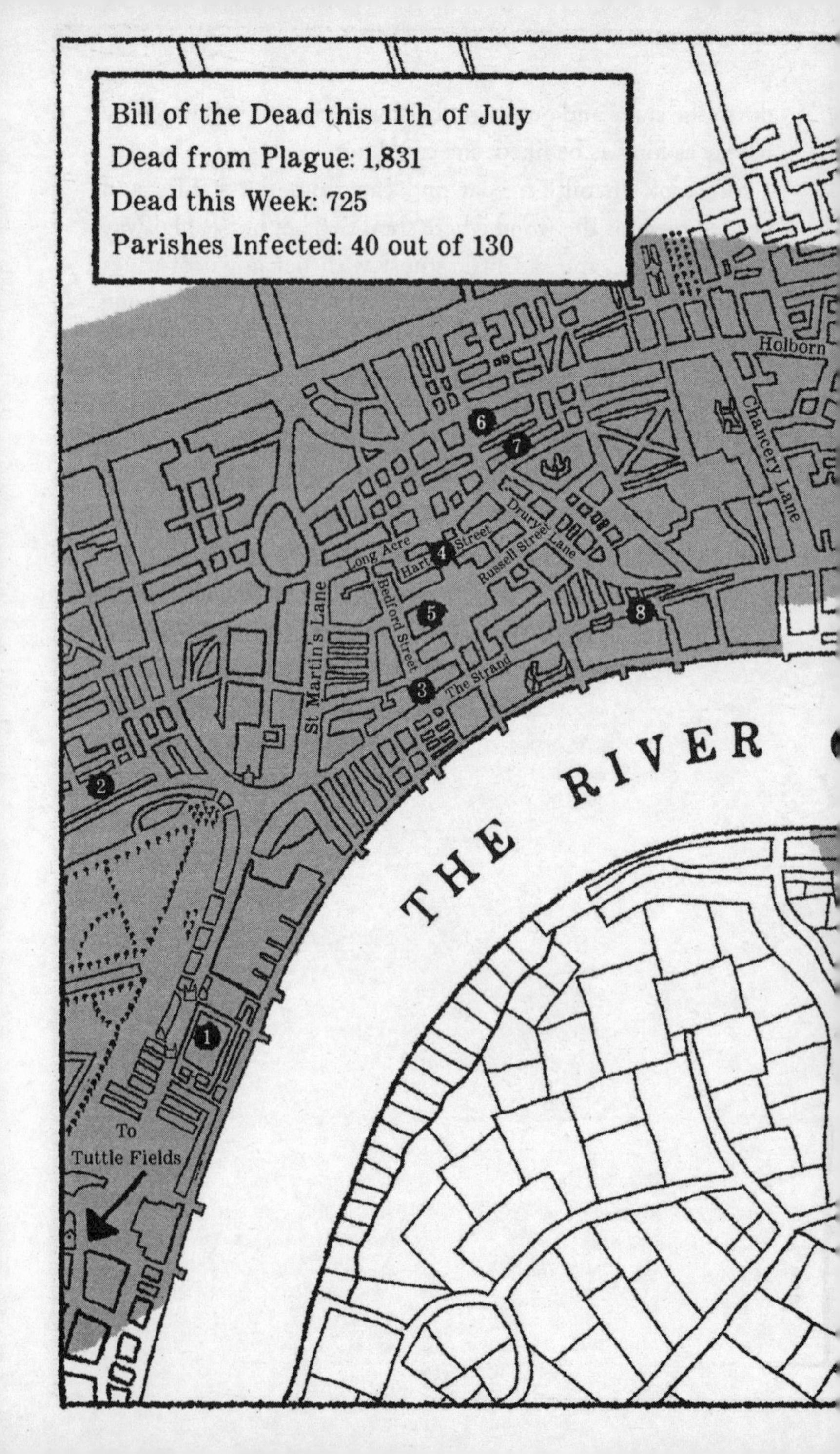
Bill of the Dead this 11th of July
Dead from Plague: 1,831
Dead this Week: 725
Parishes Infected: 40 out of 130
Holborn
Chancery Lane
Drury Lane
Long Acre
Hart Street
Russell Street
Bedford Street
St Martin's Lane
The Strand
THE RIVER
To Tuttle Fields
1
2
3
4
5
6
7
8

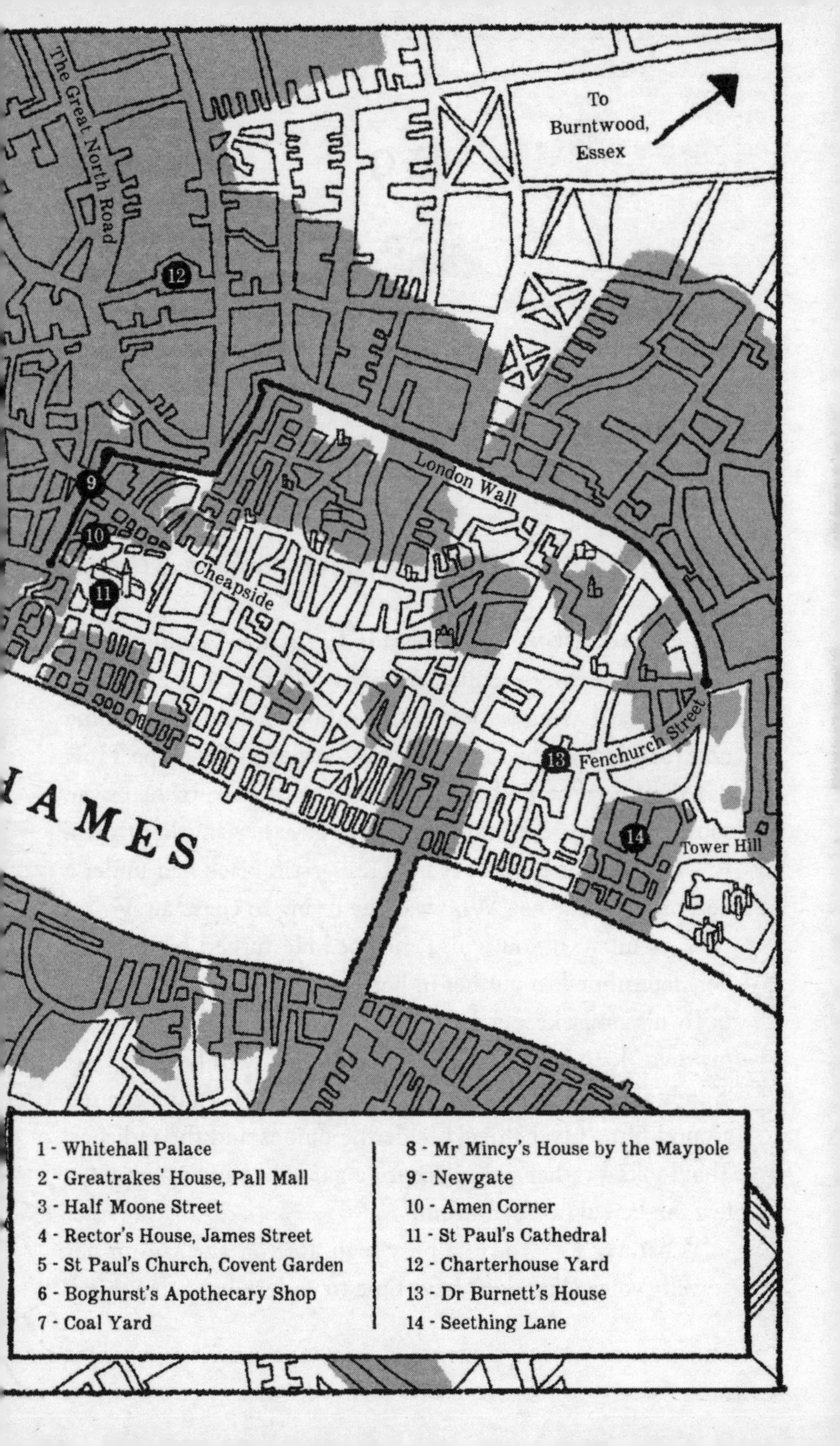
The Great North Road
To Burntwood, Essex
London Wall
Cheapside
Fenchurch Street
Tower Hill
AMES
1 - Whitehall Palace
2 - Greatrakes' House, Pall Mall
3 - Half Moone Street
4 - Rector's House, James Street
5 - St Paul's Church, Covent Garden
6 - Boghurst's Apothecary Shop
7 - Coal Yard
8 - Mr Mincy's House by the Maypole
9 - Newgate
10 - Amen Corner
11 - St Paul's Cathedral
12 - Charterhouse Yard
13 - Dr Burnett's House
14 - Seething Lane

# 19

*Tuesday, July 11th*
*Symon's House, Back Garden, Next to the Skullcap and Catnip*

'BACK SO SOON?' Penelope stood at Symon's garden gate. It was early evening, the light still high in the sky, and Symon was having a word with his housekeeper about some new plantings he had in mind. He scowled at Penelope. How did she know he had returned? She must have rushed over, soon as she heard, to chide him. He gave her another frown. A scarecrow she looked! A mud dress; stiff black hair under a flea-bitten straw hat. Who was she trying to chase away?

'A moment, if you will, Penelope.' He turned his back to her, determined to put her in her place.

To his housekeeper he said, 'I really would like a plot of my own.' Joan ignored him and continued with her weeding. 'Surely there must be room for me somewhere?' He gestured around him. 'Over there, beside the onions and the radishes. That looks a rather nice place for a garden of a few simples, a few medicinal herbs, hmmm?'

'Whatever for? You're a busy man, Rector,' she said in her gravelly voice. 'You don't have time to undertake such a thing.

Step aside, I need to get to the turnips.' Joan pushed him backward. Despite her years, the woman was tall and strong. It was no small shove – and he tripped over a duck, who flapped her wings and nipped the back of his legs, triggering an angry chorus from her brethren.

'Now look what you've done,' Joan rasped. 'See, you don't belong out here!'

He clapped his hands and shooed the ducks away. He hated them and their mocking little quacks. An awful agitation had twitched about him since his departure from Hutton Hall. Such a terrible visit. He had resolved nothing, wasted much. He'd had no more than a few fleeting moments with Elizabeth and with Mr Evelyn's last interruption that evening in the garden, he had decided he could play about no more. He'd set his mind to departing as soon as the sun was up. The party, the house. It was not a place for him. Elizabeth with her fluttery, unsettled nature had once again left him near to shattered. He'd had little sleep that second night; his thoughts racing about his brain like mice. Then there was the constant footfall outside his door, what had that been? He had thought perhaps someone was sick. And what of the shadow? The visions that seemed to haunt him the entire trip. Outside in the garden that evening; then later, as he stood before Elizabeth's door. He had heard an unholy, guttural sound and turned in a fright to see a spectre, gaunt and miserable, fly with unnatural speed down the stairs. The spectre had put a most terrible fear in his heart – that some danger had come to Penelope. In the clear light of morning, he had dismissed these anxieties, put it down to poor digestion. But there was a truth in his visit. Penelope was right; he shouldn't have gone and he felt more the fool for doing so. Aside from their one starlit moment, Elizabeth had not sought him out. What was he to make of it? And there was the matter of Evelyn. His presence at the birth of Elizabeth's baby. The baby's name. Was it possible? Symon pushed this thought away.

After supper that night and once in his bed, Symon had imagined many a thing he could write to her. He decided in the end on a short note, thanking her for her kindness and telling her of his departure. Then he had agonised over how to deliver it. A servant? Or by his own hand? He had almost gone so far as to knock, but instead slipped the note under her door. He then returned to his room and wrote a series of letters. To the aldermen of his parish. The magistrates. His patron the Earl of Bedford. He asked them all for their counsel in regards to the strange death of his servant Mary, and of the other tortured girl they'd found. A great storm broke; he hoped it would wake Elizabeth, that she would find his letter and come to him.

But she didn't.

Early the next morning, he looked in a last time on the babe, convinced himself there could be no Evelyn in her and kissed her goodbye. He walked to Burntwood for a coach without a word of farewell from Elizabeth.

And now it seemed his disappointment was not to abate, but to swell and distend in his very own household. He turned again to Joan. 'Please. It will help me find peace after a day of hard trials. A bee hive. What a world of good that would do me.' Bees wouldn't soil all over his garden like those miserable ducks.

'You want to come home after a long day and muck around in the dark and get stung?' She chuckled and bent over to pull out little sprigs of weedy green from between the turnips, then handed them to him.

'I'm sure you can find me a patch. Do let me know what you come up with,' he said a little too curtly.

'You tend the souls, Rector. I'll tend the earth.' She nodded towards a barrel near the privy; she wanted him to take the weeds and dump them. Symon's anger grew. How was it that his own household was ordering him about?

'Listen to Joan,' Penelope said. 'She's wise. You'd be much better off knocking on her door at night.'

'What?' Symon snapped. She spoke such nonsense! He handed the weeds to her and headed inside to grab his cassock; she followed close on his heels.

'When shall we expect you at church?'

'On my way now,' he said through gritted teeth.

'Good, because the smell. Lord! Even I find it disturbing. You'll want to clear it out before prayers tomorrow. Otherwise they'll lose their breakfasts!' She handed him back the weeds and rolled her eyes. 'And who would we get to clean that up?'

He let the weeds fall from his hands. Dread seeped in as he looked her in the eye. 'The churchyard? It smells even more?'

'No. The bodies in your office.'

# 20

## *A Stinkynge Office*

PENELOPE LED THE way to the church, or rather Symon chased her. As soon as he crossed the threshold, the smell hit him in the face. He let out a wail and yelled for Bernard, then cast his eyes into his office. Two forms on the floor, covered by shrouds.

'What's it now?' Bernard was standing behind him.

'You knew about this?'

'Helped put 'em here.'

'Why didn't you write to me? I would've come at once.'

'Can't write.'

Symon pulled away the shrouds. Two girls, blonde hair shorn; their broken eyes staring back at him. Lines of ink creeping out from their bodices; up their necks, down their arms.

He went outside and slid down the cool stone pillar on to the step. He was trembling all over. A black ocean crashed through his head. Who were they? Sisters, God save them? Or strangers even to each other? If nothing else, he was certain they were orphans. For if they had someone to keep them safe, this could never have happened. What was he to do?

He closed his eyes, thought of the other dead girls. Of Mary. Then of Joan. Gruff, but she had a heart far bigger than his. She took care of Symon; did he take care of her? She took care of Nell and Jack. They were growing like saplings. They needed new clothes, new shoes. Joan was always after him about this, because he took little notice himself. He never thought to invite Joan to take a rest if one day she was a little more bent, moved a little more slowly because of the pain in her joints. Never brought Jack a toy if Joan had put him to bed with a bad cough. Or even a ribbon for Nell's hair. Heavy, acid tears of failure coursed down his cheeks. He must do better. He remembered Nell's accusation when they had learned that Mary was dead. That he had promised to keep the girl and her brother safe. If he didn't, who would? Their mother and father had died a few years back, another summer, hot and muggy like this one. A fever had come through. Singing in the morning, dead by evening. Took a baby with them. Jack was still a chubby little thing himself.

Symon had met the two quite by accident over at St Martin's in the Fields. They were waiting in a pew, Jack's head buried in his sister's dark hair. Nell was holding on to him so tight Symon was sure she was drawing blood with her fingernails. Symon was there to see the vicar over their most recent boundary dispute. The man was a rotten type named Crumwell; he was arguing with some poor soul in his office. Crumwell ran out, yelling, 'Final offer!'

A big, burly man pounded after him. 'You'll take them both, you will, or the Devil take you!' Crumwell disappeared into another room across the way, slamming the door. The brute stood before Symon, tugging and pulling so hard on his hat the seams were like to burst.

'Yours?' Symon asked.

'Not mine.' The man nodded towards the girl and boy. 'They need work.'

'The lad's a bit young for that.'

The man had tears in his eyes. Symon was shocked, for the man was as much an ox as he'd ever met. 'That's what the vicar said! Too young. No use for him. Will only take the girl.'

'Surely it only wants a few years, he can work then; all will soon be well.' Symon turned to leave; he'd get nowhere with Crumwell today.

'In a few years, the boy'll be dead. All they got is each other. And that slime-arsed vicar doesn't have the charity to keep them together. A good pash and a pike is what he needs.'

Symon agreed with him. Crumwell was an awful man; Symon avoided him as much as he could. He looked over at the children. They wouldn't return his gaze. They were terrified. Well, this wouldn't do.

'They can work for me. I only have a housekeeper at the moment. A rather grumbly one. She could do with some help.'

Crumwell flew out of the room where he'd been hiding. 'Mr Patrick! You will not. They're the property of my parish. It's not for you to decide!'

'I take your point.' Symon turned to the girl and boy, asked if they would like to work for him. The girl started to answer, the boy finally looked up, but the burly man already had them by the collars and was shoving them, along with Symon, out through the door.

'Course they do. Your backside, Vicar! I've got a mind to widen it with my boot. Take care!'

'Bring them back now!' Crumwell screamed. But the brute had already closed the church door.

*This is a man of action*, Symon remembered thinking. *Why not?*

'What about you? Are you in need of work?'

'Suppose so,' said the man. 'Don't think Crumwell will have me back now.'

'You work for him?'

'Sexton.'

*Perfect*, Symon thought. 'What do you think of St Paul's over at Covent Garden?'

'Not much.'

Symon laughed. He arrived home that day with Bernard as his new sexton, and a doubling of his household. Joan wouldn't say as much, but he could tell she was pleased. She fed Nell and Jack, and Bernard, too, and didn't demand that either the boy or his sister sleep in the coal cellar. One of Symon's best days, all in all. So very unlike his life now. He grabbed at his hair in frustration. He heard someone walk up behind him. Penelope. She gave him a nudge with her boot, nodded for him to get back inside.

He followed her in, forced himself to examine every bit of the corpses, blessing them as he went.

'Tell me about them,' he said.

'Ten bodies a night now,' she said. 'Can't trace half of them. Most of them have no kin left to speak for them.' But these two, she knew it when she saw them. Their marks set them apart from the others.

Symon looked at her in awe. This girl, she was nothing but edges and tatters and mud, a walking drey, and yet she carved plague pits from the earth and rode with the dead. He noticed a leather belt around her waist, a small hand axe hanging from it. She was ready for battle, while he had been running from it. He met her eyes, the torch flames dancing in them. What did she see in his? Shame, of course. He turned away and headed out into the muggy night and over to Drury Lane. He stopped under a squashed porch roof at the rear of the White Hart Inn, kicked at the door.

'Boghurst,' he yelled, 'get the hell up.' After a few moments of silence, he heard banging, the shoving of chairs and buckets.

'What are you to accuse me of this night?' The apothecary peered angrily at Symon through cracked windowpanes next to the door.

'My dear friend, you know me for a fool. You've forgiven me before and I ask you to forgive me again, for I sorely need you now.'

The apothecary grinned and opened the door.

# 21

*The House Next to Symon's, Covent Garden*

'WE SHOULD SEE someone tonight.'

He and the apothecary were in the parlour of Sir Humfrey Tracy. Sir Humfrey lived next door to Symon in a grand expanse thrice the size of his house. But Sir Humfrey and his household had left town in mid-June. Symon had gathered everyone here because his house was filled with stench. Bernard had moved the bodies out of Symon's office as requested, but to his cellar.

'Why?' Symon had screamed.

'Your wench. Said you might vanish again otherwise.'

'Get her here, now.'

'Fetch her yerself; I've no time for this.'

'Peace!' Boghurst had said. 'She'll show up soon enough.' The apothecary went to make his examination of the bodies in the cellar while Symon broke into Sir Humfrey's and moved his entire household next door.

Not long after, Boghurst had rejoined him and was now scrounging around Sir Humfrey's cabinets for drink. The shelves bare, he sank disappointed into a purple velvet armchair.

'You look like a rhubarb in that chair,' Symon said. *A shrivelled one at that.* 'You are much greener these days.'

Boghurst glared at him, moved on to his findings. A square had been drawn around each bubo, with a letter and number. 'Our man has tried a range of techniques. On one, a caustic agent of some sort. I will say no more of that. Another he has cauterised. A third he has lanced. A fourth he has dressed with linseed oil.'

'But why?' Symon asked.

'An attempt to soften them, to draw out the morbid matter.' The apothecary ran his fingers over the stubble on his cheeks and throat, the rasping sound amplified in Symon's head. He imagined a knife at the apothecary's neck, sawing at it, his friend writhing in pain, bleeding to death before him. He caught himself, tried to organise his mind. 'Go on,' he said.

'And he has once again resorted to ulceration, though I cannot understand why he continues so. The practice has long been discredited. For it is not the pest that flows from them, but the spirit itself. If this man had any learning at all, had read any of Diemerbroeck's treatise on plague, he could have spared these poor girls considerable agony. Which is why I truly find it hard to believe this is the work of any London man of physick.'

'I know not what disturbs me more: their suffering or the ability of this barbarian to close his mind to it,' Symon said. Plague victims, tortured. It made no sense to him. Who would do this and why? These wounds were not the result of a robbery. Or committed in a passionate rage. Some of the marks had time to heal before the others had been made. The victims were slowly, methodically cut, burned, abused.

'Your instincts were right,' Boghurst said. 'What we have here is murder. Bizarre, inept, but murder.'

'Four bodies. Those are the ones we've found. There could be more, delivered to other churchyards or dumped in the pit at Tuttle Fields. How are we to stop this?' Symon told him of the letters he had written to the parish officials while he was in Burntwood. They all had long since left the city, but several had already written back. Their replies were a severe disappointment, Symon said. One had pledged money, as if he had sent a form letter asking for charity. The earl's response was a warning:

> *I beseech you to look to the stabilitye of your mind, and thus our great parish, for the tales that you send me are assuredly the deranged vysions of a lunatick. Let us heare no more of this, or I shall see the need to remouve you with utmost expedyence and place you in the care of . . .*

Symon had destroyed the note in disgust.

'Who have we overlooked? Surely someone has stayed behind?' he asked. 'Some great man who could bear witness to this brutality, who could signal to all that we speak the truth?'

'Well' – Boghurst shifted uncomfortably in his seat – 'there's Monck.'

Symon let out a long sigh. George Monck, the Duke of Albemarle, the might behind restoring Charles II to the throne. An old war hero, as grizzled as they came. He began his career at the tender age of fourteen, when he knocked in a sheriff's head for insulting his father. He was forced to flee; he said no matter, England was too soft for him, and got himself over to Cadiz to fight the Spaniards. He had been on the front line of every battle since then, fighting in France,

Scotland, Ireland and then on the seas between England and the Netherlands, and finally on England's own soil during the Civil War. He was known for his guts, an unshakeable man. He never met a risk he didn't like and was good with secrets. But the tide was against him now. No one ever knew what Monck really thought, which opened the door for some to ask, was he thinking anything? These days, in the smart circles of the new king, a king brought up in France, Monck was called a blockhead. Slow. Heavy. A mean, contemptible creature. Ravenous, selfish. A lout. And yet. He, of all the king's men, had not abandoned London.

'Let us go now,' Symon said. 'Get it over with.'

'He'll not see us at this hour.'

'He must.'

'One doesn't barge in on a duke. You know that. Besides, it is a difficult matter to explain in a time such as this, when death is everywhere. The replies to your letters are proof of this. We must be thoughtful about our approach.'

'Lie then. Tell him you ask on behalf of the earl,' came a voice from behind them. Symon jumped. Penelope. She was sitting at the foot of the stairs, scribbling in a notebook.

'You mustn't sneak,' he scolded.

Her mouth dropped open in disbelief. 'But you do!'

Symon tugged on his cravat; it was near to choking him. Or rather, this life was.

She went on, 'What a silly rule! Made up by rich folk to keep the poor ones down! Rich folk sneak all they like, in and out of all sorts of places. Kitchens. The bedchambers of married ladies . . .' She looked straight at him as she said this. 'As if all the world is their home, as if everything belongs to them.'

Symon gave a quick shake of his head, as if he would clear

it and then be able to make sense of her muddle. What was she talking about? Which would he tackle first? Her immoral nature? Her non sequiturs? That she ordered the bodies lodged in his house? Or the provenance of the midnight-blue gown she wore? He rubbed his temple. There was no time for any of it.

'I shall send the duke a note, tell him I have a matter most urgent and reveal nothing more.' He offered to find Boghurst a link boy to light his way home, but the apothecary declined.

'I can see better in the dark. Like to make observations on man in his natural environment.'

'Sun's soon to be up. Last call for thieves,' Symon warned.

'Not to worry. The secret is you walk hunched like this' – Boghurst bent over, right shoulder jacked up – 'and you swing your foot around, like the knee won't bend.' He walked in a circle around Symon, dragging his leg. 'People steer well clear of you.'

'Such tricks. Why skulk about so?'

'Always good to have a plan. Careful preparation. Makes the apothecary, makes the man.'

Symon grunted and closed the door on him. 'Penelope, there's a bed in the garret for you,' he turned to say but she was already gone. He took a cushion from a chair and settled down to sleep on the floor.

# 22

*A Shut-Up House, Leg Alley, St Martin's in the Fields*

THE OLD HAG WAS BREATHING on him, jabbing a scabby finger in the guard's face. *Most of the time, the work isn't too bad*, the guard thought. Spent his days in the shade, standing outside the houses of the sick. Not much to do other than watch and think. They rotated him around the parish; once a family died, they moved him to another house with fresh inmates. The families never lasted long, a week at most. He was in Leg Alley today, a tight little lane north of Covent Garden. Every last house shut up. He didn't worry about catching it himself. He had nothing to do with the people inside, and he chewed on a wormwood stick, kept him upright all right.

'Gimme a 'ouse now,' the hag said.

Lord she was foul. 'Get gone, old mother; get yerself washed.'

'Come on, gimme one.' The hag inched closer. 'Parish sent me to nurse 'em up, on the orders of God Almighty.'

'What's God want with a scabbed sheep like you?'

She pawed at his chest, his arms. 'Give us a good 'ouse, one with a lot of coin. A lot of fine things.'

*A walking sheep's dag*, the watchman thought. 'All right, all right, get out my face, nursey, and I shall give you a good house.'

'Get us in there, then; need to put these cheese chunks up in front of a fire. Dry 'em out.' She lifted up a large foot and wiggled it at him, bits of caked-on dung flying as she did so.

He led the hag down Leg Alley to the house furthest from his post. He stood clear of that one, they shrieked so much. 'Got a nurse for you,' he yelled as he unlocked the door. 'Stay back or I'll bash your heads open,' he added.

He held the door open for the nurse, but she waited, hand out. 'Give us the key.'

'Now, old mother, you know I keep the key. You tell me when the last one is dead and out you'll be after a fortnight.'

She rapped him on the side of the head. 'What do you have in there? The brains of a piss swallow? I'm not going to stay locked up with the dead!'

Of a sudden, she was seized by a coughing fit. She stumbled and fell against the guard, giving him a full dose of her fetid splendour.

'All right all right, here you go.' He pushed her away and handed her the key to the padlock. 'And may God rot your arse clean through.'

She stood her full height – she was much taller than she had at first looked – and swift as a bat was by his ear.

'Be careful of your curses,' she hissed, her voice low and rough. 'In my experience they make their way back to their owners, thricefold. In your case, I'll see to it myself.' She went inside and he heard the bolt slide shut. He peered through a crack between the shutters. Yes, he was sure of it. She wasn't a nurse. She was there to rob them.

He knocked on a shutter, yelled for her to open up. He would drag her out of there. The old woman opened it and leaned out.

'Go now,' she said. 'Or you'll be next.' She thrust both arms out towards him and he jumped back. She laughed at him, not a crone's laugh, but the laugh of a man. Then she grabbed the shutters and slapped them close.

He peered between the shutter slats, watched the old guard stumble away. Drunken pillock. He threw off the horsehair wig and coif he'd taken from Drury Lane. The theatres were abandoned there, the actors long gone, but their chameleon skins left behind. A doctor come to treat his patients, the guards would remember that. A sulphurous harridan, they'd forget as soon as they could.

# 23

*The Cockpit, Whitehall Palace*

SYMON HAD RECEIVED A prompt response from the Duke of Albemarle. A prompt response declining his request. 'You've lost your wits,' the duke wrote, 'for you ask for an appointment on a Holy Day!' It was an impromptu Holy Day, Symon wanted to write back. Ordered by the Lord Mayor of London, not by the Church. Every Wednesday until the pest abated, all of town was to fast and cry the Lord. But only until sundown. Details, my dear duke, details! But the duke's insults came too swiftly for Symon to gather a truly stinging response. 'What blasphemy for you to venture from the pulpit on such a day!' the duke continued. He went on to write that he thought this day of fasting was a mistake, and could the rector have it cancelled, for the world was crashing down around them, and in such a situation, a more c—t-brained idea he'd never heard of. Fasts made men weak and murderous. That is not what London needed. Then he asked Symon to bring him several loaves of good white bread and a hearty mutton stew, and to send them over no later than ten of the clock that morning. If the duke approved of the stew, he would agree to receive Symon a week later. A week's wait? Symon had thought he'd been clear in his letter, the urgency of the situation. He sighed ... *I am not the only one to crack then.*

But he did as he was asked, and several days later, he received a letter securing him an appointment with the duke for Wednesday next.

*

That (dreaded!) day had come and Symon, after spending the night at the church, had stopped home for a clean shirt. He groaned as he entered his bedchamber, for there was Penelope.

'I shall go with you.'

'No, you won't.' He went into his closet to change. 'It's not your place. There's work in the churchyard for you.'

'I see.' She pulled open his closet door and gave him a black look. 'You've got your dear friend back and so once again I'm what the cat dragged in.' She slammed the door with such a fury that a shelf collapsed and several of his treasures crashed to the floor. With a swipe of his arm, Symon knocked off some more.

*

As Symon and Boghurst approached Whitehall Palace, a miniature London sparkled before them. The king's palace a city in its own right. There was rarely a time when Whitehall wasn't hidden behind a giant veil of smoke, the whole of London for that matter. But the king had gone, taking with him his court of thousands and their sea-coal fires. Stretching in front of them now – a sky cut with gap-toothed battlements, pinnacles crowned with painted lions and dragons, gilded vanes and metal flags that blazed in the sun. Chimneys reached up like fat fingers through roofs of every sort – stone balustrades, timber gables, terracotta tiles.

'What a fabulous mishmash,' Symon said in awe.

'A heap,' Boghurst muttered.

Guard after guard, for there was no one else about, directed them through the labyrinth. One last guard, sitting outside the duke's apartments, told them to go straight through till they could go no further. They opened the very last door and Symon wished he could disappear into his hat. For inside was the duke, his bare rump nestled in a tall box covered in green velvet.

'Are you the pansy priest?' the duke asked. 'Is this your useless friend? Give me a surgeon any day. Now that is good physick.'

Symon blanched, but Boghurst stifled a laugh; he heard far worse from his family every morning upon waking, he whispered.

'Your Grace, have you been here long? Might I help? A glass of strong water?'

The duke snarled.

'Yes, of course, I will be but blunt,' said Boghurst. 'We've come to report a matter to you. Of extreme urgency. Your actions, we believe, will mean the difference between life and death.' Boghurst presented him with the facts. Four bodies. Hands and ankles bound. Shorn heads. Terrible, vicious wounds. Their suspicion of a rogue surgeon, or a rogue gang of medical men even. Black magic, possibly. Human sacrifice. Astrology taken to an extreme . . .

Symon tried to concentrate as Boghurst took the duke through their various theories, but he was finding it difficult. The duke chewed a heavy chunk of tobacco, his spit ringing into the pot next to him at regular intervals. His wig of long brown curls was askew. One of his eyelids was distorted, stuck halfway down his eye. His face was stretched, shiny, likely burned many times over in the heat of close battle. He looked like an over-roasted pig.

The duke twisted around on his box as he listened, stretching out a kink – oh, how Symon hated to think on it – in his guts.

'Surgeons,' the duke repeated. 'That's what's needed. Good, clean cutting. Cut the plague out. That Lodowick Mincy, he's the man for this. None of this bungling you're talking about. I'll recommend it to the king at once. Ban all physick save the practice of surgery.'

Boghurst did recoil at this. He looked at Symon, then back at the duke. Symon had never seen this before: Boghurst at a loss for words.

Symon took over. 'Your Grace, that may be somewhat more drastic than the situation calls for. We can't yet say who is behind these evil deeds, that is why we're here. To ask—'

'Write this down. The king orders any apothecary, quack, charlatan or physician' – he stopped to spit – 'found practising in the environs of London shall be brought to Newgate at once.'

'Your Grace—'

'Leave the order with my steward. And hand me that sword.' Monck pointed to a large scabbard in the corner.

'What?'

'Does God make all his priests stupid? I said hand me my sword.'

'With all due respect,' Boghurst said, 'I don't think a ban would help. It might, if I may suggest, make matters worse.'

'Gentlemen, you've presented your problem. I've given you a most helpful and expedient resolution. Do you refuse my generosity? Out.'

'Your Grace—'

The duke pushed up, using his sword to steady himself. He was naked from the waist down. A more hideous sight Symon had never seen.

'Do I have to beat you silly? I'd like nothing more.'

They backed out of the chamber. Symon bowed to the duke, fumbling to close the door as he did so.

'Leave it open,' the duke shouted. 'You've poisoned the air in here.'

Symon blitzed back through the warren of rooms, pulling his dazed friend with him.

'Dear God, what have I done?' Boghurst cried.

'Don't bring him into this. I've always said, you go looking for trouble and it will surely find you.'

'What are you talking about? We were looking for help, not trouble. How can we stop this? Surely he doesn't mean what he says?'

'I think he does, but I would wager the king gets half a dozen such requests from the duke a day. I'm sure it all goes into an unread pile.' He hoped. *Sitting on the pot all morning*, Symon thought as they ran out, *how is that saving the world?*

*

'We'll have to petition the plague society.' Symon and Boghurst were back in the coach. They'd been sitting in it for a good half-hour without so much as a quarter-wheel turn forward. They were both too overcome with shock to give the driver any orders. 'Though it makes me ill to think upon it.'

'We don't have many other options,' Boghurst agreed.

A more nasty, cantankerous, selfish group Symon had never met. Martyrs, one could say, or bottom feeders. Most men of physick had fled as soon as it was clear a strange situation was upon the town. 'Flight,' said Dr Micklethwaite, who had been Symon's very own personal physician in Covent Garden. 'That's what I advise my patients is the best physick.' He added, 'If I don't take my own advice, how can I expect my patients to?'

'All of my patients have left town,' said Dr Sydenham, court physician (and windbag, said Boghurst), 'whom exactly am I expected to stay behind and treat?'

Over the next few months, hundreds of medical men left London and out of the ashes came the Society for the Prevention and Cure of Plague. (SPCP for short? asked Mincy. Or SipCip? Neither, said Boghurst.) It was doubtful they would have crossed professional lines and formed a society if there had been an alternative. But they were the only ones with any real skill left. *Yet how dangerous it is to throw them together*, thought Symon. A companionship built on a putrid eagerness to cut up the dead, one that only intensified their rivalries, a close and frequent association that would undo them all, he was sure. Why, Mincy had already condemned Boghurst as a murderer. And he, Symon, followed the surgeon's lead like a pathetic sheep, so readily betraying his old friend! Symon looked at Boghurst. 'You've forgiven Mincy then?'

'Never. But this is more important.'

'Who shall we start with?'

'Dr Burnett. The head of the society. Let us find him first.'

*

They found Dr Burnett at the offices of the College of Physicians at Amen Corner near the old city's great cathedral of St Paul. He was not pleased to see them. 'Over there, over there,' Dr Burnett shouted angrily, pointing to a half-planked bench. 'Await me there!'

Every morning, plague or not, the poor gathered outside the college offices and a college member would walk amongst them, seeing to their ailments and dispensing instructions for remedies. 'A nice bit of charity,' Dr Burnett had told his colleagues, 'but increasingly impractical.' Only ten college physicians stayed behind, six of whom refused to budge from their homes, leaving Dr Burnett and three others to rotate the morning rounds. Today was Dr Burnett's third morning in a row. 'How am I to care for my paying patients?' he oft complained. He poked at his assistant, who then poked at the patient. 'Tell him to open his mouth,' the doctor barked. 'Wide! Yes, tell him to stick out his tongue. Further!' His poor assistant was dressed in nothing more than a dirty shirt and breeches. Dr Burnett wore a long, black oilskin coat and gloves; a wide-brimmed hat hid his copper hair. A long-beaked mask acted as a filter, covering his mouth and nose. Symon noticed he still wore a bandage over one eye; the other was smeared with a greasy ointment, the skin around it had shrunk back so that the eyeball protruded near to falling out.

'Whatever is the matter with him?' Symon asked.

'Everything,' said Boghurst. 'A one-eyed monster, he is, come up from a dark and jellied sea.'

They heard the doctor scream at his assistant: 'Inside his mouth! Yes, put your finger in there and press down on his tongue! Go on! Tell me what you see.'

'Fur,' they heard his assistant mumble.

'Let's go and come back anon.' Boghurst got up, gestured to the long line of patients, some lying on the ground, blankets wrapped about them even in the noonday heat. 'We can down an ale or three before he gets through that lot.'

*

Dr Burnett was relieved to see them go. He had no patience for such small potatoes. He had tried and found the rector wanting. Burnett handed his assistant a little stick and cloth, told him to scrape out the fur. He threw a final glance at the pair as they ducked in the tavern across the way. *The other one,* he thought, *he's not worth the blood his good mother spilled at his birth.* He turned back to his assistant, saw the boy was choking the patient with a too vigorous application of the stick. He knocked his hand away and yelled, 'That's enough! That's enough! Fine. Tell him he shall live, but only if he fills this tout suite and drinks it like prayer.' The doctor scribbled on a sheet, handed it to his assistant who handed it to the man. 'Tell him to drink it first thing when he wakes up, last thing before bed.' The patient opened his mouth. Dr Burnett held up a finger to silence him. 'No time for questions. Mustn't be selfish. Next!' Dr Burnett clapped his hands and a woman, teeth chattering and wrapped in a shawl, took the man's place.

He pulled his gloves up higher. He had no fear of plague here. His skin was never exposed to these wretches. His assistant de-robed him every day, then scrubbed down and smoked his suit overnight. He'd as soon die as bring that filth home to his wife again. He keenly felt the shame of having had plague in his own house and putting his beloved at risk. His Anthea. A sweeter, more selfless woman there never was.

'Deeper,' he yelled at his assistant, who was prodding around inside the woman's ear. Finally, the boy pulled something out that looked like it had legs. 'Most interesting. Drop it in the specimen bottle for later.' That time alone together, when he and Anthea were shut in, had been a blessing in some ways. Such a luxury to have time to enjoy each other, with no demands from the outside world. He was most proud of his wife. He thought she might come at him, fists beating his chest, when she heard the news. Instead, she took the flagon of wine out of his hand, his good lady, and replaced it with a quill. They stayed up late that first night, she dictating to him how they should proceed. 'We must maintain our standards . . . You needn't write that down. A simple title, "Order of Our Days" will do . . . Up at dawn—'

'Before dawn, my sweets?' he had offered. 'Wouldn't that serve us better?' Anthea smoothed one of his wiry curls back into place. 'Quite right, my love. You are forever one to improve upon a plan.' She brought in more candles, arranged them around the desk. They would start their days with a half-hour of prayer – oh, I think an hour, she corrected him – followed by a light breakfast, a turn around the garden, then to their main task: the eradication of the pest that had brought them such misfortune. (We shall never be ruined, she said, as long as we have each other. But what if . . . ? he asked. Then we shall finally gain our blessed reward in heaven, she said.) Each day they were to cleanse a new area of their home. Start with the bedchambers. Except those of the two fallen servants (who had shamed them so, bringing the pestilence into their home!), those they would seal off. 'Too dangerous to enter yet,' he said. Move through the closets. Next the kitchens, then the dining room, the parlour, the old hall. Could they get a nightsoil man soonest? his wife had asked. The cesspool in the cellar, where the household's chamber pots were emptied, the pest would assuredly be there. 'The right amount of coin will convince them,' he replied. This work, this reordering of their house, would take time. But what a sense of well-being, of purpose it would give them!

Once darkness fell, he would break from her to go to his study. There, he would call softly to the little creature that resided within him, whose name was known to no other. 'You may awake now,' he'd say, gently rubbing his chest. For that is where it lived, safely behind his ribs, next to his heart.

The creature did not want this plague time to be over. It saw the opportunity it held for its master. At no other time in Alexander's life had the doctor felt so important, so needed. At no other time had he felt so useful. When God sent forth his plagues, the physician became His most important agent. Only a physician, and one trained to the highest qualifications, as he had been, could interpret the signs and devise the cure. In ordinary times, Alexander walked the City feeling all eyes upon him. 'There he goes! A most learned and rare man! There be none his equal!' he knew them to say. His company was always sought, except by those who felt themselves inferior and not worthy of an approach. There was none so fine as the moment when he entered the house of the ill; he and his little woolly creature melting over the family's eager attentions, like butter to hot bread. In plague time, this need, this esteem of the good people of London was taken to heavenly heights. He was their only hope, and no one was more sought after than Alexander Burnett. But the plague would leave them soon enough, it always did, and then the world would balance back out, become dull again. Alexander would still walk into a room and be heralded as a man most intelligent and most wise. But it was not the same. During such an epidemic, he was wanted morning, noon and night by all. And perhaps, if he worked hard enough this plague season, he would no more be the good Dr Burnett, but the Great Dr Burnett, *He who Hath Plunged his Purifying Sword into this Most Formidable Foe, He who Hath Slayed La Peste*. Up and down the City he would forever hear them say: 'God answered our prayers. He sent us Dr Alexander Burnett.'

His little creature chittered away during those long nights of his confinement. How they would come out the other end, the shame of quarantine washed away by Alexander's discovery of a cure. How they would never again feel dirty and diminished. Anthea would only ever look upon them with pride. 'A formula,' he told his wife when she said he worked too hard, 'the likes of which the world has never seen!' He would name it after her, *Anthea Mirabilis*. She smiled. 'Thank you, my love. But I prefer *Alexander Nobilis,* after you . . .' How her generosity made him and his little creature smile.

But as their days progressed, as their quarantine lifted and he had yet to find a cure, he could see that she doubted him and she began, quietly at first, to ask him to temper his efforts. 'Your eyes,' she would say, 'if you continue so, you will ruin them!' His eyes did sting, but the pulse of the broken blood vessels in them only served to propel him forward. Still, he found he could no longer look at her directly, at anyone. For in those eyes – whether they be the fading eyes of his plague patients or the loving eyes of his wife – he would see the reflection of the other creature who was always with him now, too. He caught it once, glowering back at him in the mirror in his bedchamber. (After that he had all the mirrors removed.) He feared it was the pest, that it had lodged in his eyes. He could feel it shifting and growing in them, and he knew it had no warning for him, this suckling creature. Only a promise: death.

One long night drenched in sack, he had taken a needle to his eye; an attempt to expel the creature. The result was disastrous. His vision was gone, the eye infected, but the creature remained.

He heard a sour laugh, thought it the creature, mocking him again, but then he saw the rector and apothecary were back.

'Listen, we can't wait all day,' Boghurst said to him. 'We'd like a meeting with the society. Can you arrange it?'

The apothecary's voice filled him with loathing; he felt his creatures scratching in agreement. He looked them over, decided. 'Of course. The cost to you will be one body.'

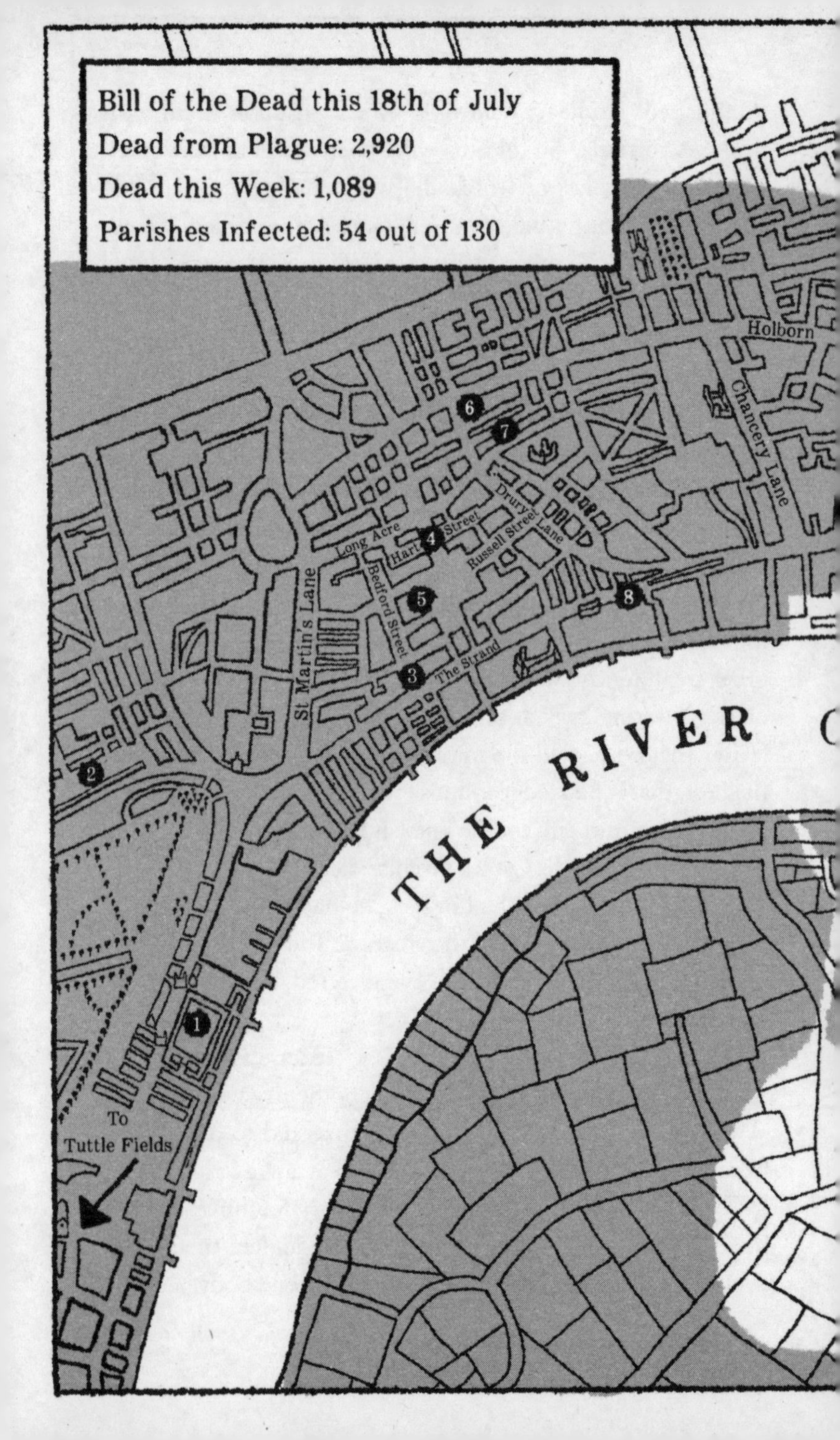
Bill of the Dead this 18th of July
Dead from Plague: 2,920
Dead this Week: 1,089
Parishes Infected: 54 out of 130
Holborn
Chancery Lane
Drury Lane
Russell Street
Hart Street
Long Acre
Bedford Street
St Martin's Lane
The Strand
To Tuttle Fields
THE RIVER
1
2
3
4
5
6
7
8

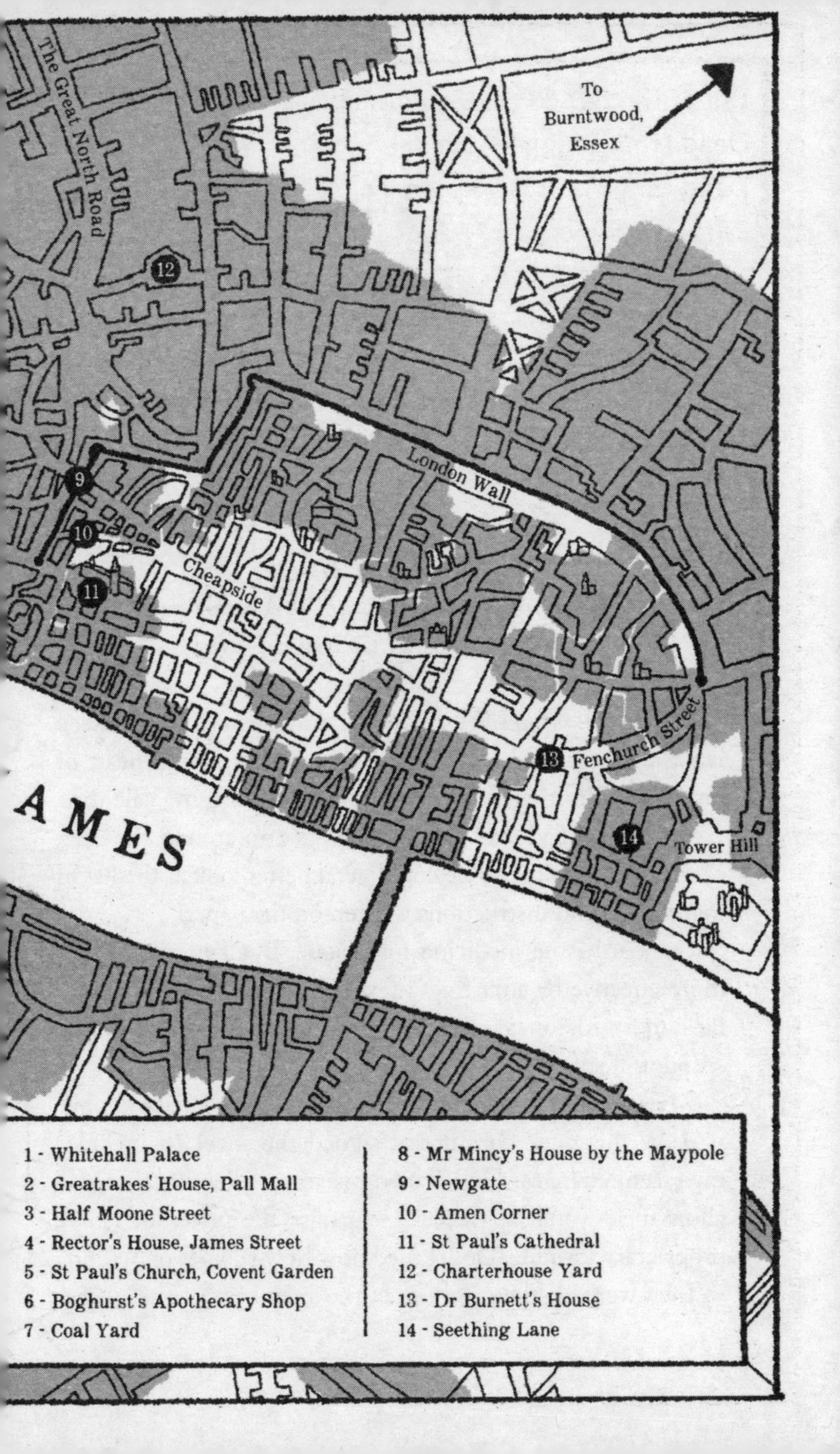
The Great North Road
To Burntwood, Essex
London Wall
Cheapside
Fenchurch Street
Tower Hill
AMES
1 - Whitehall Palace
2 - Greatrakes' House, Pall Mall
3 - Half Moone Street
4 - Rector's House, James Street
5 - St Paul's Church, Covent Garden
6 - Boghurst's Apothecary Shop
7 - Coal Yard
8 - Mr Mincy's House by the Maypole
9 - Newgate
10 - Amen Corner
11 - St Paul's Cathedral
12 - Charterhouse Yard
13 - Dr Burnett's House
14 - Seething Lane

# 24

*Friday, July 21st*
*Emergency Meeting, the Society for the Prevention and Cure of Plague, Parish of St Gabriel Fenchurch*

'NOW THIS RECEIPT for London Treacle. The college swears by it.' Dr Burnett was sitting at the head of his table, admiring a sheet of paper before him. Valentine Greatrakes glided over and draped his arm around the back of the doctor's chair so he could get a better look at the list of ingredients and instructions written on the paper.

'Standard issue medicine for plague. But I've made it far more effective by adjusting a few ingredients. I prefer viper's flesh to lizard, for example. And it pays to be generous on the amount of soporifics.'

'My word, this is incredibly complicated. May I make a copy?'

'Take this one.' Dr Burnett signed the sheet. 'It includes my recent changes.' He lowered his voice. 'Changes that also allow me – you'll appreciate – to raise the price, for it is a proprietary formula. Do let me know how you get on with it.'

They were all there to a one, the members of the plague

society; gathered at Dr Burnett's home in the parish of St Gabriel Fenchurch. The church bells struck the hour and the doctor put his remedies aside, snapped his fingers and invited them to take their seats.

'Now,' Dr Burnett said, 'who has brought a body?' He surveyed his guests through his one functioning eye. 'Hmmm, Mr Patrick, Mr Boghurst? You were to bring one, yes? Where have you put it?' Symon turned to Boghurst, who was staring at a painting over the mantel.

He pulled his cravat away from his sticky neck and feigned confusion.

'Oh, I am sorry! We thought you'd prefer to pick one of your own choosing at some later date.'

The doctor eyed him carefully, then conceded. 'Fine. Pass me your agenda item.'

Symon again looked to Boghurst for guidance, but the man couldn't take his gaze from the portrait. A lady, painted in the style of the day, made to look a feminine version of the king, or rather his spaniel dogs. Her straw-blonde hair slicked back from her forehead, then curled into shaggy puffs that covered her ears. Her eyes were round and lashless. He supposed it was meant to be the doctor's wife.

Symon huffed at his abandonment. 'Wouldn't it be more expedient if I addressed the society directly?'

'Pink-eyed twiddle twank,' someone murmured.

'Me?' asked Symon, indignant.

'Dr Burnett,' whispered Greatrakes. The Irish mystic was wearing a velvet cloak and suit, coloured the gentlest of blue, suggestive of hope, kindness, tenderness. *What a crock*, Symon thought.

The doctor shot them a look. 'Please save your gossip for after the meeting.'

'But your eye has gone oddly pink,' Greatrakes said. Then seeing the doctor's distress, he leaned over and petted the man's springy hair. 'Oh, don't pout, you know I adore you!'

At this, Boghurst finally snapped to and with a new vigour in his voice said, 'Gentlemen, we present you tonight with a simple question. Yet it is one of foul deeds. Evil deeds.'

'Good God!'

'Most unusual . . .'

Boghurst continued, 'Mr Patrick and I have stumbled across something strange, yes strange even in these strangest of times. We believe that someone may be committing murder. Torturing, if you will, victims of plague.'

The room fell silent. Then mayhem. Torture the sick? Murder them? What do you mean by murder? Accidental murder or deliberate murder? How many victims? Twenty? Ten? Where? Is there anything to eat?

Dr Burnett cut in. 'Gentlemen, Mr Boghurst, Mr Patrick, this is most unsettling, but we do have an epidemic on our hands. Wouldn't a magistrate be better suited?'

'That's exactly why we've come,' Boghurst said. 'The town authorities are in a most weakened condition. Overwhelmed, as we all are.'

Symon interrupted, 'We saw the Duke of Albemarle. He promised that he would take the matter to the king, except—'

'He was drunk. Incapacitated.' Boghurst thumped the table with his fist. 'We cannot rely on his help. You' – he looked around, meeting the eyes of each member – 'must help us. Perhaps Dr Burnett, as an official appointee to oversee the College of Physicians' business during this venomous time, could—'

'I had nothing to do with the break-in or the stolen gold. I never agreed to be their night guard,' Dr Burnett said.

‘The college was robbed?’ Mincy asked.

‘Might we stay on topic?’ Greatrakes complained, swinging his finger like a clock pendulum.

‘Yes,’ Dr Burnett said. ‘I move that this matter be put into the hands of the Lord Mayor. All in favour, say “aye”.’

‘Nay,’ Boghurst said. ‘Already presented it to him.’

‘You did?’ Symon asked. ‘When?’

‘While you went home for your nap—’

‘I did no such thing!’

‘Went right up to Mansion House. Had to wait a bit, but eventually the Lord Mayor gave me an audience.’

‘And?’

‘He listened. Then ordered that I take over all the town’s pesthouses.’

‘That would be the death of you!’

‘Nonsense. Its poison affects me not. But I did decline, for I am far too busy. I told him I had a duty to my current patients. He said I had a duty to God and Country.’

‘Such hubris!’ Symon chastised. ‘Plague or exhaustion! One way or another, you will die. Why do you not look worried?’

‘Well, he started calling me Barwick.’

‘Dr Peter Barwick? From over at Paul’s Cathedral?’

‘Yes, which means Barwick is on the hook, not me.’

‘A happy ending for all,’ Greatrakes said. ‘May we go home now?’

Symon looked at the Irish mystic. Cosseted head to toe in that soft sky blue, with ribbons of orange on his hat and sleeves and shoes. The lack of sleep, his world contracting to his church and his house, the dying, the dead, the smell. He couldn’t help himself, blurted out, ‘Why must you wear such garish things? You hurt my eyes. You mistake us for a peacock’s court.’

Greatrakes blanched, then said quietly, 'My wife loved these colours. She helped me pick the cloth, sewed my suits by her own hand.'

'My dear man, I do apologise!' He wanted to excuse himself, go home. He had never found his own behaviour more revolting. Greatrakes' young wife had died the year before he came to London. It was her death, they said, that had turned Greatrakes' hair white.

'It is known far and wide what a fine lady she was,' Symon said, knowing there was little he could say to take the sting out of his words, 'adored by all. I wish I could have met her, for surely she would have taught me much.'

Greatrakes was looking down at his hands, carefully clasped in his lap. He gave Symon a small nod of acknowledgement.

'Gentlemen,' said Dr Burnett, 'if no one has brought a body or a breakthrough, I declare this meeting over. I have not the time for—'

'Please, I beg of you,' said Boghurst, 'hear us out.' He expressed his sympathies for Greatrakes and his harrowing loss, then began again. He told the gathering about the first body, then the second, the third, the fourth. He told them about the marks. The blisterings and butcherings, the inked grids, the trinkets sewn into the buboes. That all the victims were maidens, with blonde hair, shorn off.

'Oh dear God, not that ridiculous thing,' Dr Burnett muttered.

'What ridiculous thing?' Symon asked.

'The hair. He's trying to make gold from their hair. Make the philosopher's stone.' Dr Burnett closed his one eye and pinched the bridge of his nose. 'The elixir of life. Cures everything. Makes you live for ever. Feed it to your dog, gets rid of his wind, etc., etc.'

Boghurst pointed his finger at Dr Burnett. 'That man. He understands me.'

'I should hope not,' the doctor replied indignantly.

Boghurst gave him a hard stare, and without taking his eye off the doctor, he lowered his voice and said: 'Gentlemen, are we dealing with a rogue, then? A man of physick gone mad?'

Greatrakes tapped his fingers on the table. They looked at one another in silence.

Then Mincy: 'I always said it could happen. The pressure to save lives could get to anybody. But why have you brought this matter here?' He was asking Symon. 'I already told you he did it.' He pointed to Boghurst. 'I've seen your knives. Dull and nicked. A good knife slices. Yours chew. You should be prosecuted for keeping them in such poor shape!' The surgeon turned back to the room. 'But why is he allowed to have knives at all? Apothecaries shouldn't have knives. They've had no training, and they shouldn't for that matter, for look what happens when they use them!'

Boghurst took several deep breaths. Said he owed Mincy a great apology. The surgeon had come to him once, begging him for a potion to save one of his dogs. He had failed him, the dog had died. He wished to God he had been able to save the mutt, for this was surely why the surgeon was keen to hang him. Mincy's jaw dropped open and Symon shouted out: 'He killed your dog, too?'

Boghurst squeezed his eyes shut, stretched out his fingers before him as if reaching for something. *His knives likely*, thought Symon. The dullest, rustiest he could find.

'Let us pretend,' Boghurst said, 'for just a moment, gentlemen. Who else, other than me, might have done this?'

'I agree with our plum-bottomed friend,' said Greatrakes. 'This gruesome dabbling in blood would turn anyone.' He shot a look of distaste around the table.

'Find a cure, get rich, surely you understand that, my dear Mr Greatrakes,' snapped Dr Burnett.

'I don't need money, I have God.'

Boghurst continued, 'I ask you, is this the work of a demented quack? Or a group of them?'

'A pagan,' said Greatrakes. 'A ritual to save the sick. But one gone too far. My peasants were all too enthusiastic about this sort of thing back in Ireland.' Symon nodded. He was well versed in what happened when rituals became distorted, their true meaning lost and the people they were intended to help all but forgotten. One needed to look no further than the Catholic Church. He shuddered. 'Maybe the murderer is a papist.'

Boghurst ignored Symon. 'We would like your help in reviewing the bodies to see if you recognise the work, a pattern, a tell-tale sign. If it strikes a chord, a past complaint a patient may have mentioned to you.'

'Where are they? I thought you said you didn't bring a body—' Dr Burnett winced, a tremor passed under his bandaged eye. 'Never mind. Let's see them at once.'

'Of course we didn't bring them.' Boghurst walked over to Dr Burnett. 'Would you like me to take a look at that?' He reached out to touch the inflamed tissue around the doctor's bandage.

Burnett slapped his hand away. 'If you ever touch me or my wife, I'll—'

'Would you like to see the drawings?' All eyes turned to the doorway. There stood Penelope. She wore a cream-coloured bodice and skirt sprinkled with a pattern of little green sprigs, a red shawl around her shoulders. Her hair was its usual mess, but her face was clean. ('I don't like this,' Boghurst whispered.)

She stopped between Symon and the apothecary and placed a thick roll of paper in front of them. They reeled back, coughing, gagging.

'Good God, what's that smell?' Dr Burnett waved his handkerchief in front of his face.

'Death!' Mincy was sniffing the air. 'How is it that you don't know?' He turned to Symon. 'You've been teasing us all along! You did bring a body!'

Symon stared at Penelope; his heart took another nasty tumble. She'd been working with the dead – preparing them for burial, removing their infested clothes. The clothes were supposed to be burned ... So this was, in fact, where she'd been getting her gowns. He called upon all his powers of pacification, specifically his power to pacify himself. Symon asked the society for forgiveness and hoped they would understand, given these exceptional times. He explained that all things considered, Penelope was a very fine artist and had sketched the bodies in detail. He added, 'Surely as medical men you've smelled worse?'

Eyes narrowed, one thin black eyebrow arched, Penelope looked at them as if they were a bunch of misbehaving boys. She pulled on the red ribbon binding her roll of drawings and spread them out.

'Thank you, Penelope. Most helpful. You may go now.'

'I'd rather not.'

'Penelope ...'

She started to squat, Symon knew what was coming. 'Yes, yes, you may stay, but I'm afraid there are no more seats at the table. Would the corner suit you?' There were big windows on either side of it. He could open them. He nodded to the windows. 'Gentlemen, surely now it might be appropriate to ... ?'

'Heaven help us! Please do,' Dr Burnett said.

Symon got up and Penelope turned to walk with him, revealing a dark stain down the back of her gown, which prompted another round of 'Good Lords,' and a, 'Really, Mr Patrick, such unpleasantness and you being a guest here . . .'

'Buboes,' Greatrakes loudly interrupted. He had picked up Penelope's drawings, was quickly shuffling through them. 'Buboes. All of them covered with buboes. How is this murder?'

'Pure butchery,' Mincy cut in, looking over his shoulder. 'Disgraceful! Mr Boghurst should be run out of town.'

'I've never seen anything like it.' Dr Burnett had grabbed a drawing and was examining it by candlelight.

'What a lot of great gooses you are,' Greatrakes said, tossing the rest of the drawings aside. 'Don't doctors have a licence to slay and destroy? Let's not pretend here.'

'Just like men of God have a licence to fleece the poor?' spat Dr Burnett. He left the room abruptly, came back with an anatomy book and an astrology chart. Thumbed through them, then said: 'Do we know that it is the work of one man? I see some very unorthodox practices here, but I don't see a pattern.'

'Are you blind?' Boghurst said.

Burnett snapped the book shut, his face contorted in rage, and oddly, Symon thought, fear. 'Why did I let you into my home? You always were a—'

'Oh, my head! Please, my head!' Greatrakes touched his temples. 'All of this squabbling! How is anyone to think? Now, how do we know the intent? Cutting their hair for the philosopher's stone, that wouldn't have harmed them. The rest, well . . . God knows we all struggle to figure out how to treat this evil.' He pointed to a sketch. 'It's clear they all had plague, their fates were sealed. From the moment the first token appeared, Death's chariot was upon them.'

'I find that's not always the case. If I get the patient within the first four hours of the invasion, before the tokens appear, I can save them,' Boghurst said.

'It's time you left. All of you,' the doctor said quietly.

'I warn you,' Boghurst said, 'if we don't find this rogue, no one will be safe!'

'Hardly,' Mincy snorted. 'We're talking about a few dead wenches.'

'Mincy!' yelled Greatrakes.

'What?'

'You've missed the pot! You're pissing on the wall!'

Burnett screamed and lunged for Mincy. The room erupted in chaos and Penelope yanked Symon from his chair and dragged him down the stairs.

The others – chased out by the doctor – came crashing down behind them. Once outside, Boghurst turned to face Burnett: 'Is Annie home? I must see her! I must know she is safe!'

The doctor stood stock-still, then opened his mouth and screamed, 'Never call her that!' Even after he slammed the door, they could hear him continue to scream.

*

Penelope watched them scurry off into the night, like water rats fleeing a flood. Greatrakes and Mincy headed down towards the Thames. Symon and Boghurst towards Cornhill. *Without so much as a look my way,* Penelope thought. She started to head home when she remembered. Her drawings, she'd forgotten them. She went in through the kitchen door and tiptoed up to the dining room. She could hear the doctor and his wife above in their bedchamber. He was sobbing hysterically, his wife trying to soothe him. The dining room was torn apart, the spilled wine, the piss-streaked wall, the knocked-over chairs. The mess, it seemed, would be left till morning. But where were they? Her drawings, which had been scattered about the table, were gone. She checked under the table, behind the cabinets, the grate. She put her hands on her hips. Had Burnett taken them upstairs with him? She doubted it; he hadn't the mind at the moment.

She looked up at the portrait over the mantel. 'Well, well, well, Mistress Burnett,' Penelope whispered. 'That narrows things down considerably, doesn't it?' The quacks on the plaza, the necromancers, the misanthropes, the over-eager apprentices, the frustrated parish clerks, frustrated nurses. She could stop tracking them all. She left the house and walked west towards Cheapside. She needed time to think, to plot. The streets were empty, a sight she would ordinarily have enjoyed. No one to look down upon her, no one to try to hurt her. But this night, instead, all she saw were bodies.

A frantic peal of one hundred bells ushered her through Newgate, the warning notes of London's weedy little churches all striking one. *So,* she thought, *it's one of them.* Mincy. He'd trade his own mother for a meat pie. Boghurst. How many patients had he killed in his drunkenness? Greatrakes. Slimy as a cesspit. And Dr Burnett. Perhaps the most friable of them all. She would watch them. All of them. Cold-hearted. Blind with ambition. Perverse. She reflexively patted her pocket, inside a wad of papers she had recovered from her aunt and uncle's. She checked the pocket often, to make sure they were still there, even though the pocket was deep and she had secured it with pins. They were too valuable for her to leave anywhere; she wouldn't make her aunt and uncle's mistake. She kept them on her at all times now. She had found them the other day, buried under the third shrub she dug up at her aunt and uncle's, inside an iron box. Her aunt and uncle had hidden many things under those plants – good plate but not their best plate, some coin – things that were of secondary importance to them. Things that would hurt to lose, but not much. Penelope didn't find their house deed, or enough coin to make her a lady on the spot (and sadly no jewels). She did find the old papers that detailed her father's finances and his will. Her aunt and uncle thought her just another dead wench, too.

*Hardly.*

# 25

*A Shut-Up House, Leg Alley, St Martin's in the Fields*

HER LIPS WERE DRY, cracking. 'Water,' she dared. 'Please, mistress, water.' Where had the nurse gone? Why wouldn't she bring her something to drink? The room was hot and full of shadows. A fire the only light. The girl could hear something boiling over it. Or was she imagining the fire? Was the bubbling and hissing coming from the hearth, or from the erupting sores on her brittle skin? There was a terrible pain in the side of her neck. Something huge and taut that threatened to burst with the least movement of her head. She squirmed on her pallet, slowly so as not to aggravate her neck, trying to relieve the terrible itching. She couldn't move her hands. They were tied to the sides of the bed. Why? Her ankles were tied, too. A prickling all over her head, if only she could scratch it. She didn't know why, though she knew her hair, her lovely red hair, was gone. Had it fallen out? And where was her mother? Her father? Her brothers? She heard footsteps. Please let it be the nurse. When the old woman first came to the house, she promised she would make them better. But then she heard a man in the house, not her father, someone else. He said he would make them better, too. But he didn't. She was terrified of him. She heard him yelling at her brothers, her mother; heard them cry out.

'Water,' she tried again. 'Please, mistress, water.' She squinted through the gloom. A light was coming towards her. And something large and black, beastly. A hardened face, yellow, glistening in the candlelight. Black holes for eyes. Instead of a mouth, a long, mottled beak. It was leaning down towards her. She screamed. It was the doctor. He struck her hard across the face, the violent snap of her head ripping open the tumour on her neck. She threw up, dizzy with nausea, then saw no more.

# 26

## *From Parlour to Grave*

After a dazed half-hour's walk across the city, Symon and Boghurst had arrived at James Street. Symon brought up wine from the kitchen, the remains of his household's supper. Not that he had any appetite, only a deep thirst, a need for relief. The wine would take the edge off, and the food the edge off the wine. He sighed in frustration as he sat down across from Boghurst in the parlour. 'They saw the drawings, Mincy even saw one of the bodies, and yet they are not moved to help.'

'It is fatigue.' Boghurst picked up one of Symon's pipes from the mantel and filled it. 'Of a most extreme nature. It has addled their minds.'

'You defend them?'

'Perhaps I speak more of my own condition.'

'It is greed. You heard Mincy. His talk of a few dead wenches. These girls are no more to him than a blighted pigeon. They see no profit in the matter.' Symon took out his vial of theriac and added several drops to his wine. 'Who is our man? What do we know of him? That he is merciless. That he seeks out the vulnerable, the friendless. Those who are easily enough lost in these times. That they are all girls, and thus far he requires that they have blonde hair. Who are we to seek out? Who are we to consult next?' The earl, the duke, the parish leaders, they had all turned their backs on Symon. The plague society had behaved no better. Elizabeth. He allowed himself a half-smile at this fancy. He could ask her husband. His business as victualler to the Navy gave him extensive contacts in government.

'Don't you think it strange?' Boghurst asked. 'A most odd sort of behaviour . . .'

'Not really. I expected no better from that group of madmen. The most unlikely collection I've ever met. Why did they agree to work together?'

'There's no one else of our kind left. I do believe they would like to find a cure,' he added, 'there is profit in that. And it is fashionable to be part of a society. To be part of a smart set, investigating things, making discoveries. Using big words. Bragging about your wealth, who you've dined with.' The apothecary got up and brought over a sweets tray left out for Symon by Joan. Quickly turned it into the scene of a massacre. Torn and bloodied berries. Raisins like burned little men. Dismembered tarts and cakes and ragged bits of icing. Boghurst pressed his finger into the bits one by one, licked them off his finger.

'I suspect we're all trying to make our mark and get invited to join the Royal Society. Find a cure, get an invitation – enjoy the fortune that follows both.'

'But how did they find each other? It's such a collection of odd fellows.'

'Mincy.'

'Mincy?'

'Yes, he is our stumpy linchpin. His father was surgeon to old King Charles. Had many royal connections. Passed them all on to his son. Then Mincy successfully cut the stone from the Duke of Albemarle, which brought in even more business. He now has a whole banner studded with kidney stones hanging over his door to prove his superior skill. I think it a very false show, for he does not say how many of the owners survived!' Boghurst gave a dark laugh, then paused. 'I suppose I'm the other linchpin. They all send their patients to me for the medicines they prescribe. Despite what he says, Mincy thinks very highly of my salves. And at first we were all very merry.'

'Really?'

'Of course not. We never got on. But you know we men of physick are not an easy bunch. Then one day our Irish friend showed up. We let him in because he has connections, too. And he is good entertainment.'

'Often at someone else's expense,' Symon sniffed.

'Everything he does is at someone else's expense. And I admire him for that.' Boghurst laughed again, then shook his head. 'No. Dr Burnett. This evening. That was entirely unexpected. He usually takes no side in issues. All he cares about is that things are orderly, that they follow an established routine. He is a bloodless man, unfeeling. I have always found him most annoying, most limited in thought; but rarely so obstructive. But this evening, the phlegm, the choler. The screaming! A most vituperative display. I have never seen Dr Burnett upset over debate. He's lost any pretence of objectivity. I found his erratic manner quite startling. In fact, that has been his manner since he came out of quarantine.'

'I doubt I would fare any better if I were locked up with the pest.' Symon pushed and pulled on his cheeks, his forehead, his temples. Every last bit of him ached. 'You think him transformed, then? For the worse?'

'I wonder . . . if Mincy is right, but wrong.'

'He is wrong about everything.'

Boghurst went on, 'He accuses me of murder. He is wrong to accuse me, but perhaps he is right that someone we know is the murderer. Perhaps the murderer was with us this evening.'

Symon dropped his hands. 'The murderer? At the meeting? Who?'

Boghurst took a raisin, stacked it on a berry, topped it with a bit of crust, then offered it to Symon. 'No? Fine then.' He obliterated his little tower with a finger. 'The good doctor Burnett. When someone does something out of character, it is a sign of something, is it not? Why is he so uncharacteristically passionate against the pursuit of this issue? Why did nearly every word uttered tonight send him into a rage?'

'Dr Burnett? A bloody butcher?' Symon had a difficult time seeing that. Everything about the man was immaculate. His wiry waves carefully oiled into place. Never a sign of stubble on his jaw. Never a slurp of his soup on his collar, nor a crumb to his lip. 'But we've seen it ourselves, at Amen Corner. He doesn't touch his patients. He has his assistant do it . . .'

They exchanged a look.

'So that's how he stays clean . . .' said Boghurst.

'I don't know,' said Symon. 'Why not Greatrakes? If you were looking for the morally bankrupt . . .'

'Too lazy.'

Symon agreed. Greatrakes had boundless energy for self-promotion, but that was words. He rarely saw the man physically exert himself. He was about the mind. And a beanpole. The killer had to have great strength to trap his victims, to manipulate their bodies so.

'What about Mincy, then? Perhaps he seeks to create a feint with his accusations?'

'He's incapable of sloppiness and our murderer is sloppy.'

'Have you looked at his shirt?' Symon said. 'His fingers? His nails?'

'That is different. The man's mind is well ordered, his cuts precise. He does not see fluids and excreta as filth, he sees them as natural, from God. That is why he is able to venture where others aren't inside the body. He does not fear it, he sees it as a great puzzle to be solved.'

'Dr Burnett, then?'

'Yes . . . Think about it,' said Boghurst. 'Perhaps your girl Mary wasn't the first victim. Perhaps it started with Dr Burnett's own servants. The two manservants stricken by plague back in May. You recall the story . . .'

'Indeed.' Symon thought back to that night of his first plague society meeting, his shock at finding himself inside a contaminated house.

'One of the servants was taken to a pesthouse, where he died,' Boghurst said. 'The other one disappeared. The thought was that the man had run off, that he'd decided he'd rather die out in the fresh air under a hedge than in a stinking pest-house. But perhaps not . . .' Boghurst poured himself another drink, offered some to Symon. He refused it; his stomach was feeling quite sour.

Boghurst shrugged, went on. 'It was all very odd. There had been much talk of plague at the time, but few cases inside the old city. In fact, we had all been quite shocked that the City's first cases were in Dr Burnett's own home. His manservants were the only ones to fall sick in his parish! Tell me, how did they get it? It was all rather unlikely . . . and did you know this? Some said it wasn't plague at all. That the pair had stolen from their master. That one had managed to escape, but the other was not so fortunate – and was beaten to death by Dr Burnett.'

'Good God!' said Symon, taken aback. 'Yes, I'd heard that rumour. But to apply it to Dr Burnett himself? That he could've lost his head so? It doesn't seem possible.'

Boghurst finished his glass, reached for the bottle. 'We don't really know, do we? The servants might have had plague, might have died from it. Or did they die at his own hands? As part of some hideous new experiment?' He sat up quickly, warming to his theory. 'And he was able to pass off the situation as plague because of his medical credentials, his reputation.'

Boghurst was now feverishly pacing the room. 'That first servant, he died not long after he was dropped at the pest-house. The talk that something more sordid might have happened started quite soon after that. I remember that Burnett was so upset at the accusations that he had examiners certify the man had indeed died from plague and posted their testimony at the Royal Exchange for all to see. Then at great cost to himself – personal and financial – he shut up his own house! Why would he do this? He could've left town without much recrimination – so many others had! But instead, he decided to lock himself – and his wife! – in with the plague for all of June!'

'But how are we to know? And if he were shut up in his house . . . why, the timing doesn't work out. Mary died in June.'

'Well, he says they stayed inside. But how is anyone to know? No one would insult a gentleman by posting a guard at his house.'

Symon saw the story unfolding before him. It was plausible . . . and yet. 'But what of the second servant? Where is he?'

'Yes . . . perhaps he hadn't planned it through, wasn't able to hide the first death. The second body he could have taken to an outer parish and dumped for one of the dead-cart drivers to find.'

'Like Mary.' Symon nodded. 'Like the others. But why has he only killed girls since then?'

'Because he is weak. Easier to catch them. The manservants just happened to provide an irresistible opportunity.' Boghurst cursed. 'Heartless, selfish man!' There was heat in his voice, an agony, too. 'He could've found a way to get his wife out of there, get her to safety.'

Boghurst was practically spitting at this point. Symon poured him another drink, hoping to calm him some. 'Perhaps Anthea refused. Perhaps she didn't want to be separated from him.'

This sent Boghurst into another fit. 'Annie!' He grabbed the bottle from Symon's hand. 'She likes to be called Annie!'

Symon looked at him for a minute, confused at this sudden burst of rage from his friend. Then he realised. 'Ah, I see.' He put a few drops of his theriac into Boghurst's drink to help take the edge off. 'The doctor's wife is beautiful. How long have you known her?'

'Since I first came to London. Her father was a very good City physician. I was an apprentice at the time and I met her one day delivering some medicines to him.' He slowly tipped the bottle, at just enough of an angle for the wine to pour out one hesitant red drop at a time. 'I loved her at first sight. She loved me. Her father thought Burnett the better match. Alex was older and a Cambridge-trained physician, with a lucrative business already established. God that he were still alive to see the hell to which he damned his only daughter!' The rest of the wine gushed forth in a torrent and he threw the empty bottle against the back of the fireplace, shattering it.

Symon jumped up and grabbed Boghurst's glass, kicked him violently on the leg. 'You'll clean that up! You'll not leave that for my servants. Get ahold of yourself. It worked out all right for you! You have Louisa! I've only met Anthea Burnett a few times, but she is nothing to your Louisa.'

Boghurst didn't answer, but he did seem calmer. Symon saw a smile flicker across his face. After a while he said, 'The man is soulless. I've never heard him talk of regret. Of lives lost. Of mistakes he could've righted. I've never heard him speak with any proper feeling. Only indifference.' Symon watched him walk through to the dining room; he was going to fetch another bottle of wine. *I should stop him. Why don't I?*

'I tell you,' Boghurst said when he returned, 'the gossips were right. His servants didn't die of plague. Some old crone probably watched over the one in the pesthouse. They have no trained staff there; just the dregs of the parish. They saw the body, saw that something was not right. Assumed it was a beating, a common quarrel between master and servant gone too far. But . . . I think the marks were those of a butchering. A deliberate and fatal one.' He locked eyes with Symon. It was a very convincing theory, Symon thought, and yet there was something in the manner of his friend that gave him pause.

'Symon.'

'Yes?'

'We must dig up the corpse.'

Symon spat out his wine. He knew it. 'Good heavens! You are mad!'

'It will not be pleasant. It has been two months. I do not know in what state the body will be. But I think there is a very good chance that some things will be preserved. If Dr Burnett is our murderer, his marks will be on the body. The skin would not have decomposed entirely, the ink grids should still be visible. The cuts on the wrists and ankles from the twined ligatures. And we will know the colour of the man's hair. Was he blond?'

Symon looked about him – at the dying fire. His mother's old Bible lovingly displayed on an end table. A small vase of wilted forget-me-nots, the last of spring. Was this the only way? Were these medical men right? To fight such a pestilence as plague, did you need corpses? To find a murderer, did you need to break sacred ground, to disturb eternal rest? What Boghurst was proposing was unheard of. What pretence would they use? Symon searched his memory. He couldn't recall anyone ever asking to unbury the dead in his churchyard. Except one. Bernard. But that was for a very different reason.

'You know that girl of yours?' said Boghurst.

'Mary?'

'No, not her.' Boghurst grimaced. 'Penelope.'

Symon looked confused.

'There are times when I see her behind me when I make my calls. But she does not look herself. She does not move like herself. And yet I somehow know it is her.'

'She follows you?'

'That is not my point. It is her disguise. We go in disguise. Officials. The servant would be buried in Dr Burnett's parish – there was enough attention to the matter, the doctor would have been forced to make it a proper burial. We go to St Gabriel Fenchurch. Say we need to survey the grounds to calculate capacity.' Boghurst's face lit up. 'We tell them we need to sample a grave. To see at what depth the current bodies are buried. We're there to ensure standards. Official stamps and such. We'll ask them to direct us to their newest grave. It's a small parish with an even smaller churchyard. There's a decent chance Dr Burnett's manservant is the last they put under.'

'Bah! Sextons are a possessive lot. Bernard would never allow someone else to root around in his churchyard.'

'Perhaps.' Boghurst fell silent, then began to nod as another notion filled his mind. 'We have no other choice, then.'

'What?'

'We dig it up now.'

# 27

## *A Damp and Dark Place*

SYMON GRABBED HIS HEAD, tried to hold his skull together. It threatened to split in two as if Tom, that great bell of Westminster, were clanging inside his skull. He rolled over on to his side. Everything was wet and clammy. Jack. The boy must have peed the bed again. Or worse. He seemed to be covered in a strange grit, it was in his nose, down his shirt. He sat up and dirt cascaded down over his eyes and cheeks and into his mouth. Something was very wrong, a panic began to build. His shook his head to clear away the last of the grit and did his best to wipe his eyes before opening them. Then stifled a yell as he looked around in horror. Heaven help him. He was in St Gabriel Fenchurch's yard, in a shallow grave, with much soil thrown over him. A few feet away lay Boghurst, asleep and cradling a spade. Symon jumped out of the grave and, in a rush of inexplicable fear, tore the spade out of the sleeping apothecary's hands. The bells of St Gabriel Fenchurch stopped ringing ... He tried to recount how many bells he had heard. Was it five of the clock? Six? The horizon glowed, dawn was coming, he must escape before anyone saw him, and yet he had a very strong urge to take the spade and bash in the apothecary's brains. *Do it*, a voice hissed inside his head. *Do it.* Symon dropped the spade and ran. Tried to piece the night together as he bolted from the safety of one dark street corner to the next. What had happened? Why was he in a grave? Why did Boghurst have the spade? As he crossed on to Cheapside, he allowed himself to slow a little, there was safe enough distance now from the church. He would be unable to explain to anyone why he was up so early in the morning and running about this end of town covered with dirt, but then he was unlikely to meet anyone, he reassured himself. His head continued to throb, and it was from something other than too much drink. He took a moment to look at his reflection in a shop window and flinched. A gash ran across his forehead, a good several inches long. What had caused that? Boghurst had insisted they take another bottle with them and the last Symon remembered they had arrived at St Gabriel Fenchurch and by that point were shamefully intoxicated. Well, he was. He couldn't say for Boghurst. The apothecary was not much different drunk or sober. He remembered stumbling around, looking at the graves, trying to sort which one might belong to Dr Burnett's manservant. And then? A blur. Symon picked up his pace again; he must make it home before his own servants were about. He couldn't let them see him like this. He reeked of drink, they would think poorly of him. He remembered a feeling of jubilation, but he could not remember the cause. The feeling he had now was entirely of a different nature. Mistrust. Had he fallen and cut his head? Or had Boghurst hit him with the spade . . . and tried to bury him in a grave? He stayed off the main streets, made his way home through passages and side courts. *Think, Symon,* he said to himself, *you must remember. And you must find Penelope.*

# 28

*Symon's Bedchamber*

'DO YOU THINK HE TRIED to kill me?' Symon asked Penelope.

'It's possible.'

He looked at her, struggled to push down his panic. 'But you set him free! You said he was innocent.'

'I've made mistakes before.'

She had been gone for several days, left no word. He had started to worry. Then, this morning, he'd come home from another night at his churchyard to find Penelope in the closet off his bedchamber, slurping away at her breakfast and barking with laughter as she read his letters.

'Put those down! Come out of there right now!' She ignored him so he grabbed the letters and pulled her out of the closet. 'When this is all over, I'm having this torn down.'

He plopped her in the middle of the floor and started yanking open the windows. He hoped to find a morning breeze; instead, he was hit with the heavy heat of July and with it, he was sure, the miasma that was like to steal their breaths.

'Could we be so wrong about Boghurst? There he was hugging the spade, the very weapon in his hand!'

'Well, you tend to be wrong about most things.'

'What?' He gave her a sharp look.

'The things you get up to at night! Nothing but trouble!'

She was in a surly mood. He should have known better than to consult her.

'If he had wanted to kill me, what stopped him? He fell asleep next to me!'

'You mean collapsed in a drunken heap. That is your problem, you know. You look at a vulture and tell yourself it's a turtle dove.'

'Penelope, has something upset you?'

'Of course not.' She turned and started rifling through the chest at the foot of his bed. 'You should stop drinking. Then you won't find yourself in these situations.'

'Situations?' He put his hands on his hips, impatient, tired of her roundabout ways.

Penelope mimicked him, put her hands on her own hips. *What have I done now?* he thought.

'Really, Symon. I saw you, in Burntwood. At Hutton Hall.'

He cocked his head in confusion, dropped his hands. 'What?'

'I came to fetch you. And what a ridiculous and perverse party I found! Such frivolity, when half a day's ride away in London, all the world is ending.' She had turned her back to him and looked out of the window. Her voice was shaking, in tears or anger he couldn't tell.

'I saw you. Go into Elizabeth's room.'

Symon put a hand on her shoulder, tried to turn her towards him. He felt her shoulders tense even more, then she shrugged him off. 'Penelope. I do not know if you are telling the truth. I never can tell, actually. But what you claim is most decidedly not true. You are right. I shouldn't have gone there. I deeply regret it. But this accusation—'

'I saw you.'

'I do not know what spies you employ. But you need better ones.' He could not say he had never done such a thing; he desperately wanted to end this conversation. Who was this girl? Who was she to ask for an accounting?

'I am my own spy. There is none better. I saw you. Outside her room. I saw you knock on her door.'

Symon searched his mind for the details of that night. No, he hadn't knocked. He was about to . . . yes, but thought better of it. Then there was that unearthly noise from down the hall passage . . . Ah . . . of course. She had been there. The wraith flying down the stairs. The face in the garden earlier. Penelope. How . . . ? He was both furious and confused. She was dangerous. She crossed all boundaries. And yet . . .

'Penelope, I will say this only once. And then we are never to speak of Lady Gauden again. You are not my confessor, nor my conscience. I owe you no explanation. But in the interest of peace, I will say this. I did not go into her room. I put a note under her door. To tell her that I would be leaving early the next morning. Though you are right. That alone was an impropriety.'

'You talk to me as if I'm a child!' She started throwing everything out of the chest and on to the floor.

He stared at her crossly. 'Stop it. What are you looking for?'

'Gloves!' she spat. 'Anything of yours that could be useful.'

'Useful for what? No, never mind.' He walked over and closed the chest. 'Listen. I must go. Bernard has sent word. Down at the churchyard, there's another girl. Mutilated, like Mary. She came in overnight.'

'I already know.' She swatted a stray bit of hair from her eye, sat down on the chest. She seemed somewhat calmer. Perhaps his explanation had helped? Though why he should care at all what she felt . . .

'Symon, I don't know if Boghurst is behind this. If he tried to kill you at St Gabriel Fenchurch. But I do know this: the killer is one of the plague society.'

He took out a handkerchief, wiped at the sweat dripping down his brow and neck. Would his head, this conversation, ever stop spinning? 'What do you mean? How could you know that?'

Seeing his distress, she got up and poured him a drink. Gestured for him to sit down with her. 'You see, after the plague society meeting broke up the other night, I went back inside, I had left my drawings behind. And everything in that room was exactly as it had been when we left. Mincy's piss on the wall, Boghurst's broken wine glasses, Dr Burnett's meeting notes. But can you guess the only thing that wasn't there?' She didn't wait for him to answer. 'My drawings.'

Symon closed his eyes. Could she be right? 'Perhaps they were only borrowed. For study.'

She raised an eyebrow. 'Unlikely. They have no real interest in the matter. Besides, they see plague all the time. Why take my drawings?'

'Well, you are an exceptional artist.'

'You really think so?' Her gaze softened.

'Most certainly.' He hesitated. 'Is that what you wanted to be when you were a little girl? A painter?'

'No.' The edge returned to her voice. 'A lawyer.'

Oh. A squit of a girl with an exquisite eye who saw herself arguing before the King's Bench. Then he realised. She wasn't a street urchin at all. She had been someone's daughter, someone very fine. 'Penelope, where do—'

'And if someone wanted to make a study of them, why not say so? Why hide it? But there is a simple way to answer that question.'

He was looking at the sticky bits of her hair poking out from under her cap, the dirt under her nails, the ink stains on her fingers and chin, and imagined her as she was supposed to be, a young lady with a promising future. Who had stolen that from her?

'Symon, if you wouldn't mind following along? To answer that question, you go to them, one by one. Bring up the drawings. Indirectly. Ask them what they make of the marks. If one of them did take them for good enough reasons, they'll tell you. If no one confesses, well then, I'm right. But I'll tell you now, the murderer took those drawings.'

She told him about Greatrakes and Mincy; how she had been following both of them. How they both liked bed companions with fleas, except Greatrakes' had two legs instead of four. 'And I found this.' She handed him the letter she had taken from Mincy's desk. 'It's worth a read.'

He scanned the letter and shook his head. 'It's in German.'

'Shall I translate for you?' She took the letter back. '"My dear brother, I rejoice at your continued success in Hesse . . ."'

Symon stared at her, waiting for her to smile and acknowledge the joke, but she did not falter.

*These chocolate hounds you have sent me are most marvellous. They, like our English hounds, are resistant to the pestilence. I have infected them several times over, and they frolick as happily after as they did before. (If only those of our own species could respond alike when a dear man of physick comes to their aid!) I have decided, however, that it would be fruitless to experiment upon them any more, for their bodies are so tiny and unlike ours, their physiology renders no comparison. The English mastiff is more suited to the purpose. As you warned, I find these dachshunds to be most excellent companions and it is my utmost desire to breed my own family of them once this plague has taken its leave of us. There is nothing I desire so much as this. Perhaps I shall retire once this season is past us.*

*My patients are most ungrateful, they complain of my methods. I say to them, 'I must take that leg or that arm.' But they refuse the procedure, for they say it shall hurt too much. I do not understand them. Of course it will hurt. But pain is preferable to death! They do not truly want me to help them. There is no connection. I find only headache and heartache from this work and the constant rejection it brings. Now a life of breeding dogs. That would be most rewarding. They know I mean the best for them, and agree readily to my proposals. This is how I imagine heaven. Surrounded by appreciation and a lingua franca; not complaints and disagreements and unpaid bills!*

*I have written you much of my attempts to bring an early end to this onslaught and I must disappoint you once again, for I have yet to find even a toehold on a possible treatment. It is a most distressing business, for one toils for days, weeks, months and is met only with defeat. I find solace only in these hounds and the pleasure of giving shape and language to their lives through our sessions of instruction.*

*You have heard, no doubt, that all such beasts are to be put to death in this most wicked of cities, therefore I must keep them within. But upon my roof, I have set up such an entertainment for them, and at regular intervals throughout the day I teach them many a trick! There is no smarter dog than these hounds (perhaps our poodles), they have taken quite readily to the hoops and tunnels I have set for them. How they dance under my orchestration! These trainings I keep with me as I search for a cure for this most horrid affliction, for with it, order shall return, and along with it, the constant companionship you have often spoke of, that comes from these miniature souls.*

'Penelope,' Symon interrupted. He swallowed the question most on his mind, which was how was it that she knew German, and chose instead to follow his suspicion that the letter was so puerile in nature that she might be making it up. 'Is there much more to this? I do not think his obsession with animals furthers our work.'

'Shh,' she said. 'I come to the best part.'

*When a promising treatment appears to me, I oft think I should try it on our mother (the most désagréable of them all! Did you know she still insists on cutting my hair? I regret not having followed you to the German lands! Be it too late? If ever there were a body ill-ruled by passions, 'tis madame . . . ) for she is the patient most readily available to me and no one in the world other than we should miss her. But do not worry, Mother is safe! My work has not advanced far enough yet to tempt me down that path. (It is a wonder, though, that Father was never tempted to enlist her in his experiments. Or did he? That would explain much, would it not? Ha ha!)*

*With these lines, you see the state I am in. I do not handle these disruptions well; I long for a return of my small days. I fear a melancholia shall settle on me soon if there is not an end to this matter. A return of my old spirits is most needed; you recall the unpleasantness that followed the last time I descended so. I thank you for the medical treatise you recently sent. It is indeed rare and the knowledge within it unheard of on this isle. You will thus understand why I ask you with all expediency to send me the enclosed list of materials and any further works that could illuminate the matter. As for its shipment, if it would please you to send a boy along with it, one who speaks no English and who may assist me in my search. I know it a sin, but I have no desire to share my secrets with any other than you. If you would see fit to bring the items yourself, I would also welcome you most heartily. The two of us would indeed lay this beast to rest. There is one other delicate matter I must seek your advice on, a rather sordid situation that*

'That?' said Symon. 'That what? Go on . . .'

'That's it. He hadn't finished it.'

'Ah, if only you had waited then!'

She scowled at him. 'How was I to know? Now, what do you make of it?'

Symon thought for a moment. 'Why is the letter in German? Mincy comes from a long line of English surgeons.'

'It is a bit odd, isn't it? Perhaps his mother is Hessian? But then why write in her tongue so she can see all the vile things he says about her?'

'Perhaps he doesn't care if she reads it. Perhaps he's more worried about others. A type of code, although a feeble one.'

'Not so feeble. You can't read German.'

'Yes.' He looked at her. 'How can you? Or is this another trick of yours? Did you have someone translate it for you?'

Penelope folded up the letter and put it in her pocket. 'I feel as if I know what it is like to be Mincy's mother,' she sighed, 'to have those around you be a constant disappointment.' She surveyed herself in the small looking glass hanging on the wall; straightened her bodice. 'Have you anything helpful to say before I go?'

Symon gestured for her to stay. 'I am sorry, Penelope. Won't you tell me how it is you know German?' She gave him a hard look. He relented. 'I think Mincy is a man of many perversions. His mother cuts his hair as if he were still a little boy. Thus he wishes her dead, by his own hand. These are matters of the family, however. Does it follow that he is capable of killing others?'

'Ordinarily no. I hear that is a common enough sentiment, to do away with one's mother. But if he doesn't want her to cut his hair, he should simply say so.' She frowned. 'But what if you are a surgeon and spend your days cutting away at human flesh and, as he has admitted, canine flesh?'

The letter was most confusing. A man whose most treasured companions were dogs and yet he also killed them in service to physick. Who thought little of the pain of his patients except the inconvenience plague brought to his life. How far would Mincy go to restore the order he wrote of? But the methods of torture they'd seen upon the victims. They seemed too fanciful for Mincy. Perhaps these methods came to him from his brother, from the heart of some great, dark Germanic forest.

'But why should he condemn Boghurst so quickly as the culprit?' he asked, thinking back to the unfortunate night he had, at Mincy's insistence, locked Boghurst in the crypt. 'Why not agree these were unorthodox but tolerable practices? That would indeed give his own diabolical work cover if he is the murderer.'

'Or scapegoat Boghurst. Six of one, half a dozen of the other . . .' She took a comb from his table and raked it through her hair.

*Could she be any queerer*? He'd been to Cambridge; how was it possible she spoke a language that he didn't? What tragedy had befallen her? He'd never met anyone like her, man or woman. How had she become so impoverished and alone? And why had she attached herself to him? To these murders?

Surely her survival would be all consuming. He knew what happened to cast-offs like Penelope.

'Here is what you are going to do.' She hadn't stopped talking. He heard the church bell strike.

'I'm sorry, Penelope, I must go.'

'I'll come with you.'

He shook his head, lied. 'No, Joan needs you. Said to send you down if I saw you.'

'Oh.' She was quiet for a moment. 'If I wash can I come with you?'

He stifled a laugh. The comb was stuck in her hair, the snags too gnarled for it to get through. Her apron was soiled, but at least there was no blood on it. It would almost be worth it, to have her wash. But no. 'Not this time.'

'Fine. I have an appointment with our killer anyway.'

Nausea flooded through Symon. He couldn't keep letting her put herself in harm's way. Penelope had no protector, no father or brother or husband to look out for her. She was doomed to pass her life – likely a short one – wandering around the edges of things, never invited in. He sat back down, overcome with shame and guilt. He'd barely given her much thought at all, other than to puzzle at her brashness. He saw now that he too was taking advantage of her by not watching over her. 'Penelope, really, all of this must stop now. We must keep you safe. It wasn't that long ago that we took you for dead. These bodies, it's not a matter for you.'

'Apparently not for you, either,' she said. 'Because why else do you sit here, doing nothing?' She threw at him the heavy gloves she'd found in the bottom of the chest. 'Here, take these. May God preserve you, you fool of a man.'

# 29

*Shop at the Sign of the White Hart Inn, Parish of St Giles in the Field*

BOGHURST SPAT ON THE church gate as he passed by. *Conspiring against me, every last one of you*, he thought. No matter where he went in London, he was surrounded by saints. All those St Margarets. St Marys. St Andrews. Those blasted St Pauls. They refused to make him taller or richer or turn his hair, with its tint of bile, the colour of the noonday sun. They refused to give him smooth manners and a tongue that would convince all to do as he said. They could, however, unite him with his lost love, Annie, they said. St Giles offered to hold him until he died, and they would let her know where he was when she arrived. He shook his fist at them. The saints were in collusion, he had no doubt of it.

He was walking back from the Bull Inn and in a terrible mood. He had woken up alone in a charnel ground, cold and wet with his own piss. A low even for him. He could not fathom why Symon had left him there, it was very unlike him. Especially after all he'd done for him. Boghurst had made his way home quite quickly that morning, changed his clothes and washed out his mouth with some stale-tasting water. Tried to calm himself with work, but then the experiment exploded on him, leaving nasty burns on his hands and singeing his shirt. He'd fled his shop in frustration. He wanted to go to Symon and ask for money, but knew he would get a lecture with it, so he'd decided to take a candle holder with him and hoped it would do for payment. The Bull Inn up the road was one of the few places in the parish still open and serving. He'd bought some bread and cheese; he didn't have the stomach for much more than that. *Too many late nights, too much drink,* he thought as he stumbled back towards his shop. But nothing to be done about that.

As he made his way down Lion Street, a dead cart came out of the passage ahead of him. The bodies in the back jumped as the cart banged down in a rut in the road. A man walked in front of the cart, ringing his bell, calling for the dead. Boghurst looked down the narrow ways as he went and saw more of the same. A slow dance of footmen to the dead, coming out from a court, nipping into a yard, visiting up the street, then departing for the burying places.

No one was out, no one running to fetch loaves from the bakehouse, no children scampering about before their mothers called them home. The sounds of his once merry parish replaced with creaking wheels, the sluggish clops of tired horses, monotonous calls for the dead and bells – church bells, hand bells (but no shop bells) – hoarse with tolling. The air around him was stifling, thick with late-afternoon heat, miasma. There was a tension to it; so many near to death, sucking in their last breaths, each taking a bit of the world with them as they went.

He crossed over Holborn, saw watchmen guarding the

entrances to the passages splintering off the street. They leaned, they scratched. He knew what they were thinking about. Relief. Ale.

Of a sudden, an almighty yell ricocheted off the buildings. Boghurst ducked as something flew out of a window nearby; he heard it land with a crunch. It was a man, jumped free from his house. The guards snapped out of their daze and ran towards him. He lay in the middle of the street, and they stopped just shy of him, unsure what to do. Boghurst watched as the man pushed his broken body up with a roar. The guards jumped back. He shouted and hissed and growled to keep them away, and then, in nothing more than his shirt, hobbled away.

Boghurst took the nearest turning away from the howling man. His keepers should have tied him up. God have mercy on him. Boghurst knew where the man was going. To the Thames. They all wanted to go there. It was the fever, the heat building inside them. They dreamed of the Thames, they told him often enough as he sat by their sick beds, they wanted to submerge themselves in its water. He allowed himself a grim smile. Only the nearness of death could make those waters delicious. Two of his patients, who had broken free from their constraints, had managed to come back from those waters, supplying him with his latest theory. They were cured, their buboes soft and shrunken down to the size of grapes. Once they got in the water, they told him, they swam about, the chill of the water giving them a new vigour.

His theory was this. The pest liked to lodge itself in certain places in the body, under the arms, in the groin. But a rapid and vigorous swinging of the arms and the legs forced the pest out, forced it through the body and thereby denied it powers of concentration. Now, circulating in a more diluted form, the pest was weakened and the body better able to fight it. Its strength was in numbers. Divide and conquer, he was saying these days.

Mincy and Dr Burnett had laughed at his theory, but they had little to counter it from their own findings. Greatrakes, however, agreed with him. 'A form of stroking!' he said. 'Now you see! I tell everyone it's a cure-all.' He asked Boghurst to show him the motions of the arms and legs, but he refused. *I'm not going to watch Greatrakes get rich off my cure*, he thought as he unlocked the door to his shop and stepped across its stained threshold. The place smelled of onions. Had he used onions earlier? The gush of liquid from the glass pot that exploded that morning had since slowed to a drip, sure to leave a permanent black stain on his floor. His wife would have thrown a fit. But what did he care? There was no one to tend to customers, no one to impress, so why waste his precious time cleaning up? Perhaps he should borrow one of Bernard's boys, get him over here to clear some space.

He kicked at another broken pot in frustration. The plague society meetings. He hadn't seen Dr Burnett this much in years; he enjoyed provoking him. Boghurst had never understood what Annie saw in the pop-eyed pillock. *A steady income. An orderly man*, he lamented as he shoved away the remains of yesterday's supper from a table; Burnett wasn't one to make a mess. Cleanliness was held in too high esteem, Boghurst thought. Fastidiousness stifled the mind. A man who went to church regularly. But so many more exciting things to do on a Sunday morning! No, he could not say that Annie had chosen wisely by agreeing to marry Alexander Burnett. Yes, a mistake for everyone that was, all around. Everyone but the doctor.

Boghurst tore off a chunk of hard cheese, smashed it into the bread. The night had not turned out well. They had all ridiculed him, torn his arguments apart as if he were an ignorant child. Sided with Dr Burnett. And then that godforsaken journey to St Gabriel Fenchurch.

He heard a knock at the shop door, ignored it. This was not a place for visitors.

# AUGUST

*It was dark before I could get home, and so land at Churchyard stairs, where to my great trouble I met a dead corpse of the plague, in the narrow ally just bringing down a little pair of stairs. But I thank God I was not much disturbed at it . . . This day I am told that . . . my physician, is this morning dead. Poor unfortunate man!*

Samuel Pepys, Naval Clerk, Seething Lane

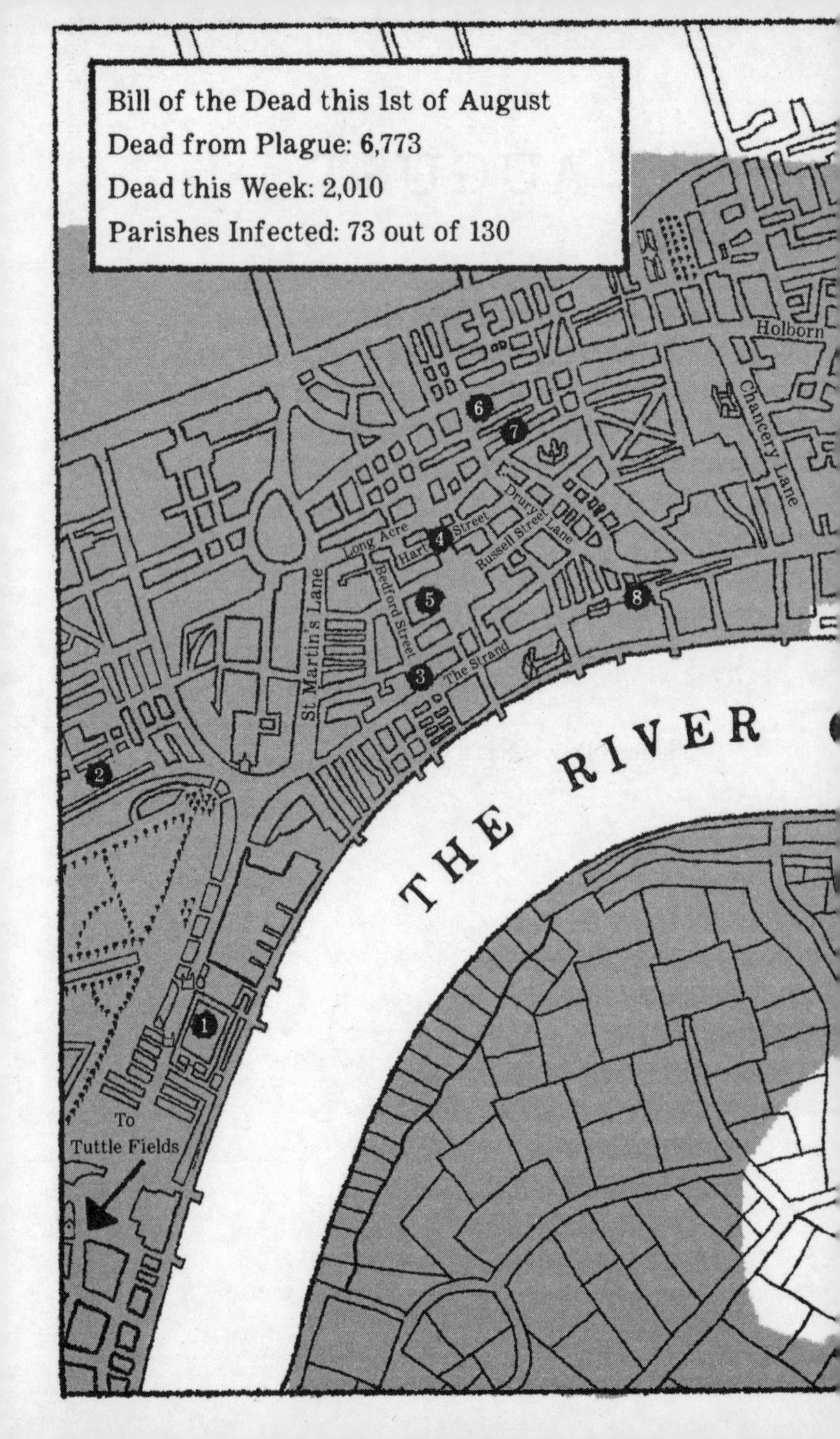
Bill of the Dead this 1st of August
Dead from Plague: 6,773
Dead this Week: 2,010
Parishes Infected: 73 out of 130
Holborn
Chancery Lane
Drury Lane
Russell Street
Street
Hart
Long Acre
Bedford Street
St Martin's Lane
The Strand
THE RIVER
To
Tuttle Fields
1
2
3
4
5
6
7
8

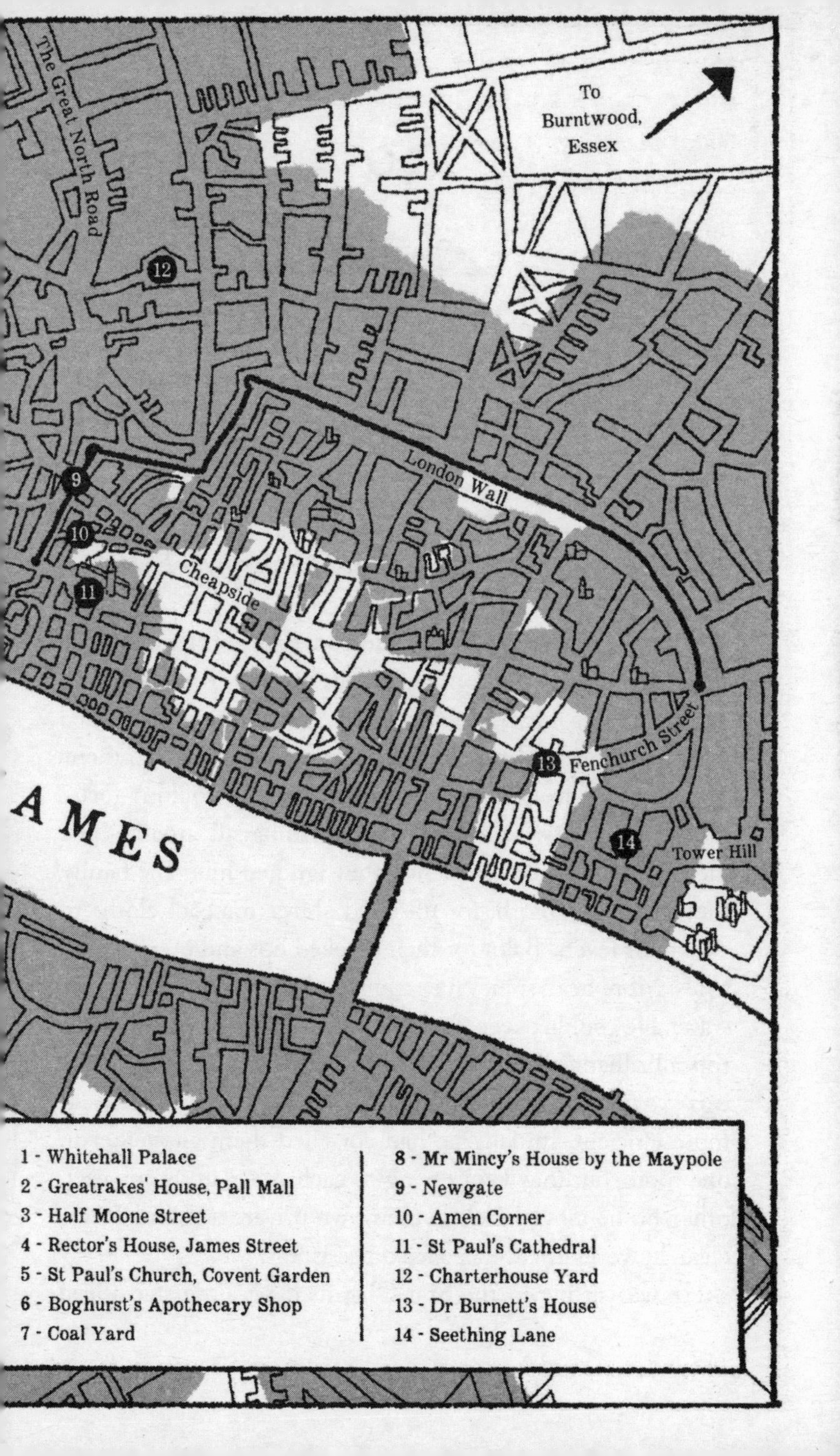
The Great North Road
To Burntwood, Essex
London Wall
Cheapside
Fenchurch Street
Tower Hill
AMES
12
9
10
11
13
14
1 - Whitehall Palace
2 - Greatrakes' House, Pall Mall
3 - Half Moone Street
4 - Rector's House, James Street
5 - St Paul's Church, Covent Garden
6 - Boghurst's Apothecary Shop
7 - Coal Yard
8 - Mr Mincy's House by the Maypole
9 - Newgate
10 - Amen Corner
11 - St Paul's Cathedral
12 - Charterhouse Yard
13 - Dr Burnett's House
14 - Seething Lane

# 30

*Tuesday, August 1st*
*A Shut-Up House, Leg Alley, St Martin's in the Fields*

IF ONLY HIS PATIENTS would cooperate a little more. He picked up a book from his pile of reading. Kircher's work on blood – his microscope had revealed the liquid to be filled with tiny worms. Vermicules, the German priest called them. He struggled to examine the images, but he couldn't focus. His headache was growing; the moaning all around him, incessant. He asked for silence, they ignored him. The family, they asked for broth, for unsoiled shifts, for cool cloths to ease their fevers. Balm for their cracked lips and their painful sores. More heat, something cooling. And always water, more water. He couldn't keep up with them. At first he had thought this a brilliant idea. Working with only one patient at a time was proving too slow. A houseful of active cases would be far more efficient. Initially he had corralled them altogether in one room, but they kept crying to each other, upsetting each other. So he moved each to their own private quarters. It was clear, however, that he needed an assistant.

He was sitting in the Star Chamber; his little star asleep

on the bed. He hadn't been so blessed as to get a blonde in this batch, but there was such fire in her hair. Surely there was some strength in it, if he could get the distillation right. Each room he tried a different theory. The Star Chamber, second floor, was home to astrological workings. The father he kept in the garret. The Hall of the Barber-Surgeons, he called it. The mother just below him in the Van Helmont Chamber, named after that wonderful chemist who said the only real way to know anything is by trial and error. The sons behind her in the back, where he practised the teachings of Galen and the College of Physicians. In any one of these rooms his advance might come. If it didn't, all of them, every last soul in London, would be dead. And there would be no salvation for him. He tried to explain this to them. Why they were so very important, why he needed their cooperation.

What he really needed was rain. There was a most rare plant, *Coelifolium*. Flowers of Heaven. A summer rain could bring it down. It was said to be the spiritus vitae of earth, of life. *Materia prima.* But you needed a wind from the south-west and a rain that fell in the evening and stopped long before the middle of the night. The plant was but fragile. Once it fell to the soil and took root, it only lived for a few hours, the sun's rays destroying it. From it, you could make an oil, *Aurum Potabile*, the elixir of life. A thimbleful of it would sell for five pounds. He did get hold of a few leaves in the spring and was able to make a small batch. It was shite – a nasty, fetid oil. He desperately needed more of the plant, so he could add it to the gold or fire he distilled from the hair, and then he might just have it, a potion that could cure anything. And be relieved of these dirty, bloody explorations.

But it hadn't rained in months.

Moss that grew only on a dead man's skull. That was another

route. Life from death. Very strong medicine. He needed his own charnel yard, instead of sending the corpses to the priest. But where to put it?

He gently put the back of his hand on the girl's forehead. Her fever was still high – a good sign. That mess she had created on her neck was drying up. But her sores were multiplying and she wasn't responding to the charms. The mercury-filled walnut he placed over her heart. The dried toad over her lung. The amulets of arsenic – to draw out the poison by its magnetic virtues – he placed over the carbuncles on her left leg. The amulets of spices – said to invigorate the body's own defences – he placed over the carbuncles on the right leg. None of it worked.

He would try sweating it out of her next. He was sure the pestilence came from the heavens and the stars. Carried here in the fumes of the great comet that streaked the sky December last. Sweating held some promise. If the seeds of plague surrounded the body in an invisible cloud – whether from heaven or hell – they would enter the body through the pores. The pores thus would be the best exit for the poison, too.

He threw more coals on the fire and heaped more blankets on his young patient, closed the shutters. He snagged his sore thumb on a latch and sucked on it to ease the sting. It was bleeding again. He had cut it earlier while dissecting the mother. A great swelling had developed under her chin and had settled there, very hard and very large, so big it hung down like a bag upon her chest. It had choked her to death when he wasn't watching. He decided to use her to search for the archeus – the spot in the body that holds the spark of life. He was rooting around for it in her stomach (and only turning up dross) when the dishes of burning brimstone he had set next to the table to cleanse the air started smoking uncontrollably and temporarily blinded him.

He sighed. He really should go up to the top room to check on the patriarch. He had been applying too many blistering cataplasms, it appeared, for the man did nothing but piss blood and rave. He had meant to create only a handful of ulcers this time – each just big enough to fit about eight peas, as the French surgeons recommended – but he had been tired and forgot himself and the next thing he knew he had burned dozens. He was fed up with the surgeons anyway. Their methods were hard-going and mucky and had got him nowhere.

He must rest first, he was feeling uncommonly drained. He looked over at his little star, her face glistening with the glow of the coals. Her breathing was hoarse, uneven. A terrible sign. He would attend to her shortly. But for now, he curled up in a corner, rolling up his sack for a pillow.

*

He woke up hot and vomiting. Something sharp and burning in his throat. He got on his knees and crawled over to the bucket of water. He took a sip to cool his throat, sat back against the wall. The girl was awake, candlelight flickering in her eyes. She was watching him. Smiling.

He had to get home. A deep cramp in his abdomen, his bowels near to exploding. He couldn't risk falling ill here. Sack tight in his fist, he crawled over to the table by her bed, swept what he could into it and blew out the candle. He took hold of the bed frame and pulled himself up, lurched over to the wall and out of the door.

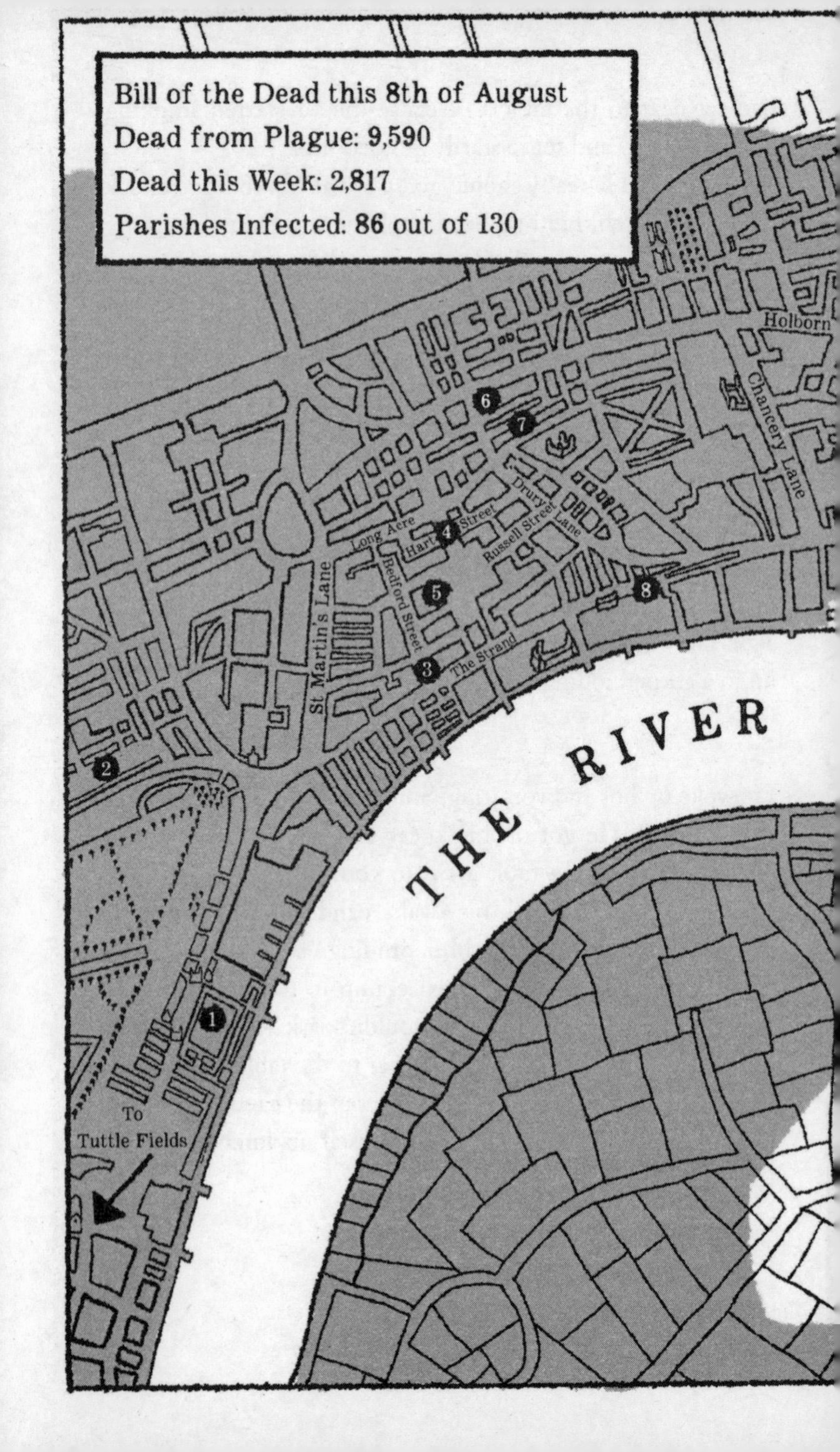
Bill of the Dead this 8th of August
Dead from Plague: 9,590
Dead this Week: 2,817
Parishes Infected: 86 out of 130
Holborn
Chancery Lane
Drury Lane
Russell Street
Hart Street
Long Acre
Bedford Street
St Martin's Lane
The Strand
THE RIVER
To
Tuttle Fields
1
2
3
4
5
6
7
8

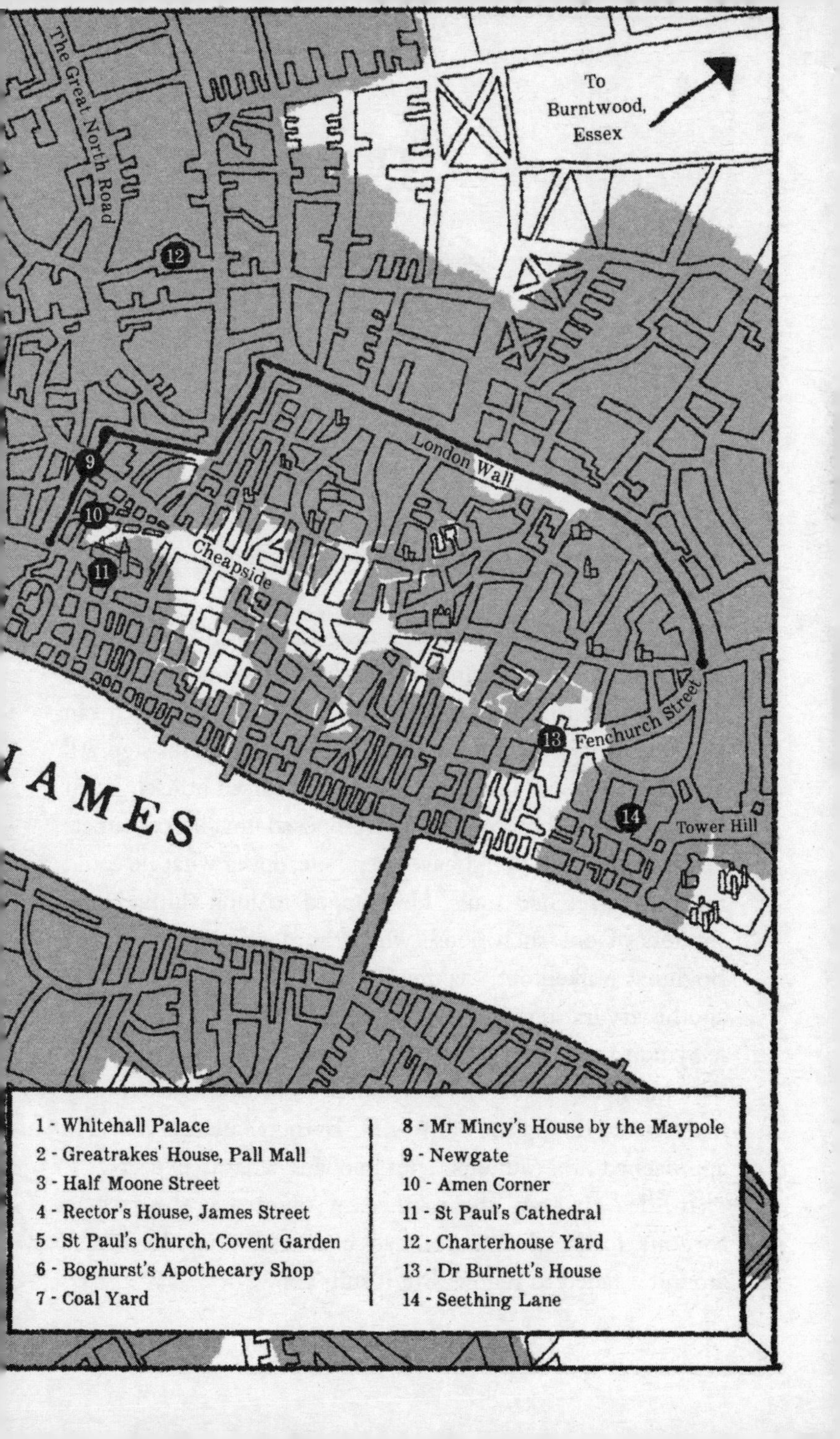
The Great North Road
To Burntwood, Essex
London Wall
Cheapside
Fenchurch Street
Tower Hill
IAMES
1 - Whitehall Palace
2 - Greatrakes' House, Pall Mall
3 - Half Moone Street
4 - Rector's House, James Street
5 - St Paul's Church, Covent Garden
6 - Boghurst's Apothecary Shop
7 - Coal Yard
8 - Mr Mincy's House by the Maypole
9 - Newgate
10 - Amen Corner
11 - St Paul's Cathedral
12 - Charterhouse Yard
13 - Dr Burnett's House
14 - Seething Lane

# 31

*Wednesday, August 9th*
*A Dish of Coffee, Served in a Shut-Up City*

SYMON WAS ON HIS WAY to the Lord Brunkard's at the bottom of Drury Lane; he had decided to once again plea for help with the high, mighty and mad gentlemen that ran England. But as he crossed Bow Street, he slowed his step. All of the houses were shut up or vacant. He cursed himself; what had he done with his morning? Composed imaginary sonnets to Elizabeth. He should have been here, doing what he could for these wretched souls. He stopped to look through the shutters of one such house when the door burst open and Boghurst walked out, shaking his head. 'God save them,' the apothecary muttered, looking back over his shoulder.

Symon took a deep breath; he hadn't seen Boghurst since that night in St Gabriel Fenchurch's graveyard when they had tried to dig up the body of Dr Burnett's manservant. He approached him cautiously, not knowing what to expect.

'It'll leave a scar.' The apothecary squinted at the gash in Symon's forehead. The cut had hardened over, the bruise around it faded to yellow. 'But it suits you.'

Symon pulled his head away from the apothecary's prodding fingers and scowled.

'You're turning into a rotten fellow.' Boghurst chased after him. 'Why did you leave me in the churchyard? Why didn't you wake me up? I caught a nuisance of a charnel fever and you're to blame.'

Boghurst had lost a good stone, possibly two. He was wasting away, drenched with sweat, his shirt sticking to him in translucent blotches. His long pale locks were gone, cropped close to his head, like a fever patient. Like the victims. Fear crept through Symon's veins. 'What has happened? Your hair . . . You are well, I hope?'

'What? Oh. Cut it off. Too many things living in it. Tell me, why haven't you come to apologise? That's all right. You can make it up to me now. Buy me a drink.' He cocked his head towards the coffee house on the corner.

Boghurst clearly thought he had been wronged. Symon wasn't having it. 'Do you know where I woke up? In a grave. With this cut on my head.' Symon pointed to the gash. 'I found you holding the spade. It seems to me' – he took a step towards the apothecary – 'that you were trying to kill me. And the only thing that saved me was that you were too drunk to finish the job. Thank heaven for vices, I say!'

'You are quite wrong. I was trying once again to save you. You were digging up a grave, the only fresh one in the yard. You thought Burnett's man was in it. Every spadeful you dug up you flung back on yourself. When you hit yourself in the head with it, I took it away from you. You, my dear friend, were the victim of vice, not me.' Boghurst stopped shouting, took Symon's hands into his own. 'Ah, I see, this is quite serious. You still don't trust me. What damage that fiend Mincy has done to us. Symon, you must believe me. My conscience is clean. You are my dear friend. My only friend. Come, let us get out of this heat and talk this through.'

Symon looked at him. The man seemed sincere and deeply troubled at the accusation. He hadn't yet told Boghurst about Penelope's stolen drawings, that the murderer was quite possibly one of the plague society. Which meant that he was very much a suspect. And as a suspect, he had motive to kill Symon. The cut on his head, it may have been an accident as the apothecary said. Or it may have been a failed attempt to stop his investigation. But if he had been trying to kill Symon, why hadn't he carried it through? There had been nothing to stop him. Besides, he could just as easily poison the tonics he mixed for Symon.

'Yes.' Symon didn't want to reveal his thoughts. 'There are few we can rely on at the moment, and so much about us. We must see each other through. Let us forgive each other. We can talk more of this later, but I—'

The apothecary grabbed him by the elbow and pulled him into the coffee house.

It was dark as a mole hole inside, the only light a few low candles and the flicker of the hearth coals under a vast boiling cauldron of coffee. Symon was surprised to see such a crowd, that this many people indeed were still in London. He came to a halt when he saw who was in a back corner. Penelope. He hurried over to her. 'You shouldn't be in here! They'll think you a—'

She waved him off. 'Tut-tut. Who is around to fuss about that now, who will be left to remember it?' She added with a wicked smile, 'Besides me?'

A boy came by, tossing dishes of coffee towards Symon and Boghurst. Penelope pulled Symon's towards her. He sighed and signalled the boy for another. He sat down and looked at his company. A sooty waif and a pushy wastrel. The boy flung another dish at him; he sniffed it, took a small sip and grimaced – it was a gritty concoction of cinnamon, clove and liquid ash. The door slammed open and Symon skittered along the bench like a rabbit.

'Have you any news?' the apothecary asked Penelope. 'Have you found our murderer?'

The door banged open again; Symon wanted to throttle something. The constant commotion scraped at his nerves. One patron in, one patron out, a regular stream of merchants looking for comrades and gossip. They weren't leaving town as long as there was money to be made, abandoned connections to take over. He turned to see a squat man with bow legs silhouetted in the doorway. Symon shrank back. 'Sir Denis. That's Sir Denis.'

'Lizzie's husband?' Penelope asked.

Symon frowned at her. 'You'll regret these forward manners soon enough, I tell you.'

'Does Lizzie regret hers?'

Symon shook his head and looked over at Sir Denis. He had sent his family out of town, but had stayed behind for his work with the Navy. The man headed for a table where several rather severe-looking men were sitting. Likely a business meeting of some sort. Should he greet him? Perhaps not. He and his companions looked quite disturbed. In fact, Sir Denis looked uncommonly ill. His face puffy and ashen; a bloated bullfrog. He was talking rapidly and as if in great pain. Symon couldn't see any visible sores. A pity. Bags under his eyes. In need of a shave. He recalled the whisperings at Elizabeth's dinner in Burntwood. A hundred thousand pounds in debt. Unfathomable! As he watched Sir Denis, he felt hate and happiness at the same time. He scowled. The proper thing to do was to go and talk to him, not spy from a corner. If the man were ill, Symon could be of comfort to him.

He forced himself to take another sip of his coffee, then excused himself. A sour smell hit him as he approached the table, a smell he knew well – nerves gone weak. He swallowed, put on his best manners, and laid a hand on Sir Denis' shoulder.

'Sir Denis, how fare you? Your family?'

Elizabeth's husband looked up, confusion on his face as he struggled to place him, then softening as recognition set in. 'My dear Rector! It is you!' He pushed himself to his feet, caught Symon up in a bear hug and gave him a kiss on the cheek. 'They're alive, my good man! They're alive! Is there anything more wonderful to say than that? Best thing I ever did was send them out of town.' He let Symon go and sat back down, offering him a place beside him. 'I bless the Lord every day for bringing me such a fine woman. Her letters do ease my heart.'

Symon had started to sit down, blinked. She writes to her husband? Symon thought they barely talked. But of course she would, how foolish of Symon to think otherwise.

'And Rector, thank you for being a most constant friend to her. She does struggle at times. She reads me your letters, you know.' He smiled jovially. 'They do keep her faith strong!' At this, Symon had to cough. To hide the utter look of bewilderment crashing across his face. 'These days, though, I have to make do with copies. She likes to highlight your best phrases when she sends them. What a gift you have with words! I do envy you!'

A punch to the gut. Did Elizabeth really share his letters? Their private letters? He nodded, smiled; he was too stunned to do anything but. He decided to make a hasty retreat. He asked Sir Denis to send his blessings and love to his family, invited him to stop in and walked slowly back to his table.

'You look like you've been struck,' Penelope said. 'Did he hit you? I didn't see him hit you.'

'He said Elizabeth sends him my letters.'

Penelope and Boghurst barked in laughter. 'She does worse than that,' Penelope added.

'What? What do you mean?'

She shrugged, sipped at her coffee.

Had she seen something else at Hutton Hall? He eyed her carefully. 'Is there something you would like to say?'

'Who me?'

He sighed. They didn't understand. His letters to Elizabeth were that of one dear friend to another, or at times, a spiritual father to a struggling soul. There was nothing illicit in their correspondence, no, he was very careful about that. But he still thought them private. Intimate. How could she?

The coffee-house door flew open again. This time, a boy burst through.

'Dead bills!' His voice cracked. 'Advance copies! Fresh from the Hall!' He waved one of the huge bills in the air. 'Thousands dead. Five hundred in St Giles Cripplegate alone!'

The boy was mobbed within seconds. Boghurst ran up to grab a sheet for them. 'It's eating us up entirely,' he said as he scanned it. 'And yet. St Gabriel Fenchurch. Dr Burnett's parish. Not one dead of plague.' He handed the sheet to Symon. 'He is indeed not the type to make the same mistake twice. He's made sure his hunting grounds are far from home. What's this?' The apothecary was looking back at the door, the room had gone quiet. Another man had come in behind the boy; he hadn't moved beyond the door. He rocked in place, his gaze listless. In his hand, he held a paper that threatened to slip to the floor. *Plague*, thought Symon. He saw the apprehension in the faces around him. *That's what we're all thinking. He is going to fall down dead.*

Then Symon watched in horror as Penelope walked up to the man, straightened his wig and took the paper from his hand. She read it to the room: 'The City is Closed. By Order of the Lord Mayor. By Order of the King. The City is Closed.'

She had broken the man's stupor. He looked around, gasped. 'We are locked in. God Save Us.'

Benches scraped and crashed to the floor.

'The king has abandoned us! He's sealed our doom!'

Men crushed around the messenger. Symon thought they were like to kill him, they tugged and pulled on him so, attacked him with their frantic questions.

'What does this mean? Is it the old city that's closed? Or all of town?' Symon asked. Penelope had managed to free herself from the mob and brought the king's order back to the table. They read down through it. No one was allowed out of town. No one was allowed in.

'This indeed is our death warrant,' Boghurst said. 'The king adds that anyone who breaks out of a shut-up house shall be sent to Newgate. Why bother, when he has turned the whole town into a prison?'

Symon couldn't quite grasp the situation. His fingers fluttered, a tremor was building in his upper lip.

'I can't say I disagree with him.' Boghurst sighed, leaned back. 'When I saw the first cases, I told my patients, you're not to worry, you may very well recover. I was indulgent. But these past weeks, I see something else. The distemper has changed.' Sweat was beading upon his brow. 'Once it is in a house or neighbourhood, all die. No longer in days, but in hours. A terrible, bloody cough takes them. What I see ahead of us is a most terrible slaughter.'

A man snatched the king's order off the table; they made no move to stop him. Boghurst shoved his dish forward for a refill as the coffee boy rushed by. Symon declined, covering his with his hand. The boy poured it over Symon's hand. He yelled, shaking the boiling liquid away.

'Better get something cold on it,' said Penelope. 'You' – she pointed at the apothecary – 'fetch some lard from the kitchen. Be quick about it.'

Boghurst stared at her, then pulled his hand back to strike her. 'You foul shrew—'

'Peace!' Symon caught his hand. 'It's of no consequence. A small burn.'

The apothecary rose. 'I'll see what I can find. Something to stop her mouth, too.'

Penelope's eyes followed him as he grumbled towards the kitchen. 'We're trapped,' she whispered. 'With the murderer. Death is inching ever closer to us, my dear Symon.' She took his hand and blew gently on the web of white blisters forming below the knuckles.

Boghurst came back with a bowl of lard. Penelope snatched it from him and applied it to Symon's hand. He closed his eyes, allowed himself to imagine for a sliver of a second that it was Elizabeth gently ministering to him. He could be at Hutton Hall by the end of the day. The town was closed, but not for people like Symon, people with connections. He could go across the river to Lambeth Palace, get a special pass from the archbishop. Have his household – Joan and Nell, Jack – moved to Elizabeth's empty house in Clapham. Bernard could surely manage without him, would probably prefer that Symon clear out. He took a breath and thought of the cool English wood surrounding Hutton Hall, the scent of moss and the moist, rich earth hiding beneath it. But when he imagined himself at Lambeth, then in a coach on the road to Essex, then walking under a starry sky with Elizabeth, another feeling swelled in his body. It was deep and barbed, unbearable. He saw himself take Elizabeth's hand, find a reprieve in her eyes, a moment of wholeness. But then she would say goodnight and the thrilling ache of his passion would give way, he knew, to the ache of irritation. And after that, shame at abandoning his parish. The look of disappointment in Penelope's eyes. That he had left them – the dead, the murderer, Penelope – all behind for something as ephemeral as a kiss from Elizabeth.

Boghurst took a last sip from his dish and said he must get on.

'Please do,' said Penelope.

The apothecary gave her a stern look, shook his head. 'Symon, you do have such strange companions these days. Ones that are certain to lose you friends, and I do not think a man in your position can afford that.'

'He can afford to lose you,' she said.

'You don't know as much as you think you do,' Boghurst said, then turned to Symon. 'I bid you farewell. My patients need me. They need me to watch them die.'

'Yes,' Symon replied softly. 'And after that, they come to rest with me. What a business it is that fills our days.' He looked at his hand, then made a fist, stretching and tearing the blisters on the back of it. He wanted to feel the pain, to remind himself viscerally how much more others had endured. Those on their death beds at that very moment. The murdered girls in his churchyard.

He sat in silence for a few moments. The coffee house was emptying out. The news that the king had abandoned them had put an end to any false cheer. Then turned to Penelope. He could not let her continue on such a dangerous path. 'Please do explain,' he said. 'For I cannot fathom your behaviour.'

'We must bait the killer. Put him off guard. If I antagonise these men, in ways that make no sense to them, they will do two things. One, they will discount me as a lunatic. Two, they will be angered into rash action. Both situations work to our advantage.'

'That is my point. They will either lock you up in Bedlam or kill you.'

'I have considered that. That is where you come in. You are to keep me alive, and I am to do the same for you.'

He laughed at the absurdity. 'Then we are both very much in trouble.'

She didn't smile back. 'I'm most serious, Symon. I'm counting on you. You most certainly can count on me.'

He saw that he had upset her. All too often people had laughed at her. Failed to see that underneath the muck was a strange and wonderful intelligence. A beautiful and kind heart.

'Of course, Penelope. Of course. I put myself most gratefully in your hands.'

# 32

*At the Scene of Several Break-Ins*

'STOP! BEFORE YOU TAKE another step, I want you to think.' Penelope put her hand on Symon's chest. 'You walk like a big stupid dog. Everyone can hear you coming.' They were on the stairs at Symon's house – a suffocating set of stairs. It was a hot August day; the beeswax polish on the banister melted and dripped on to the stair treads. Penelope rubbed the sole of her shoe in it. 'Do this, it will help you slide, instead of that clomping you do.'

'You're making a mess. Joan won't like it. I don't have much time. What is it you wanted?'

'You have much to learn,' Penelope sighed. 'So little aptitude.'

'Penelope?'

'Right. Today, that great flapping fluff of angel cake is our target.'

'Greatrakes?'

'Indeed.' She smiled. 'I do not know where we will find him. He flits about so. But I have to get something from my rooms first.'

'How long will this take? And what do you mean your rooms? In the church?'

'I have rooms all over town. That is the way of a good intelligencer. Come, and please do try to be quiet. It is important.'

She led him over to Little Piazza across from Symon's church. The apartments of Lord and Lady Wittwrong. 'My lady left behind quite a wardrobe,' Penelope said as she took him around the back. She saw Symon's confused face and laughed. 'You thought I got them all off the dead, didn't you? What do you take me for?' She pushed open a window and crawled through, then opened the door for Symon.

He baulked. 'This is trespassing. We could be hanged if caught.'

'Caught by whom? Now, when spying,' she continued, 'you must pick your disguise. How is it you want people to perceive you? We have to make inquiries of servants and shopkeeps and such today, so we will want to appear respectable, but not haughty. If you are too shabby, they'll worry that you're contagious and they'll shoo you away. If you appear too proper, they'll clam up. The dutiful daughter of an honest tradesman, that would be appropriate. Now wait here.' She left Symon in the parlour while she exchanged that morning's gown of violet silk for a modest but well-made suit of fine grey. In the right light, it gave a hint of silver. She made sure to transfer her papers into the skirt pocket. It was possible that her aunt and uncle, although removed from London, might not survive plague. It was outside of London now, she heard. It would make her case against them much easier if they died. But she would be cheated of the satisfaction.

She tucked her hair under a linen cap and slipped on my lady's shoes. Where to start then? Pall Mall at Greatrakes' house? See what they could get out of his servants. See what his local haunts were. Haunt. She didn't want to even think the word. It always brought the ghosts, they were so eager for attention these days.

Fear of plague kept most servants from wandering. If they were like their master, Greatrakes' servants would be sunning themselves on the back steps, ordering in most of their provisions. Things like a fat dinner of prawns and lobster. That's what he had the other day. She saw the lobsters being delivered. She wrapped a crisp white kerchief around her neck and shoulders and slid its edges into the bosom of her bodice. Wonderfully soft. But what was that? A patch of angry red spots on her chin stared back at her from the looking glass. She blamed it on the apothecary. She had taken a dewy skin potion from his shop. She had been searching for his notebooks and had seen it high on a shelf, in a pretty little indigo jar of Venetian glass, with an etched brass lid. It had promised radiance; a *visage magneticus*. She should've known by the smell. Another poor formula, its root ingredient spoiled butter, like all the others.

She left the bedchamber and rejoined Symon in the parlour. 'Here, I'll sketch what I know.' She went over to Lord Wittwrong's desk, took out some paper (scented with orange) and drew a map. Here is where he worked. Here is where he slept. Here is where he went to church.

'Who are his main connections?' she asked.

'Anyone with money.'

'Who are his friends?'

'Anyone with money.'

'Could you be a little more helpful?'

'Yes of course, I'm embarrassed because I know so little about him. He pops up when I least expect it, behaves as if we are dear old friends, asks me for something, then disappears.

That is most of what I know about him. But I can do this. He has mentioned dining with Lord Brunkard. He's an old Navy commissioner, he's stayed behind and opened up his house to the sick.'

'He lives with the plagued? He sounds promising. Have you asked him for help with the matter?'

Symon frowned. 'Yes, I saw him after I left you at the coffee house. He brushed it off, as so many others have. Said something very war-like: that collateral damage was to be expected in a battle with plague and that we must focus on the living, not the dead. I got a lecture. People are fond of lecturing, aren't they?'

'Well, go back soon. Before he's dead, so he can tell you about Greatrakes. I'll ask his servants. They may know the mystic's haunts—' Damn, she'd said it again. She looked around to see if any of the ghosts had heard her.

'What is the matter?' Symon asked.

'Oh, I thought I heard the neighbours . . . But you know, this gown isn't right. A moment, please.' A bewildered Symon watched her run back upstairs, where she dumped the grey suit for a tattered gown dyed an artless black. The costume of an urchin. No one noticed the homeless. She of all people knew this. The smell was a bit high and the gown itchy. A shift and underskirt of silk would help. She transferred her papers again, then topped her new suit off with a lace shawl that was more hole than stitch.

Symon scowled when she returned. 'Really, Penelope, it's time you left the rags behind.'

'These rags are my dear friends, you'll see. I'll get you your own set.' She led him up a skinny back stairwell to the roof, walked three houses down to the Earl of Sussex's. He had a much nicer roof, was fond of entertaining up here. There was a house of necessity, as well as one of those glittering, glass banqueting houses, like the one at Hutton Hall. Penelope had spent the other evening here, enjoying the sunset while making marzipan sweets. A figurine of Elizabeth. Whose head fell off when a ram of candied fruit rudely butted her. But my Lady Wittwrong had much better taste in clothes and a fatter bed of feathers than my Lady Sussex. She headed down into the earl's house, stopped to take some books off a shelf but Symon made her put them back. They left through the kitchen door and hugged close to the garden wall, out by the empty stables and into the alley. She threaded through the back ways and courts and down to the Strand, where she waited for an agreeable hackney driver. 'Too cocky, that one. Too lusty, him. The third, now he's a gentle soul.' The driver doffed his cap. 'Yes, he's a chap to help us out.' She nodded and told Symon to hop on the back, which he did, very awkwardly, and off they went towards Pall Mall.

The Lady Ranelagh's townhouse, where Greatrakes was a guest and after the lady's flight the only resident, was a pale yellow trimmed with a brilliant white wood. It sat back from the street, one in a string of grand mansions. Topiaries lined a merry path to the front door, but she knew it a false welcome – the heavily curtained windows were closed and blank in the August heat.

Undaunted, Penelope checked her dress, straightened her coif, buzzed her lips and sang a scale like she'd seen the actors do at Drury Lane.

'Wait across the street,' she told Symon. 'We look an odd pair otherwise.' She watched him go, then walked down the path to the front door and knocked.

A girl answered, a few years younger than she. Crisp white smock, crisp white cap. She looked at Penelope like she was a week-old cabbage. *And that poor manner*, thought Penelope, *is why God left your face lopsided with only one dimple.*

'Message for your master.'

'You're a messenger? Who would send you?'

'Is he at home?'

'No.'

'Down at the tavern? I could take it there.'

'No, he's at the yard.'

'The yard?'

She looked Penelope up and down, then shrugged. 'Charterhouse Yard. Outside the hospital. He gets good business there he says.'

'Of course,' said Symon when Penelope had rejoined him. 'Charterhouse Hospital. He's mentioned it before. He treats people there, there's always a crowd. Mostly the poor and disfigured, trying to get into the hospital and get a bed. I'm surprised he works there, they don't pay. He's not one for charity' – he looked back at Lady Ranelagh's house – 'unless he's the recipient.'

They hopped on another coach and headed into the City. Charterhouse Hospital sat outside old London's northern wall. The dry summer had turned the orchards and gardens around it yellow and sickly. The coach dropped them at the hospital's main entrance, a stone arch off Charterhouse Lane. As they walked under the arch and into the yard surrounded by the hospital buildings, Penelope waivered, took a step back. Symon reached out to steady her. 'What is it?'

'Let's wait back in the lane,' she said, turning away.

'Are you all right?'

She gave a weak smile. 'You know what this place was, don't you?'

'Yes, an old priory. One of the first Henry took from the Pope.'

'Right.' Penelope kept her eyes down. 'The yard there was a burial yard. And at one point, long ago, a plague pit.'

'How do you know?'

'I can see them all, standing there.'

Symon looked around. 'Yes, the beggars; I'm surprised they're still allowed to gather there.'

'No, the plague dead. Hundreds of them. And dead monks. That's what I see.' The dead stood out amongst the living with their exaggerated faces and their funny clothes. The men wore long belted tunics and hose; the women shapeless gowns that trailed behind them, their hair hidden beneath hoods. They screamed in the faces of the living, tried to push them and kick them, bite them. Their words made no sense, but Penelope knew what they were saying. 'Get gone, there's no more room! Go find your own pit. Ours is full up.'

Symon took her hand. 'The dead? You see them? Penelope?'

She didn't answer; she was looking down the lane now. 'I'll perch over there, wait for Greatrakes to leave. You sit under that tree.' She ran down to a market stall, took several deep breaths to recover, then bought four bunches of wilted flowers and a bent-up basket to hold them in. She set herself up as another beggar selling rotten goods, someone to avoid, and squished herself against a wall to get a little shade from the eaves. She kept her ears open, but her eyes down. She didn't want to make contact with any of those wretches hovering in the old charnel ground. She took out *The Friar's Complaint* – she'd managed to get a few books past Symon – and started in the middle. Wesley has just found the friar naked in bed with his wife. (*Sounds too familiar*, Penelope thought glumly.) But Wesley had a magical flute and piped them out of bed, still naked, and out of town. Everyone came out to watch their humiliation. Where could she get such an instrument? She nibbled on some cheese while she read and waited. A turn of the page, an empty street before her. She sat for about two hours with only the beggars and ghosts shuffling in and out of the gate. Symon had fallen asleep against his tree. She took out a second book.

Right around the time the king's son inexplicably pulled a black pudding from his breeches, she caught a bit of motion at the door of the hospital. Two rabbits popped out. One old, stubby, rich. The other tall, skinny with a bulbous white head. Greatrakes. They bowed and parted ways. And Penelope began her hunt. She looked over at Symon, but he was still asleep. She had no time to wake him, Greatrakes was almost out of view, turning the corner at Smithfield. She rushed to catch up until he was only a few dozen yards ahead of her. He wandered down Cow Lane and Cock Lane, on to Snow Hill where he passed by the Dolphin, the King's Head and then disappeared into the Angel. It was dinnertime. Penelope crouched down and peered through a windowpane. The tavern was sectioned into small alcoves, almost all empty. She backed across the street, set up with her flowers again and worked on an apple to pass the time.

A strike of the clock later, he was out. Greatrakes walked into the old city through Newgate and over to the massive old cathedral of St Paul's. He browsed amongst the stalls surrounding the cathedral and then passed under an arch into a side alley off Paternoster Row. Penelope peeked around the corner. The sign of a unicorn. An apothecary's shop. He came back out a few minutes later, a large parcel wrapped in brown paper under his arm. She couldn't see a purpose to his walk, he looked aimlessly through windows, stepped into random shops. *An unhurried stroll through a doomed city, a very odd walk indeed*, she thought. He stopped and looked around him before turning into a dark old passage. *This could be promising*, she thought. Tiptoeing up to the corner, she squatted down and poked her head around. He was making water. She pulled back and counted to thirty, then peered back down in time to see him disappear. She followed, picking him up as he stepped into a baker's on Bread Street.

He was in there for a good half-hour and yet he came out with no bread. Did they misplace his order? From there, he threaded his way back through the old streets to Charterhouse Hospital. Symon was gone. Penelope took up her position well outside the arch and saw Greatrakes leave two more times over the course of a very long day. Once to the Golden Fleece, a silk shop back at Paul's churchyard. She made a list of all the places he had visited, and planned to return tomorrow to see if she could discern any pattern to his behaviour. The bells began to ring all around her – St Bartholomew the Great, St Bartholomew the Less, St Giles Cripplegate – they were tolling the closing hour, the curfew. Night was falling, she should find Symon. And yet . . . she was not often near the old city, perhaps she should go home, her real home. Not far from her aunt and uncle's. A house on Chancery Lane. The lawyer who lived there these days likely had fled. She'd only been back a few times since her parents died, it was too painful. The furniture had changed, the wall hangings, but the smell was still that of her childhood: of happiness, the smell of warmed sugar that comes from age-old oak floors. She could find a blanket and curl up in the master chamber and remember her mother and father and the loving world they had built around her.

She bit her lip. Sometimes, though, when she returned, she got lost in thought and it might be sun-up before she knew it. She would come back another time. Soon. She needed rest, to recover from the Charterhouse spirits pressing on her all afternoon.

She would try Cheapside, instead. She often dreamed of living there. When she first left her aunt and uncle's and had not yet found her bearings, she would crouch outside the Cheapside homes, watching them with longing. Cheapside was a grand boulevard of merchant houses, the windows alive with candles, the rooms packed with merry families, and oh around the festive days how these families made her heart ache. She often spied on a friend she'd had when she was little. A girl named Charlotte. How Penelope envied her life! She hadn't really had a friend since Charlotte. When you're alone in a city full of people all too eager to take advantage of you, it's not easy to trust. That was why she liked Symon, he was kind to her, and asked nothing in return.

Penelope came upon the Cheapside house through a lane behind it. It was four storeys, the ground floor the family's shop, the floors above covered with an intricately carved oak façade and glittering bay windows, windows so big that Penelope would sit across the way and watch the family for days on end; watch them take their breakfast, bend their heads to their work, watch Charlotte laugh as she chased her baby brother around. When Penelope had taken to swallowing pebbles, hoping to trick her stomach into thinking it was full, when she had cried herself sick because she knew she would never hear her mother sing her to sleep, she thought of knocking. Surely they would remember her, take her in. And then tell her aunt and force her home. Charlotte, a married woman with children now, still lived in the same house. Penelope took out a hairpin, fiddled the lock and went up to Charlotte's room. A fine room panelled in oak, velvet bed curtains lush as a peach. She would sleep here tonight, and she would imagine a life in which her parents hadn't died; a life in which she was still surrounded by love, a love so rich that she felt made of honey.

*

Early the next morning, Penelope waited for Symon in his kitchen. She had put out bread and butter and herring for him. This had been her father's favourite breakfast. Butter to ease the heart, herring to wake the mind, he'd say. She had decided to put that night at Hutton Hall behind her. Was Symon telling the truth? Had he only slipped a note under Elizabeth's door? It mattered not. He was foolish for going, foolish for ever putting pen to paper and writing to Elizabeth. But Penelope could not spend any more time on Symon's weak heart; she must use him as she could. He was a flawed instrument, but the best she had available to her.

He sat down next to her at the old trestle table. 'Penelope, I had a thought.'

'Did you now?' she said. 'You look pale. Eat more herring.'

He shook his head, pushed the plate away. 'Yesterday, at Charterhouse. You really saw ghosts?'

She got up and fetched the herbs Joan had brought in from the garden that morning. Rosemary, thyme, sage. She ran her thumbnail down a stem of rosemary, paring off the leaves as she went. 'Here.' She handed Symon a knife and pointed to the growing pile of leaves. 'Chop these.' She took a deep breath. They were so angry, the ghosts. Dead for centuries but their ire as alive as anything. One was so frustrated, he was banging his head on the stone wall. She'd never seen so many at once, even *she* was daunted. They were like a hive, the strongest emotion of any given ghost running through them and changing them all. Even the mothers, mourning their missing children, who had been buried perhaps in another pit, had faces turned to rage instead of grief.

'You believe me, then.' She had never told anyone she saw ghosts, never was close enough to anyone to speak of it.

'I don't rule it out. Ghosts were banished out of England with the Catholic Church. But who am I to say what is real? God has delivered to us, or allowed, a pestilence that kills the poor and spares the rich. If that is possible, why shouldn't ghosts be?'

'I don't like to think on it,' she said. 'No good comes of meddling with them.'

'But if you can see them, perhaps they may be of help.'

She took the knife out of his hand, pulled over some turnips, began chopping. A crisp cut into something solid and resistant, this was far more satisfying than talk of the hereafter.

'Ah, you think I can talk to them.'

'Can't you?'

'No more than you can fly.' She'd never seen a ghost before her parents died. After they died, it was her most fervent wish. To see them again, to have them with her. Instead, little by little, the others started coming. In her darkest moments, she had sought out necromancers, witches, asked them how to communicate with the dead. The good ones counselled her to think no more on it. The bad ones talked of blood sacrifice; Penelope knew that would be a mistake.

'But we must try. Surely there is a way. They will want to help us, if . . .' Symon looked at her carefully, 'they are real.'

She continued to chop. Had moved on to potatoes. Looked around the kitchen to see if there were any joints of meat about; she had an urge to flay flesh off bone.

'I have tried. There is no good way. You bring yourself only trouble. You call to one, and they all come. Then they stick to you for days, the most stubborn, for months.'

He took the knife out of her hand; she was using it now to carve into Joan's table. 'If they want to follow you, I'll deliver a prayer to banish them, but we must try because we have so very few options. We can track these men, but we cannot be everywhere they are at all times. It is easier for them to know us and our routines, than for us to know them. Tonight we'll go into the churchyard, to the paupers' grave. We shall sit and ask. And see what appears.'

She gave a sad laugh. 'Symon, I do think I'm rubbing off on you. To think you'd suggest a midnight communion with the dead.'

'I am so well acquainted with their bodies these days, why not their parted souls?' He ran his hands through his hair, forcing it up into great clumpy tufts. He laughed, too; he was becoming more like her. 'Perhaps you are right. Or perhaps it is Boghurst's tonic, disrupting my mind.'

'Let's pour it out, otherwise the day will come when you will truly be in need of the poppy and it won't work. I'm surprised the apothecary still gives it to you.'

'You needn't worry, he dilutes it greatly, if he adds any at all. Still charges the same, mind you.'

'It is a cracked plan,' she said at last. 'They are the most erratic creatures, even more so than your Lizzie. They walk in circles. They go in and out of my vision. It's possible they see a different world, one that makes sense to them, for they make no sense to me.' She wiped the sweat from her brow; the August heat had breached the cool of the cellar kitchen. Was there no refuge? She dipped a corner of her apron in the water bucket, closed her eyes and put the damp cloth to her cheek. Yes, they could try. If nothing else, the girls might rise from the grave and she could study their bodies. Search for a clue that perhaps she had overlooked. She took the knife back from Symon, started to chop the vegetables again. 'I'll have a think.'

# 33

*A Chance Meeting on Hart Street, the Parish of St Paul Covent Garden*

'CALL OFF YOUR RAGAMUFFIN.' Valentine Greatrakes had come up behind Symon in the street. He was dressed in a suit of rose silk; a matching hat presided over his pearly ringlets and a band of excessive white lace hung from his neck. He looked like a giant powderpuff.

'Peanut. Putty. Nutty. What's her name?'

Symon swallowed hard, looked for a way to escape. He was heading home from Bow Street, had just finished the day's visits to the sick. He and a small army of yard boys usually crossed the parish each morning, taking stock and delivering goods. The guards would unlock their doors and pass to the sick – or their nurses, if those inside were blessed enough to have one – bread, beer, meat, clean linens. Symon and the boys would stand outside the windows and pass them gossip or sing with them, pray with them. He had more lists these days than he ever did see in his life, lists for who to visit next, what nurses were needed where, whose house needed to be cleaned. And a list kept close at all times, one for a secret trade in bodies. He was appalled at the order to shut in the well with the sick. So if the children were yet healthy, he had Bernard and Penelope steal them away to a safe house, and added their names to a list of which boy or girl was placed where.

But he also used this morning's visits to scout out Penelope's hiding places; she had disappeared again. The south side of Hart Street was taken up with the stables of the grand houses that fronted the next street over. He was peeking through a carriage-house window, wondering if he was brave enough to break in and check the house, when he had felt an abrupt smack on his shoulder.

'She's taken a liking to me, follows me around,' Greatrakes said. 'Has done all summer. It's annoying.' He gave Symon a hard look. 'As a matter of fact, she's been in my house. Spying on me. Does she think I'm her murderer? Wouldn't that be something?'

Symon stalled. 'Did you see that, over there?' He pointed down the street. So Greatrakes had seen Penelope, had he seen Symon too? He had gone in with her once. A disaster. He looked back at the mystic. 'There are a great many thieves about these days. I was just checking these houses for signs of a break-in, as it were. My word! Do you think that's what happened to you? A robber! What a fright that must have been!'

'Hmm. Constable in all matters now, are you? Now, your girl. What's she about?' Greatrakes tapped his cane impatiently. 'Was this your idea? As part of your little investigation? I'm offended.'

Symon kept his smile wide and polite. 'Come now.' He put a placating hand on Greatrakes' arm. 'Let us get out of the heat. A cup of punch, that's what's needed.'

'Suit yourself,' said Greatrakes. But he pulled Symon back when he tried to walk away. 'But here's how you can make it up to me. You can come to one of my shows.'

'Well, I—'

'Fabulous. Sunday next. Noon. Paul's churchyard, the real St Paul's.' Symon flinched. 'I expect a handsome turnout. And afterwards you can write a testimonial.'

*I'll do no such thing*, Symon thought. 'Not Charterhouse?' he asked.

'Nothing more I can do there now. Plague's taken hold of the place.'

Symon tried not to stare at the man's spidery fingers darting in and out of his sleeves as he straightened and fluffed his white lace cuffs. 'Plague makes me look bad. My talent only works on the run-of-the-mill stuff – at the moment. Don't go spreading that about!'

'But there's plague inside the City walls too. And a ban on crowds. Your shows could make things worse, all of those people packed together.'

Greatrakes waved a hand. 'I leave that to God. Besides, no one else is obeying the rules.'

'What will you do if someone with plague shows up? Will you turn them away? I don't think that would go over well.'

'No, you see, my dear, it can be quite a nice selling point. I can honestly say I've never had a plague patient come back for a second treatment.' He winked. 'Ulcers, palsy, usually I see them a second time. Not plague. I do try, you know. Spent all afternoon at my Lord Brunkard's, giving my plague preventative to his servants and those poor coconuts he keeps locked up there.'

'Locked up? The sick he's taken in? I didn't know he was locking them up.'

'Whatever you call it. They wouldn't sit still for me, nasty plops. Not a one. Would you like some for your household? I call it *Greatrakes' Arrows of the Almighty*.'

Symon looked at the row of modest homes on the north side of Hart Street – the dwellings of minor sea captains, shoemakers, barbers. Tried to ground himself in their plain building and uncluttered windows. It made his head hurt to try to follow Greatrakes, there were so many false turns in the conversation. 'I didn't know you liked to brew potions,' Symon said offhandedly.

'I don't. It's only . . . people are a bit shy about the stroking at the moment. No one really wants anyone to touch them, such a shame. Touch can be so healing, wouldn't you agree? But God does want me to make a living. Now, I grant you, and only you – because you are charged with keeping confidences, are you not? – that my water is more of a paper arrow at this point. Haven't got the knack of it yet. But I will.'

It was probably rat piss. Well, watered-down rat piss. Greatrakes was economical if nothing else.

'I'm working other lines, too. Something will come. Now let me ask you. Why would you think I am your killer? This disturbs me greatly. Not to mention what it could do to my purse if such a suspicion were made known.'

How direct he was! Symon feigned a nonchalant wave. 'Now I am offended that you would think me capable of such a thought! But this is rather fortuitous that you found me because I've been wanting your advice on this matter. Who do *you* think the killer is?'

'It's interesting you should ask, because I have thought about this. Namely when I saw that nightjar of yours fleeing my house the other evening. She was with some other halfwit too, do you know whom? I couldn't place the fellow. Oh, I'm not accusing you! Everyone knows you keep early hours!'

So he had seen them. A few days after Charterhouse, Symon had let the girl talk him into sneaking into Greatrakes' house. There they were, on Pall Mall, the middle of the night, it was all going well, they were as stealthy as cats, just as she'd taught him. They were nearing his bedroom – when Symon sneezed. They heard Greatrakes grumble and get out of bed at the noise. To their great luck, he tripped over something in his room, buying them time to slip down the stairs and out of the back door. They thought they had made it out unsighted. Apparently not.

Symon turned towards James Street. Time to get out of here, before the very ground turned to mush under him. Greatrakes followed behind.

'Really, Symon, are you sure you know what you're doing? You have a bloody butcherer on your hands. A dangerous person. I myself wouldn't go near someone so adept with knives. For one, I see the tiniest dab of the red stuff and I'm near to fainting.'

Symon scoffed. 'You treat the ill. You see blood all the time.'

He laughed. 'You have me there, don't you? You see, before God first spoke to me, I would vomit at even the smallest of wounds. I still feel the tendency, to tell the truth, but I'm better able to suppress the bile now that I see the wonders God works through me. And as you and your friends all too freely point out, I have other concerns that help me push past the queasies. Coin, my darling, coin. I need to keep it coming, in large amounts. I have hundreds depending on me back on my estate in Ireland. Poor wretches. But I digress. What would I do? Well, it's not a matter of what would I do, but what *will* I do, for I am as obligated as you are to get this menace off our streets.'

'You're offering to help?'

'Indeed I am. I've seen this kind of thing before. You're quite right, we must put a stop to it. And I think I can help you, you know.'

'In London?' Symon asked. 'There have been others?'

Greatrakes shook his head. 'No. Back in Ireland there was a faith healer working amongst my peasants. Blended several traditions to the point where I thought he was making it up. A bit of Celtic ritual, some Viking touches. New World things, too. Bizarre sacrifices all around. Mostly their clothes. He liked to bury them and build altars over them. I thought, "Those are perfectly good shirts and blouses! Has he gone mad?" Not like they had spares. I would say to my people, "Why would you give away the clothes off your back?" But they swore he was a miracle worker. I was right, though, he had gone mad. It wasn't only clothes he was burying. The sacrifices took on a more corporeal nature and I shall leave my story at that. In the end, it was a most gruesome business.'

'How did you end it?'

'Once he got word that I'd got word, he fled.'

'You didn't catch him? He is still out there?'

'Awful, isn't it?' His spidery fingers gave Symon a light drumming on the shoulder. It was meant to be friendly, but Symon cringed. They had reached his house, and Symon wondered how to keep Greatrakes out. 'But we shall catch your beast, you can count on me. You needn't rely on that spoiled bit of pudding any more. Shameful, that's all you've had for help.'

'I wouldn't say that,' Symon said. 'She's rather resourceful. Ingenious, one might say.'

Greatrakes laughed. 'Oh my. You're not developing a taste for her, are you? How your interests vary.'

A most unpleasant man. Had Greatrakes murdered the peasants on his estate? Was Symon witnessing a man whose mind had been cleaved in two? A murderer unknown to himself? Or the most clever of liars?

'Oh, stop your fidgeting,' Greatrakes said. 'You don't have to invite me in! I'm behind schedule, too. My point is this: as with my peasants, my networks in this town run deep. One doesn't spend all day treating the poor at Charterhouse and not learn the local gossip. This fellow will not be able to hide from me for long. He's too distinct. The poor, they'll protect a pagan. But a barbarous one for only so long.'

Symon looked at him. He sounded convincing, confident. What would Penelope make of this? He knew the answer. She'd throw him down a well.

'You think there is some sort of religious ritual involved, then? A lost or forgotten practice resurfaced?'

'Yes. Or a nurse. Mimicking her betters. Like that Mistress Mess of yours. Some poor old lady thinking she's doing her part, getting carried away. Putting on airs.' He reached out and made a show of inspecting Symon's face and hands. His touch was warm, soothing, Symon hated to admit. 'I *am* worried about you. When you first came back from that spa, I thought you were looking as fit as a flea. But now, those circles under your eyes, they're as dark as January. Brandy, that's what I suggest. Often as you can.'

'All out.'

'Sack then?'

'Gone.'

'My, my, you are playing with your life. Oh, don't get sniffy! Silly doctor's tales. Why if that stuff worked, we wouldn't be in this bother. My favourite is carrying one of Queen Bess' gold coins in your mouth and rolling it around with your tongue.

Absurd! If you're so foolish as to suck on a coin instead of spending it, then I say Britannia is better off without you. Besides, I don't need any prevention. I've got it all taken care of.'

'You do?'

'God needs me, haven't you been listening?'

Exasperated, Symon looked at Greatrakes. The ribbons on his hat, on his sleeves, on his breeches, his shoes; ribbons that would shoot out and cover Symon too if he didn't get away soon. He opened his front door, smiled at the fat packet of letters waiting for him on the table. Blessed be, there was one from Elizabeth. He opened it while Greatrakes prattled on. He read the note, frowned.

Greatrakes took the letter out of his hand. 'Dear me, moping over my Lady Gauden again? That won't do at all. Say . . . you should see her more often! She misses you! It must be terrible for her out there! All alone with a new babe, separated from its father . . .'

'Indeed,' Symon said through gritted teeth. He snatched the letter back and they stared at each other for a moment. Symon tried to read the man's face, that gleam in his eye. No, there was no way Greatrakes knew anything. No one knew but Symon and Elizabeth. This was his way. Greatrakes thought such talk amusing. A distasteful sort of companionship. Symon wasn't having it. 'Your conversation, you do manage to stray so in your talk.' He turned around and held the door for Greatrakes. 'I thank you for your offer, and please, anything you discover, tell me, for we have no time to spare.' *Your innocence may very well depend on it*, he thought.

'My show at Paul's churchyard, I'll start there. It'll be a rare gathering during these plague times and a wonderful opportunity to ask a good many people a good many questions.

And no one can work a crowd like I can.'

Symon sighed. Greatrakes was indeed a master showman. He'd seen it himself. But did God truly work through his hands? And, if so, why Greatrakes' hands and not Symon's?

'I know what you're thinking,' Greatrakes said, one foot out the door. 'I've seen that look many times in my life. Including from my dear wife, God rest her soul. It sounds preposterous, I grant you, and she didn't believe me at first either. But then she woke up one morning and her finger had shrivelled on itself and bent under. I put my hands on it and began stroking and I chased it right out of her and ever after she was my truest supporter.' He turned as if to speak to someone next to him. 'Weren't you, my dear?' He laughed as if sharing a joke, then looked wildly around him. For a moment, Symon thought he was about to cry.

Greatrakes settled his eyes on his great lace cuffs and continued. 'Indeed. Now my mother refused me until the bitter end. She had a poor sick kitten and I tried and tried but I couldn't make it better and she said God wouldn't give me a gift that only worked on people.'

'Was she a stubborn woman, your mother?'

'Not particularly. I was very fond of her, you know. When I was little, I remember going to a house near ours. My mother said I was to meet my very first friend. I was so excited. Thought of all the fun we would have. This boy, when he sees me, he says, "Why you look like your mother." And of course that made me happy for I thought the world of my mother. Then he says, "You both look like trolls." Said we had big ears, big fingers and teeth. Well, so you see, he didn't want to be my friend. Quite hard for a little boy to hear really. And to have someone say such awful things about one's mother. Life really is cruel, isn't it?' He sighed. 'Such hopeful little things we are, we expect to be loved, not hurt, and when it happens, the force of that first blow, well, it's unrivalled, isn't it? I like to think of it as God's first test of me. And once he got started, he didn't want to stop!' He gave a half-hearted laugh. 'It only got worse. No one really wanted to be my friend. It was a rather lonely life, until I met my wife. She thought I was wonderful. My wife and God.'

*He must wonder*, Symon thought, *why God intervened to save his wife's finger, but not her life.* That would most certainly test the faith of anyone. 'He meant for you to be with her,' Symon offered. 'He knew you were worthy of her.'

'No,' said Greatrakes, finally heading down the street. 'I most certainly was not.'

# 34

*Sunday, August 13th, Paul's Churchyard, the City of London, High Noon*

THEY'RE ALL HERE, *every member of the plague society*, Symon thought as he scanned the crowd gathered in front of St Paul's Cathedral in the heart of old London. (*Yes, the real St Paul's*, he could hear Greatrakes saying.)

The Irish mystic had drawn a most magnificent crowd. It seemed all of town – what was left of it – had come for the spectacle. A respite from their morbid thoughts, a hope that miracles still existed, to see God work through Valentine Greatrakes' hands. For the murderer, a chance to find a new victim.

'There is no person who knows me, but will acquit me of being excessive!' Greatrakes shouted.

*That couldn't be further from the truth*, Symon thought. He stood near the front, sweating like a mad bull under the noonday sun. Behind him, there looked to be several hundred people, plague be damned. It was a mixed group – merchants, servants, beggars. To the right of Greatrakes' travelling stage was a platform with a canopy for shade. Several very pretty ladies sat underneath, sipping what Symon imagined to be cool, thirst-quenching drinks.

'I invite any who disbelieve to purchase the knowledge of Truth. If you take me up on my offer, you shall learn that I have no further design than to distribute that Talent which the All-healing God has entrusted in me. No further design than the Honour of our Maker, and the good of His poor fellow creatures, whose distempers – and you have many of them! Yes you do! – neither Art nor Physick can reach.'

Mincy was in the back of the crowd. Dr Burnett at the edge closest to the cathedral, and Boghurst was up by the stage, in the shade of the ladies' canopy.

Greatrakes' little stage put him three feet off the ground. He was dressed rather soberly and looked much more like Symon.

'It is with great cheer, that upon hearing God's voice, I cast all worldly pleasures and delights behind my back' – *For this one moment*, thought Symon – 'that I ran myself into the midst of all diseases' – *Except plague!* – 'to make my House a Hospital' – *His house? What would Lady Ranelagh say about that?* – 'to forsake my own interests and advantages, to labour Day and Night, and oftentimes run the Hazard of my Liberty and Life by mingling with crowds like you with your pressings, steams and stinks and multitudes of Ulcerous Persons. But I say this because, as you know, few men can brook or bear to be near the ulcerous. I am one of the few!'

Murmurs spread through the crowd. They had come to see miracles, not to be insulted. Symon began to doubt the mystic's claim that his networks could reveal anything about these murders at all. If the man were a healer, the power did not extend to his words.

'Pass us the beer! Where's the beer?' someone shouted. 'We're like to stroke ourselves in this heat!'

Greatrakes, in the only sign of discomfort Symon had ever seen him make, fluffed away the white curls stuck to his neck.

Symon looked towards Boghurst, who was whispering to one of the ladies on the stage. He watched him carefully for a moment; he was still struggling to understand that night at St Gabriel Fenchurch's when they tried to dig up Dr Burnett's manservant. Ever since, Symon had been trying desperately to make his mind work, to recall the events of that strange situation. But he could remember little past the door closing behind them at his house as they set out.

'It has been seven years since I first had the impulse,' Greatrakes went on, 'the strange persuasion of mind, suggesting that God had bestowed on me the Gift of Curing. I have in that time cured thousands of poor souls through God's blessing. The king's evil! Ague! Deafness! Palsy! Violent Pains! Dropsy! Wind! Lameness! The Falling Sickness!'

'Can you cure her?' A man stepped forward, his arms around the waist of a woman hanging on to him for dear life. Her head was leaning on his chest, her eyes closed, her face marred by agony.

Greatrakes jumped down from his platform and helped the man around to the stairs. They carried her up together and lifted her on to a long table.

'From what does she suffer?' he asked the man.

'A swelling in her guts.'

A yell from the crowd: 'She's with child, you rabbit stink, get her down from there!'

The man turned to them. 'It isn't so! It comes and goes, swells to such a degree on a sudden that it's like to burst her!'

Greatrakes spat into his great hands and rubbed them

fiercely. He lay them gently over the woman's stomach and then his hands jerked upward as if he had been shocked.

'The man speaks the truth! I shall chase this ill humour out!'

He put his hands back down on her belly and traversed her body. 'It flies up to her throat! Do you see? Do you see the swelling now at her throat? The size of a pullet's egg!'

The people around Symon were pushing on each other, standing on tiptoe, trying to use him as a post to climb up to get a better view.

The woman gagged. 'It swells before us, it almost chokes her!' Greatrakes laid his hands down on her throat.

She screamed, 'I'm blind, my eyes, I'm blind!' She went silent and then her head lolled about, foam coming out of her mouth.

Greatrakes' hands jerked down to her chest and over to her shoulder and down her arm. 'I shall chase it out, out through her hand!' Symon was close enough to see rivulets of sweat streaming down the healer's face.

'It is stuck,' he cried. 'Stuck in her fist.' Her husband moved over and tried to open her fist, but couldn't get a finger to budge. Greatrakes wrapped his hands over her fist and squeezed hard.

'It is gone! NO . . . wait.'

The woman's tongue was sticking out of her mouth now, writhing in the air.

'It is where I want it. The tip of her tongue! I shall push it out from there!'

He ran his hands along her clothes, up from her waist, up through her throat and he stroked up around the curve of her chin. He repeated the motion. The woman violently belched, Symon had never heard anything so revolting in a woman. Her eyes were wide open now, darting from side to side. She stared at the crowd, her crazed eyes skipping from one person to the next. Then a church bell struck and the entire crowd jumped and the woman's body went limp.

'It is out,' said Greatrakes. 'It is OUT! Let us rejoice and praise God! This is His extraordinary doing, He has appeared before us, wrapping our souls in wonder and amazement, filling our heart with praises and Thanksgiving to the Almighty and Merciful Lord God, to whom be the Glory, the Power and Praise for Evermore After. My heart melts in Tears!'

His assistant, a small fusty-looking man, came up to Greatrakes and pressed a cloth to his forehead, mopping up the sweat. The woman was helped off the table by her husband, whom she hugged over and over. She turned to the crowd and smiled and waved. They walked down the stairs, still hugging and kissing. The crowd was overcome with joy, too, clasping hands with each other, taking the treats they had brought with them out of their sacks and sharing them. Huge mugs of beer were passed around, each person taking a sip and handing it to the next. *This is better than church*, Symon thought. *That's a problem.*

'Who be next?' Greatrakes asked after taking his own restorative sip from a (private) mug.

Someone was pushing through the crowd. Symon couldn't see who, somebody short and stepping on people's toes from the sound of it.

'Me,' it screeched. 'You can help me.' An old woman stumped out of the crowd. She was covered in rags and wearing a patched cap over her scraggly hair. Her left leg and arm were locked straight. And yet she looked familiar. *God save us*, he thought. It was Penelope.

'Help me up now,' she yelled when she reached the foot of the stage. 'Where's yer manners?'

Greatrakes and his assistant scrambled down the steps. They lifted her up and on to the table as if she were no more than a pile of sticks. He beamed at the audience, spread his arms wide and motioned towards her. 'Dear mother, tell us what tortures you?'

'Me leg, me arm. Born on the side of a hill and they never bent none since.'

Greatrakes turned to look at her and cringed. He recognised her. He looked out into the crowd and found Symon. Gave him a murderous squint. Greatrakes whispered something into Penelope's ear, then took a deep breath. 'Let us see what we can do.' He spat in his hands and rubbed them again. He reached over her prostrate body and put them on her left arm. He stroked around the elbow, then ever so slowly bent it into a right angle.

''Tis a miracle! God be praised!' Penelope shouted. Then she frowned. She reached over to feel her right arm with her newly cured left. 'Now this one is stuck! Can't bend it.' She was sitting up now, holding out a stiff right arm. Greatrakes moved over to it, stroked it with his hands. As the right arm started to bend, the left arm snapped straight. The crowd gasped. 'What's going on here?' she asked. 'Can't you make them both work?' Greatrakes crossed his arms, gave her a calculating look.

'Maybe try the legs?' The left was sticking straight out, the right, bent and dangling down off the table. Symon put a hand over his eyes, sneaked a glance from between his fingers. He could hardly bear to watch. Greatrakes spat and rubbed his hands and stroked along the left knee joint. It began to bend, and then her right calf snapped up.

'You got it all wrong!' Penelope said.

'Brother Croker, will you help me?' Greatrakes turned to

his assistant. 'Hold her bent leg, while I work on the affliction.' Croker moved over and put one hand on Penelope's calf and the other hand on her thigh.

'Scoundrel!' She slapped Croker's hand away. 'How dare you!'

*This is also better than church*, Symon thought. Croker adjusted his hands to wrap them both around Penelope's calf and Greatrakes began working on her right leg, snapping it bent. Both of her arms shot out, smacking him and his assistant in the head, knocking their hats off. The crowd roared with delight. Greatrakes swooped down to pick up his hat. He put it back on and turned to the crowd. He stretched out his arm and held one finger up as he locked eyes with them. He waited, motionless, until they were silent. He held them a few seconds more with his gaze, then said: 'I have seen this before. A difficult case.' He bowed his head in prayer, then looked up and said in a stage whisper: 'Possession.'

The word ran through the crowd like wildfire. Screams came from the platform of fine ladies; one of them had fainted. The others circled around her to fan life back into her. Symon's heart landed like an anvil on his feet. This was a treacherous game Greatrakes and Penelope were playing. Healing disease was one thing. But where there was a demon, there was a witch. Greatrakes might be angry enough to say Penelope was a witch, commanding her own demons. England didn't go in for burning witches these days, but it didn't mind hanging them.

Greatrakes rubbed his hands some more and touched her arms. She shrieked again. 'That hurts! Get away from me, you charlatan.'

The crowd was back on her side. 'Didn't pay her enough, did you?' someone shouted. 'Get her some silks and velvets next time!'

Greatrakes was looking at Symon again. He mouthed the words: 'Do something. Now.' Symon edged through the crowd towards the stage. What he would do once he got there, he didn't know.

'Brother Croker, hold her down. We may have to knock her out to cure this most trying of cases.'

'Will not,' Penelope yelled. 'Ow, he's pinching me! How is that godly? How is that good physick? Quack!'

The crowd booed and Penelope scooted off the table and thudded down the steps, playing the role of most aggrieved. 'To the Dolphin! I'll seek my comfort there!' She spat behind her. 'Shame on you! Pinching and pawing like that!' She headed towards the tavern; the crowd slowly peeled away, some following her, some heading back to work.

Greatrakes vaulted off the stage and landed nearly on top of Symon. 'I warned you. Keep your dross bucket away from me.' Symon looked around for an ally, an item to defend himself with if needed. 'She's near to ruining me with that stunt. If I ever see her again, I'll hang her myself.' He span around, leapt back up on to the stage and called for more volunteers.

# 35

*Calling the Dead, Symon's Churchyard*

IT WAS FOUR IN THE MORNING, yet there was no sweet relief of dew from this fetid August heat. Sweat streamed down Penelope's temples; Lord, she'd take off her skirts if she could. Symon kept his cassock on; she didn't know how he managed it.

'You must cease this business at once,' Symon said to her for the thirteenth time. 'You must not trifle with these men. They are powerful and they are low-minded. Not one would lose a wink of sleep if they damned you a witch.'

'You fear the wrong things.' She had chosen a spot near the old paupers' grave, where the first victims were buried. She sat down, arranged the paper and ink around her. A Bible. A crucifix, for who knew what would answer their call. They had sat for hours in Symon's office – he had lectured her most of that time; he was quite angry about what she had done to Greatrakes – waiting for the yard to clear, the boys to go to sleep in their shacks off the church alley, for Bernard to decide he could do no more for the world that night and head home.

But they were not alone. Out of the corner of her eye, she could see them standing outside the church gate. The yard boys who had died, somehow they'd got word, overheard Symon and Penelope perhaps as they talked. She had gone over to them, implored them to stay quiet, to not to speak of it, for if word spread of what she was about to do, they would be inundated with spirits wanting to get their messages across. The dead boys looked at her with hopeful eyes; she knew what they wanted. A promise. That if they behaved, after she was done, she would listen to them. 'Yes,' she said. 'I'll try.'

'What?' Symon asked.

'Not you. Now listen. You must stop your barking about those dreadful men, or the ghosts won't come forward. Remember, they've all killed someone! Either through their inept bungling or, in this most pressing case, through diabolical means. Now peace! Stop interrupting or we'll get nowhere tonight.'

Symon fell silent. 'No pouting, either,' Penelope added. She looked about the torn-up churchyard. The lush grass, the honeysuckle, the roses, the borders of red and white currant bushes. All of that was gone. In their place, dirt and rocks, scattered bits of bone and wood from old coffins dug up to make room; grave wax smeared over everything. Fresh burial mounds pushed up, the dead trying to break out belly first. Tombstones tilted at every angle, some soon to fall flat over in protest at the disruption. Much of the ground sat a few feet higher than it had in June. The bodies got closer to the surface with each new one stacked on, the gravediggers forced to throw ever more soil around to keep them buried. And in the far corner, a raw hole. The plague pit. The old paupers' grave was in another corner, and that is where she and Symon now sat. There was some comfort in this, that she would not have to cast her net widely over a pit of dozens, but over the grave of a few.

'We begin.' She wasn't afraid. They could bring forth a demon and she wouldn't be the worse for it. She'd known many a living demon in her life. Beleaguered was a better word for how she felt. That she would fail in this, as she had so many times before, and be left with a horde of phantoms to hound her for God knew how long.

She took Symon's hand. At least she had that. 'Here we go.'

She sat back on her heels. Closed her eyes and took a last deep breath, then stared at the paupers' grave. Called to it. 'Dearest Mary. Your sisters in woe. Are you there? Will you awaken? Come. Speak.' Her palm grew sweaty in Symon's hand, she saw his head nod a little, he was trying not to fall asleep. She closed her eyes again. It was actually pleasant to be out here with him, under the moon, holding his hand. *Bah*, she thought, she would not allow him to distract her. No matter that he smelled of hay, of meadow grass, of goodness.

Neither she nor Symon had stirred for some time when he asked, 'Is that it? That's all you say? Perhaps they didn't hear you?'

She opened her eyes, looked around her. 'Oh, they heard me. A good many. They stand all around us, waiting most patiently. The yard boys must have told them I had my rules.' One of them was wishing her dead. It was the baker's man. He was sitting in a manner not appropriate for a churchyard. 'That one over there, I used to work with him.' She minded the ovens and baked the loaves while he did the heavy lifting – wood, sacks of grain, the baker's wife, no doubt – over at Half Moone Street. She stopped taking her meals with them because his slimy looks put her off her food. His rather fond opinion of himself led to her eventually carrying a knife with her at all times. If it wasn't the baker, it was his man.

She faced him full-on. 'Oh, I see the blood in your eyes, I do,' she said calmly. 'And I see that bloodstain over your heart.' When the baker and his family fled town in the middle of the night, leaving them behind with orders for his man to watch the bakery and Penelope to fend for herself, it had only been a matter of hours before he had tried to pin her to a wall.

'Didn't like my farewell, then?' she said to the ghost. 'Think you're not finished with me, eh? Move along, there's nothing for you here.' The ghost growled at her, she growled back. Symon gripped her hand tightly. 'Do we growl at ghosts?'

'What an absurd question,' she said. Then, 'Can you see them at all?'

'I see the air shimmer . . .'

'Yes, that's them. They are without ease.'

'No, it is the heat coming off the braziers Bernard keeps lit to cleanse the air.'

She gave Symon a sour look; he softened his tone. 'What about the girls?' he asked. 'His victims?'

'They're all here.' Symon's servant Mary, the others – they looked at each other in surprise as Penelope spoke, as if they hadn't known until now that they were part of a sad sisterhood. Their inked lines, their brutal wounds, shorn heads, their heavy eyes, they stood out even amongst the damned.

'Try.' Penelope felt her strength waning; the misery surrounding her was oppressive. 'You speak to them, Symon.'

He looked about, hesitant. Then closed his eyes. For far too long. Penelope poked him. He let out a heavy breath, began. 'Mary . . . It was my duty to care for you. I should have been here. I . . .' His voice faltered. 'Help us find him. Stop him from hurting any more girls . . . Let us protect them as I failed to protect you.'

The girls all began talking at once. Penelope grew frustrated, for they spoke of loose stitches, of lame horses, curdled milk, coals that wouldn't light, hammers that hit backward. It all came out garbled. They so desperately wanted to talk, and when they couldn't be understood, they became irritable or sullen. Some shouted, some cried. Some started to leave, some shoved their way to the front. One was the ghost Penelope had seen out in Burntwood. The young woman, dressed in ashes. 'Who are you?' she asked. Fine blonde locks pinned in intricate curls. Then the ghost reached out her arm. She was asking Penelope to follow.

# 36

*A Wild-Ghost Chase*

THE MYSTERIOUS GHOST LED them all over the parish. Or was it Penelope who led them? Symon could see nothing and many times over wondered if Penelope was lying or hallucinating. Every now and then, he imagined a flicker ahead, or an icy touch. Was it real?

The sad young woman first led them into the church, or so they thought. The ghost had walked right through the church wall, Penelope said. They searched the crypt, for one of the girls had been placed there during Boghurst and Mincy's examination, then the offices, the gallery, the attic, even the belfry, but found no trace of her. They went out into the piazza for a breath of night air, and Penelope found her waiting for them. The ghost headed north and disappeared into an empty house. Penelope found a way inside, dragging Symon with her. They searched the house from top to bottom; every step of the ghost a potential clue. Was the house the site of a murder? The home of one of the victims? Only for Penelope to find yet again the ghost waiting in the alley behind the building. And on it went. It took an hour to get to Long Acre, and then the ghost turned back south, walking straight through shops, houses, carriages, never understanding that Penelope and Symon couldn't do the same. They were sitting at Charing Cross, amazed they had made it that far and also weary with the stops and starts. As they went, Penelope had been gathering bottles and odd morsels from the places they searched, and so as the sun rose, they sat a moment to share her hard-earned but illicit feast.

'When I first started seeing them,' she said, 'they were my dearest friends. It was after my mother had died. I was alone in my room, and thankful to be alone, for my aunt and uncle were poor company indeed.' This was the first she had talked to Symon of her past. He made not a move, for he was eager to hear more and afraid that the slightest disturbance would cause her to retreat. 'And one night, I had been crying, I opened my eyes and there was an old woman, sitting next to me on my bed. Her hand was on my foot, a loving touch, and she smiled at me, nodded, and stayed with me for hours. But when the sun came up, she was gone.

'She filled me with such hope, but over time, I grew to hate her. I thought if I saw her, surely I would soon see my parents. That they would appear to me and comfort me. But they never did. Of course, in my child's mind I thought it meant they hadn't really loved me. Oh, how I tormented myself. But over time, I realised something else. For I saw every manner of ghost, and most of them were not pleasant as this woman had been. And then one day . . .' She stopped, wiped her eyes. He took her hand, whispered for her to go on. 'I finally understood why I couldn't see them.'

'Ah, I think I know why,' Symon said with a gentle smile.

'Yes . . . they weren't ghosts. They were together. They

weren't stuck, and they were waiting for me in a happy place.' The morning sun had peeked over the gables, throwing a pink wash on the world around them, on Penelope. Despite their sleepless night, she seemed to glow. 'And that kept me alive. For I knew if I were to let myself go, I wouldn't be able to join them. I would be stuck, like the others.'

And then Symon felt his own tears, thankful that she had realised this, for if she hadn't, she would not be here with him now, and he had a blurry sense that without her by his side during this plague season, he would be completely lost. As she spoke of her past, it seemed the most natural thing in the world for him to lean over and kiss her. And so he did. She kissed him back, and then he gasped in pain. She had grabbed him by the crotch. 'We'll have no more of that, Rector,' she said before letting go. She got up and started walking down towards the river. 'Time for a bit of rest. If you feel a brush of fingers across your neck, 'tis our ghost, and come find me.'

'Where?' he shouted after her.

'Don't worry. I'll make it easy for you.'

*

Symon was actually quite terrified of seeing her again; he shouldn't have kissed her, it was a trespass, an abuse of power. She was right to stop him. He paused. For a moment, however, before pushing him away, she had kissed him back. Hadn't she? Should he speak of it? Or pretend it never happened?

He would apologise anyway, he had no business treating her so. He found her sleeping in the bedchamber next to his later that morning; felt himself as confused as ever. She was lying on her back, boots still on, one of Symon's cassocks wrapped around her. He was surprised to find himself thinking she looked quite lovely. He hadn't noticed earlier, but her hair was smooth and lustrous; her alabaster skin rather striking against the black of his cassock. She had washed and yes, looked almost a dark angel. One who had not shunned him because of his many failures and shortcomings. Yet.

He sat a cup of whey on the table next to the bed for when she awoke and slipped out of the room. He had been alarmed, of course, to find her sleeping there, and had gone down to the kitchen to ask Joan what he should do. His housekeeper shrugged, said the girl had been sleeping there for some time now and she thought Symon knew and it was too late to fuss about it now, wasn't it?

He climbed back up the stairs and considered whether to force Penelope to at least sleep in the garret with his other servants. *But she isn't my servant*, he thought as he looked at her. He didn't know what she was. Besides, there could be no real harm. There was no one to gossip about Covent Garden's rector and the scandalous liberties he took with his household. The vicar over at St Martin's, who would gladly tell all the world, was dead.

He picked up a letter on his desk. He had started writing it the day before. It was to Elizabeth. She oft wrote these days that Symon wasn't telling her the truth, was holding something back. He thought this rather coy of her, considering . . .

*You enquire what ministers are dead. For you heard of some, and would know the truth.*

He looked down the list he had written:

*Mr Peachell, St Clement's*
*Mr Mandrill, at Benet Fink*
*Mr Austin, of St Mary Stainings, I think*

*Mr Stone, minister of Alphage, I think*
*Mr Bastwick, preacher at the Counter in the Poultrye*
*Mr Welbank, minister at St Saviour's, Southwark*
*Mr Throckmorton, curate of St George's, Southwark*
*Mr Phillips, who officiated for Mr Hall, St Michael Basishaw*

He added:

*Mr Crumwell, vicar, St Martin's in the Fields*

The news of the vicar's death had come to him early this morning, after prayers. He was not sorry for the man, though he was sorry for the family he had left behind and what would happen to them. He dipped his pen in ink, continued:

*I may well suppose you are in good health and put yourself to little trouble on my account. You are right that I have not told you many things that have happened here.*

He had not written of late because he knew not what to say. How to explain any of it? For his part, he read each of her letters with a growing resentment. She said little of the baby, and left him with the feeling that in the ways that were important, she had abandoned him.

A loud snore came from the other room; he put down his pen and listened, then thought about what he would do when Penelope awoke.

# 37

*A House That Boasts No Fewer Than Nine Hearths, Fenchurch Street, the Old City of London*

'We must leave now,' Symon hissed.

Penelope squeezed his hand. 'No, they'll never know we're here. They do this every night.' They were inside Dr Burnett's house and could hear the doctor and his wife shouting above them. 'Shh, we may learn something.'

It was one in the morning. Penelope had sent Symon a note, asking him to meet her outside Dr Burnett's house on Fenchurch Street in the City. She took him in through the kitchen, and they wound their way up the servant stairs.

'How many times?' he heard Dr Burnett's wife shout through tears. 'How much is enough? When will you think us safe?'

'He has ordered her to fumigate the house yet again,' Penelope whispered. 'He fears he brings it home with him every night, he wants her to clean the house top to bottom each day.'

Penelope had been there that morning to watch the latest scrubbing. The chimney sweeps came at sun-up – even the flues were to be scrubbed daily – and from the moment they arrived, the house was filled with the clang of buckets, furniture scraping across the floor, and the cries of Mrs Burnett. His wife often had to find new help, to replace those who had disappeared or died, and Penelope that morning had managed to get into the house as a maid. She had helped the other girls pound the rugs and flood every crack in the walls or furniture with vinegar. They sanded and scrubbed the floors, the pots, the pans. She had mistakenly picked up the wrong wax and turned an oak cabinet black, so the mistress had sent her out to the garden to work. She had been on her knees, washing each leaf by hand, when another maid brought her a bucket of fresh water.

'They're queer ones, aren't they?' Penelope had said to the girl. 'Never been asked to do this before.'

'Next is the stones,' the girl replied.

'Lord, we'll be here day and night.'

'Better in here washing stones, than out in the streets,' the girl said.

'Been here long?' Penelope asked.

'Not too long.' A week, she said. The last girl before her, she didn't know much about her, or the girl Penelope had been hired to replace. She knew there were lots of servants abandoned by their masters ('Happened to me, too,' Penelope told her), and no one was eager to take in a stranger, so she considered herself blessed to get this position.

'Still, it is odd master wants this done every day,' Penelope continued.

'He can ask me to do whatever he wants,' the girl replied. She got up and brushed her dirty palms on her apron. 'Gives me a roof and bread. And for that I'm grateful. You should be grateful, too, and stop that tongue of yours.'

Penelope had watched her walk out of the back gate to dump her bucket of dirty water into the street. Gratefulness was an emotion Penelope could not abide. It was insidious, led you to put up with all sorts of wrongs. There were two other girls working in the house but they had toiled with their heads down, silent. They were afraid, Penelope knew, for their lives, for the loved ones they hadn't yet lost.

As she worked her way around the house, she would slide a drawer open, look under a stack of books, unfold a letter. She had offered to clean the doctor's study; were her drawings in there? But the doctor's wife said no, she would take care of that herself. She offered to do the wash. No one else wanted to touch the doctor's clothes. She put on gloves and inspected each collar, each shirt, each cravat carefully for stains. But they were all spotless. She didn't see how this was possible. How could one treat patients every day and not have a single drop of blood or phlegm upon them? Dr Burnett must be hiding his soiled clothes, changing into clean ones before he came home, she told Symon as they crouched in the doctor's hall that night.

'He makes his assistant do it,' he replied.

She and Symon both jumped as they heard a crash above them. Something had fallen – or been thrown – to the floor. Penelope felt Symon's hand grab hers. She shook it off. They hadn't talked about what had happened the other night. She was quite pleased about it really. But she didn't want him to know that, and she wasn't about to encourage him to try again. It was all too easy for him to behave as such under the cloak of night. How would he treat her in the light of day? She flinched again; Dr Burnett's wife had thrown something heavy against the wall. 'Chamber pot is my guess,' she whispered to Symon.

'All you care for,' they heard his wife scream, 'is order, cleanliness! That the paintings aren't crooked, that the sheets are crisp! But why? Why! How will this save us? Why must we allow these slatterns to come into our house? Is it not better to let the house be as it will than to bring stranger after stranger and God knows what filth they carry into our most private of spaces?'

They heard a brushing sound on the ceiling above them; it was probably the doctor sweeping up the pieces of whatever his wife had smashed. His wife paced about him, they could hear her dainty steps tracing a circle. The doctor got up and murmured something, they heard him walk out of the room then come back. He spoke to her in low, loving tones; Penelope strained to hear what he said, but couldn't make it out. His wife stopped crying, there was silence. Then a scream and she ran to the door and threw something down the stairs. 'Blood! You bring me blood?!' A trinket of some sort, small and round, bounced down the steps, flashing in the moonlight as it went. Penelope tiptoed over to catch it. She held it up to the window and caught her breath. It was a ring, a polished ruby snug in a bed of gold; a perfect bubble of blood.

*A poor choice indeed for a doctor's wife, but it suits me fine*, Penelope thought, putting it on. She crooked her newly bejewelled finger for Symon to follow and they crept into the doctor's study, all the while listening to the cries rise and fall in waves from above.

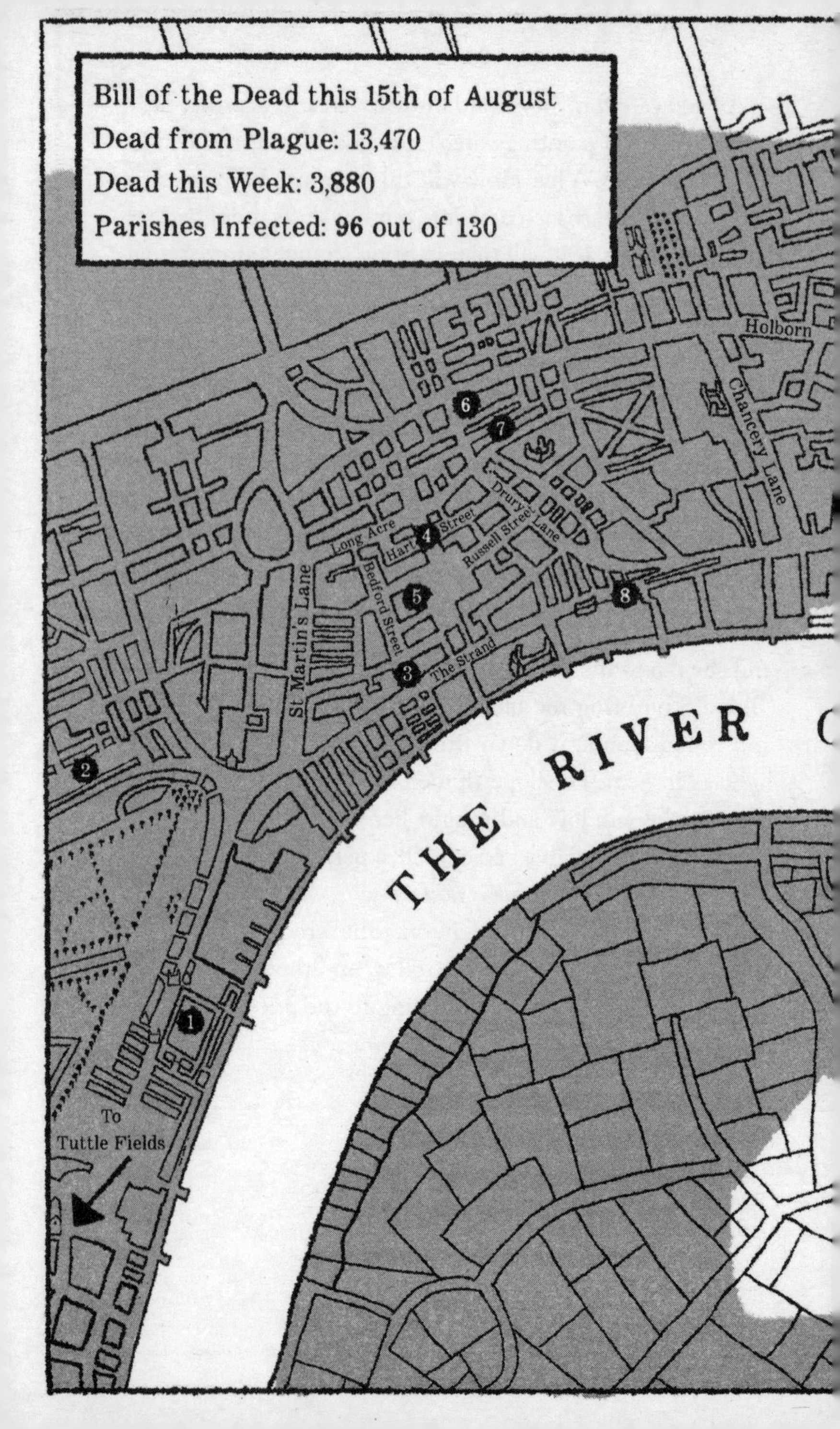
Bill of the Dead this 15th of August
Dead from Plague: 13,470
Dead this Week: 3,880
Parishes Infected: 96 out of 130
Holborn
Chancery Lane
Drury Lane
Russell Street
Hart Street
Long Acre
Bedford Street
St Martin's Lane
The Strand
THE RIVER
To Tuttle Fields
1
2
3
4
5
6
7
8

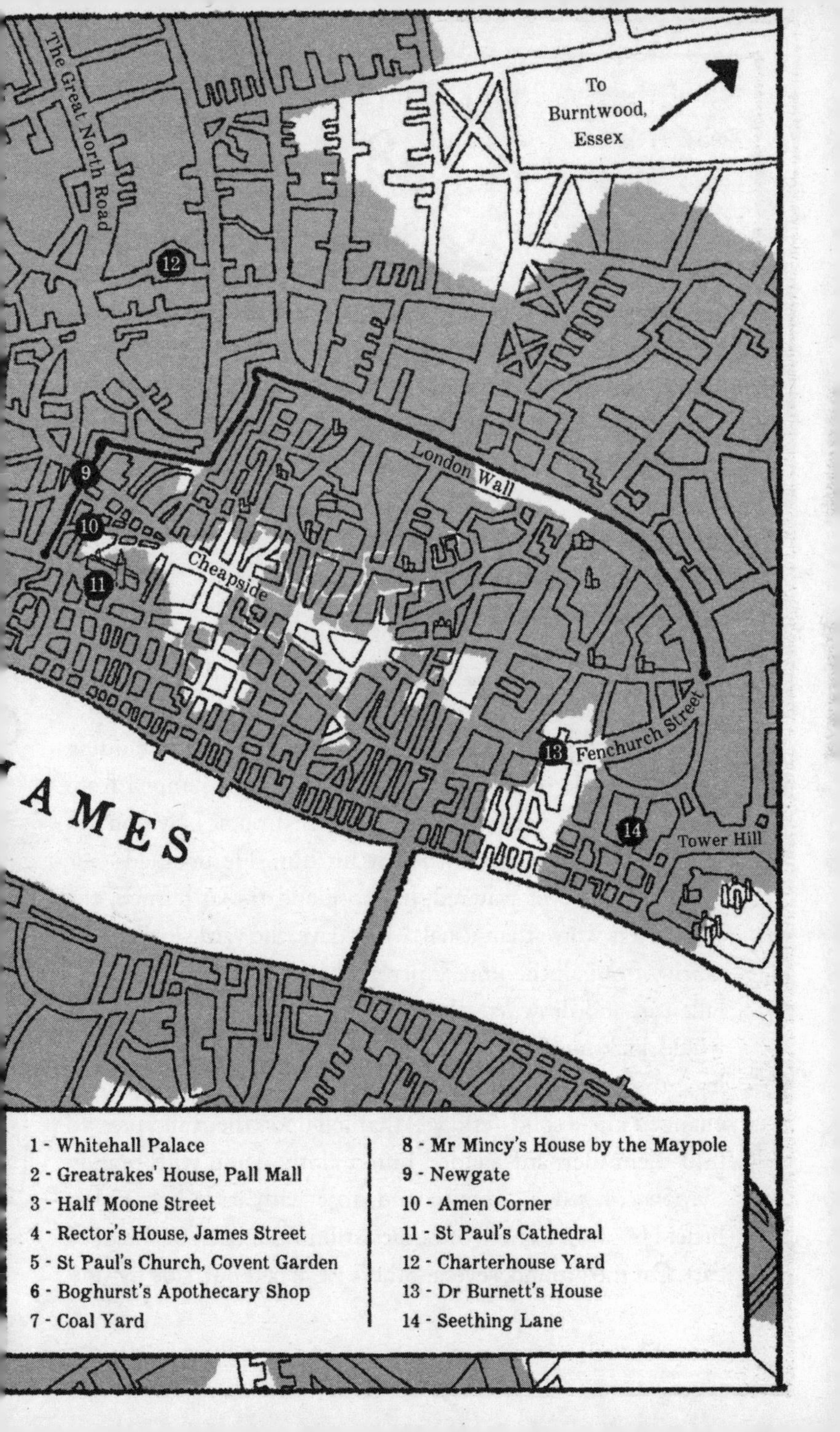

The Great North Road
To
Burntwood,
Essex
12
London Wall
9
10
Cheapside
11
Fenchurch Street
13
AMES
14
Tower Hill
1 - Whitehall Palace
2 - Greatrakes' House, Pall Mall
3 - Half Moone Street
4 - Rector's House, James Street
5 - St Paul's Church, Covent Garden
6 - Boghurst's Apothecary Shop
7 - Coal Yard
8 - Mr Mincy's House by the Maypole
9 - Newgate
10 - Amen Corner
11 - St Paul's Cathedral
12 - Charterhouse Yard
13 - Dr Burnett's House
14 - Seething Lane

# 38

*Thursday, August 17th*
*The Churchyard, Covent Garden*

THE NIGHT WAS DEEP. Torches flamed down the stone path, with more circling the plague pit that was once Symon's beautiful, orderly churchyard. He could see a cluster of bodies next to the hole, but the gravediggers were standing on the far side of the yard. A sparkle of light jumped from one man to the next – a bottle for their troubles. Symon got halfway down the path when it hit him. He doubled over, retching. His eyes watered, his nose and throat burned; the stench was worse than usual. Most days, the yard smelled like a privy from all the lime, a privy where many an animal had fallen in and drowned. Breezes were insufferable; the winds would kick up the stench and send it twining around their legs, their arms, their bodies. But this eve, the vapours had changed into a solid, fetid veil that fell upon them and pressed into them. Bernard handed him a cloth, damp with brandy. Symon covered his mouth and nose with it. It helped but little. He saw a tumble of bodies still in the back of the dead cart. On the ground, several others were laid out, side by side, a cloth draped over each. Penelope was already there, standing motionless beside them.

'They are like the others,' she said. 'Only worse.' He bent over and pulled back the shroud on the first one. The man's face was a purplish black, the skin shiny and taut. The cheeks and jaw were so swollen that the lips and eyes were compressed to black slits. Yet he recognised him. The draper, from over on Long Acre. A sickening feeling crawled up from his stomach. How could that be? They left town. Didn't they? There were ulcers of different depths near the buboes on the man's neck. Around each one he could see the dark lines of an inked square.

Symon felt a growing heaviness, as if his limbs were turning to stone. He counted the other bodies. Five. A family. The three in the middle, smaller than the man. A dainty foot arched out from the shroud; the toes slightly pointed, as if waiting to slip into a dancing shoe. He looked at Bernard. 'Is that . . . Theodora? Theodora Thurgood?'

He had said goodbye to them. Under the church portico. It had been his first service back after taking the waters. He had kissed Mrs Thurgood goodbye; wished them a safe journey. They were leaving that afternoon, the mother had told him; they were to wait out the plague with family in Kent. He remembered his reaction when pretty (but ever so pushy!) little Theodora told him that upon their return to town, after the distemper was gone, she would hold him to his earlier promise of daily spiritual guidance and would arrange a Bible study with him for every day at three of the clock.

Bernard was shaking his head. 'Thurgood fell down in the street before they even got home that day. The damn fool shoulda waited until they were inside, given the family a chance to escape.' He pulled the shroud back over Thomas

Thurgood's face. 'People saw him rolling in the street. Swarmed 'em and shut up the whole family.'

'Why didn't you tell me?'

'I did.'

Symon felt the blow of those two words as if Bernard had used his fist. Had he told Symon? He searched his memory for what else had happened that day, and as he remembered, a fireball of pain exploded behind his eyes. For that was the day he had fled town for Hutton Hall. For Elizabeth. He forced himself to pull the shroud away from Theodora. Her red curls were gone. Her bodice was cut open and she was wearing several twine necklaces of differing lengths. There was a pouch tied at the end of each and laid atop those nauseatingly familiar inked squares. One at the base of her throat, one over each lung, one at the top of her abdomen. One over her heart.

'The necklaces were all a tangle when she came in,' Penelope said in a tight voice. 'I sorted them out, to see what he was doing.'

'What's in them?' Symon reached over to pick up one placed over her chest.

'Amulets. There are more tied to her legs and arms. The ligatures are there too, on her wrists and ankles. On all of the bodies.'

He opened the pouch, tilted it to catch the torchlight so he could see inside. A dried powder with some larger pieces. He reached in and pulled one out. A small white bone. A leg bone of some sort. 'From a bird?' he asked.

'No. A toad.'

He dropped it in revulsion. Reached for the one over her heart.

Penelope stopped him. 'Don't touch that one. It's a walnut filled with mercury. Poisonous to the touch.'

Symon looked away, to hide his face from Penelope. He had failed them. His mind began painting pictures, unwanted pictures. He saw the murderer, torturing them all together. They would've heard each other's screams, powerless to help. An endless terror, until it wasn't. He dragged himself away from the bodies, stumbled out through the front gate; his body barely responding to his orders. He tried to recover his breath, tried to ground himself in the stars. It was a clear night, the moon waning. There was the swan high above him, its wings stretched and soaring down the middle of the sky, the dragon lurking right below it, ready to break its neck. The heavens were as violent as earth.

He heard Bernard come up beside him, hand him a flask. Symon took a deep swig, felt the life return to his body. Bernard pulled him up and they walked back. Penelope was rearranging the torches to throw more light on the bodies, a pot of ink and a board with paper on the ground. 'Get out of here, girl,' Bernard said. She ignored him, squatted down next to Theodora and began to sketch her. But then for some reason she changed her mind. Penelope rolled up her paper, picked up the ink pot and left.

Symon heard the slow clop of horses behind him, fell again to his knees beside Theodora's corpse. Another dead cart had arrived.

*

'Last man standing, I am.' Boghurst showed up as the yard boys had put the third round of dead that hour into the pit. 'Present company excluded.' He looked at Symon, his drawn and haggard appearance. 'Maybe.'

Symon didn't have it in him to respond, he sat staring at the ledger before him; the names of the dead in it. He was in his church office, had just written down each of the Thurgoods. The apothecary stood by him near the window, flapped the edges of his shirt to circulate air around his torso. 'A flaming, weeping mother of a day,' he said. 'Greatrakes is gone. Word is the king requested him at court. Left right after his show. I'm sure that's a lie, spread by Greatrakes himself. More likely he made a run for it. Coward.'

*That is curious*, Symon thought. *Mildly.* It was no great surprise the mystic had left town. All his paying patients were gone and he didn't hide that he wouldn't touch plague.

Boghurst flopped down on the chair next to Symon, then covered his mouth and started coughing, as if something were caught in his throat. Symon pounded his friend on the back, and once he had settled, Boghurst picked up a Bible and fanned himself with it. 'Lost count of how many died on me. One woman, I thought she was a rare one to pull through. Saw her yesterday, she was raving like a lunatic. Talked about how crowded the chamber was with all her relatives coming for Sunday dinner and how she had nothing to feed them. But no one was there! Just her husband, whittling away in a corner, and a nurse. She kept on talking, saying how good of them it was to stop by and she sent her boy to fetch a roast duck and some cakes from the Rose. But there was no boy! He had died a few days before. Then she sat up in her bed and wrapped her arms around the air and kissed it. She said it was her dear father, whom she hadn't seen in years. She scared me so! Every time I moved she told me to be careful, I had stepped on so-and-so's foot. I thought she would be dead by nightfall.' He took a drink of the brandy on Symon's desk, spat it out. 'Tastes like rot. Everything does.' He started coughing again and tried more brandy once the fit subsided. 'Went to her house this morning, just in case. And she was up and out of her bed, sweeping the floor, a good soup on the fire. Said she was feeling fine. I took her pulse, it seemed strong and steady. Her tokens seemed softer, lessening. I was going through my bag, trying to remember what medicines I gave her – I throw stuff at them these days – when there was a knock at the door. She went over and opened it. There was no one there, least not of the kind that I could see. But she started smiling and said, "Wonderful . . ." and then fell down dead on the spot.'

Symon watched the apothecary closely as he went on to tell of another patient, another death. He made himself seem a martyr, to stick so closely by the dying. Was he? *The man has seen so many plague patients*, Symon thought. Had for months. With no one watching over his shoulder. Until now. Penelope had spent some time visiting Boghurst's patients after he left them. Said he had a surprisingly gentle touch and did very little other than to cool their fevers with cold cloths and gave them a special concoction that he said would take away their terrible thirst. She had taken a sip of it; said it tasted of nothing more than sugar water. What was disturbing, however, she had reported, was that like Mincy, he had taken to drawing grids if he used a balm or amulet on a sore to more accurately track results. Penelope said she was rather stumped by this, had told Symon that while she had no doubt that Boghurst was as amoral as Mincy, that he wouldn't think twice to adopt a method from a murderer if he thought it effective, she could not illuminate the timeline. Had Boghurst adopted the practice of grids? Or was he in fact the source of it? The answer eluded them. And Boghurst was clever. He knew Penelope had followed him, he had told Symon so that blasted night they tried to dig up Burnett's manservant. But Symon also knew that Boghurst didn't take her seriously. No one did. Symon looked at the little spikes of his friend's hair, his bloodshot, sleepless eyes. Could the man have two sets of behaviours, two sets of treatments? This time, when Symon showed him the bodies, he would watch his reaction very closely. He said little as he led Boghurst outside to where Theodora and her family lay. He nodded for Bernard to pull back their shrouds and turned to look at his oldest friend's reaction.

Boghurst stared blankly at the bodies, scratched at his head. Finally, he turned to Symon and said, 'Burnett must be stopped. Symon, you must go there now. Take Bernard. Force Newgate to take him. He won't last long, every rotted fever known to man breeds there.' He made a hasty gesture for Bernard to cover them back up. 'Otherwise, we'll have to kill him ourselves.' He turned to go but doubled over as a coughing fit came upon him again. He grabbed his thighs to steady himself, then spat out something Symon refused to look at. 'I must go home, I'll come back tomorrow. I need rest. It's this charnel fever. The one you gave me by leaving me to rot at St Gabriel Fenchurch that night. Thought I had it licked, keeps coming back.'

Symon followed him as he stumbled towards the piazza. 'How do you know? Why are you so sure it's Dr Burnett?'

'I know him.' He was wheezing now. 'His inhumane nature. His poor medicine. He's realised his training is useless. It's all words and theory and calculations. From books, fancy degrees. As a physician, he was taught never to touch the body. That it was beneath him. All too late, he's understood the failings of his training. What we see before us is a desperate man, trying anything he can.' He coughed again, this time the fit turning to vomit. He rested for a moment by the side of the church gate. Symon handed him a clean handkerchief; the apothecary pushed it away, wiped his mouth with the back his hand.

Symon frowned, deeply worried about his friend. What ailed him? Coughing was rarely a sign of plague. But Boghurst had mentioned that perhaps the disease was changing. 'What can I get you? More brandy? Sack? Wait here; I'll be right back. It will help.'

'Can't wait.' He paused, doubled over again. 'He thinks himself a saviour, all knowing. But he does not truly care for life. For if he did, he would not have desecrated the first law of physick. Do no harm.' The apothecary's voice had grown hoarse. 'I'll be back. Soon as the sun's up.'

As Symon watched him go, Penelope stepped forward out of the shadows.

'Was that a confession?' she asked. 'Was he talking about Dr Burnett? Or himself?'

Symon let out an anguished sigh. He didn't want to think it.

Penelope picked up a torch. 'Leg Alley is where the Thurgoods lived. This time, we know where he butchered them. Let us pray he left something behind.'

*

Leg Alley was a tight passage not far from Symon's house. The alley was no wider than a horse; the cobbles thick with rubbish. Most of the houses were shut up, red crosses bleeding on the doors. A night guard stood watch about every seventh house. The Thurgoods had lived at the far end; the door to the family's apartments on Leg Alley, the shop front on Long Acre. Symon held up his lantern, surveyed the building. The wood panels and trim were done up in burgundy. Elegant gold letters swirled across the top of the shop front, announcing, 'T. Thurgood & Co.' The windows below were smudged; tattered sheets thrown across them for curtains. Theodora would be horrified.

Symon and Penelope started with the guard nearest the house. He looked no bigger than a boy, the top of his head falling well short of Symon's chin. But this was no youth. His hair had long gone grey, his face had the collapsed look of a miner, there wasn't much to him but a stunted frame of thin bone.

'Aye, watched that house most nights,' the guard told them. The father was the first to fall ill, the grandmother the first to die, he said. 'She went in a day, buried her over at St Martin's.'

'The south side of Long Acre belongs to my parish. Why was she sent over there?' Symon asked, indignant.

The man looked at him out of yellowed, drooping eyes; shrugged. 'She liked things proper, the old lady did. They see you right at St Martin's.'

Symon ignored the slight. 'Then what happened?'

For a while, all was well, the guard went on. The father seemed to be recovering. The family regularly sent the watchmen on errands for them, to fetch food and such. Then all within a day of each other, the rest took to their beds. The guard hadn't heard anything out of there for at least a week.

'They died? They'd been left in there – dead – for a week?'

'Makes no difference to them.'

Symon stared at him, guilt flooding through him. If he had known – if he had paid attention – they might still be alive. They at least wouldn't have been tortured to death.

'You didn't think to check on them, ask them to the window?' Penelope asked.

'Nights are for sleeping. Not for me to disturb 'em.'

'You knew they were dying,' Penelope said, disgusted.

The guard looked past her, chewed on the unlit pipe he had between his teeth.

'Did you see anything at all unusual?'

The guard shrugged. 'Just that nurse. Mother of the Devil, she was.'

'A nurse? What nurse? Who sent her?'

The guard snorted, looked Symon over head to toe. 'Who did you say you were?'

'I'm the rector!'

'Not my rector. This here's St Martin's. Where've you been?'

'No, it's not.' Symon wanted to brain him. The man was wrong. Long Acre was shared by both parishes, the north side belonged to St Martin's. But the south side was Symon's. The old folk might like to dispute it, but a boundary was a boundary.

'The nurse. Where is she now?'

'If God has any mercy, she's dead. Never seen such an ugly woman in all my life.'

Symon cursed under his breath.

'I agree,' said Penelope. 'He's a real rat-fucker.'

The man scowled and spat at Penelope's feet; she shoved her torch in his face as if to burn him. Symon pulled her towards the door, told the guard to stay there, he hadn't finished questioning him. But he wanted a look inside first.

'Can't. They locked it back up.'

'Never mind,' Penelope said. 'We'll come back tomorrow.' She looked at Symon. 'There'll be more light then. Let's go.'

She led him out on to Long Acre, then ducked down the first passage that led to the back of the Thurgood house. The door was ajar, the lock and hasp hung from its hinge.

Symon looked at Penelope. 'Did the guards forget to lock the back door?' he whispered. 'Or did someone get here before us?'

'It was me. I came over earlier.' Inside, the shelves were empty of fabric. Looted, by the guards most likely. A broken dressmaker's dummy lay at the foot of the stairs, its hip caved in. They went up to the family rooms, the top of Symon's head brushing against the dark timber beams as he went. The air was closer up here, years of coal fires in small rooms giving the place the smell of cured ham. A simple table was under the front window, once the centre of everything for the family. Eating, writing, games. A cupboard against the staircase wall was filled with dirty trenchers, bowls and cups, all smothered in flies.

They searched each room; it was slow going, the night was dark, they had little light to see by. They moved chairs and benches, looked under tables and in cabinets. Upstairs, in the garret, the roof was so steep they could only stand up straight directly under the ridge.

'Dead-cart driver told me the father was found in this room,' Penelope said. Symon held up his lantern and looked around. A hearth on one side, a pile of clothes and blankets in a corner, a bed in the other. He headed for the hearth to search through the ashes for bits of unburned paper, after that he would sort through the clothes. Penelope went straight for the bed. She dropped to her knees and looked under it.

'What's this?' She held up her torch for Symon to hold it for her. He started to cross the room but as he passed the door, it swung shut and he felt something crash into his head. The room began to spin; he lost his balance and fell to the floor. He felt a kick to his side, tried to reach around and grab at a foot, an ankle, whatever he could get a hand on. But he was dazed and slow; the man began kicking him about the neck, his head. He heard a yell and then suddenly he was free again. He saw someone run towards the door, Penelope chasing after him. He saw her throw something, heard a thwack and saw her disappear down the stairs. He scrambled to his feet after her. She was at the bottom of the stairs, had stooped to pick something up, then was off again. He caught up with her as she sprinted out of the house and collided with the guard.

'Hold on, now!' the guard yelled, wrapping his arms around Penelope.

'Symon! Take this, go after him! He went down Long Acre.' He looked down at her hand; she was holding a small axe.

Symon ran to the corner, looked down Long Acre. It was pitch black; not a flicker of a movement. Whoever it was, he had probably escaped down the nearest passage.

Symon ran back to Penelope, who had just slammed her head into the guard's nose. The man let her go and she grabbed her axe back from Symon. He put an arm out. 'It's too late. He's gone.'

The other guards had gathered around; the one whose nose Penelope had bloodied was ordering her to drop her axe.

'Listen here,' Symon said. 'You're going to stand back and keep watch. That man, he killed the Thurgoods. You're going to do as I say, or you'll be out of work within the hour. All of you, stand outside these doors, don't let anyone in. And yell if you see something.'

Penelope followed Symon inside, her back to his, hand axe raised as a warning in case the guards changed their mind.

They climbed back towards the garret. 'Did you see who it was?'

'No,' she said. 'It was too dark. Could've been a common robber. Why would the killer come back now? The Thurgoods have been dead for days.'

Symon slowed his step, thought back to earlier in the night. Boghurst in the churchyard. Ordering Symon to arrest Burnett that night. Then his sudden change in mood, the cough, the wheezing. Had he been acting? A cover? A reason to leave and get to Leg Alley before Symon did?

'Something could've forced him to act. The discovery of the bodies.' They reached the garret and looked behind the door where the man had hidden to see if he had left anything there, a boot print, anything, but there was nothing but dust and straw. Penelope sighed, then held up her torch towards the bed. 'There,' she said. 'That's where she sat.'

'Who?'

'Our ghost. The woman. She was sitting on the bed.' Penelope walked over to the wooden bed frame, motioned for Symon to help. They picked it up and moved it away from the wall. Penelope bent down, picked up a piece of paper stuck in the corner.

She unfolded it, held it up to read in the torchlight. Symon stood behind her, reading over her shoulder. 'A receipt for plague medicine, for treacle,' she said. A single sheet of paper. Title and authority sprawled across the top.

*London Treacle, Prepared according to COP.*
NEVER FAILING *Preservative against the Infection*
SOVEREIGN CORDIAL *against the Corruption of the Air*

'COP,' said Penelope. 'College of Physicians.' She ran her finger down the long list of ingredients . . . red coral, pearls, unicorn, viper's flesh, seeds of turnip . . . and stopped at the bottom:

*On the Order of Dr Alexander Burnett, 6p an Ounce*

'So it is the good doctor,' Penelope said slowly.

'He was right, then. Boghurst was right all along.' Symon took the parchment from Penelope, folded it back up and put it in his coat pocket. They quietly walked down the stairs, passed back over the other rooms in case they had missed something. In a room on the middle floor, a pile of sacks had been bunched up into the shape of a makeshift bed. *Dr Burnett doesn't seem the type to sleep on the floor*, Symon thought. But Boghurst would. Something niggled at the back of his mind. What was it?

'Maybe the sacks were for one of his patients,' Penelope offered.

Symon sat down at the table. The room was stifling; the night air did little to cool it. He tried to steady himself by focusing through the dim light of his lantern on the items on the table: a jug of ale, cheese rinds, a mouldy, half-eaten loaf of bread. A lone almond. That was unusual. He picked it up. Almonds were quite expensive. They weren't a pocket food, something to nibble on in a death house. Had he ever seen the doctor eat almonds?

He reached for the jug of ale, he needed a drink, something cool on his throat, he didn't care how old it was. As he put it to his lips, an insect climbed out. He threw the jug away in disgust. 'What are we to do now? It seems we may know who the killer is, but this receipt, it is not enough to hang him. And who was this nurse?' He thought back to what Boghurst had said. That Dr Burnett didn't like mess; couldn't stomach touching patients himself. Was the nurse his assistant? Who was she?

'We are close, Symon. We cannot give up.' Penelope twisted the ring on her finger . . . the ruby Dr Burnett had given to his wife as a peace offering. Penelope stroked the box-shaped bezel trapping the ruby, its gold edge perfectly flush with the gem.

'He'll come for us now,' Symon said. 'There's no reason for him to think we didn't recognise him.'

'You're right. He will come for us. So we must be prepared.' She started chipping away at a beam in the wall with her axe. 'In fact, I think we can decide the time and date of that meeting. We let him know that we have found something very damning, and that we intend to make it public. Three nights from now.'

Symon gave a nervous laugh, put his hand on hers to stay her axe-work. 'He'll kill us before then.'

'Indeed. We are the trap.' She waved the axe in front of his face; the ruby-fingered hand that held it. 'And you are the bait.'

# 39

*James Street, Covent Garden*

*A* MURDERER *Shall Bee Announced*
*May it Please You to* ATTEND
*A Meeting of The Society for the Prevention and Cure of Plague*
*Where* EVIDENCE *Shall Bee Proffered*
AND A MURDERER [*By God's Grace*] PROCURED

*The Reverend Symon Patrick Requests Your Presence*
*James Street*
*Nine of the Clock*

Symon had written up three such invitations. One for Boghurst. One for Mincy. One for Dr Burnett. He thought of sending one as a courtesy to Greatrakes care of Lady Ranelagh's house, but Penelope laughed at him. 'To use the word "courtesy" in the same sentence as "Greatrakes"?! Why bother? You said he fled town. He's not worth the paper.'

They set the date for three nights hence and Penelope

delivered the notes to each of the remaining members of the plague society. She and Symon then began their vigil. For the next several days, Symon was not to be outside the company of Penelope, with her hand axe, or Bernard, with his stick.

'Dr Burnett will come for you at night,' Penelope said. 'He'll use the darkness to his advantage; therefore, both Bernard and I will be with you once dusk falls. But hidden. I will be in a corner of your bedchamber and Bernard shall be tucked away in the parlour.' During the day, she and Bernard would keep at a distance at all times; they wanted the doctor to think that Symon was alone, vulnerable, naïve as ever.

On the second night, Symon sat at his makeshift writing desk in his bedchamber, opening two letters from Elizabeth. Both had arrived that day.

> *. . . I scarce find myselffe able to lift my Eyes, for when I do, I see not Cloudes, not Ayre, not Vapour, but a Flamyng Sword held in a Hande, with a Point hanging directly o'er us. I called out for my babe. I gather'd her to mee, shewed not my tears . . . I forced myselffe to look againe and my Eye caught a Herse, then another, and Coffins in the Ayre, carryng many to be buryied. I shut fast my Eyes and there I shrank, poore and miserable . . .*

Elizabeth had sunk into another of her melancholic states. She was alone at Hutton Hall, she said, her guests gone, the merriments over, and so she was left to think on the poor condition of her soul. While she was at a remove from London's troubles, her mind ceaselessly ran upon images of the town's death and destruction. Symon's death and destruction. He cursed himself; he shouldn't have sent her that list of the parish priests who'd passed. She ended the letter with a request: an afternoon of his time to assure her he still breathed.

He had given her an afternoon, more than an afternoon, and how she had abused him. He took a knife savagely to the seal of the second letter. This one was dated several days later, the other had been held up – in Penelope's apron. He threw her a stern glance; she was sitting on the floor behind his bedroom door, sharpening her axe. He grunted. Ridiculous creature! She looked up, saw the letter in his and said, 'Lord, I meant to burn those!'

'Were there others? How many have you burned?'

'If I'd only had the time! How do you have the time to read them?'

He scowled at her and turned back to the letter. *At least*, he thought, *here is some good news.* Elizabeth had recovered her spirits.

> *... there is not in the Christian worlde better Wynes than their Midland ones or their Sherry or their Canary. Their water tastes like Milke, their corn Whyte to a Miracle, and their Wheet makes the sweetest and best Breade in the worlde. Bacon beyond beliefe goode, the Segovia veale much larger, Whyter and Fatter than ours. Mutton most exsellente; capons much better. They have a small Bird that lives and Fatens on grapes and corn, feasted so fatt that it exseedes its quantity of flesh.*

Lord and Lady Dorset. Her neighbours in Burntwood. They'd been away in Spain and Elizabeth was writing of their return. She had been invited to a dinner at their home, for a Spanish-themed amusement. How could one host an amusement in these times? She was back to her false friends, Symon once again forgotten.

*. . . they have Olives whych are nowhere so goode. Their Perfumes of Amber exsel all the Worlde in their kynde, both for clothess, householde Stuff, and fumes.*

She was sending a jar of olives and a thimbleful of the amber, as well as a venison pasty and a new silk cassock she had sewn for him. He looked again at Penelope. What had she done with his gifts? He scanned down the letter, looking for another assurance; another plea for him to visit, or some mention, please God, of the babe. But she was too distractible. More about her guests' travels, their discoveries, a strangulation of the guts by Lord Dorset, eased by a cup of olive oil . . . He stopped cold.

*Of course Lord and Lady D. come back to a householde overrunne with mice. A Most Disturbing Situashon and they looke to ridd themsylves of their Stewarde who so verilie mismanaged it all. They are quite desperate, how they find themsylves!, and can nott go to their London home. I thought of you and knewe at once what you would have mee do. I gave to them yours to helpe return Peace to their householde. For you know your Creatures are exseedingly goode at catching thyngs and will bryng much relieffe to Lord and Lady D.*

She had given away his cats. As easy as that. She writes him of a merry life, sends him fanciful presents. Did she not think? He set the letter alight and threw it in the fire.

'See, you agree with me,' Penelope said. 'Her words are waste.'

*

Joan knew of their vigil, though Symon had not told her why, he did not want her to fear, and so she had him made a coffee drink before she turned in. Symon sipped at it while Penelope slept. He listened to the night around him, the pulsing buzz of insects, the peeps of frogs in a nearby ditch. Inside his house, only he and the mice were awake. He heard them scurry across the ceiling, down the walls and back again. They were part of his guard, too, he thought, for they stopped their scurrying at the slightest noise. With each night moan of the house, he caught his breath. Was it him? Was it time?

He took out a packet of old letters from Elizabeth, bundled together with twine. He thought back to his paralysis of the spring, when his mind and his energy had been consumed with her and the thought of their baby, and he could think of little else. These days, life felt very different. He had taken the world of the living for granted. Every time he saw Penelope, calling for him at the door or drawing at his desk or ordering Bernard about the churchyard, he felt relief that she was also still here, with him. He was ashamed that he had kissed her, a momentary thoughtlessness, he wouldn't do it again. She was not to be trifled with. He was thankful that she had not mentioned it either. He stoked the fire, rousted the coals back to life. And one by one threw in Elizabeth's letters.

# 40

## *A Resignation*

'NOT EVEN A GENTLE FART.' Penelope shook her head in dismay. It was the third morning since they had sent the invitations, the day that they were to publicly call out a murderer. And yet there had been no sign of Dr Burnett. He had not attempted to kill Symon. For the first time, Penelope was afraid. Dr Burnett had avoided their trap; would they fall into one of his?

'We should have been more forceful. More direct about the evidence, driven him to act. Now, he will arrive with the other members of the plague society; some chaos will result, it always does with them, and then he will use that to escape. Unless ...' She slashed at the air with her hand axe, then danced around him, swinging it high and low as she went, as if she were destroying an oncoming horde.

'That's most annoying.' He tried to grab the axe from her, but she jerked it back. 'And you wonder why people dislike you so!'

Penelope rolled her eyes and slung it back on her belt. 'If

someone dislikes me, it is because they know I speak the truth.' She patted her pockets, which now contained not only her father's will, but Dr Burnett's signed receipt for London Treacle, which she'd swiped from Symon.

'Enough! The murderer shall be in my home this night. And we are once again without a plan. Any suggestions?'

She shrugged. 'Poison the wine. Kill them all. The world will thank you for it.'

'Penelope, I beg of you! Don't abandon me now.'

'There is this, then. We bring them together. We say we found an important document at the Thurgoods' house. Written by one of them. Signed by one of them. Then we pause. And look at the good doctor.'

'That is a poor plan,' he said. 'We must cancel the meeting.'

'No. We bring them here. We lock the doors. No one leaves until the doctor cracks.'

*

A shout outside snapped Symon away from the rut he was wearing in his parlour floor. He pulled a curtain back. It was Dr Burnett and the surgeon Mincy. They had arrived together and were already quarrelling. 'They're here,' Symon said. Penelope and Bernard headed down the hall to listen from the garden, underneath the dining-room window.

'It is Mincy,' Dr Burnett said when Symon opened the door. He was holding a handkerchief to his nose.

Symon looked at the surgeon, worried.

'He keeps breaking wind.'

'My father always said never keep it in.' Mincy brushed past Symon and headed down the hall. 'It could damage the organs. In my family we always break wind freely and I would add have had few complaints of that order as a result. Are we in the dining room tonight?'

'Disgusting!' Dr Burnett called after him. 'Did your father also tell you that plague is carried by steams and fumes? And these expressions of yours could be spreading it? Chew horse mint. And take no onions with your meat.'

Symon followed them. Dr Burnett was indeed cross, but he did not seem nervous. Merely offended at Mincy's impropriety. They continued to bicker as they stood by the sideboard, where Nell was pouring them wine. He had told her to keep the glasses full this night, hoping the wine would loosen their tongues. The girl had not been pleased with the situation; having strangers in the house during such a time, particularly strangers who came into contact with plague every day. But he gave her little time to object. He found himself embarrassed as he gave her the instructions, because it was only then that he realised how much she had changed since the beginning of summer. Joan had made her a new dress that fit her beautifully, accentuating the change all the more. Nell was no longer all elbows and ears. She was rounding out, becoming a woman. She did not wear her hair so severely; and her squinchy eye no longer seemed to cast suspicion on all. Rather, it spoke of a keen intelligence. *She's finally settling in,* he thought, *letting her guard down a little. And here I've gone and thrown her in with these vile men.* He sighed as he watched her quickly splash out a drink then jump back, as if Dr Burnett and Mincy were contagious. This was his fault, for he couldn't say they weren't.

He decided he would pass the tarts around himself when Greatrakes strode in, looking as peeved as the others.

'What are you doing here?' Symon blurted out.

'What a nasty thing to say! About as nasty as forgetting to invite me to your little do.'

'I was told you left town,' Symon stammered. 'You'd been summoned by the king.'

'A brief sojourn. And not an excuse for your rudeness, Mr Patrick.'

Symon started to protest, but a hand had timidly reached around from behind him. Nell, using Symon as a shield.

'A drink, sir?' she mumbled, holding out a cup of rum and milk punch for Greatrakes.

'Come, girl, there's no need to be afraid,' Symon said gently, encouraging her forward. 'He shan't bite.' But even this turned to disaster. She summoned up too much courage, it seemed, for she leapt out from behind Symon and her outstretched arm collided with Greatrakes, who was reaching for the punch. The cup flew up in the air, dousing everyone. Greatrakes dropped his bag and whipped the apron off Nell to dry his satin suit.

'Sir! Forgive me!' She bent down to pick up his satchel, its spilled papers.

'You clumsy cow,' Greatrakes said as he moved to yank the wet pages from her hands. Symon dropped down to help, knocking heads with Greatrakes in the process.

Greatrakes started swearing at them both, and Nell looked at Symon, eyes wide with fear, unsure of what to do. He let out a sigh of exasperation. 'Have some sense, girl! Fetch a cloth, go on!'

She stumbled a curtsy and ran from the room.

'Really, Symon, you attract such dim creatures.' Greatrakes tied up his satchel and straightened his ruff. 'If they haven't any graces, best to keep them outside, yes? A good hoe in their hands?'

Symon bit his tongue, went back to the sideboard to fill another cup of punch for Greatrakes.

'No thank you,' Greatrakes said. 'I've had enough, haven't I? Now where did she go! My breeches have milk fat all over them!' He stalked off to find her.

'Symon!' It was Mincy, tugging at his sleeve. 'Are we all here? Could we start, please? I have had a very long day, and my dogs miss me. They never get out any more.'

The sun was down behind the house now, so Symon quickly lit the candles and turned his back on his guests to sip from his flask. He heard the front door open. Ah, Boghurst at last.

'A holy terror,' the apothecary shouted, throwing his bag at Nell, who had come back into the room. She screamed and ducked, but the bag snagged her cap as it went by. She frantically ran her fingers through her dark hair. Symon groaned. *She's searching for blood. She'll probably quit tomorrow. Tell everyone how I abused her.*

'You're all right, girl,' Symon said, a little too sharply. He picked up her cap and righted it on her head. 'Help him now.' He pointed to Boghurst, who was picking up the spilled contents of his bag.

The apothecary took no notice of the girl. 'Drury Lane! Holborn! St Sepulchre!' he shouted to the room. 'All gone! I know not what to do!'

'Try staying at arm's length from me,' Greatrakes said.

*Enough*, thought Symon. He would get this over with. He looked around at his guests. Greatrakes, tall and gangly, back to mopping punch off his sleeves and breeches with what looked like one of Symon's shirts. Boghurst at the sideboard, filling not one but two glasses. Dr Burnett at the head of the table, a bigger bandage than ever over his eye, talking to himself and scribbling in his ledger. Mincy, filling a plate with tarts and cheese.

He took a deep breath, said a small prayer.

'My dear friends. For these many months now, we have been tracking a murderer.'

'I do not recall agreeing that was the case,' Dr Burnett interrupted.

'The facts are this,' Symon raised his voice. 'Someone is murdering the sick. At first, he preyed on maidens, experimented cruelly on them. And though it seems not possible, he has become even more depraved. Most recently, we found an entire family, mercilessly destroyed by this man. The Thurgoods. Many of you knew them. One of you knew them all too well.'

'I have consulted with my two brothers,' Dr Burnett cut in again, 'Dr Reason and Dr Experience, and took a voyage to visit my mother Nature, by whose advice, together with the help of Dr Diligence, and warned by my cousin, Mr Honesty—'

'I don't give a whore's pocket who you're related to,' Boghurst said.

'—that this was a theory,' Dr Burnett said. 'One which led to a long and substantive discourse but ultimately could not be proved.'

'Oh, come now.' Boghurst put his drinks down and walked over to Dr Burnett. 'We most certainly did agree.'

'I did not agree.' Dr Burnett fixed his working eye on his ledger. 'What is more, I reject the theory. These victims – if in fact they exist, for we have not seen the bodies – died of plague. As so many others have in this time, God rest their souls.' He whipped a folded paper out of his pocket. 'The latest bills! A thousand more dead this week than last!'

'We must not turn away from Evil!' Symon answered back. 'Be it great or small. We have two threats upon us. One we may never stop. The other one we can. This very night.'

Dr Burnett cocked his head, looked at Symon. 'All right, Mr Patrick, you brought us here to announce a murderer. And that you have evidence, real evidence, not only of these alleged murders but of the perpetrator. So be quick about it. Show us your evidence.'

Symon looked over at the window; he wished Penelope and Bernard would jump through it at this moment. What an appalling gathering! Boghurst, wilted and green, his whole being the colour of an infection; Greatrakes appeared tired too, even his white curls had gone flat; Dr Burnett, so red in the face, so swollen with anger, he looked to pop. And then Mincy. He was whispering conspiratorially to the plum tart before him. Symon took another deep breath. *It might be my last*, he thought, *for one of them may slay me once I speak.* Out of the corner of his eye, he saw a darting movement at the window. He blinked, for he thought he saw a most sorrowful young woman, unwinding the curls in her blond hair. Was this Penelope's ghost? He blinked, rubbed his eyes, looked again. It was only Penelope, mouthing the word, 'Strike!'

'MR PATRICK! Are you with us? Or did you call us here to watch you flux apart?' spat Dr Burnett.

Symon squared his jaw ('The appearance of confidence, that is all one needs to succeed,' Penelope had coached him), and said: 'The evidence is this. A receipt for physick. Found in the home of the Thurgoods, after they died. A receipt signed by one of you.'

'Cock of Christ,' Boghurst said. 'You never told me!'

'Signed by Boghurst!' Mincy snorted. 'Why doesn't anyone listen to me?'

'Lunatics!' Dr Burnett yelled. 'Every last one of you! We have our killer and it is PLAGUE. May I remind you of our true *and only* purpose. The preservation from' – he slammed his hand on the table – 'the prevention of, and the cure of plague! For every minute we spend talking of Mr Patrick's phantom murderer, the true murderer is out there, this great distemper, laying siege to one and all.'

The doctor stood up, unbandaged eye bulging, cheeks puffing, curls shaking. 'A receipt for medicine! Proof of murder? Surely you jest! Unless you mean to find us guilty because we cannot cure? Yes! Then I am a murderer. Hang me now!' He laughed, a high-pitched, maniacal laugh, then stopped abruptly. He turned and looked out of the window behind him; a foul stench had blown in. 'You really should keep your windows closed, Mr Patrick. You are a man deaf to all good sense.' He shook his head. 'Now, you've taken up enough of our time with this nonsense. I bid you goodnight.'

Symon swallowed hard, then heard Penelope's voice in his head, 'One good shove, that's all he needs. We've got him; he's ready to break.' Symon opened his eyes, whispered: 'The receipt. It is yours. It is signed by you. You killed the Thurgoods.'

Burnett's jaw fell open. His eye darted about. Hand shaking, he took a sip from his wine glass. Cleared his throat. Tidied his cravat. 'I see, Mr Patrick,' he said quietly. 'A receipt for plague water signed by me? I give them out by the dozen every day at Amen Corner. I don't even charge any more because they're useless.' He called for his things; took his bag, his coat, his hat from Nell. 'You shall hear from my lawyer on the morrow. I cannot let this calumny stand.' He fitted his hat on his head, gave a final look around the room. 'Gentlemen, one other thing: you've made a mockery of these proceedings. Every last one of you. I resign my post as head of this society.' He made a shallow bow and left.

'Oh, don't sulk, my dears.' Greatrakes moved to the head of the table, took up Burnett's seat. 'I shall be your new secretary!'

# 41

## *Inside a Hell Pit*

THE REMAINING MEMBERS of the plague society had left and Symon had retrieved his theriac from his bedchamber and downed half of it. Then finished his flask of brandy. Then started on the wine. He would put a new purpose to his life: to spend the rest of his days drunk.

Despite this pledge, and a painful head, he was up betimes the next morning. For one, he didn't want to wake to see Penelope standing over his bed chiding him. He wanted to at least meet her on equal ground. He spent the day in his charnel ground, praying over the dead, waiting for her to turn up with some clever word, some clever plan about what to do next. But night came, and still no Penelope. *I have let her down*, he thought. *She does not want to see me.*

Late that afternoon, Jack arrived with a note from Joan. The boy was crying. Symon took the note and as he read it, fell against the nearest gravestone. Nell was gone, his housekeeper wrote. His first terrible thought: *I was right. I did drive her off.* But the housekeeper wrote that the girl had left her clothes behind. And why would she leave her brother? She wasn't such a cruel girl as to abandon the boy without a word. Symon scooped up Jack in his arms, whispered to him, 'We'll find her, not to worry; we'll get her back. I'm sure she's with a friend.'

'A friend? She hasn't got any friends,' Jack said, his quizzical eye trying to figure out Symon's logic.

He took the boy's hand and walked him home. Joan greeted them at the door, her eyes red and swollen from crying, too. She sent Jack out to shell peas in the garden, a chore to occupy his mind. 'Could it be a man?' Joan asked as they watched the boy from the kitchen window. The old woman was taller than Symon, but this new grief seemed to hit her in the middle, stoop her to half her size. 'Someone sweet on her, promising a better life?' Her husky voice dissolved away as she spoke words they both knew to be false. Joan was even more bereft than when she had learned Mary had died. She had known Nell longer, had begun to think of her like a daughter.

He put his arm around her. 'Let us hope,' was all he could say, worried his own voice would betray him. Nell was another young maid. Vulnerable. Often about the streets alone. The killer had shown a preference for blondes, and Nell had dark hair. But that was no longer an assurance, for Theodora had not been fair, either. *No*, he thought, *the Devil couldn't strike this household twice.* Unless someone had been stupid. Had tempted, baited, confronted the Devil as Symon had. *Good God*, he thought, *what have I done? What have I done?*

The girl had been gone since sun-up, Joan said. She had sent Nell down to the earl's gardens on the south side of the piazza, asked her to steal in and pick some herbs, some vegetables. Whatever they had. 'I know it's a sin, Rector. But the markets are closed and we have to make do, don't we?' The girl shouldn't have been gone long. After a few hours, Joan started to worry. 'Perhaps she got caught. They won't hang her for thieving, will they? They'll understand, won't they?'

He could see the woman hoped it was that simple. 'I'll check right away, Joan. I'm sure that's all it is. She'll be fine.' *Please God.* Let him find her asleep in the earl's gardens, curled up in the arms of a strapping young man. Symon rushed back to the church to get Bernard, sent him to find the earl's guards while Symon searched the gardens. But he didn't find Nell.

*Please God,* he thought. Perhaps there was still a chance. Perhaps she was stranded in an alley. Had twisted her ankle and couldn't get home. He and Bernard ordered the yard boys to scour the parish. They were to look in all the passages, the courtyards, every last house. Call on the neighbouring parishes, set them to it. Symon didn't care about the cost. *Please, let me find her. Before he does.*

*

He walked the west end of town all that day and all that night; shouted himself hoarse. Yelled for Nell. Yelled for Penelope. Where was she? If anyone could find Nell, it would be Penelope. He tapped on the shoulders of couples in dark corners, hoping one would be Nell. He checked the pesthouses, courts, peered in windows. *If she were ill, she would have crawled out of the hot sun,* he thought. *Climbed into a cellar. If she had been kidnapped,* he forced himself to think, *she would be hidden away. But where?* All of the victims thus far had been brought in by the dead-cart drivers from St Martin's and St Giles, and Covent Garden, but these parishes covered an area far larger than the old city. He skirted around the plague pit at Tuttle Fields. An abomination standing in the shadow of the great abbey. Corpses stacked up on carts, waiting to be thrown into the deep pits cut from the earth. He could almost see the shades, drifting around, directing the workers to have more care. Had there been other victims? Had they been taken here? Would this be Nell's fate? She, too, an unknown girl dragged out of an abandoned house, thrown on to a cart and forgotten by all. *Stop it, Symon. You will find her.* He walked back to his own plague pit, fighting thoughts of death with every step.

A thousand a day were dying now. More like two thousand, said Bernard grimly. Symon's mind couldn't hold it all. There were so many dying now that the carts were overflowing by noon. The Lord Mayor's order to bury only under the cover of night had long been lifted; there were just too many bodies. As he watched the cart horses traipse through his church gate, he glanced up at the backs of the houses edging the churchyard. All were empty, except for one stubborn old woman who had refused to leave her home. Lady Digby hadn't stepped a foot outside since early July; she was there, every day at her window, scowling and cursing. Even though it was past midnight, she sat there yet, looking at Symon.

'Must you insist on killing us all, Mr Patrick?' she squawked, her lacy nightcap flailing around her shrunken face. 'Is that what you are planning? To bury us all in there? You bring this on us, you do, you wicked man!'

*She's right,* thought Symon. *I have been wicked.*

He saw Bernard walk over and raise his stick to her window. 'Only a fiend would want such a seat! Be gone, you frogged-mouth witch!'

Lady Digby screamed for Bernard's hide. The sexton walked back to Symon, shaking his bedraggled head in disgust. Even in the best of times, the sexton was unable to tame his hair. Most days it flew out from his head, always as if he had suffered a terrible shock. (The shock of being Bernard, Symon used to joke.) But now, it was turning in on itself, matting into knots. The lines on Bernard's face were deeper, and he was shrinking under his clothes. *Someone is letting the air out of him*, Symon thought.

Another dead cart came in off Bedford Street, the horse and driver aimless, as if they turned by chance through the front gate. Bernard directed the cart up to the pit, counted the bodies as the yard boys used long poles to hook around a shoulder or leg and tug them off the cart and into the mass grave. The driver got down and walked over to the pit's edge, looked in and grimaced. Then he swayed, let out a moan and toppled in head first.

'Oh, heaven help us, not again.' Bernard rushed over to the spot where the man had fallen. 'Another one dead on the job,' he said to Symon. 'Used to have to get down in there and check on them.'

'You're not going to? Look, he's still moving.' The man's arm was slowly unbending; a leg unfurled.

'Happens all the time now. God save 'em.'

A ladder, that's what he needed. Symon brought one over, slid it down the side of the pit. He could hear Bernard behind him. 'Don't, Rector. It won't help! Rector!' He was down the ladder before Bernard could stop him, before he could stop himself. In rapid fire, he chanted the Lord's Prayer, never fully getting past the first line. He had to walk on the bodies; he told himself it was like picking out rocks when fording a stream. Look for hard things – shoulders, knees, but not the heads, oh please no, not the heads. He searched for guidance in the night sky, but the moon and stars had been obliterated by the lime dust. He could hear Bernard cursing. Each step kicked up a white cloud of lime, coating his clothes and stinging his skin.

He reached the fallen cart driver, squatted down, put fingers to the pale neck. Nothing. *You could stay with them*, he heard a voice say, *wait here for Nell. Wait here for all of them.* He sat down, without much thought about what he was sitting on. Out of the corner of his eye, he saw someone coming down the ladder. He squinted through the dust, heard her yells. Saw writhing hair, a crooked smile. *Oh*, he thought, *exactly who I want to see. Penelope.*

'Where have you been?' he demanded as she pulled him to his feet with a mighty heave, and dragged him back to the ladder. Bernard was holding the top, waiting for them.

'Take your boots off and your breeches,' the sexton said after he climbed out. 'That was a damned fool thing to do. We'll have to burn them.'

'He really doesn't deserve such nice things,' Symon heard Penelope say. He looked around, but couldn't see her through the darkness, the lime eddies kicked up by the wind. 'Where did she go?' he asked.

'Who?'

'Penelope.'

'Haven't seen her. Now get out of here, before I throw you back in.'

Symon stumbled to his church office, threw his vial of theriac on the floor and crushed it with his foot. Last thing he needed was hallucinations. Had she been in the pit? She was one for popping up when you needed her. Then vanishing just as suddenly.

*

Symon slept with his head on his desk, woke up before the sun and put on a dirty shirt to start his search again. Around noon he returned to find Jack waiting for him, eyes down. The boy wanted to join the search. Symon refused. *He's afraid to look at me*, Symon thought. *Afraid I might tell him something awful.* Symon gathered him up in his arms. This evening he would write his will, he needed to make sure that his lovely little boy was taken care of. Why had he ever thought him a servant? Jack was his ward. And he would do the same for Nell when she was found, for he would find her. He hugged the boy tighter, buried his nose in his sandy hair.

'Came to the house,' the boy said, breaking away and handing him a note.

'Who is it from?'

'Don't know. Mistress gave it to me. Said it might be important.'

Symon dreaded to open it. There was no such thing as good news these days. Sure enough, inside, a hastily scratched:

*Make Haste. Another body. Coal Yard. Holborn*
*– B*

The killer had struck again. Symon cursed himself, it was all happening too fast. He should have had someone watching Dr Burnett. He put on his cassock and picked up his prayer book; saw the alarm in Jack's face and stopped. 'Oh no, no. It's not that. It's all right.' He put a hand on his shoulder. 'There's nothing to worry about. Mr Boghurst is calling. You know how he is. Annoying.' He kissed Jack on the head, smiled. 'We'll find our Nell yet.'

*

Coal Yard was an unloved place. The weeds were hip high, the handle was off the water pump in the centre of the dirt court. Most of the doors were padlocked, the residents long gone. Symon saw one open and said a blessing for the poor murdered girl he knew he would find inside.

He stepped through the front door, called out to Boghurst. Another ransacked room, like half of London. Called out again, but there was no reply. He pushed deeper into the room, knowing that at any moment he would see some irrevocable horror. His mind flashed back to the attack the other night. He looked around for a weapon, picked up a poker from the hearth. And the ash shovel. He headed up the stairs and at the top, called out one last time. Hearing nothing, he slowly turned the corner and collapsed against the door frame as he felt lightning strike his chest.

There she was. Sprawled on the floor. *God, no. Please God, no.* He forced himself forward, his legs heavy as lead, fell to his knees by her side. Touched her thick, dark waves of hair; the sleeve of her grey dress, the one that fit her perfectly. He found himself staring at the white kerchief around her neck; it was tied too tightly. He leaned over to loosen it, a final gesture of love – and saw the bruises. She had been strangled. He pulled Nell on to his lap, cradled her, kissed her. He deserved to die for this. He yelled again for Boghurst. He had the notion that he was yelling for quite some time, but finally he heard running, shouts from the street below. A herd of men, coming up the stairs, bursting into the room, led by a man with a crooked wig and a half-melted eyelid. It was the Duke of Albemarle. *Thank you, Lord.* Boghurst had sent help. Real help.

Symon held Nell's body tighter to him, shouted at the duke, 'If you had only listened, she would be alive; they would all be alive.'

'Seize that man,' bellowed the duke. The guards dragged Symon away from the body, clapped irons on his wrists.

'He doesn't mean me!' Symon yelled at them, struggling to break free. 'What are you about? This is my maid!'

'I do mean you,' the duke growled. 'You're that floppy-haired priest, the one railing about a rogue cutting up the outparishes.' He looked Symon up and down, gave his hair a flick. 'It was you all along. You've been watched, your depravity and lunacy finally revealed. Your friends turned you in. You should thank them for saving you from any further destruction to your soul.' He signalled to the guards. 'Take him to Newgate.'

Symon shouted that he was rector of St Paul's Church in Covent Garden, the Earl of Bedford's man, that they were making a horrible mistake. Why would he kill his own girl?

'The Earl of Bedford's a sissy. You look a sissy. And this' – the duke pointed to Nell's body – 'the work of the most cowardly of sissies.' He turned to his men. 'Get him out of my sight before shit erupts out of my arse and I use him to wipe it off.'

# 42

*Nestled Between Friends, Newgate Prison*

SLITS OF LIGHT CAME THROUGH window grates at the top of the cell wall. At first Symon could only hear the coughs and moans of his fellow prisoners, but now he was starting to see the bundles on the floor all around him. Some writhing. Some not.

Bile rose up from his stomach, eating him from the inside out – his body's reaction to his failings. He looked at the bundle nearest to him. Sharp bones sticking out from under a sack. Symon wished him death. That would bring him peace at last. He hoped.

What would he tell Jack?

*The Lord is my shepherd; I shall not want. He maketh me to lie down in green pastures; he leadeth me beside the still waters.*

Psalm 23. Such beautiful words. They came to him unsummoned. But what did they matter?

*He restoreth my soul. He leadeth me in the paths of righteousness for his name's sake.*

He had tried to help, and failed horribly. Who was behind

this? His friends had turned him in. That's what the duke had said. Friends. Friend. Another trick of Dr Burnett's. The note had been hastily scrawled, signed only B. It was designed to make Symon think it was Boghurst. Whoever wrote it knew Symon well. Knew that he would follow any summons from Boghurst. There, of course, were any number of reasons to believe that the note had been sent by Boghurst himself, that Mincy had been right all along. The apothecary's original reluctance to help. That night at St Gabriel Fenchurch's charnel ground. The shallow grave Symon awoke in, the gash on his head. His instinct had told him that Boghurst was responsible; had tried to kill him. Symon shook his head. No, it made no sense. There was still the matter of the theriac. Symon was going through a bottle a week now. Boghurst mixed it for him, a far easier way of getting rid of Symon than building such an elaborate trap . . . and killing Nell. Nell! Why Nell? Because she was another poor servant girl in the wrong place? Available, defenceless, like the others? But her circumstances were unlike the others. She had been killed shortly after she disappeared, and Symon had seen no signs of torture. Nor did she have plague. So why kill her? Was she killed simply to warn Symon, to trap him? Was that what her life, her warmth, her vitality had been traded for? *I am a monster*, Symon thought, *for I did not keep her safe. I have not kept anyone safe.*

He started to list his blessings, which had so often helped him recover his strength, his purpose in the past. By remembering the good, he could find the courage to confront evil. Yet why was it so hard to recognise those sweet moments while they were happening, to fully feel them, soak them in? Nell. Nell and Jack. Jack. Alone. His fault.

He tried again.

*Yea, though I walk through the valley of the shadow of death, I will fear no evil: for thou art with me; thy rod and thy staff they comfort me.*

It wasn't always the case. There were moments when, at the time, he felt fully connected to joy. The many wonderful days he'd spent at Elizabeth's house in Clapham. The moment when she told him she was with child. And oddly, yes, that too – sitting by a grave, waiting for the dead to rise with Penelope. The surprising softness of her hand, that kiss that tasted of liquorice.

He needed to get out of here. He owed it to Jack. He owed it to Theodora Thurgood. To Nell. To Mary. He had as good as killed those girls himself. The killer would come after Penelope next, if he hadn't already got her. Where was she? He must get out of here. But how? No one ever got out of Newgate. As Symon watched the light grow dim, watched the little windows become as black and solid as the walls around them, he began to worry that Newgate had already swallowed him up and was starting to digest him. He might be found, years from now – *Oh, Symon, you wouldn't last that long*, he thought – weeks from now, a pulpy, decaying mess. The guards would look at him, a blob, scratch their heads and ask, 'Now, what did that used to be?'

'Give us yer coat,' a voice said.

'Sorry?' Symon looked down at his cassock, confused.

'Too warm in here for a coat like that,' said a shadow creeping closer. 'You'll be wanting to get that off. I'll take good care of it for you.'

Symon couldn't see his would-be servant. But he could smell him. Raw onions. The tang of iron – blood.

'I'd rather like to keep it.'

'Won't be needing your stockings. Or your shoes.'

'I wouldn't agree with that,' he ventured.

'What's your name?'

'Symon. The Reverend Symon Patrick.'

The man cackled. 'No, your devil name!'

'I don't know—' The creature punched him in the jaw, tore off his cassock. Ordered him to take off his shoes. Symon did and then threw them hard at the man; they would help him little.

*Thou preparest a table before me in the presence of mine enemies: thou anointest my head with oil . . .*

It wasn't a complete oubliette, he discovered later, as the bars in the windows took shape again with the rise of the sun. Not yet, anyway. A few guards remembered them, came in with buckets of water. They took them around, splashing out sips. If a bundle didn't move as they approached, they kicked it. Still no response and they'd drag it by the ankles out of the room. He used to think his churchyard at night was one of the ghastliest places. He now realised it was indeed a home. One worth protecting, one worth watching over. One he had failed to honour.

*

He fluttered his lids, but everything remained black. His arms were pinned to his sides and the smell of rotten breath, rotten meat was all around him. Every which way he turned his head, the smell was there. He tried to elbow his way free and something thumped him back. *Oh, dear God. The bundles.* They had moved around him, nestled up next to him. There was no question about it. He would soon die in here.

He wriggled out from between the bundles, got on his hands and knees, started to crawl. One hand out, one finger feeling in front for obstacles, then another. Something wet there, recalibrate course, something oozing there, turn, turn, turn, something damp there. He could smell it, he knew what that was, and so on until he found a dry, bundle-free patch. *Surely, surely, surely goodness and mercy shall follow me all the days of my life, SURELY . . . and I will dwell in the house of the Lord for ever.* He hoped, if nothing else, the psalm's rhythms would trick him into sleep.

His last thought, *God's will be done.*

Except then he had another: *This isn't it. This isn't over.*

# 43

## *A Broken Home*

WORD QUICKLY SPREAD around the parish. Their beloved rector was the Prince of Hell himself. Killing sweet young girls, including two of his own maids. Penelope rushed to Symon's house, stabbing herself in the thumb with a loose pin in her pocket for penance; she would come up with a far crueller punishment later. *How could you, Penelope?* she thought. *How could you let this happen?*

She found them huddled in the dark in Jack's room, Joan stroking the little boy's hair, softly singing to him. Tears tore down Penelope's cheeks. She was too late, they had already heard.

'It's not true, he didn't do it,' she said, barely bringing herself to look Joan in the eye. 'You know that, don't you?'

'Yes,' said Joan, 'but she is dead and he is gone from us.' She kissed the boy on his head. 'May the Lord forgive us.'

Penelope went downstairs. She warmed some stew for them, buttered some bread. She cooked bacon for Jack (isn't that what little boys loved?), but he wouldn't touch it. She tucked them into bed together and said she would have Bernard send someone to care for them.

'We'll be all right, Penny, you needn't worret,' said Joan.

'I'd do it myself if I could. And one day I shall.' She handed Joan a warm drink to help her sleep. 'But there is something Symon needs me to do.'

Penelope's heart felt as thick as a bog. She had never seen Jack so pale and lifeless. She'd been proud and paid for it. She had baited the killer, tried to push him into action. But she had misjudged him. Thought he would walk right into their trap. Instead, he had been patient, taken his time. And now Nell was dead. But why Nell? Why not Symon? Or Penelope?

Bernard told her about the note Symon had received, that it was signed *B.* Was it Dr Burnett? Or was it Boghurst? What did it matter? She would gut and roast them both.

She looked again at Jack, he was crying in his sleep. What could she do for him? Nothing. His mother and father gone, his sister murdered. She and Symon had lied to him. Told him he could trust them, that he could be happy and safe. Penelope knew his future. To have felt love, then have it taken away. It would be a daily struggle not to succumb. But she also knew one could survive. And that is what she would do for Jack. Show him how. How a biting wind or a rough blanket could support you. To find marvel in a shoe that flaps apart as you walk or in the cold mud that seeps in. How to lose yourself in these things and, for a moment, push aside the pain, long enough to get through the worst of it. She brushed the boy's hair away from his eyes and kissed him goodbye; he didn't stir.

*

She found Boghurst at a sick house in Moor's Yard. He came barrelling out of the door, then stopped cold when he saw her.

She was crouched down, had been biding her time by carving large tombstones into the dirt. On one, she had written his name.

'Is that a threat?' he asked.

'How are we going to get him out?' she asked quietly. 'What are you going to do?'

'I have no connections. Who am I?'

She stood up, wiped the dusty axe blade on her skirt and started walking away. 'He's your only friend. Think on a life without him and maybe then it shall come to you.'

'He's *your* only friend!' he shouted after her. 'You mangy magpie,' she heard him add under his breath.

She turned and threw the axe at him.

# 44

*Amidst the Charnel Gas*

Boghurst jumped clear of Penelope's axe; she waited out his curses before she fetched it back. 'Next time, I shan't miss,' she said, holding it up an inch from his face.

He gave her a cool look. As much as he disliked her sour ways, Boghurst knew she was right. They had to act quickly. There wouldn't be a trial for Symon till after plague abated, but gaol fever would have him within a fortnight.

She drew her finger lightly across his forehead. 'I shall get you right here. A nice, big, bloody gash. Like the one you gave Symon.'

'You're a bit much, don't you think?'

She paused, staring at him with her unsettling pale grey eyes. 'Yes . . .' she said slowly. 'What about that night in the churchyard? You were there to dig up Burnett's manservant . . . The one you claim was his first victim. Why haven't you gone back?'

Boghurst nodded, broke into a grin. 'You're right. We must see what that corpse has to say.'

*

'What a horrid little church,' Penelope said when they reached Dr Burnett's parish. St Gabriel Fenchurch dated back to the Crusades; vast blooms of frothy lichen covered nearly all of its coal-blacked stone. 'It looks like a crusted leviathan beached upon the street.'

'Well, let's see what we can do about getting the doctor buried here,' said Boghurst as he opened the iron gate to the churchyard and led them towards a far corner.

'They haven't had to dig a pit,' said Bernard, looking around the yard. They had stopped to grab him before heading across the city. 'God may be with us yet,' said Boghurst. He pointed to a fresh mound unmarked by stone. 'That's where Dr Burnett's servant is buried. It was the only fresh grave about when Symon and I came here.' He laughed grimly as he inspected it. 'I see they've retopped it after our failed exhumation.' He turned to Bernard. 'What do you think? Shall we be polite? Send a note, ask permission? You have some authority, do you not, as a sexton? And perhaps I do as well, as a medical practitioner. They might—'

Bernard knocked him on the back of the head. 'What a halfwit you are.'

'Yes,' agreed Penelope. 'We've no time for manners.'

*

They waited till the other side of midnight, when all but the church mice would be asleep. They carried spades and a pickaxe; Boghurst had a small box and a bag of tapers slung over his shoulder. 'Most powerful,' he said. 'They burn up the corpse fumes; can't be too careful, especially with a plague body. I add crushed coach-horse beetles to the wax.'

Bernard took one out and sniffed it, made a face. 'Never

miss a chance to cheat someone, do you?' He broke the taper and threw it back at Boghurst. 'But these you've brought at your own expense, and I'm always obliged when someone else is paying. Let's get on with it.' The sexton took his spade and made the first cut in the grave of Dr Burnett's deceased servant.

Penelope sat next to a pile of broken and discarded gargoyles. She absentmindedly stroked a snout as she watched the hole grow deeper, all the while keeping an eye out for a light that wasn't theirs, a sign that someone else was awake.

'You might help,' Boghurst called to her in a loud whisper.

She didn't reply. Within the hour, they would have exhumed the body of Dr Burnett's servant and the corpse would speak its truth. Did the lad die of plague, as Dr Burnett testified before all? Or would a tale of murder be imprinted upon his corpse? What would they need to incriminate the doctor? Blond hair, shorn. Restraints around the wrists and ankles. Perhaps the only true tell-tale sign would be a grid of ink around the various sites of treatment. Neither Boghurst nor Mincy had ever seen such a practice, even though she had since witnessed both using it. Little other evidence would be left at this point. Who could tell a blister from holes left by decay? She looked up at the sound of a great crack; Bernard had hit the lid of the coffin.

'Get your tapers and climb down in there,' the sexton grumbled to Boghurst as he pulled himself out.

'What,' said the apothecary, 'we're not to bring it up? It's dangerous to be in such a confined space with a corpse.'

'Small boys do it every day in my yard. And I'll not risk my back. Light your fancy tapers now, I'll hand you the crowbar.'

Boghurst grimaced but grabbed his tapers. He also opened the box he had brought, which had several glass jars inside.

'What are those for?' Penelope asked, coming over.

'Two birds with one stone,' Boghurst said. 'Collecting jars. While I'm down there, I'll gather a few samples from his skull. Moss from a dead man's bones! A most potent ingredient. Good as gold.'

Penelope shook her head in disgust and started lighting the tapers. The sooner they got this over with, the better. Boghurst jumped in but the coffin was cheap and his feet crashed through the thin wood lid. He howled as a thick stench filled the air. Penelope quickly dropped to her knees and thrust several of the tapers into the grave to help burn the charnel gases.

'Get me out, quick,' Boghurst yelled.

'Shut the hell up,' Bernard said, throwing an axe down into the hole. 'Or I'll stove in your teeth. You'll wake the whole town!'

Boghurst gave him a dirty look, then picked up the axe and started chopping at the coffin lid. Bernard tossed him the crowbar and he started to prise back the wood. Little by little a face was revealed, a most horrible rictus. 'What can you see?' Penelope hissed down to Boghurst.

Before Boghurst could reply, Bernard bellowed, 'My good man! A hearty welcome to you!'

Penelope turned around and saw a slight, crooked shape sloping towards them. The nightwatch.

'Francis Bernard, is that you? Never thought you a grave robber.' The man was heavily wrinkled with rheumy eyes and receding chin; he looked as old as the church. He shone his torch over them questioningly. 'No, never thought you fit for church work,' he lisped, 'but never thought you a thief, neither.'

Bernard gave a small bow, 'Mr Un—'

'You should have come to me, I would have helped. And

such a lousy crew you've fallen in with. Oh, your poor mother, God rest her soul!'

'Ever the gushing spout, Mr Unthankes.' Bernard, his patience gone, drew himself up to his full height, a good thrice the size of the man before him. 'We're here on urgent business. If we had time, I'd have sought you out. But we don't.' He put his finger up to silence the little man. 'We need this body.'

Unthankes looked past Bernard at the gaping hole. 'Dr Burnett's boy? But why? He had the plague! You'll loose it upon us.'

'The boy was murdered. By Dr Burnett.'

Mr Unthankes gave them a dubious look. 'Why, I knew there was trouble about! I heard the stories. But fie! Dr Burnett is a most excellent man! He brought my grandchildren forth! He never stints the parish. I can't see him murthering.'

'That's not for you to decide,' said Bernard. He bent over, looked Mr Unthankes in his watery eyes. 'But I'll guarantee you this, if you attempt to block us, you'll find yourself in the dock with him.'

'Well . . .' said Mr Unthankes, drawing back and putting a pensive hand to his pruney chin. 'I'll have a think on it. Letters will have to be written.'

'Mr Unthankes,' Penelope cut in, 'forgive me, but was the lad – Dr Burnett's servant – was he fair-haired?'

The man slowly turned to her, confused that she should dare to speak to him. He looked back at Bernard, who nodded in encouragement. The man seemed to relax, then broke into a beatific smile, his chin now all but disappearing. 'Oh, like an angel!'

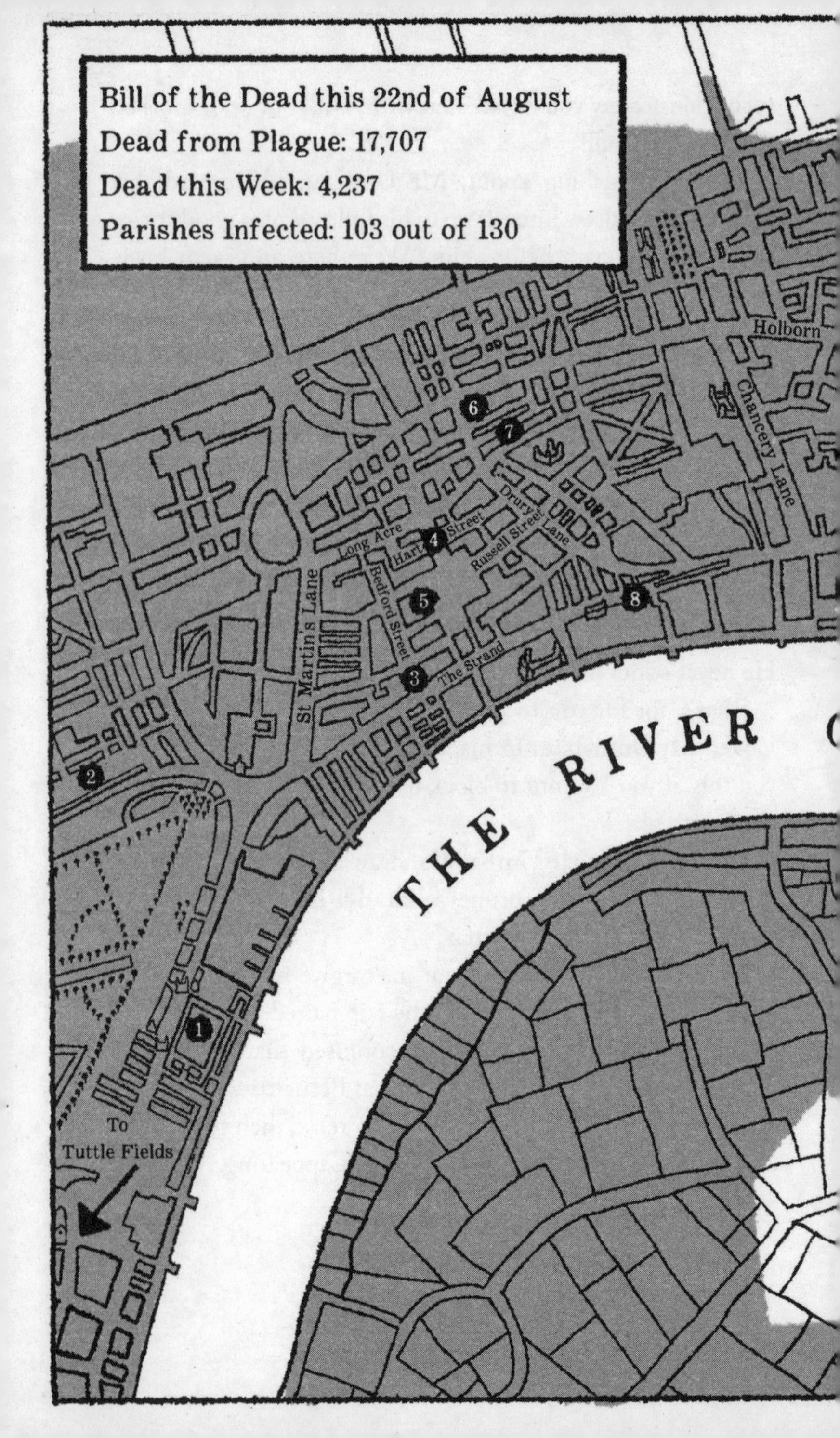

Bill of the Dead this 22nd of August
Dead from Plague: 17,707
Dead this Week: 4,237
Parishes Infected: 103 out of 130
Holborn
Chancery Lane
Drury Lane
Russell Street
Hart Street
Long Acre
Bedford Street
St Martin's Lane
The Strand
THE RIVER
To
Tuttle Fields
1
2
3
4
5
6
7
8

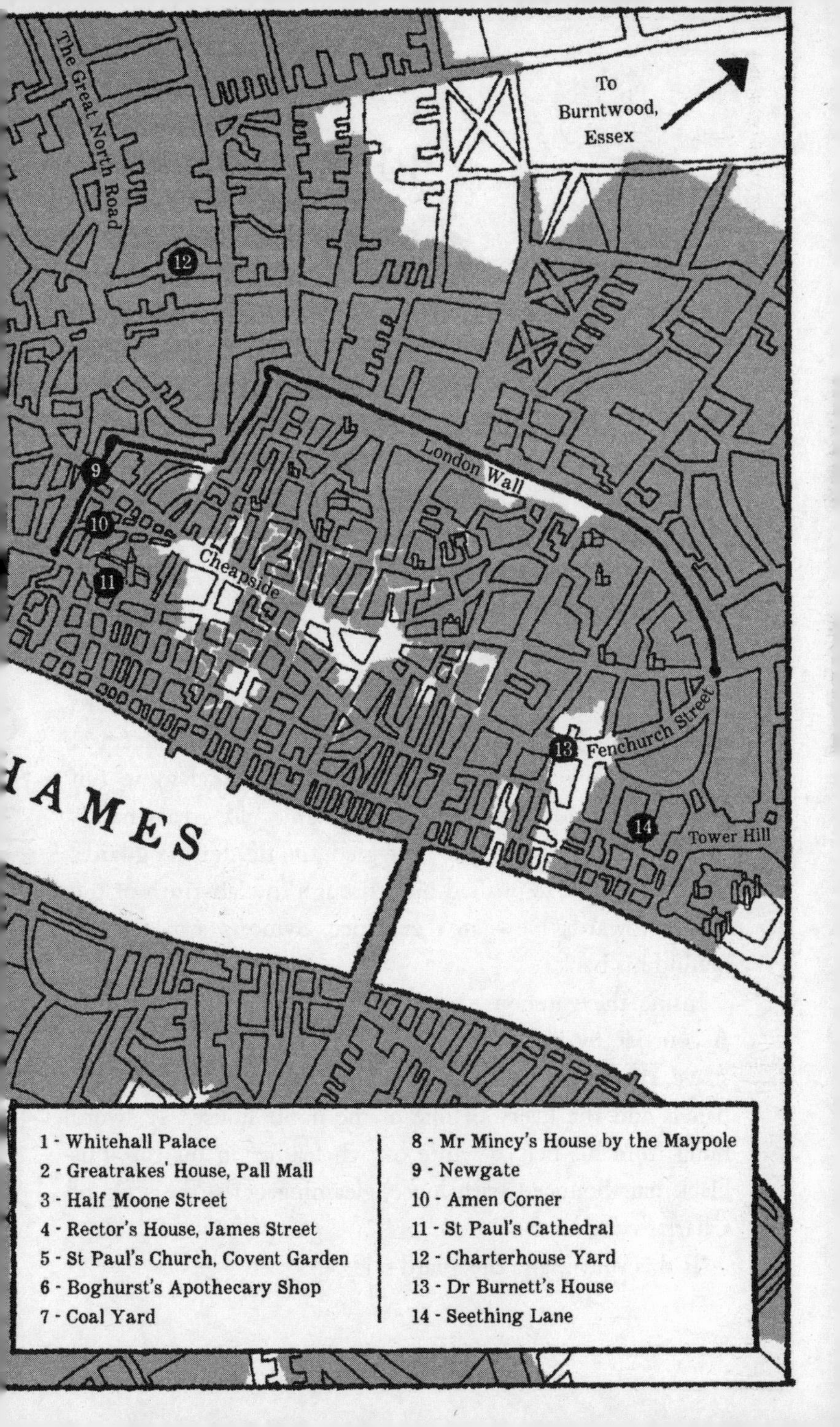
To Burntwood, Essex
The Great North Road
London Wall
Cheapside
Fenchurch Street
Tower Hill
HAMES
12
9
10
11
13
14
1 - Whitehall Palace
2 - Greatrakes' House, Pall Mall
3 - Half Moone Street
4 - Rector's House, James Street
5 - St Paul's Church, Covent Garden
6 - Boghurst's Apothecary Shop
7 - Coal Yard
8 - Mr Mincy's House by the Maypole
9 - Newgate
10 - Amen Corner
11 - St Paul's Cathedral
12 - Charterhouse Yard
13 - Dr Burnett's House
14 - Seething Lane

# 45

*Thursday, August 24th*
*An Escape to Hell*

SYMON HEARD HIS NAME being called. A call to death? Or salvation?

'You look a preacher all right, my pretty pet,' the guard said, pulling him to his feet and dragging him up the spiral stairs. 'Don't get your kind often. Shoulda had more fun with you.' Symon tried to push the man's cold, greasy hands off him, but the harder he struggled, the tighter the guard's grasp became. He pushed him through the labyrinth of the prison towards Newgate's entrance, Symon's arm twisted behind his back.

Inside the gatehouse, a young gentleman awaited them. A courtier, by his looks, and not much older than his first shave. He wore a most expensive suit of red silk cut with gold panels and the livery of one of the noble houses. A sword hung from his belt; a white ostrich feather in his cap. His black hair bounced with loose, gleaming curls, the style of Charles' court.

'Is this your man?' the guard said.

'No,' the courtier said, a look of revulsion on his face. 'I'm here to fetch a clergyman.'

'Back you go.' He turned to take Symon way.

Symon looked down in confusion. He wore only his shirt, torn and soiled. His face was thick with stubble, his hair with vermin. He looked back at the courtier, ready to beg; then he realised who it was.

Symon stood as tall and imperiously as he could. 'Enough of this. You know very well who I am. Your master will be furious if you leave me here.'

The courtier curled his lip in disdain, looked him over again. 'I'll have to send for a separate carriage. I shan't ride with him.'

'That's nowt to do with me.' The guard gave Symon a great kick with his boot towards the courtier.

'His breeches, please.' The courtier stepped away at the stink of him. 'Or would you like us to believe he came to you in his God cloth?'

'It matters not,' Symon said, his anger rising at Penelope's foolish delays. 'I'll gladly walk home bare-arsed to the world.'

Outside the gate, the guard still watching them, she prodded Symon with her sword. 'Stand at the rear, I'll not have you inside with me.'

It was Bernard in the driver's seat; he had the horses moving before Symon even had a chance to grab on. Once their carriage was safely away from the City, Symon yelled for Bernard to stop and jumped into the carriage to hug Penelope.

'Get your foul self away from me,' she cried.

'How did you do it? How?'

'It was not easy.' She handed him the change of clothes she'd brought. 'Went to see the Duke of Albemarle. It took some time to clear up his muddled head. He blamed you for all sorts of mysterious crimes, including a venison pasty gone missing from his cook, and a sore on his mistress's . . . well, anyway. Lord! That man doth talk! Said something about the Church being the centre of all evil. Eventually, he paused and I shoved a note into his hand. He had only to read it once, so I will give him that; he does know the pecking order of the kingdom.'

'What did you write? I can't imagine . . .'

'It wasn't from me. It was from Lady Castlemaine. Said you were a favourite of hers, and to call you a murderer was a violation of her very soul.'

'The king's mistress?' Symon said in disbelief. He had a sudden urge to kiss her again. Those lips always twisted in disappointment at him. Those startlingly clear and reproving grey eyes. A thousand times over. 'You most wondrous beast. How ever did you make such a connection? How did you convince her to write a letter?'

'I didn't. I forged it.'

Symon's jaw dropped. 'But . . . how did you get her seal?'

'I had a seal I'd got earlier, from the earl's house. Fixed it up.'

Symon shook his head in dismay. 'And the duke believed it?'

'His eye's goopy. He can't see very well.'

Symon sat back in his seat, closed his eyes, smiled. The only thing that kept the fatigue and strain at bay was a mad desire to bed Penelope. He rather liked her in breeches.

*

Symon washed off the filth of Newgate and quickly drank some broth. He met Penelope and Bernard up on the roof (Airing you out, the sexton said). He took a thirsty look up at the sky, watched as dark clouds moved in and blotted out the evening's first stars.

'Is it possible it will finally rain?'

'Please God, yes,' said Penelope. 'That would make for a most promising night.'

'Why is that?'

'Never mind. Now listen. All the arrows are converging on Dr Burnett. There is the note that condemned you. It was signed *B*. You assumed it was Boghurst, but it was Burnett. He knew he would profit from your confusion.'

'I don't understand.' A mixture of rage and sadness coursed through him. 'Why kill Nell? Why not kill me? Why make such an elaborate trap?'

'Too many questions would be asked if you disappeared,' said Bernard. 'No one cares about missing girls. A dead rector from a rich parish, you can't ignore that.'

'But why her? The dead are everywhere. He could have used any number of bodies to entrap me.'

'That last night, the plague society meeting,' said Penelope. 'Perhaps she saw something. She handled everyone's coats, their bags. I've asked Joan if Nell said anything to her, but she didn't. Or,' Penelope sighed heavily, 'it was an act of pure cruelty. He did it to wound you. Kill someone you love. Condemn you for their murder.'

Symon looked wildly about. Who would be next? How were they to stop him?

'Then there is this,' Penelope went on. 'While you were in Newgate, we dug up the body of Dr Burnett's servant.' She leaned in. 'He was fair, like the other victims. There were ropes on his wrists, his ankles. There was much decay, but the signs were there; that he had somehow been abused.'

'We have him then.' Symon stood up, ready to rush down the stairs with the news. 'Such depravity. Such blackness of soul. I have never seen such a thing. Why aren't you coming?'

Bernard was standing with one foot up on the roof's stone balustrade and smoking his pipe as if he wasn't even listening. Penelope was looking at Symon with great pity.

'It's not enough. The markings were too vague. The ink grid would have sealed it. But the skin was too degraded.'

'Filthy business,' said Bernard. 'Let me alone with him an hour. I'll squeeze it out of his balls.'

Penelope brightened at this.

'The two of you can be quite terrifying,' said Symon uneasily.

Bernard let his heavy boot fall from the low railing and strode over to the door. 'When you're ready to do something other than sit on your arse, come find me.'

Symon started to call him back but Penelope shook her head. 'Let him rest a little. He'd never admit it, but he was worried to death about you. And poor little Jack. Since you've been gone, he's been taking all his meals with the boy.'

Symon's head started to throb again at the boy's name.

'Now,' Penelope continued, 'everything points to Dr Burnett. His dead servant. The receipt we found at the Thurgoods'. But it is not a perfect fit. He is a cold man. A factual one. But he is fanatically fastidious. I've been at his house. The daily cleaning, his white-as-snow shirts and collars. His refusal to touch patients; we watched how he ordered about that poor assistant of his. Our murderer, however; he does not mind gore. He bathes in it.'

'There is the matter of the nurse at the Thurgoods' house. An assistant of some sort is Boghurst's theory.'

'There wasn't a nurse.' Penelope was pulling at threads in her skirt, the hem getting ever shorter as she went. 'I went back while you were in Newgate. Searched the place some more. Found an old wig and a dress of rags.'

'A disguise, then?'

'Yes, I suppose that is how he was able to come and go without the guards taking any notice.'

'So there may not be an assistant?'

Penelope shook her head.

'Then . . .' He was afraid to say it. He grabbed at one of the threads on Penelope's skirt and started pulling on it too. 'It might be Boghurst after all?'

She flicked his hand away from her dress. 'I've thought about it. The man we chased after at the Thurgoods'. He was not a short man. Boghurst is.'

'Heels,' said Symon. 'A good heel on his boot.'

'Maybe.'

In the distance, Symon's church bell rang the hour. Penelope sprang up and shook out her skirts. 'I've discovered something else curious about our good doctor.' She snapped her fingers at him. 'Now get off your muckety piles. For we have an appointment at eleven of the clock this night in Seething Lane.'

# 46

*An Empty Storehouse, Seething Lane, the Parish of Alhallows Barking*

THE MEN WERE HUDDLED around a table, a lifeless body before them. Through the smudged window, Symon could see Dr Burnett shouting orders in between violent coughs.

'He's not well at all,' Symon whispered to Penelope. 'How pale he looks!' While Symon was in Newgate, Penelope had found out something the doctor had hidden from them. He was moonlighting with another plague society, another group of healers trying to find a cure for plague. This group had been more productive and more energetic than Symon's, for here before them, the body of a lad.

The shadow society met in a small storehouse on Seething Lane. Penelope had broken into the silver shop next door and taken Symon up the stairs and out over the roofs to get to an upper window of the storehouse. They could see straight down into a small near-to-claustrophobic room, boxes and sacks piled up against the sides. In the middle, the table.

Symon squinted through the dusty windowpane. It appeared the group had not yet made the first cut; Symon felt his throat seize as he looked at the boy on the table. A lad of about fifteen, his corpse adorned with buboes. He had a full head of hair, and no ink grid or other strange marks that Symon could discern.

'What are they about?' he whispered.

'Dissection.'

'Did they kill the boy?'

'I can't be sure.'

Dread took hold as he watched the scene before him. How many more victims had fallen to Dr Burnett's knife? How many had been sent to other charnel grounds? He flinched as one of the men sliced into the abdomen.

'How did you find them?'

'Intercepted a note. I've taken to opening his post. Now shut up.'

Suddenly, the men stepped away from the table, erupted in exclamations. What had they seen? That they dared to look at the very roots of the disease itself, Symon could not fathom.

'Don't look at the corpse,' Penelope said. 'Watch their faces. Memorise their features.'

Dr Burnett doubled over, racked again with a cough. He groped for the corner of the table to steady himself, then shouted something and the men returned to resume their work. Two of the men, one on either side of the table, did most of the exploration. The doctor leaned against the table, the corpse's bare foot brushing against the cuff of his sleeve. Burnett seemed to shake all over for a moment, recovered himself then pointed and directed them towards something in the boy's abdomen.

Symon was about to ask another question when one of the

surgeons dropped his knife and fell to the floor. The other surgeon pointed to the corpse's abdomen, then turned to vomit. Another man staggered away from the body, screaming and scratching at his eyes, his throat, as if attacked by an invisible demon. He reached out to Dr Burnett, seemingly to beg for help, but the latter's cough had worsened, his whole body convulsing. Symon watched with dismay as the doctor gave a last great shout and fell to the floor, the other man falling atop him.

Symon grabbed Penelope and looked about for the quickest way down.

'Let's go,' Symon said. 'We must help them!'

She pulled him back. 'I think not.'

# 47

*Symon's Kitchen*

SYMON SAT AT THE TRESTLE table with Penelope, staring at a piece of bread and contemplating how he was supposed to eat it given all he had seen that night. He was roused from his stupor by the sound of someone shouting his name.

'God damn! Symon, are you down there?' Boghurst came running in, smacked the table with a rolled-up bill of mortality.

'Must you?' said Symon. 'There's enough shock about.'

'God damn! The man is dead. The doctor is DEAD!' The apothecary flew around the kitchen swatting everything he could in his glee. 'Have you heard? Shall I tell you?'

Symon thought back to the scene they'd witnessed. The doctor was dead? He recalled what the doctor had shouted as he fell. What Symon now knew to be his last word. 'Annie.'

'I was right!' Boghurst continued, grabbing Penelope in a hug then shoving her away before she scratched him. 'That hound of hell, that fiend! That most Unchristian of Souls! That Imposter of Physick! He killed them, killed them all!

Shall I tell you more?' He didn't wait for an answer. 'He was found this morning, he and a secret fraternity of fiends! All dead. And next to them, a poor lad they had cut into.'

'All dead?' Symon gasped. 'How is that—' Penelope squeezed his hand, willing him to stay quiet. Symon looked at her. What had the men unleashed?

The apothecary shrugged. 'Dead. Or dying.' He took Symon's bread, buttered it and stuffed it in his mouth. 'The ones still breathing have all but an ear in the grave. It's all over town! These fine fellows, they were some sort of shadow medical society. Well, they got a body off a dead-cart driver. A lad from Petticoat Lane. A good boy, by all accounts, a shame. His corpse was still warm, they say. Well, they opened him up – I saw Mincy this morning, he told me this – digging around for the seat of the pest, found it near the stomach. Tried to cut it out. Well, they poked the pest too much, didn't they? And it burst! Imbeciles! The very heart of plague. It gave forth a most venomous juice and a stench that rose up and infected them all! The Devil's aeyres itself!'

He started to sit down next to Symon, made a face at the chair as if he'd eaten a bad piece of fish, and jumped back up. 'Mincy says our dear Dr Burnett fell dead immediately. Two others still breathe, but the Devil has already marked them for his own. I visited one this morning. I wanted to see him before he died, beat the truth out of him, that he helped Dr Burnett with the murders, he and this most wicked shadow society. But he could not be roused except to spew blood.'

Boghurst leaned against the wall, gasped for breath, exhausted by his own tale. Then he recovered himself, eyes burning like the sun itself, and gave Symon a double smack on the head with his bill. 'Well, what do you think of that? Done and dusted, that's what I say.' He began to laugh.

*A laugh of relief*, wondered Symon, *that the murderer truly has been caught?* Or that the inquiry was now sufficiently deflected from the apothecary's own actions?

Symon looked over at Penelope. Her back was to him. She'd gone to the sink, was cleaning vegetables she'd gathered from the garden with Jack that morning.

'It's all rather remarkable,' Boghurst went on, still gasping. 'That this is how it ends. God's Destroying Angel found him and meted out justice. You were right, Symon! Right all along! Trust in God!'

Symon walked over to the kitchen window. Watched the play of light on his garden as the wind blew through his little trees. 'Most strange indeed. Most unexpected,' he murmured. Is this how it ends? Had God tired of waiting for Symon, decided to handle it directly himself?

'Do you really think the pest reached out of the corpse and killed them all?' he asked.

'Or charnel gases from the corpse. Or a contagious and fatal hysteria brought on by the black waters they chose to enter.'

'I'd seen him recently,' Symon lied – he would not tell Boghurst he had witnessed the scene – 'he had a quite violent cough.'

The smile vanished from Boghurst's face at this.

'A cough? A persistent one? Was he coughing up anything? Did he appear feverish?'

'He looked very sick, to tell you the truth.'

'Dear God, no.' All the colour had drained from Boghurst's face. 'It's another incarnation of the pest. It seizes the lungs instead of the blood. It kills quickly. And spreads like lightning. I must go. At once. Annie.' He ran from the room; Symon had never seen him move so fast.

He turned to Penelope. 'All dead! I had no idea. We should have stayed.'

'Then we might be dead, too,' Penelope said.

He shook his head, still trying to sort it all. 'Good God. Just like that.' He paused. 'Is that it, then? It's all over? Can we be sure?'

'No.' She put a knife in Symon's hand, motioned for him to chop the vegetables.

'No? Why not?'

She nodded to the chair next to Symon, the one Boghurst had attempted to sit in. 'Because she is still here.'

# 48

*Where a Cursed Rain Falls*

'WAS IT DR BURNETT?' Penelope asked the ghost. 'And if not, then which one of them? The surgeon? The mystic? The apothecary?' The woman looked at her forlornly, held out an oyster shell.

Penelope sighed. The ghost was almost always with her these days. But they still had no ability to communicate. Penelope could not figure out the woman's connection to the murders; but whenever she and Symon talked about the deaths, the woman with her gown of ashes appeared. She had been on the roof with them on Seething Lane, looking over Penelope's shoulder down on to the dissection.

When Boghurst had come into the kitchen with his news, the ghost had no reaction. Instead, she sat quietly at the table, mimicking Penelope, using a carrot to slice the plates and cups. If Dr Burnett were the killer, wouldn't the news of his death have registered with the ghost somehow? Perhaps not. Perhaps there was to be no communion at all with the dead.

*

Evening was upon them. Another hot, stifling August eve. S*urely the sky will burst soon*, she thought, *a storm must come*. She was sitting in the front pew of the church, with only a single candle to cut the dark. Symon came in from the churchyard, a break from the burials.

'What shall we do now?' he asked.

'I don't know.' She stared straight ahead, as if trying divine the truth from the gloom around them.

He hesitated, then took a letter out of his pocket. 'It's from Lady Gauden.'

'I know,' she said flatly. 'Read it yesterday.'

'Ah, well, then you know what she asks. That I come, that she will tell me about the child.'

'She can't tell you,' Penelope said. 'She is incapable of the truth.'

'Such harshness—'

'I must speak the truth.' Her voice dropped, almost an afterthought. 'Otherwise, I am lost myself.'

Symon took her hand. 'You must rest, Penelope. Go to my house. Eat something. I will be home soon.' He got up and headed back out to the burials, his outline fading into the dusk. She looked down at where he had been sitting; he'd left Elizabeth's letter on the bench. She took it with her as she left the church through the little door behind the altar that opened on to the piazza. As she dropped the letter into one of the smoking braziers lining the square, she felt a tiny splash on her head. Rain, finally. It had come. Not a drop all summer. She knew what this meant. She sat down on the church step under the shelter of the portico. The rain, this changed things. Her mind switched. She needed to be sure. That with Dr Burnett's death, they really were finished with this business. If the killer still walked this earth, she knew where he would be tonight. The lure was too irresistible. It was what these men of physick had been waiting for all summer, how they had prattled about it during their meetings! Their desire for rain; a summer rain that would carry with it the seeds of a plant that could save them all. *Coelifolium.* Flowers of Heaven. A plant that grew only in particular conditions. In the mist of the night, destroyed by the harsh rays of the first light. A fresh harvest of it in the right hands, with the right formula, could be turned into an elixir that could cure any ailment. No need of gold or golden hair if one had this golden plant. No one had managed it yet, but they said it was only a matter of time. She had looked up pictures of the plant in one of Boghurst's books. *A grubby little thing,* she thought. *To have such fantastical hopes pinned to it!* It grew up in cracks in the streets. If the killer lived yet, he would be out there, searching for the plant. And once he had it, his butchery would begin anew.

She watched as the heavens opened. She waited for a lull, then with one of Symon's cloaks as cover, she wandered through the back courts and alleys of the outparishes, the liberties, peering around corners, staying in the shadows, looking for the men who were looking for the plant. She had wanted to borrow a horse from the earl's stables. She could cover more ground that way. But then they would see her, hear her coming.

It did not matter in the end, for she found them all out there, on the hunt for the tiny plant. Mincy. Greatrakes. Boghurst.

Another idea came to her as she watched the apothecary. He was on his knees, back to her, digging between the cobbles in Heathcock Court. They would be out all night, collecting. Which meant their homes, their bedchambers, their private papers would be unguarded. This time she did not hesitate;

she took a horse from the earl's stables and rode as fast as she could.

*

The stars were with her, for she found them in the very first house she looked. They were in the closet off the bedchamber, as she had expected. Her drawings. Every last one. Along with a stained and water-warped notebook of experiments. She didn't want to touch it, afraid of the misery the book would tell. She took the collection straight to Symon's, but he was not there; his bed hadn't been slept in. *Still down at the church*, she thought. A crash of thunder shook the house; the rain would return soon. She looked for a place to put the drawings and the book for safekeeping. She needed to go out and find its owner. There was every chance he already had a new victim. She would find him and follow him back to his lair. Burn him in it.

She returned her horse to the stables and headed towards the passages off the Strand. She turned down Katherine Street, but a mist had settled in, obscuring her vision. Her eyes were growing heavy with fatigue and a chill ran through her as the wind picked up, pressing her wet clothes against her. She crossed the Strand, picked her way down a little lane.

'Hello again,' she sighed. The ghost had come forth from the mist, bits of ash flying off her dress and disappearing into the wind.

Penelope smiled at the poor woman, started to walk past her, but the ghost grabbed at her arm and tried to pull her into the wall.

'You know I can't go there.'

She grabbed for Penelope's hand, pleaded with her eyes for her to come.

'It's a wall. I haven't time for this.'

Suddenly the woman stiffened, her empty eyes flew open with fear. She screamed.

Penelope felt the hair on the back of her neck stand up, a dreadful cold down her backbone. Behind her, she heard: 'Penelope, I'd like a word please.'

# SEPTEMBER

*My meeting dead corpses of the plague, carried close to me at noon-day through the City in Fanchurch-street. To see a person sick of the sores, carried close by me by Gracechurch in a hackney-coach. My finding the Angell tavern, at the lower end of Tower-hill, shut up, and more than that, the alehouse at the Tower-stairs, and more than that, the person was then dying of the plague when I was last there, a little while ago, and I overheard the mistresse of the house sadly saying to her husband somebody was very ill, but did not think it was of the plague. To hear that poor Payne, my waiter, hath buried a child, and is dying himself. To hear that a labourer I sent but the other day to Dagenhams is dead of the plague; and that one of my own watermen, that carried me daily, fell sick as soon as he had landed me on Friday morning last, when I had been all night upon the water (and I believe he did get his infection that day at Brainford), and is now dead of the plague. To hear that Mr Sidney Montague is sick of a desperate fever at my Lady Carteret's, at Scott's-hall. To hear that Mr Lewes hath another daughter sick. And, lastly, that both my servants, W. Hewer and Tom Edwards, have lost their fathers, both in St Sepulchre's parish, of the plague this week, do put me into great apprehensions of melancholy, and with good reason.*

Samuel Pepys, Naval Clerk, Seething Lane

# 49

*James Street*

SYMON WOKE EARLY, despite not getting into bed till near four in the morning. Had he slept at all? He listened for sounds of his household moving about, but all was quiet. Penelope was sure to be up and out already. He had come home last night to find a puddle of water inside his front door. On the landing, a wet cloak, one of his, and a trail of wet footprints up the steps. She would've slept in his guest chamber, he was sure, after drying off with his best linens.

He went to see if she was still there and found the bed tidy, her wet things gone. He walked down to the kitchen, the puddles cleaned up, too. *Thank God she cleaned up after her mess,* he thought. Otherwise Joan would have words with them both. Penelope delighted in provoking Symon, but never Joan.

The kitchen was quiet save for the burbling of a pot over the fire. The tenor of his house since Nell's death. He looked through the back window and there was Joan in the garden, with Jack, picking flowers. He went out and gave them both kisses and all the warm words he could muster. He promised the boy he would be home for dinner, and that they should all sit around the table together, and plan a service for Nell. Bernard had made sure the girl had been buried in a good spot, one of the last plots near the piazza and far away from that horrible pit. 'You must pick out a poem to read,' Symon told Jack, 'I shall help you.' He gave the boy another kiss on the top of his blond little head and left for the church.

*

Noon. Symon wiped at his mouth, stood back up. He'd had another fit, though there was nothing left in his stomach. The stench was so high, the horror so unavoidable, it was impossible not to vomit. Symon had thought that if he stopped eating, the fits would stop too, but that hadn't been the case. The rains had returned and now his churchyard was a morass. The yard boys slipping and sliding as they went about their work. *Where is she?* he wondered, looking about the churchyard. He hadn't seen Penelope all morning.

'Have you seen her?' he asked Bernard.

The sexton started to reply, then took off at a run: a yard boy had fallen into the pit. The ground had been so dry from the summer heat that the rain made short work of the edges of the mass grave.

Symon checked to see that the boy was all right, then returned home, finding Joan and Jack at the kitchen table. 'We're making biscuit bread for Nell,' the boy said. ''Tis her favourite. I want to leave it for her in her room. She was sitting on her bed last night and she looked sad. This will cheer her up, won't it?' Did the boy see her ghost? Was he like Penelope? Or was it because of Penelope he thought such things? She shouldn't be spreading such nonsense. He would have to speak with her about this, he thought as he gave the boy a wan smile. 'Throw in an extra spoonful of sugar. That will indeed cheer her up.' He turned to Joan. 'Has Penelope been in for her dinner?'

Joan shook her head. 'She knows better. The mess she made last night! You ought to knock some sense into that girl.'

'Oh, Joan, I am so sorry. I thought she cleaned up after herself. She left it for you?'

The housekeeper banged her wooden spoon on the edge of the bowl. 'In and out like that, mud all over the stairs. As if I don't have enough to do!'

Symon winced, put a hand on Joan's shoulders. How could Penelope have added to the woman's troubles? 'May I help in some way? Send a boy up to help with the washing? I can only imagine the state of the bedclothes.'

'She's not gone completely mad, she knew enough not to touch my good white sheets, I'll give her that.'

Symon frowned. 'You never spoke to her? She didn't sleep here?'

He saw the colour drain out of Joan's face. He quickly looked at Jack, who had put his cup of flour down and was staring at Symon.

'This really won't do,' Symon said rather sternly. 'You're right, Joan. When I see her next I shall chide her thoroughly! She was down at the yard an hour or so ago,' he lied. 'I should have boxed her ears!' He ruffled Jack's hair. 'Now, if you don't mind, Bernard begged me to bring him a plate.' He went into the larder and put his hands on the shelf to steady himself. Not a word from Penelope since yesterday. It might be nothing. It might not.

*

'I fear she's gone,' he said to Bernard. 'I fear he's taken her.'

'But the doctor's dead.'

'No one's seen her since yesterday.'

'You know the girl's ways. Mad as a March hare.'

'It's only that . . . what if we were wrong? Look what happened to Nell . . .'

'I see. I'll send 'em all out now.'

*

The rain came down in a fury, so hard that Symon could barely see more than a foot in front of him. But that didn't stop any of them. The diggers, the yard boys, Bernard. They spread out around the parish to search for Penelope. One of the boys had come back from the river, an axe in his little hand. 'Her one, in't it?' he said.

Symon took the axe, felt its weight, felt his anger boil into a rage. How many times could he be a fool? How many would die because of it? He ran through the rain, up James Street, over to Drury, numb to the hard drops pelting his head and shoulders. *This anger*, he thought, *it is my ally*. It would push him through this most dreadful task.

He was drenched by the time he reached the White Hart Inn on Holborn. Boghurst's shop was on the corner, a board outside advertised his speciality:

*A Plain And Easie Method*
*for the*
*Plague*
CHEAP *And Absolute* REMEDIES
*For*
*Prevention And Cure*
*Thereof*

The door was unlocked. He went in and paused, listened for a breath, a stir, the scrape of a chair across the floor, but there was nothing. With each step he took, something crunched under his feet. He spied a candle on the table and lit it. He was shocked by what he saw. The shop was a wreck. Candied rose petals and vials of cherry syrup were scattered across the floor, pots of alum and sulphur tipped over. A jar of dried earthworms lay smashed on the counter. What had befallen this place? His foot slipped on a pestle.

'Boghurst? Are you here? Come out.'

The shop looked as if it had been closed for weeks. He made his way to the back. Dusty, dirty, a makeshift bed in the corner by the hearth. He ran over to it in horror. It was like the sack bed they'd seen at the Thurgoods'. Where the killer had slept. A new wave of nausea swept through him. Where was Boghurst's wife? His children?

He closed his mind to the pain, searched around for blood, for writings, for Penelope's missing drawings – anything that would condemn his friend. He walked over to the filthy bed. Picked up the pillow, threw it across the room. Picked up the blankets, felt something clunk against his leg. He shook the blankets to free whatever was in them, then looked down. A night cap, with something sticking out, a hard object, something heavy. He pulled the cloth back; inside was a stained, dog-eared book with leather covers. He turned the pages; they were filled with writing and diagrams, every last inch of space taken up. It was Boghurst's casebook. He read through the first pages; they detailed the coming of the plague with elaborate notes on his earliest patients and treatments. Was this it? Symon looked around. *Patience*, he thought. *Think, Symon. Think.* There might be other evidence. Most of the bodies had come from streets around Boghurst's shop. Coal Yard, where he'd found Nell, was just down the way. If he had Penelope, she would be somewhere close. Symon listened, heard nothing but the rats scurrying overhead. He looked at the wall the shop shared with the inn. Could it be? The White Hart Inn. Was she in there? The inn had been abandoned for months; it was a perfect hiding spot. Large, cavernous, empty. He took the book and used Penelope's axe to smash his way through.

# 50

## *A Sick Bed*

SHE HEARD YELLING, SHOUTING. It was coming from below. Penelope was locked in a garret, had been there for some time without ever hearing a single sound from downstairs. But now she could hear voices. A party? Or another wicked meeting of those godless men? Would any of them help her? Every bit of her itched. She couldn't tolerate this much longer. First he had infected her with plague. Used the rough tip of his quill to draw a square on her upper arm and label it '1'. Then took a knife and sliced three deep cuts inside the box. He talked to her as he did this, told her every step of the way what he was doing and why he was doing it. He showed her a little stick, its tip covered in plague matter from an active case. He stuck the tip in each of her cuts. He said that he had always liked her, and recognised in her a kindred intelligence, no matter her impoverished upbringing, dismal appearance, poor manner and terrible choice of friends. Penelope let him talk, encouraged him to. For she did want to know. Her father often said, stay silent but interested, and people will soon talk themselves into the noose they deserve.

He kept her well fed. Asked her constantly how she was feeling and took copious notes – he was awaiting signs that the pest had awoken, had started to consume her. He passed the time by reading to her from his medical books, told her the theory behind his treatments. Said if she had any ideas of her own, he would welcome them. He did not believe in rank, he said. His success, he was sure, depended on having an open mind when the minds of so many others were closed. 'Let us be friends,' he said. 'Please. This is a lonely business.' He stressed that he meant to cure her. He considered untying her, for he knew she had a strong enough mind to see the benefit of his work. But he also said he knew she was an unnatural girl, that she had an unwholesome tendency towards slipperiness, so for now, he would leave her fastened to the bed.

Slipperiness. *He was too right*, she thought, *and that would be his downfall.* She hoped. She had found the killer, she could find her way out of this. She had even found out who the ghost was. The woman hadn't left Penelope's side since she had been captured. She was there now, crying and holding Penelope's hand. On the other side of the room, a small painting hung on the wall. A young woman wearing a dress of gold silk to match her golden ringlets. He had noticed her staring at the portrait. 'That's my love. My one true love. Beautiful, isn't she? I miss her so. I used to see her all the time, but she's gone from me now . . .' Penelope felt a pressure on her hand, the ghost. The woman was crying harder, the kind of tears Penelope had often known in her life. Tears of impotent rage.

He gave her a few days, then began his treatments. Giving her physick before symptoms might lessen the severity of the illness, he said. This morning he had given her an injection. Not long after, the itching began and a rash erupted over her skin. He carefully mapped its spread, his quill connecting the pattern on her skin, then documenting it in his book. Downstairs, she heard another shout, a crash. A chair falling to the floor? Then another big laugh. A party. He was having a party while she was dying. He would soon know what a mistake that was. She turned to the ghost. 'Now, like we've practised, yes? You pick up the knife, you cut the rope. Come on, you can do it.' The ghost reached for the chair instead. Then she opened her mouth and screamed in frustration, and Penelope almost felt sorry for her. She knew how badly she wanted to help. Penelope took a deep breath and bent her thumb back against the table. She said a quick prayer and made the strongest, swiftest jerk with her arm that she could; bit her lip to keep from crying out in pain. It didn't work. She would let the pain pass, then try again.

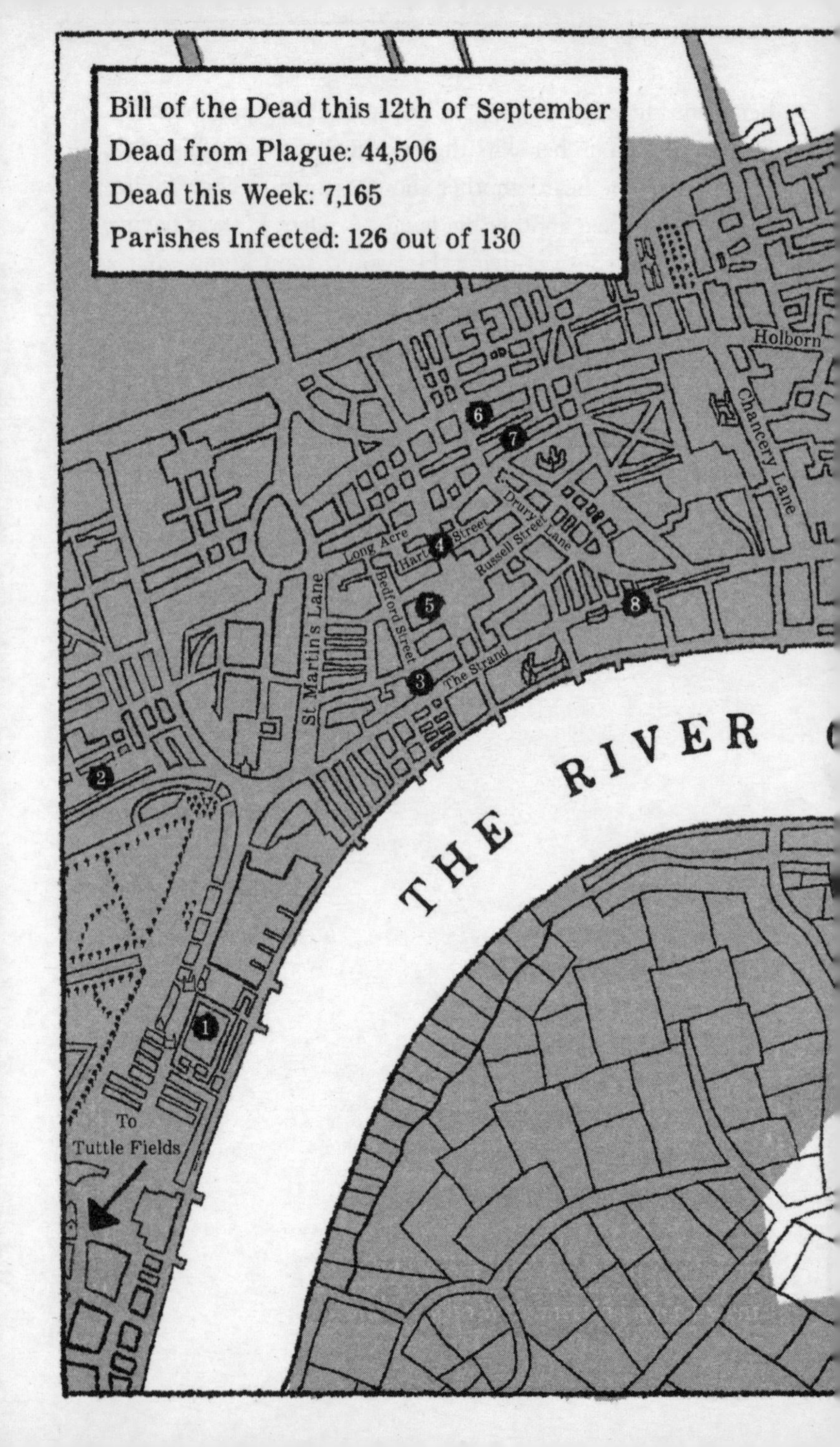
Bill of the Dead this 12th of September
Dead from Plague: 44,506
Dead this Week: 7,165
Parishes Infected: 126 out of 130
Holborn
Chancery Lane
Drury Lane
Russell Street
Street
Hart
Long Acre
Bedford Street
St Martin's Lane
The Strand
THE RIVER
To
Tuttle Fields
1
2
3
4
5
6
7
8

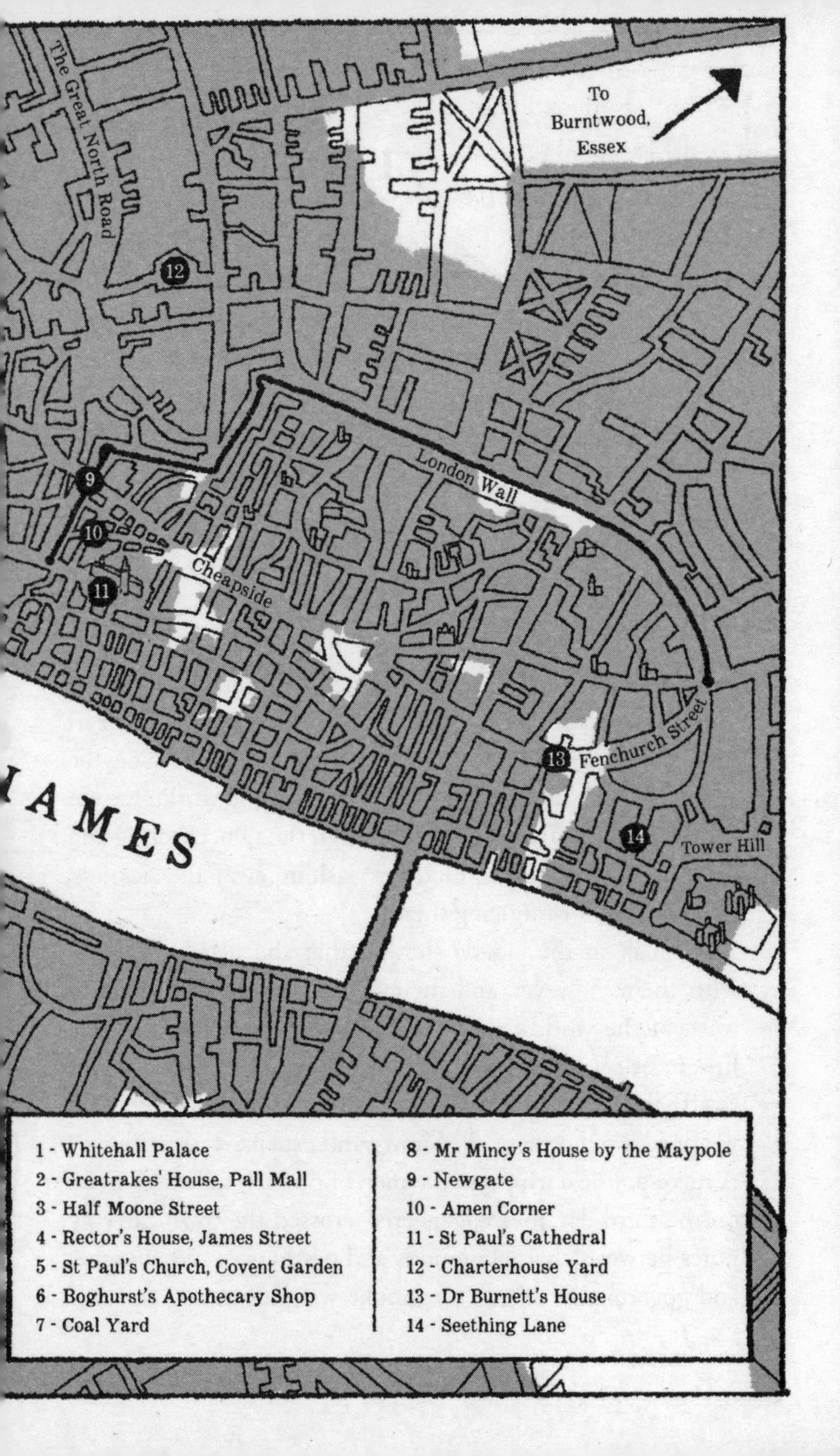
The Great North Road
To Burntwood, Essex
London Wall
Cheapside
Fenchurch Street
Tower Hill
THAMES
1 - Whitehall Palace
2 - Greatrakes' House, Pall Mall
3 - Half Moone Street
4 - Rector's House, James Street
5 - St Paul's Church, Covent Garden
6 - Boghurst's Apothecary Shop
7 - Coal Yard
8 - Mr Mincy's House by the Maypole
9 - Newgate
10 - Amen Corner
11 - St Paul's Cathedral
12 - Charterhouse Yard
13 - Dr Burnett's House
14 - Seething Lane

# 51

*Tuesday, September 12th*
*James Street*

A COLD, MISLING MORNING, a gloomy time indeed. September had brought no relief to London's suffering, only a biting, furious rain and a promise to destroy any heart that dared to still beat. The few people Symon saw on the streets walked like they had taken leave of the world. Except for the fanatics. They marched through the rain, cheering and blowing horns, praising God for washing away the sickness, the torment; for forgiving them.

A break in the clouds showed that the plague was still with them, however, and their cries changed once again to warn of the world's end. The Lord Mayor ordered sea-coal fires to be set across the entire town. Fires lined both sides of the Thames and all the major streets, and black smoke soon wrapped around them all. 'Showy and expensive, superfluous! A mere political frippery!' the men of physick railed. By noon on the third day, messengers criss-crossed the town carrying notes between charnel grounds and pesthouses and churches and government offices: the smoke was suffocating the sick.

Even the heavens wept at so calamitous a mistake, and on the third night of fires, the skies opened up to extinguish them. It had been the most fatal day that plague season. Four thousand dead between one rise of the sun and one setting of the moon.

Symon pulled the curtain back to look out of the window of his bedchamber, the world before him a solid sheet of grey rain. He could see no one and nothing. He let the curtain fall shut. Perhaps he was dead.

He couldn't find Penelope. She wasn't trapped in the White Hart Inn. The place was empty, the rats the only vermin he found there. Bernard had not given up the search. He and his boys were out looking for her day and night. They checked passages and sheds; broke into houses, knocking and calling and kicking in doors, but to no avail. 'She's gone home that's all, left us,' Bernard said, trying to comfort Symon. Home? Symon had never even asked her where that was. He tried to fool himself, let himself think that she was angry with him. He left her a letter a week ago, in the church loft where she stored her things. An apology. But the letter was still there. He would write her a dozen others. Put them everywhere he knew her to go. Allowed himself to dream that all of this was a misunderstanding. How could he have let this happen again?

The rain clawed at his window; the phantoms wanted in. Symon turned back to the papers on his desk. Above him, he heard someone walk across the floor. Joan, with Jack. Symon felt the rupture heave in his heart. His boy was sick. On the third day of the fires, the boy was one of those who had fallen ill. He should have sent them all away early in the summer. Or any day since. He was losing them all. Their deaths were on his hands.

He picked up his pen and wrote another note to Penelope. He would tuck it under the pillow in the guest chamber.

*I must make amends. Your counsel is now and always wanted. Your loss causes all of us great hurt.*

The curtain billowed with a gust of wind. He didn't want to look down at the street. More dead than living moved through the town these days. He heard the distant chime of a bell. It was time to search for Penelope again.

Symon had spent much of his life searching for kindness, wondering why it was so short in the world. And now he saw that he was as guilty as any. Penelope had been kind to him. Bernard. Joan. Jack and Nell. And he taken them all for granted, traded their kindness for the company of people like Elizabeth. He finished the letter.

*For what am I without you?*

*Your most humble and affectionate servant,*
*SYMON PATRICK*

Symon had read through the notebook he had taken from Boghurst's. He and Bernard had gone back to the shop and inn, turned it over several times. They found nothing to damn him. The apothecary's book was indeed thick, a record of patients he had seen since December when the first cases appeared. Near to a thousand of them. Each entry had details of their complaints and the treatments he had tried. Lozenges, sweatings, theriacs, cordials, amulets, cutting of the sores to ease the pain. But no burnings, no blisterings. Eventually, squares of ink drawn on the skin, but not until after Symon had found those first tortured girls in his churchyard. No frogs sewn inside wounds. Boghurst had detailed where the patients lived, who else was sick in the house, how long the sickness lasted, whether they survived, the conditions of the house. Damp or warm? Cleanly or dusty? Sweet air or foul? There was nothing untoward in the book. An apothecary, practising his trade. Symon read the book over and over, looking for any sign. Any code, any hint. He'd found nothing. But where was Boghurst's family? What had happened to them? On the last page, Boghurst had written his final thoughts on how to treat the plague, and Symon had used that in his care for Jack. Fresh air. Good broth. Rest. Compassion. A potion, perhaps of heated wine and cinnamon. 'It doth warm the heart,' the apothecary wrote, 'and that be its secret.'

Symon picked at the corner of his desk. A list he had made long ago with the names of the plague society on it. The suspects. Dr Burnett at the top. Then Boghurst's name. Both crossed out.

He pushed back from his desk; he must go, nothing good would come from counting his mistakes. He moved to get up when he paused, he heard jaunty steps on his stairs. Too light for Bernard. He rose to greet his visitor and scowled.

'Valentine Greatrakes. So you live.' God's favourite, indeed.

Greatrakes walked in, bright as sunshine in a suit of gold. The suit he had worn that day in church, when he sat with the Thurgoods. Symon had never asked how he knew Theodora. It mattered little now.

'Brought you some peach preserves. Thought it might cheer you up.' Greatrakes held out a jar of cut glass, the jam a tawny and flecked hue. A crisp cloth cover over it, held tight with twine. What a cheerful gift. It made Symon sick.

He refused to take it so Greatrakes put it down on the desk, then stepped closer, tilted Symon's head back and pulled at the skin under his eye. 'My, you do look glum. Why the frowny face? Still pouting over your murders? Shouldn't you be out hunting, leaving no piss pot unturned? I know your girl is.'

Symon tore his head free and grabbed his wrist.

'You've seen Penelope? Where?'

'Everywhere, you know how she follows me,' Greatrakes said, shaking Symon's hand off. 'Thinks I'm a bloody murderer.'

'Where have you seen her? When? You must tell me. Was it recent?'

'Oh, I can't recall. Here and there.'

Symon collapsed back down into his chair, his heart racing, his anger building. Another taunt. 'You haven't seen her, then, really. You shouldn't say such things.' He took a knife out of a box on the table and began to sharpen his quill.

'Why? What's the matter? Anyway. Rather dangerous thing for her to do, you know; surprised you let her run around for you like that.' Symon winced, his greatest mistake thrown so casually about.

Greatrakes saw the list of names on Symon's desk and picked it up. 'What's this? Your suspects? Why am I not crossed off? I knew it! For shame! Every last member of the plague society. How could you turn on us so? Fie! Ah, but I see here, our good doctor Burnett is crossed off. Because he's dead or because he was your man?' He let the list fall dismissively. 'Highly unlikely. Everyone knows Burnett fainted at the sight of blood. A terrible doctor, God rest his soul!' He gave Symon a pitying look. 'Oh, what a great goose you are! They said his heart stopped with his first look inside that corpse. Died of fright! Did you spend your entire summer coming up with that?'

Symon didn't respond, continued to sharpen his quill. He wouldn't let Greatrakes see his doubt. Had the doctor died of fright? Or of a most potent miasma they'd unleashed? Or had he already been ill, as Boghurst suspected, with plague that he'd caught from his victims?

Symon put down his quill, rubbed at his weary eyes.

'I see. Sore subject. My apologies. Any news from my Lady Gauden?'

How long would this go on for? 'I don't mean to be rude, but I'm not at all feeling well. Would you mind? Perhaps another day . . .'

Greatrakes put his hand over his heart and bowed. 'I understand completely. Just making the rounds today. Checking on my friends. Seeing who I've got left.'

Symon finally managed to meet Greatrakes' eye, then looked closer. 'Did someone hit you? Is that a black eye?'

'Of course not. A little stage acting earlier. Follies to amuse ourselves. Must have left some grease on.' He went over to check his face in the looking glass next to Symon's wardrobe. 'You know, Evelyn's back in town again. God's work he does, trying to save all those dying sailors! So gruesome, the Thames these days. Nothing but a floating morgue. Anyway, ran into him yesterday, mentioned he met you, said you were a fine gentleman. I thought to myself, of course they get along, because like you, he couldn't stop singing Lady Gauden's praises! And that babe of hers! He said it's a dear little thing, a whole head now of thick black hair. She'll be a beauty. Her beaus will line up from four counties over, like mother like daughter!'

He caught Symon's eye in the mirror and the corner of his mouth crooked up. A lazy smile? Or a smirk? Symon felt like he was swallowing poison. Black hair? Elizabeth's hair was auburn. Sir Denis' blond. His own hair was brown. Mr John Evelyn. Naval commissioner. Member of the Royal Society. With those long and flowing ebony locks. His eyes stayed on

Greatrakes as the mystic walked to the window and gathered up the curtain to tie it back. Was he teasing him? Or telling the truth? So Evelyn really was the father of Elizabeth's baby?

Greatrakes took a step back to admire his work. 'Much better. So dreary in here, how do you stand it? Afraid I must go now.' He patted Symon on the head, frowned. 'You do worry me. Try to rest.'

The mystic danced down the steps, leaving Symon to stare at the curtain, his mind trying to sort through it all. Elizabeth and Evelyn. The baby's hair. Symon's blood turned to ice. Penelope. Greatrakes knew something. His taunts weren't empty. They never were. He was mocking Symon. Penelope had said it had to be a member of the plague society. If it wasn't Burnett, and it wasn't Boghurst, that left Mincy. And Valentine Greatrakes. He heard the front door slam shut and with it a great crash came from his closet. The rest of his weak shelves had finally collapsed, sending his treasures crashing to the floor. He ran into the little room to survey the damage. His broken seashells, pieces of a French dish, his beast's jaw, cracked in half. He crushed them even more under his foot. He took a deep breath and leaned against his desk, his hand resting on a thick pile of papers. He picked up a sheet, then another. His heart seized. A face, a leg, a torso. Bruised and mutilated. Penelope's drawings. She had found them, put them here. When? The night of the storm, when he'd found her muddy prints all over his house. How could he be so stupid? There, pinned to the top portrait was a note from Penelope:

*Found them!*

Goddamn him. Damn him to Hell. He ran down the stairs, out of the door. Then everything went dark.

# 52

## *A Vase Is Broken*

Symon tried to sit up, but pain rocketed around his skull and he fell back. Boghurst was standing over his bed, shining candlelight in his eyes.

Symon pushed him away. 'What's going on? What's happened?'

'You slipped in the mud. Banged your head on your front step. That's where I found you, seems I can't leave you alone.'

Symon eyed him warily. 'Where have you been?'

'Essex. Went to check on the family.'

'Family,' Symon whispered. 'Your family. Is that where they are? They're not . . . ?'

'Not yet,' Boghurst said grimly. 'They're with Louisa's cousins. Sent them in July, it was senseless of me to have waited even that long. But they had a scare. The little one had a fever, they sent for me and I went right away. But she's fine, thank God, she's fine. A wee cold.'

'Why are you here?' Symon asked. He fought against the pain in his head; he had to get out of here.

'I came to check on you. And thought you might be worried about me, too. Would have sent you a note,' he said darkly, 'but look what happened the last time.'

Symon grabbed him by the arm. 'Listen, we've got to go. Get Bernard.'

'You're not going anywhere. That's a nasty bump you've got. Besides, it's raining like banshees outside.'

'We must go now. Find Bernard, the others. Stay here or come. Your choice.' Symon left the room without a look back. He knew the apothecary would follow.

*

Brother Croker, Valentine Greatrakes' assistant, let them in to the house on Pall Mall. Greatrakes soon after came down the stairs, wrapped in a purple velvet banyan and matching nightcap.

'A bit early to call it a night?' Boghurst asked.

'Apparently so,' Greatrakes said, staring at them with wonder.

Symon's heart skipped a beat. He felt like a hedgehog before a lion.

'Penelope,' he blurted out. 'Where is she?'

'Why, I have no idea. Something wrong? Oh yes, you were worried about her earlier. She hasn't gone missing, has she?' He took another step down the stairs, surveyed the group. Boghurst had sent word to Mincy, too, who had just come in through the door behind them.

'Is this a search party?' Greatrakes asked. 'Would you like me to join?'

'You have her,' Symon said. 'Where is she? Tell us now.'

Greatrakes laughed. 'Indeed! And what did you have for your supper, Mr Patrick?'

'Murder,' said Symon. 'Murderer. Nell. Theodora. Her family. Mary. The others. You killed them all. Now, where is Penelope? For your sake I hope she is still alive.'

'Symon, is that what this is about?' Mincy stepped forward, irritated. 'Another wench gone missing? I'm beginning to think we'd be better served if your brains were chopped and moussed.'

'Indeed!' said Greatrakes. 'Murder? Me?' He put a hand to his chest, feigning mortification, and looked at Boghurst. 'Is our dear Mr Patrick all right? Should we offer him a seat? Brother Croker, a brandy for our guest.'

Symon felt a paralysis moving up his body. What was he to do? What *could* he do? This scene had already played out once before, when he accused Burnett. Nell's last night alive. He had failed then. What was he to do now?

Bernard had a crowbar in his hand, awaiting Symon's signal. Boghurst only stared at him in dismay; he didn't understand what was going on. Symon had never told him that Penelope's drawings were stolen by someone within the plague society, or that she had disappeared the night she found the drawings in the murderer's home. Symon trusted no one at this point.

'You're to come with me,' he stammered, 'you're to answer for your crimes . . .'

Greatrakes came all the way down the stairs and halted in front of Symon, towering over him with his big white curls and knobby cheeks. 'You are quite like a moth in the cloth, Mr Patrick. And I'm thinking of throwing the whole chest out if you keep this up.'

'. . . for the most fiendish and most terrible abuse of your powers as a healer.'

'Abuse my patients? *Au contraire*. I heal my patients. Just like the rest of you.' Greatrakes threw a limp finger in Boghurst's direction. 'Or try to. Not my fault this plague thing. Nothing works. I must admit I've been up night after night with worry over what to do. I'm exhausted and out of ideas. A good sleep should help. I recommend the same to you. Now if you'll excuse me . . .'

'You tie them up, you mutilate them, you torment them. You kill them.'

'Dear me.' Greatrakes crossed his arms, looked again at the others. 'Your friend has gone on a most awful witch-hunt and I'm afraid he's close to irrevocably damaging our relationship. Are all of you in on this? I will have to seek reparations. Perhaps some good Spanish wine. And new testimonials, from all of you. But I must think on it. I have an early day tomorrow and must ask you to leave.'

All eyes were on Symon. He looked down, stared at the slippers on Greatrakes' feet. Pale purple, embroidered with gold thread. Silly.

'Look, Greatrakes,' said Mincy, clearly angry, 'do you have Symon's wench or not? If so, is she still alive? If not, lead the way. The corpse might still be fresh enough for a good dissection.'

Symon recoiled in horror.

'What a headache you are! All of you!' said Greatrakes. 'Go on, then, out you go. Tout suite.' Greatrakes dismissed them with a flick of his hand and turned away.

Symon felt as if pierced by a sword as he watched him head for the stairs. 'You most foul monster,' he shouted after him, 'you most foul demon.'

Greatrakes turned back, his genteel façade dropping. 'Name calling? So that's your talent? I really was wondering what it could be. You're not much of a godly man at all, are you? Why, even your little wench has more godliness than you do. Is it any wonder that she's left you? How embarrassing. Come to think of it, you should be defrocked for your behaviour. This cavorting with any lady who smiles at you. Playing about with the dead and accusing everyone under the sun of murder.' He was standing right in front of Symon now, poking viciously at his chest. 'You've quite lost it. The duke had it right when he threw you in Newgate. Only it should've been Bedlam!' He jerked his hand up and Symon stumbled back, thinking Greatrakes meant to hit him. He fell against a chair, knocking it over.

Greatrakes laughed. Boghurst stepped forward, shouting, defending Symon. The room was spinning around him, then he felt something wet spreading over his leg. One of Mincy's badger dogs was pissing on him. Symon shoved the dog away, pulled Penelope's axe from his coat and swung it back to brain Greatrakes. But right before the axe met its target, his arm was violently jerked backward. He turned around in confusion. Croker stood there, Penelope's axe now in his hand. Greatrakes stepped away, still laughing at Symon.

*I don't need it,* thought Symon. He yelled and ran forward, fingers stiff as knives; he would gouge out his eyes. Greatrakes threw up his hands to shield himself. But just as Symon reached Greatrakes, the man fell to the floor with a crash, pieces of porcelain showering all around him.

There, standing where Greatrakes had been, was Penelope. Panting, her eyes ablaze, triumphant – the broken bottom of a large vase in her hands.

# 53

*Midnight*

THEY TIED UP GREATRAKES and his assistant. Bernard had used the momentary chaos of Symon's charge to grab the axe from Brother Croker and knock him out with the butt of it. Mincy and Boghurst had stood watch over the pair while Bernard went to get a cart and Symon tended to Penelope. They hauled them back to Symon's church and locked them in the crypt. Boghurst said it was as sound a place as any.

Penelope had asked for fresh air, so they were now all gathered on the roof of Symon's house. It was the best they could do these days.

They were waiting. Symon and Mincy had sent messages to the duke, the Lord Mayor, anyone with authority. But the sickness raged worse than ever, their requests so far had been met with silence.

'We'll give it a day. After that, we'll take care of him ourselves,' Boghurst said.

'Why wait? I'll do it now,' Mincy said flatly. He had

Penelope's axe in his hand, had been inspecting it. 'This is a good blade. We'd be doing them a favour. And I hate sitting idle.'

Boghurst grabbed the axe out of his hand. 'I wasn't serious.'

'Oh, all right.' Mincy looked truly dejected. 'I'll fetch the duke myself. He is in my debt. There was that kidney stone I cut him of.'

'For the love of God!' Boghurst seethed. 'Go!'

After Mincy left, Penelope told them her tale. She had been held in a room on the uppermost floor of Greatrakes' house. She told them that she'd heard the commotion downstairs, knew it was an opportunity. She'd been trying to break her thumb, so she could slip out of her bindings, and when she heard the voices below, she gave the biggest jerk she could muster and was free. She untied her other hand and ankles and sprinted for the back stairs, but changed direction when she recognised Symon's voice.

'I don't know if I could break my own thumb,' Boghurst said as he cleaned a deep puncture wound on her lower lip; she'd nearly bitten through it to stop her screams. He had already set the broken bone and dressed her other cuts and wounds the best he could.

'You could if your life depended on it,' Penelope replied.

She did not yet show any signs of plague – a miracle on many fronts. Greatrakes had not been able to deploy his most invasive treatments on her. He awaited physical signs of the disease, he had told her, otherwise he could not evaluate the effectiveness of his treatments.

Symon had tried to get her to sleep, but she had refused. Said she'd had enough lying down. She did let them burn her clothes and submitted to a bath. She even let Joan wash her hair. A hot supper returned some of the colour to her face, but dark stains remained under her eyes.

He stirred the nearest smoke pot and threw in more pine needles. A sudden wind had thrown up the scent of rot, coated in lime. It burned the skin, refused to let go. A reminder. The world was still in chaos. The distemper was full on in the old city now. Near to 15,000 dead this week. Unfathomable.

Symon sat back down next to Boghurst, who, having finished for the moment with Penelope's injuries, propped his feet up on the balustrade.

'Perhaps Mincy is right.'

'Symon.' Boghurst was shocked at his friend's turn. 'Don't fall prey to my black humour, or Mincy's careless whims. We'd never get away with it.'

'But once he's out of our hands,' Symon went on, 'Greatrakes may find a way out of this, what with that tongue of his. He'll deny knowing anything about the murders. That his assistant Croker was behind it all.'

'I agree. He will try that,' said Penelope, 'though I never saw his assistant until those last moments. The man is quite thick. I do not think he knew anything, except that he should defend his master against the marauders.'

The bells had stopped ringing – on the order of the Lord Mayor. Too much noise, he said, disturbed even the dead. They fell quiet for a moment, sinking into the sounds of the night: the rhythmic chirps of the grasshoppers, the night song of a robin – the snores of Bernard. He was asleep in his chair.

There was still such a heavy weight about this business. The tension of keeping a prisoner. The path to catch him, marred with shame. Distraction. Obsession. They were mighty enemies. Boghurst's fixation on Dr Burnett's wife, Anthea. Annie. He had carried that hatred for years, their professional rivalry only making the pain of that loss worse.

Eventually, his antipathy had led him to pursue the man without thought that any other could've been behind the killings.

'There were too many pieces that fit,' Boghurst said. 'The mysterious death of his manservant; the other one missing; the signed receipt you found at the Thurgoods'; his hostility towards our investigation. It was all there.' He chipped away at a flake of stone with the toe of his boot. 'If I had set my passions aside, would it have changed our course?'

'Who am I to say?' Symon had spent half the summer thinking his old friend was the murderer, and the other half daydreaming of a life with Elizabeth. And lost Nell for it. Mary. And nearly Penelope. He closed his eyes. He was too tired, damned by his own recklessness to fault the apothecary. He had built a most mighty and fine fantasy around Elizabeth. Around the baby. He had looked forward to holding the little girl again, but had stopped shy of truly thinking she really was his. A part of him had always known she wasn't.

How bright and shining Elizabeth had been in his eyes. He had thought her smiles and words were real; that she could offer him the life he had always longed for. He had mistaken her looks, her touch, her need. That he alone had awoken something in her. Such serpent thoughts! He had seen the reality at Burntwood ('Oh you'd seen it before, then!' he could hear Penelope scolding), and he had still struggled to believe it. Elizabeth was unmoored, even more so than he; she bounced from one false delight to another, refused ever to let her feet touch the ground. She clung to anything that could lift her from her own pain. *What happened to her*, he wondered, *to make her so fragile? To behave so rashly?* He had only known her façade.

Through the garret window below, he could hear Joan

chiding Jack, and then a little laugh from the boy. The quiet, mundane conversation of true connection. Symon had come home to find Jack alert, his fever broken. It had not been plague, said Boghurst, a summer ague was all. Two miracles in one day; Symon didn't know what he'd done to deserve that.

'He's sharp, our Jack. Brave,' Boghurst said. 'He's shown quite an interest in my work. I'd like to take him on as an apprentice. Could do with a fine young man about.'

Symon hesitated. He had thought about the church for Jack. But he would let the boy choose, help him any way he could.

'I think, when he's better, I shall get him a dog, too. He would like that.' Mite and Tripe would have to learn to share. They were back. He had come home to find them waiting for him, with a note from Mr Evelyn:

*Your treasures will bee much safer with you. As mine are with mee.*

*Yrs affect.*
*John Evelyn*

*Indeed*, thought Symon. Evelyn had Elizabeth. The baby. But for how long? He burned the letter in the coals of a smoke pot.

'How is Annie?'

'Utterly devastated,' Boghurst said. 'But well. It looks like Burnett knew he was gravely ill; he had not been home for several days. In some ways – hell, many ways – I was wrong about him. He stayed away to keep the pest from contaminating her. But he sent many letters to her those last days

– nearly one an hour, she said – telling her of his love for her. His hopes for her if he were to pass over.'

Symon let out a deep sigh. 'I must go to her. See what I can do.'

'She would like that. I stop in as often as I can; send someone when I can't. You know, they really did love each other.'

'As do you and Louisa.'

'Ah, I know it, man! Spare me the sermon!' he grumbled. 'Are you to leave your false thoughts behind too, then? Leave off this business with Elizabeth for good?'

'Beat me if I don't.' He stared at the whorls of smoke rising from the brazier. With every letter Elizabeth had written this summer, had Evelyn been sitting next to her? Who came before Evelyn? Before Symon? Who would come after?

He looked over at Penelope. She was squatting, knees tucked up under her chin, pouring little drops of milk into bowls for Mite and Tripe. Her lips were cracked, an angry rash all over her body. But not plague, said Boghurst, not yet. He had made an ointment of comfrey and she was now covered in a thin paste of it.

Symon nodded towards her. 'Will she be all right?'

'She has a decent chance. It's unlikely she has plague – it's rare for such an infection to take twice in one season. Only time will tell. But she is a strong one. Stronger than you or me.'

Symon looked at Boghurst with marvel. His friend had changed this plague season, indeed. As soon as he thought this, recollections of his own behaviour rushed back in to haunt him. 'We should have seen it. I'll never forgive myself.'

'Yes, we should've.'

'I spent most of my time avoiding Greatrakes, he was so thoroughly unpleasant. If only—'

Penelope cut in. 'I think he killed his wife trying to save her. He told me a terrible fever came through their village. When I saw her, she wore a dress of ashes. I don't know how to explain it. A sign of the fever that took her? Or did he burn her in an attempt to cure her?'

'Let's go burn him, then,' said Boghurst, getting out of his chair.

'Steady.' Symon pulled him back down. 'We've already been through this.'

'He seemed utterly unaware of how evil he was,' Penelope said softly. 'He told me Nell was my fault. He killed her because of me. Said she had seen my drawings in his satchel, the night he was over here.' She took a long, ragged breath, coughed. 'I suppose he's right, for I did invite a murderer into Nell's home.' She kept her eyes down as she said this, brushed her skirts and pulled one of the cats onto her lap as if she sought to distract herself, too, from thoughts that were too painful. 'He really was quite mixed up, about everything. He said his experiments, he did them out of love. That his search for a cure, that it was all for God and for his wife. He said he lost his wife because he had done something to displease God; that he'd lost his power to heal because of it. He said if he found a cure for plague, then surely God would forgive him. That she might forgive him too.'

'Do you think she will?' Symon asked.

'No.'

'He truly thought that what he did to those girls would lead to a reunion with God? I don't see how he could make such a connection.'

'Oh, I do. I see such distortions all the time. Perhaps not on that scale. But they are there.'

Symon didn't reply, ashamed of how convoluted his own

thinking had been. They had caught a most evil man, but Symon could not get the visions of the victims, the sick – of Nell, of Mary – out of his mind, of the pain they had suffered. And there was still much to fear. He looked around at his company; they had survived so far. But any one of them could be dead by the morrow. London hadn't seen such a great plague in centuries.

As soon as they could pack, he was sending Joan and Jack to his mother's in Lincolnshire. Bernard and several of his boys were to travel with them to keep them safe. Symon would get a pass from the bishop; a private carriage from the earl's stables. He wanted Penelope to go, too, but he could no more control her than he could a wild cat. Symon would stay behind and close up the pit. It could take no more bodies. There were few left living in the parish anyway. There was Lady Digby, but he would gladly send her to Tuttle Fields if it came to that. After he had sealed the pit, he would go to the east end of town and offer what help he could.

He stole another glance at Penelope, allowed himself a small smile. Joan had brushed and braided her hair, but he had to admit, even when it was a squirrel's nest, she was radiant. He thought of their kiss. He had thought of it often these past weeks, and now, of how he could get another. He desperately wanted that, he realised. She gave him hope. She made him believe, queerly enough, that there could be a sweeter future.

Tripe was mewling, trying to knock the milk jug out of Penelope's hands. 'How many times can a man be a fool,' he said softly.

'We shall see, Symon Patrick, we shall see,' Penelope replied.

She knew what he was thinking. Could she be as strong as she seemed? Could he take her as she was? Penelope gave the cats a final scratch. She bid them all goodnight and threaded her way through the chairs, the smoking pots, the empty cups towards the roof door. She must think to her future, seek her fortune. She would no longer hide, nor work under others. Symon would be her friend, as he always had been, even before he knew her name, and enlist his earl to set her fortune to rights. She would live as if this were already true. She would open a shop. What would she sell? Potions? Paintings? Advice? She would wear crimson satin every day, except on those when she preferred plum or emerald.

Or she would deal in exports. Sail the high seas, her skirts tied up, the salt thick on her tongue and in her blood, her hair wind-whipped into a helmet the colour of a black dragon's eye. Symon and Joan and Jack would be safely below deck, playing cards, writing letters, singing songs, while she set about freeing the whales and the savages, discovering lands. Or maybe she'd tie her hair back in a man's queue and talk in a low voice and wear breeches. Become a clergyman, get her own parish. She'd run it far better than Symon. She'd like that. To be in charge. To care for others. To have them care about her.

'Fie,' she said to herself. She traced her fingers along the cool, smooth oak banister as she walked down the stairs. 'That's very fancy thinking, indeed, Penelope.' But where would she call home until then? She dropped a letter on a step. From Elizabeth. She threatened to come to London if Symon didn't write to her soon. Penelope thought about destroying it; she would enjoy seeing Elizabeth in town, in the muck. But she had also tired of their affairs. Once Joan and Jack left, Penelope couldn't stay in Symon's house. He would expect her to cook and clean. And he really didn't deserve that. She had any number of other houses to choose from, but they were empty. She would be lonely. What to do, Penelope, what to do?

She headed to the guest chamber next to Symon's. At least for tonight, she would sleep in a soft bed, in a safe house. Tomorrow she would wake up, put away her disguises and get back to work.

# HISTORICAL NOTE

The epidemic of 1665 peaked in London around the last week of September. The bills of mortality put the death toll at 68,000. But there were many missed or hidden cases, and the true death toll is thought to be 100,000 out of a city of half a million people – an inconceivable loss in modern times. Another 100,000 died outside London as plague spread throughout England before burning out in 1666. Today, the leading infection theory is that fleas, through their bites, carried the plague bacillus, *Yersinia pestis*, from rats to humans. In 1665, there was no suspicion at all that fleas and rats were responsible for spreading the disease.

Many of the characters in this book are based on real people. The Reverend Symon Patrick stayed with his parish during the outbreak, writing to his friend, Mrs Elizabeth Gauden, who had fled the plague for safety at her sister's house, Hutton Hall in Essex. Several dozen of Symon's letters to Elizabeth have survived, but only three of hers are known. Elizabeth was amongst some 200,000 people who are thought to have left London. A third of those who stayed behind died.

While many medical men also fled the plague, Mr William Boghurst and Dr Alexander Burnett did stay behind to treat patients – and compete for a cure. It would have made little difference if more medical men had stayed, since there was no known effective treatment until the discovery of antibiotics in the mid-twentieth century. Dr Burnett did have two man-servants who reportedly had plague early on in the outbreak, and there were rumours that foul play at the hands of Dr Burnett was behind the death of one and the disappearance of the other. But it's not clear how Dr Burnett himself met his death. He did die at the end of August 1665, as Samuel Pepys recorded in his diary. But Pepys says nothing more than that he died of plague. Two letters written shortly after Burnett's death – one from the Reverend John Allin to a friend and another from John Tillison, a clerk at St Paul's Cathedral, to the dean, William Sancroft – tell of a dissection that the doctor was allegedly present at and that was fatal to all attending save one, George Thompson. Thompson denies this story in his own plague treatise. He says he was the only one present at the dissection, though acknowledges the others named were his friends and medical colleagues and that within a few weeks of each other they all died of plague.

Valentine Greatrakes was not in London during the plague but arrived a year later. After being greeted with initial enthusiasm, he soon left town. The historical record shows him to be a devout and civic-minded man, but cursed for the purposes of this book with an irresistible name.

# ACKNOWLEDGEMENTS

This is the hardest part of the book to write. Because there is no way to convey with mere words all of the gratitude and love I feel for the following:

To my editor Miranda Jewess at Viper and my agent Victoria Skurnick at Levine Greenberg Rostan. Thank you both for your sharp guidance, your wisdom, your darkly brilliant insights and the salty, ingenious language you both toss at me in every correspondence. (If there is a clever or original – or outlandish – phrase in my writing, chances are I borrowed it from one of these ladies.) I am your affectionate servant now and forever.

Thank you to the incredible team at Viper and Profile Books and their dedication to making this book the best it could be, with the excellent Graeme Hall leading the charge. To Sam Johnson for such a texturally rich and evocative cover, to Steve Panton for maps I want to live in. To Rachel Nobilo, Flora Willis, Jane Pickett and Drew Jerrison for making sure Penelope and Co. get to meet their readers. And also at LGR, thank you to the crew who gave Penelope her first real shove into the world: Beth Fisher, Courtney Paganelli and Cristela Henriquez.

Thank you to Dr Andrew Wear, my former professor at University College London, who put me on the path to this book. To Dilys Cowan, fellow student in my history of medicine master's programme there, for all of your cheer and kindness.

To my mother and father, Pam and Colby Valentine, for being such good, honest people, and for plunking me down on this earth near so many fantastic cemeteries and haunted old farms. And for taking me to the library every week to check out so many books about witches and ghouls.

To a wonderful new friend, Jennifer Ryan, and a wonderful old friend, Bridget Bentz, for taking the time to read drafts and giving me the best feedback! And to Alison Richards, for all of your support along the way in this and in all of my efforts!

I apologise to the Reverend Dr Nicholas Fisher, biographer of Symon Patrick; I've created a character who shares little in common with the real rector. Thank you for answering my questions! Also many thanks to ecologist Dr Tim Gardiner for your help regarding the historical flora and fauna of Essex.

To Anthony. To Manny. Yes. To Mery.

To Gisele Grayson. Eliza Barclay. Michaeleen Doucleff. Jessica Goldstein. Lin. Damn! So big and so bold, ladies! More, please.

To Pia Harold – extraordinary, fantastical Pia – who made my plague dreams come true. And Sonya Artis and Tracey O'Halloran. So many good adventures. I am the luckiest person in the world to have grown up with you as my best friends!

And my Big Boy Sylvan Cat. You said the other day, 'I don't think our Halloween decorations are scary. I think they are *adorable*.' You also said your favourite part of the book was the pirate – the graphic of the skull and crossbones on the chapter headings. I love you so much, kid.

# ABOUT THE AUTHOR

V.L. Valentine is a senior science editor at National Public Radio in Washington, D.C., where she has led award-winning coverage of global disease outbreaks including Covid-19, Ebola and the Zika virus. She has a master's in the history of medicine from University College London and her non-fiction work has been published by *NPR*, *The New York Times*, the *Smithsonian Channel* and *Science Magazine*. *The Plague Letters* is her first novel. Her next novel, *Begar's Abbey*, will be published by Viper in 2022.

@valentinevikki
@ViperBooks
Viper Books